Riot
POLITICS

Praise for the book

'Outbursts of communal violence in India are often portrayed as aberrations, as moments of collective madness interrupting a lively liberal democracy. Nobody can maintain that position after having read Ward Berenschot's meticulously researched and robustly argued study of local politics and violence in Gujarat. Berenschot demonstrates that organizing, preparing and imagining communal violence—real or potential—is endemic to the way democracy, identity and political power function at the level of neighbourhoods and streets in India's economic powerhouse. A must read for anyone interested in the political sociology of violence.'

—Thomas Blom Hansen,
Professor of Anthropology, Stanford University

'The 2002 genocidal violence in Gujarat has remained partly unexplained. Focusing on the city of Ahmedabad, Ward Berenschot's book throws new light on these events, drawing on unique fieldwork emphasising the role of grassroot leaders. This is a remarkable addition to the literature on communalism in India.'

—Christophe Jaffrelot,
Senior Research Fellow, CNRS, CERI

'Ward Berenschot explains how the neighbourhood-based agents of the commanding party heights tried to segregate people on the basis of their religious identity. His excellent study shows that communalism is a political act rather than a state of mind.'

—Jan Breman, Professor Emeritus and Senior Fellow
Amsterdam Institute of Social Science Research

'An exciting new study of the relationship between political mediation and violence in Gujarat, this work is ethnographically rich, well written and theoretically ambitious.'

—Professor Samira Sheikh,
Vanderbilt University

This volume provides a rich ethnographic account of the modus operandi of grass roots political actors in communal (ethnic) violence. Berenschot provides an insight into everyday politics and the state in Gujarat, India. Highly useful for students of Indian politics and society.'

—Ghanshyam Shah, National Fellow,
Indian Institute of Advanced Study

HINDU-MUSLIM VIOLENCE
AND THE INDIAN STATE

WARD BERENSCHOT

RAINLIGHT
RUPA

Published in RAINLIGHT by
Rupa Publications India Pvt. Ltd. 2013
7/16, Ansari Road, Daryaganj
New Delhi 110002

Sales Centres:
Allahabad Bengaluru Chennai
Hyderabad Jaipur Kathmandu
Kolkata Mumbai

Originally published in Great Britain in 2011
by C. Hurst & Co. (Publishers) London

ISBN: 978-81-291-2375-6

10 9 8 7 6 5 4 3 2 1

CONTENTS

PREFACE AND ACKNOWLEDGEMENTS

The origins of this book can be traced back to an interview I conducted in 2001 with a student on the campus of Mumbai University. It was my very first interview in India. I had just landed, and was still adapting to the sights and sounds of the country in which I would spend so much time in subsequent years. I was glad I could to sit down with Rohan, a bright sociology student who offered to help me orient myself. He patiently answered all the naïve questions that I fired at him. I had come to Mumbai with the aim of doing a research project for my master's thesis on the Hindu-Muslim violence that had occurred in 1992–93. After an hour of talking, with a brusqueness I felt ashamed of later, I started questioning Rohan about his experiences during these violent days. It turned out that Rohan had lost a friend in the riots, killed by a violent mob. Rohan wanted to tell me how this friend was killed by a mob when he had gone out to buy some milk, but halfway through the story he choked up and said he could not continue. I remember how I clumsily tried to comfort him, angry with myself for touching upon this topic in such an insensitive way. Rohan told me later that it was the first time he had spoken about his friend after the riots. For almost ten years he had not shared his grief with anyone.

The incident gave me a first glimpse of what an open nerve Hindu-Muslim conflict still is in India. After Rohan I met many people who carried very painful memories with them, feeling they had little other options but to bury these memories and carry on. It is not just that their daily struggles leave them with little time and energy to reflect on the grief and anger that Hindu-Muslim violence leaves behind. It is also that the political atmosphere in a number of Indian states actively discourages people from discussing and reflecting on past incidences of violence. Political leaders routinely construe criticism of the handling of communal conflict as an insult to national or regional pride. Brave journalists and documentary makers who try to stir up public discussion about India's communal tensions are being harassed and censored.[1] India's active censor boards have prevented films on communal conflict from being screened,[2] arguing that such work could stir up further communal tensions.

I disagree. The large pool of fear, hatred and grief that lies hidden beneath the surface still forms the combustion for more rounds of violence. A lack of public discussion about communal prejudices makes it easier for political actors to invoke these prejudices for their own ends. Soon after my interview with Rohan it became apparent how dangerous this lack of public introspection still is. On 27 February 2002 a new round of horrific Hindu-Muslim violence erupted in Gujarat, one even more deadly and gruesome than most of the previous outbursts. This violence highlighted once more the dangers of the way social divisions are being politicized in India. These events also showed—to me at least—that social science still had an urgent responsibility to lay bare the processes that produce this violence.

That conviction eventually led to this book. Between January 2005 and March 2006 I lived with my wife in some of Ahmedabad's most violent neighbourhoods. I gradually integrated myself—to the extent that a white *burio* ('foreigner') with a funny Gujarati accent can ever be integrated—into the local political networks that call the shots in these streets. In the daytime I sat with local politicians on the street corners where they held their 'roadside offices', I accompanied neighbourhood leaders on their visits to government offices, I joined the workers of political parties during their canvassing for the municipal elections and I did *cha-nasto* with local police officers. In the evenings I sat out on the *otla*s—raised stone platforms at the side of the road—drinking *chai* and listening to my neighbours and friends gossiping about the latest exploits of local *goonda*s ('criminals') and other political hopefuls. In between, I conducted interviews with journalists, civil servants and academics to make sense of it all. The material gathered during these fifteen months forms the bulk of this book.

Ever since that interview with Rohan I felt compelled to try to write a book for two audiences. On the one hand this book targets certain academic debates about communal violence and about Indian politics. In particular this book addresses weaknesses in the available approaches in the literature that focus on political machinations as an explanation for the occurrence of communal violence. By focusing on the local networks through which people gain access to state services this book offers, I believe, a better understanding of how and why political leaders are capable of mobilizing people for violence. With its analysis and ethnographic material about the everyday mediation of the state, this book also aims to boost debates about the functioning of India's democracy and its pervasive identity politics.

On the other hand this book was also written with some hope of contributing to a wider public debate on India's communal violence. It is intended to support the work of activists, journalists and scholars in India who try to stimulate public discussion about India's Hindu-Muslim divisions. In particular I hope that the book can serve to steer this debate away from the angry and, in my view, often unhelpful finger-pointing at political leaders (not that some politicians should not be brought to justice for what they did during Gujarat's 2002 violence). But the focus on the innocence or culpability of certain political leaders has politicized the public debate on communal violence to such an extent that it precludes a broader and more personal introspection into the roots of communal violence. The current debate stimulates people to condone communal violence for the sake of defending one's political preferences and, worse still, enables political leaders to construe any criticism of the handling of the Gujarat violence as 'anti-Hindu'. For instance, as long as debates on communal violence have the character of being about Congress versus BJP, voters as well as politicians will be stimulated to defend and legitimize the occurrence of violence. With its focus on the historical processes behind Gujarat's current communalized politics, I hope this book can offer an occasion for more reflective debate on how and why all sorts of politicians—none of India's major parties can be said to be above instigating violence—feel the need to invoke and manipulate social divisions, and on how the structural conditions that give rise to such identity politics might be changed.

One of the rewards of this research project has been the large number of wonderful people I got to meet. There have been so many people who have helped me along the way that I fear forgetting to mention some of them. I should start with the protagonists of the coming chapters, the people who live in the three localities I studied. They made this study possible by letting me into their lives. I hope they will recognize in following pages how much I learned from them, even if they might not agree with everything I have written. Many of them became good friends with whom I have shared wonderful moments. I also have fond memories of the many evenings when I sat out with my neighbours—always only men—on an *otla* near my house, where we talked, laughed and played chess until late. The stories that were told there, as well as the endless political discussions, helped me to get valuable insights into the nitty-gritty of the functioning of local patronage networks, and I gradually acquainted myself there with the language and the expressions associated with local politics.

Because of the sensitive nature of some of the material in this book, I have tried to protect the anonymity of my informants as much as I could. I have changed the names of two of the three neighbourhoods that this book focuses on, Isanpur and Maneknagar. I felt it was unnecessary and unpractical to change the name of the third neighbourhood that won prizes for its capacity to avert violence, Raamrahimnagar. I have also changed the name of all the protagonists in this book. That includes some otherwise well-known politicians that figure here under different names. I felt that using their real names would inconvenience a wider range of informants and would thus be an ungrateful way of repaying the debt I owe them. Furthermore I wanted this book to stimulate discussion about the nature of local politics, not about the actions of particular politicians.

Fortunately there are some people in Gujarat whom I can name. I am very grateful to Prof. Raymond Parmar for teaching me Gujarati. I thank him and Kiritbhai Bhavsar for their insights on Gujarat's culture and history and their help translating Gujarati texts. I was able to overcome the more difficult moments because of the kindness, support and wonderful company of Shahrukh Alam, Mahesh Langa, Achyut Yagnik, Brijpal Patel, Roma Pandya, Riyaz Tayyibji, Rafi Malek, Sharoop Dhruv, and fellow travellers Carolyn Heitmeyer, Ton Groeneweg, Welmoed Koekebakker and Thijs Turel. A special thanks to our neighbours, the Soni and Varma families whose warmth never failed to lift my spirits. I have been very lucky to meet Shaival Thakkar, who has been a wonderful research assistant as well as a wonderful friend.

The Amsterdam School for Social Science Research (ASSR, now AISSR) at the University of Amsterdam has been a great home base for this project. At the ASSR I wrote the PhD thesis that eventually led to this book. This book has benefited from many discussions I had there, especially from the comments and support from Malini Sur, Marie Lindegaard-Rosenkrantz, Justus Uitermark, Maarten Poorter, Devika Bordia, Cressida Jervis Read, Mohammed Azca, Michiel Baas, Deasy Simandjuntak, Jamie Cross, Lotte Hoek, Victor Toom, Gerben Korthouwer, Eelke Heemskerk, Luc Fransen, Johan Goudsblom, Thomas Blom Hansen, Reinoud Leenders, Francesco Strazzari and Mattijs van de Port. I thank Ton Zwaan, Willem van Schendel and Johannes Houwink ten Cate for helpful ideas and particularly for stimulating me to undertake this project. I am particularly indebted to Ghanshyam Shah, Mario Rutten, Abram de Swaan and Jan Breman for their support throughout this project. It has been an immense pleasure to learn from them, and their insights and experience have contributed much to the book.

The research for this book has been made possible by a grant from the Dutch research council NWO. Some of the material in this book has been published elsewhere; parts of Chapter 9 have appeared as 'The Spatial Distribution of Riots: Patronage and the Instigation of Communal Violence in Gujarat, India' in *World Development* (2011). A more elaborate version of Chapter 5 has been published as 'Everyday Mediation: The Politics of Public Service Delivery in Gujarat, India' in *Development and Change* (2010, 41 (5)). Some material in Chapter 8 also appears in the article 'Moneypower and Musclepower in a Gujarati Locality: On the Usefulness of Goondas in Indian Politics' in *The Journal of South Asian Studies* (2011). And my article 'Rioting as Maintaining Relations: Hindu-Muslim Violence and Political Mediation in Gujarat, India' in *Civil Wars* (2009, vol. 11 (4)) contains material from the introduction and Chapter 9. I thank the publishers for their permission to reprint this material.

I also want to thank Job Verhaar, Eran Nagan, Anna Schoemakers, Jan de Laat, Fleur Berenschot, Rutger van den Breemer, Marc de Wilde, Henk Tieleman, Monique van Ede and Leni Noteborn and my parents Cathrien Dieperink and Adriaan Berenschot for their particular contributions to the writing process and for putting up with my distracted state of mind during this period. And then here is finally the font styles I picked for Suzanne and Kas. I think they know why.

GLOSSARY AND ABBREVIATIONS

adivasi	Tribal communities.
AMC	Ahmedabad Municipal Corporation.
Bajrang Dal	Militant youth wing of the VHP.
bandh	The closing of offices and shops.
BJP	Bharatiya Janata Party ('*baajap*') is the political wing of the Hindu-nationalist movement and Gujarat's biggest party.
chawl	Housing block with small houses and narrow lanes, build around textile for textile labourers (also referred to as *chali*).
chamar	Dalit caste traditionally engaged in leatherworking and skinning of the hides of dead animals.
chamcha	Sycophant or 'yes-man'.
cha-nasto	Tea with snacks.
cha-pani	Commission or tip—also used to refer to a bribe.
Congress	The Indian National Congress Party, the main party in India's current ruling coalition. In Gujarat an opposition party.
corporator	A municipal councillor. The word is derived from 'municipal corporation', the word used for big city municipalities.
crore	Ten million.
dada	Thug.
Dalit	Literally 'downtrodden': those occupying the lowest rung in India's caste hierarchy.
Don	Leader of a (criminal) gang.
Isanpur	A locality of predominantly Dalit and Muslim textile labourers, housed in *chawl*s.

goonda	Thug.
hapta	Bribe (in Gujarati: *hafta*).
Hindu rashtra	A society and polity based on Hindu values.
Hindutva	'Hinduness', the term used to denote the Hindu-nationalist ideology that relates India's national identity with a homogeneous Hindu faith.
jaatvat	Casteism.
Jati	A subcaste (also known as Gnati).
karsevaks	Religious volunteers.
karyalay	Office.
KHAM	Kshatriyas, Harijans, Adivasis, Muslims.
kitli	Tea stall.
lakh	100,000.
mahajan	Guild.
majburi	Difficulty.
Maneknagar	A middle-class locality in the old city of Ahmedabad with mostly upper-caste residents.
matabhare	Literally 'heavy-headed': stubborn and prone to fighting. Term used for *goondas*.
MLA	Member of Gujarat's Legislative Assembly.
MP	Member of Parliament, i.e. of the Lok Sabha, the national parliament in Delhi.
number two	Refers to illegal activities.
OBC	Other backward castes.
otla	Raised stone platform on which people sit in the *pols*.
paan	A snack served in a betel leaf that stains the mouth red
Patel	An upwardly mobile and politically prominent caste in Gujarat.
pol panch	The neighbourhood committee of a *pol*.
pol (*pole*)	The typical gated 'mini-neighbourhood' in Gujarat's main cities, traditionally housing people from the same occupation or caste.
prabhav	Authority.
Raamrahimnagar	A slum on the eastern side of the river Sabermati that houses Muslims as well as Dalits.
RSS	Rashtriya Swayamsevak Sangh (National Volunteer Corps): the 'mother' of all Hindu-nationalist organizations, founded in 1925 with the purpose of establishing a *Hindu Rashtra*, a Hindu nation.
samadhan	A compromise between disputants.
Sangh Parivar	The 'family' of Hindu-nationalist organizations, including the BJP, VHP and RSS and the Bajrang Dal and

	numerous other organizations for students, labour, farmers, women, etc.
Saurashtra	South-western peninsula of Gujarat.
Savarna	Upper-caste Hindus (the 'twice-born').
shakha	Local branch of RSS.
TLA	Textile Labour Association (or Majoor Mahajan Sangh)
Vankar	Dalit caste traditionally engaged in weaving.
VHP	Vishwa Hindu Parishad, the 'World Hindu Council' that aims to promote Hinduism worldwide with a range of religious as well as social programmes.

PART ONE

INTRODUCTION

1

INTRODUCTION

RIOT NETWORKS IN AHMEDABAD

On the afternoon of 1 March 2002, hundreds of people gathered at a central square in Isanpur, a neighbourhood on the eastern side of Gujarat's largest city, Ahmedabad. The atmosphere was agitated, people were talking about a train coach that had been burned in a town called Godhra. Apparently Muslims had set this coach on fire, killing more than fifty Hindus. As one informant relayed, this tense atmosphere quickly turned violent: 'When the news about Godhra came, people went out on the street. Just to watch what would happen. Then the rumour spread that Muslims were about to attack. So people felt the need to attack. People became afraid, so they started to attack. Many people came out, most of them just to see what would happen, while only some did the work. They carried the [gas-] cylinders and set things on fire'.

Two days earlier a train had come to a sudden halt just outside the train station in Godhra. The 'Sabermati Express' had been carrying RSS (Rashtriya Swayamsevak Sangh) and VHP (Vishwa Hindu Parishad) workers; the members of these popular Hindu nationalist organizations had been campaigning for the construction of a temple to Lord Ram. As their train came to a halt, one of the coaches caught fire. It is disputed whether this fire originated from inside the compartment or whether it was lit from the outside, but either way the result was tragic: as the coach burned out completely, 58 people died. Politicians from Gujarat's ruling party, the BJP, jumped on the incident, convinced that Muslims were to blame. Chief Minister Modi called the incident a 'pre-planned, violent act of terrorism', and others alleged that Pakistan's secret service, the ISI, was involved. The VHP called for a *bandh*, a strike, on 28 February, and its general secretary Pravin Tagodia said, 'Hindu society will avenge the Godhra killings. Muslims should accept the fact that Hindus are not wearing bangles'.[1]

The *bandh* marked the beginning of one of the worst incidents of communal violence since India's independence. It was hardly the first time riots erupted in Gujarat, but the violence was exceptional both in scale and in brutality. Large mobs went on a rampage in 20 out of Gujarat's 25 districts. The mobs pillaged, looted, and killed for over three months, resulting in a great loss of lives and property. According to official figures 790 Muslims and 254 Hindus died and 2,500 people were injured as a result of extremely brutal acts or torture, burning, raping and maiming.[2] Human rights organizations estimate that at least 2,000 people perished.[3] Factories, shops, tombs, bore-wells, textile looms, rickshaws, warehouses and restaurants were burned in what seemed deliberate attempts to damage the livelihoods of the victims. The total economic loss is estimated at almost two billion euros.[4] More than one hundred thousand people were displaced.[5] The violence was, on the whole, very one-sided; as most of the incidents amounted to a coordinated assault by Hindu mobs and the police on isolated Muslim localities, it is warranted to speak of an anti-Muslim pogrom.[6]

Isanpur was one of the many neighbourhoods where the incident in Godhra exploded like a cluster bomb. Inhabitants soon felt that violence between the Muslim and Dalit[7] populations of the locality was inevitable: 'On hearing the news … that a bogie of 'Sabermati Express' had been torched … we felt a vertigo-like sensation and smelled a big carnage by Hindus in the offing'.[8] In the afternoon of 1 March the large mob encircled a small Muslim locality and showered its houses from all sides with stones, crude bombs and bottles filled with petrol. The police on the street did not deter the mob. On the contrary, the small police force supported the rioters by supplying petrol and by firing on the inhabitants of the besieged locality, killing and injuring several Muslims who ventured out of their houses. Meanwhile the mob used gas cylinders to burn down the shops on the main street, and a group of rioters managed to enter the local mosque and set its interior on fire.[9]

This incident started a period of rioting that lasted, intermittently, for four months. Large mobs numbering up to five thousand people gathered at a number of places throughout Isanpur, and attacked several—mostly Muslim—localities. Although reports also speak of some clashes between Hindu mobs and Muslim mobs, most of the incidents that took place were attacks on isolated Muslim localities by Hindu mobs in cooperation with the local police force. The attackers assaulted their victims with unnerving cruelty; women especially fell victim to maiming, torture and mass rape.[10] Instead of restraining the mobs during these attacks, the police often fired indiscriminately on the inhabitants inside the besieged localities. As one witness recalled one such incident: 'until five o'clock there was peace in our *chawl* [housing block]. Then the police and the RAF [Rapid Action Force] broke down the gate of our *chawl* and entered in the chawl and they started to destroy things in the houses. [Yusufbhai] hid himself under the charpoy [bed]. The policemen caught him and took him to the terrace and shot him through the back of his head'. In all, 29 people were said to have died in and around Isanpur, 22 of them Muslims.[11]

By way of explanation for the violence, Chief Minister Narendra Modi described the riots as a 'spontaneous reaction' to the events in Godhra, arguing that 'every action has an equal and opposite reaction'.[12] This 'Newtonian' logic of action and reaction was repeated by other politicians, the police as well as the vernacular media. All spoke of mobs 'being out of control', 'carried away by the general sentiment',[13] because of a 'natural outburst of anger and grief over the Godhra massacre'.[14]

However, conversations with those who participated in or witnessed the rioting leave a different impression of what actually happened in March and April 2002. Three years after the riots I lived in Ahmedabad to do research for this book, and during this time I found a home in one of the *chawls* ('housing blocks') in Isanpur, where many of my neighbours had either witnessed or participated in the rioting. The experiences of my new neighbours and friends during the riots belie the idea that the communal violence in Isanpur was just a spontaneous outburst of violence. Their experiences suggest that the violence in 2002 was in fact a planned and organized event, coordinated by a relatively small group of people.

Take, for example, the experiences of Akashbhai. Akashbhai is a committed social worker who spends most of his time solving all sorts of daily problems for his neighbours; through his wide range of contacts he helped me find accommodation in Isanpur, not far from his own house. After the first few weeks of rioting in Isanpur, Akashbhai took up an active role in organizing of what he saw as the 'defence' of his area. This is how he recollects his experiences during those days:

> When two boys died in this area, the situation was very tense. It was against my principles but I thought if the atmosphere becomes worse, then these people [in my neighbourhood] do not have weapons, they do not even have a good stick. I went to BJP representatives [and asked] 'in case there are riots in the area at night, what are the safety measures you have taken?' So they took me to places where weapons could be bought. In the middle of the riots we went there secretly. At these places I saw [municipal] councillors, a member of parliament, MLA's, local respected leaders and religious people. If I had not abandoned my principles and gone out there, I would not have found out all these things.

Jagdishbhai is another prominent social worker in Isanpur, who was an invaluable guide for me in the fifteen months I stayed in Ahmedabad. Together with a friend, Saamaben, he has an office in one of Isanpur's narrow streets, where they receive visitors who solicit their help to settle a dispute, repair a clogged gutter, arrange paperwork, deal with the police, etc. Jagdishbhai's good contacts with local Congress politicians enable him to pressurize the local bureaucrats to solve these issues. This is what he observed at the time of rioting:

On both sides there are only five percent [who commit violence]. During the riots I saw this when I was sitting on the terrace of a three-story building. In the beginning only some anti-social elements are there, and there are some VHP workers. And there are some naïve boys, about 25–50 people; they give them weapons, they give them money. They feed them *masala* [tobacco]. They make them drink alcohol. Then they move around the area saying, 'Those people will come, they will kill us, they will do this, they will do that!'. These 50 people keep moving. The rest of the people feel terrorized, they feel what will we do if we are attacked? So what I believe is that [those who commit violence] are just a small group. On both sides. The rest of the public [in the mob] is just afraid.

Pradeepbhai made similar observations. He used to be one of the many small-time *goonda*s (criminals) in Isanpur; he earned his income selling liquor to residents, which is illegal in the dry state of Gujarat. He stopped selling alcohol in 2003, when the police raided his warehouse. Thanks to the intervention of Shailesh Macwana, the local MLA (Member of Gujarat's Legislative Assembly), he narrowly escaped incarceration. He comments on the close cooperation between politicians and local *goonda*s:

The politicians have met them [the *goonda*s] before [the riots]. At night they call them to their place. [During the riots] such a meeting was held in the next *chawl* [next to his house], a *parishad* [VHP] meeting with all the *goonda*s of the area. The politicians do not contact anyone directly; for example Durga Vahini [VHP's women wing] would contact the women, and VHP would contact the men. So different people contact different people and they keep on giving all the information to the *corporator* [member of the municipal council] and the MLA. Only if someone is injured or killed—then the *corporator* or MLA steps into the field in order to instigate people.

Pradeepbhai's protector, Shailesh Macwana, is one of Isanpur's most important politicians. This VHP activist and BJP leader distinguished himself during the riots of 2002. Throughout the first month of the rioting he gave anti-Muslim speeches inside Isanpur's Dalit-dominated localities, and he led several attacks on Muslim areas. He was seen ordering people to burn Muslim huts, and he is held responsible for the killing of several inhabitants. The police registered a number of cases against him, for rioting, arson and the possession of illegal arms as well as the murder of three people.[15] He was arrested on 31 March 2002. At that time Shailesh Macwana was still a minor political figure; he had lost the municipal elections in 2000. But his speeches, his participation in the rioting and his subsequent arrest made him famous. Large groups of his supporters started to demonstrate in front of police stations to demand his release. When, after more than three days in jail, the police succumbed to this pressure and released him, Shailesh Macwana became a local hero. Six months later he won the local elections and captured a seat in Gujarat's state parliament.

These observations by Isanpur residents provide glimpses of a fairly closely-knit network of municipal councillors, MLAs, the police, party workers, VHP and RSS activists and local neighbourhood leaders, all involved in the planning, instigation and perpetration of violence. Such observations are consistent with the available documentation of other incidents of violence. Most of the incidents that various reports[16] describe were organized and led by BJP politicians and members of Hindu-nationalist organizations (VHP, RSS, Bajrang Dal), often in cooperation with both local *goondas* and the police. In the often unnerving descriptions in these reports, as well as in the remarks above, a division of labour emerges: some actors were involved in spreading rumours and accusations, some occupied themselves with the logistics of the mobilization, some instigated and led the mobs while others kept up morale and support by providing relief and by securing the release of those arrested. Throughout, Gujarat politicians seem to have played a pivotal role in these activities. Politicians like Shailesh Macwana not only took the lead during the actual rioting, they also maintained close contacts with local *goondas*, provided weapons to local social workers and directed BJP and VHP workers during their relief efforts. They kept in touch with police officers in order to prevent the police force from taking action against rioters and to secure the release of rioters that had been arrested. The testimonies of eyewitnesses suggest that these politicians worked together with local Hindu-nationalist activists and party-workers to distribute weapons, select targets and mobilize crowds. There is even evidence to suggest that organizations like the VHP and the Bajrang Dal had stepped up their activities in the months before the violence, in apparent anticipation of communal violence[17]—during my research I came across indications that this was indeed the case.

Such observations led most of the investigative reports to the conclusion that many of incidents of violence were 'engineered and launched' (CCT 2002: 23). The conclusions of these reports were corroborated by an undercover report carried out by a journalist of the magazine *Tehelka*. In a series of secretly videotaped interviews, participants in the violence as well as political leaders describe with a chilling sense of pride how they organized and perpetrated the violence, and how they were supported by the police as well as high-level politicians: 'It was [Chief Minister Modi] who gave all signals in favour of Hindus. (...) If the ruler is hard, then things can start happening'.[18]

Between instigator and instigatee

This study aims to understand the capacity of these 'riot networks' to organize and instigate such gruesome acts of mass violence. It relates the outbursts of communal violence in Gujarat to the way political actors function as mediators between state institutions and citizens. I will discuss the day-to-day functioning of the networks around local politicians in three different neighbourhoods in Gujarat's biggest city, Ahmedabad, in order to understand the formation and operation of the networks of people involved in the orchestration and perpetration of communal violence. How can we understand the existence of these riot networks and the way they function? How and why are they capable of mobilizing such large groups of people? And why do they succeed in instigating riots in some localities and not in others?

Commentators have long argued that politicians play an important role in creating communal tensions and provoking violence (see for example Engineer 1984, 1989, 1995). While scholars have related India's long history of communal violence to various factors—in Chapter 2 I will review the wide range of approaches to the study of India's communal violence—most authors focus on the political processes behind the occurrence of violence. In recent literature one may identify (Chandra 2006) an emerging consensus about the sequence behind this political instigation. Although approaches differ, several recent publications have discussed how a trigger—a procession, a local dispute, a shocking political event, etc.—'lands' in local settings (Tambiah 1996) where, depending on the local political context, the event may be taken up by local political actors to serve their interest in polarizing the electorate (Wilkinson 2004, Brass 2003) or deflecting tensions between upper and lower castes (Shani 2007, Shah 2002a, Breman 2003). Violence seems most likely in areas where there are politicians who perceive communal conflict to be advantageous and where these politicians are supported by local networks of (extremist) organizations and individuals who specialize in creating and maintaining communal tensions. These networks are, according to Brass (1998, 2003), 'institutionalised riot systems' that specialize in the creation of communal tensions and the organization and instigation of violence (see also Shah 2002a). As such actors have kept communal tensions alive throughout the years through a steady infusion of communal ideology (Jaffrelot 2003a), a precipitating incident can easily be interpreted as an instance of broader communal conflict. If the activities of these networks are not kept in check, either by the police or by civic bodies (Varshney 2001, 2002), large-scale violence may develop.

This book addresses a number of questions that this literature evokes. Although today most authors agree that many communal riots are instigated by political actors, there is little insight into the actual mechanisms that underlie the mobilization for, and the instigation of violence. Lacking documentation and an understanding of these mechanisms, the available literature about the political instigation of violence cannot account for the capacity of politicians to induce large mobs to commit violence: those who make up the mobs are depicted as docile followers, who can easily be swayed with the help of a little alcohol or money. This is unsatisfying: Kakar (1996: 151), for example, criticized this 'picture of evil politicians and innocent masses' and argued that 'in concentrating on the instigators, it underplays or downright denies that there are 'instigatees' too, whose participation is essential to transform animosity between religious groups into violence'. The focus on the electoral incentives behind the violence (in for example the work of Brass, Engineer or Wilkinson) is, in itself, insufficient to understand why these (political) actors can count on the cooperation of local residents who do not share these incentives. As Pandey (1992a: 41) put it, this literature creates a 'sanitized history' of innocent people led astray by power hungry politicians because the mass of 'the people' appear to account for very little in our analysis of 'riot' situations'.

What is needed is an account of how and why political leaders can tap into the existing fears, hopes and drives of those who actually perpetrate violence. As Horowitz (1985: 140) argued, 'attention needs to be paid to developing theory that links elite and mass concerns and answers the insistent question of why the followers follow'. These concerns drive the focus of this study on the actual organization and instigation that take place during riots: how can we understand the processes of mobilization and instigation through which large groups of people are induced to contribute to communal rioting?

This research question goes hand in hand with three sub-themes that will return throughout this book. First, the book will focus on the formation and functioning of the networks of local actors involved in the rioting: how do these 'riot networks' that foment violence actually form? How do they operate in different localities? How can we account for the coordination and cooperation of quite a number of different individuals at the time of rioting? How can we account for the local authority of those who spread rumours and accusations? Why are the words of those who appeal for calm not heard in localities where violence erupts?

Secondly, this study aims to deepen our understanding of the electoral benefits that politicians gain from communal rioting. It has been repeatedly observed that the groups involved in the instigation and organization of riots are later rewarded at the time of elections. The violence in Gujarat showed a similar pattern: the BJP swept the polls in the state assembly elections ten months after the outbreak of the riots. Analyses of the results have shown that the BJP increased its tally by 10 per cent in riot-affected areas, whereas in riot-free districts its share of the votes dropped on average by 3 per cent (Kumar 2003, Prakash 2003). Much of the available literature explains this electoral effect of communal violence by pointing to the electoral polarization that riots provoke: as a result of the riots, the argument goes, voters tend to vote more along religious lines, that is, for parties that claim to represent a religious community. This study focuses on how and why the nature of politics in Gujarat rewards such manipulation of the political salience of religion.

Thirdly, this study aims to offer an approach to understand why some cities (or parts of cities) stay peaceful for many years while neighbouring areas see repeated outburst of violence. The 2002 violence did not spread in a uniform manner throughout Ahmedabad: as various investigative reports indicate[19] the violence was concentrated on the eastern side, being particularly intense in the localities to the east and south of Ahmedabad's walled old city. The more posh neighbourhoods of western Ahmedabad were largely spared, while the poorer neighbourhoods that had suffered from the collapse of the textile industry in the 1980s (see Breman 2004) were worst hit. This variation in levels of violence has received increased attention in recent years.

While some authors concentrated on explaining variation between cities (Varshney) and states (Wilkinson), I agree with Brass[20] that only by focusing on variation between neighbourhoods can we get a better grip on the actual mobilization processes underlying the outbursts of violence: how can we understand the relative calm in some parts of the city, and the repeated outbursts of violence in others?

I will argue in this book that the answers to these questions lie in the more routine, day-to-day functioning of politicians and their followers as intermediaries between state institutions and citizens. I will argue that the daily functioning of the networks around politicians as mediators between state institutions and citizens shapes the mobilization and instigation that take place during communal riots: the dependence of both citizens and state institutions on networks of various intermediaries generates the network's interests in, and their capacity for, instigating and organizing communal violence. In this way, Gujarat's communal violence can be seen as the outcome of the historical process through which the state has come to be embedded in Gujarat's society: as wide-ranging networks of various brokers and intermediaries have formed to facilitate the interaction between state institutions and ordinary citizens, politicians have acquired the necessary local authority, contacts and incentives to foment violence.

It has often been observed that the hold of politicians over the daily functioning of the bureaucracy makes it difficult to see the state as an actor discrete from society, since through these political mediators societal elements seem to penetrate the state from all sides (Hansen 2005, Fuller and Harris 2001: 22). Indeed the terms 'state' and 'society' already suggest a false dichotomy of two bounded entities in opposition to each other (Nugent 1994): seen from up close it is very difficult to describe one as external to the other, as they are demarcated by a 'blurred boundary' (Gupta 1995) or a 'spongiform interface' (Harriss-White 1997). An awareness of this interpenetration of state and society led a number of authors to call for more ethnographies on the everyday appearances of the state (Gupta 1995, Fuller and Harris 2001, Hansen and Stepputat 2001, Barkey and Parikh 1991, Das and Poole 2004) and the everyday functioning of political actors as intermediaries between state and society (Manor 2000, Harriss-White 2003, Wilkinson 2007).

Several chapters in this book may be seen as such an ethnography of the 'everyday state'. To understand the actual embeddedness of the state we should not just focus on the symbolic 'language of stateness' that shapes the everyday experience of the state, we should also study that 'blurred boundary' between state and society as a 'field of power', (Bourdieu 1977, 1991, 1999: 58, Bourdieu and Wacquant 1992) marked by an intense competition for access to state resources. This field has its own structure of incentives and rewards that shapes the behaviour of those who aim to make a living from mediating between state institutions and needy citizens: the various strategies that individuals employ to develop some control over the resources of the state can be seen as a product of (their perception of) the structure of the competition in this field, as well as a product of the specific resources that they dispose of. While discussing the characteristics of this specific field I will speak of 'political mediation', 'mediators' and 'intermediaries' to denote the everyday facilitation by political actors of the interaction between state institutions and citizens. This mediation between state institutions and citizens consists of three different but related practices: (a) brokerage—the facilitation of the flow of information between state institutions and citizens, (b) patronage—the practice of exchanging access to state resources for political support; and (c) particularization—the practice of undermining the uniform application of laws and legislation to the advantage of private interests.

This book argues that an understanding of the nature of the competition and cooperation between various intermediaries is essential to understand the outburst of communal violence in Gujarat. We would misinterpret the nature of riot networks if we viewed them solely as 'institutionalized riot systems', because these networks were not created for the specific purpose of fomenting violence; they formed themselves in response to the difficulties that citizens face when dealing with state institutions. The networks behind the perpetration and organization of communal violence are, in fact, versatile patronage networks engaged in daily facilitation of the interaction between state institutions and society. The co-operation between the various actors in these networks stems from the financial and electoral benefits that can be derived from developing the capacity to facilitate the interaction between citizens and institutions: it stems from the daily necessity to get things done. Riot politics is an integral part of a larger game of capturing (state) resources and developing the capacity to facilitate the interaction between state institutions and citizens.

In that light one can read my choice to retain the word 'riot' ('*hullad*' in Gujarati) to describe Gujarat's 2002 violence, instead of using 'bigger' and more rhetorical terms like 'pogrom' and 'genocide' (the latter being, in my eyes and in this case, an unjustified term). As I hope to show in this book, the connotation of spontaneity and unruliness that the word 'riot' carries is largely unwarranted; but I retain the term to challenge these assumptions. We should not be led to believe that a distinction can be made between a 'normal', more spontaneous form of communal violence called rioting and an exceptional, unspontaneous form like Gujarat's violence. I posit that the smaller outbursts of violence between Hindus and Muslims that take place every year throughout India display the same characteristics highlighted in this book—riots are never fully spontaneous and are generally fuelled by the need to maintain and strengthen relationships with influential and useful people.

The dependency on local patronage channels is particularly intense where government jobs and resources form an important part of local livelihoods. The intense politicization of the neighbourhoods that we will encounter in the coming chapters is also a product of the lack of alternative sources of income for the inhabitants. In this way Gujarat's increased integration into the global economy has contributed to making the poor neighbourhoods of eastern Ahmedabad particularly riot-prone: the collapse of the textile industry in the 1980s and the resulting informal nature of much of the remaining livelihoods increased the dependence of inhabitants on political patronage networks and the government jobs they could provide (Breman 2002). Add to this the discrimination that many young Dalits experience when trying to obtain a private sector job, and one can understand why many youths hang around the residences of influential politicians to offer their services. Thus Gujarat's communal violence is also a product of its lopsided economic development of the last decades: the liberalization of its economy, while proving a boon for Gujarat's well-educated middle class, has intensified efforts to reduce labour costs to the lowest possible levels, which has made poorer neighbourhoods more vulnerable to political manipulation.

This focus on the everyday mediation of the state offers an avenue to bridge the division between those approaches to communal violence that emphasize political machinations and those that advance broader societal factors, such as the nature of civil society or a changing economy, as explanations. A focus on political mediation can help to understand how and why politicians, *goonda*s, political workers, social workers and the police contribute to the occurrence of communal violence: the capacity of these actors to instigate and perpetrate violence, as well as their interests in doing so, is closely related to the different positions they occupy in the patronage networks that provide access to state resources. The structure of the political field in which these different intermediaries—men and, to a lesser extent, women—operate, generates incentives to contribute to the violence, and their capacity to access state resources lends these actors the necessary local status and authority to engage in the instigation of violence. Their capacity as well as their willingness to instigate violence, I will argue, should be interpreted in the light of the interdependencies generated by the everyday mediation of the state.

Similarly, the arguments in this book can provide an avenue to interpret the appeal of Hindu-nationalist ideology in recent decades, which has contributed greatly to Hindu-Muslim tensions in Gujarat. There are good reasons to relate this appeal to the anxieties caused by an increasingly competitive economy and by the growing fluidity of social hierarchies. The message of 'Hindu-pride' that the numerous local outfits of the RSS, the VHP and the Bajrang Dal in Gujarat are spreading, together with a barrage of anti-Muslim prejudices, generates a sense of self-esteem, of pride, and perhaps these ideas also serve as a source of reassuring stability at a time when the pressures of increased competition and accelerating social change can seem overpowering (Basu *et al.* 1993, Nandy *et al.* 1995, Hansen 1999, Punyani 2004, Anderson 1987). However, the strength of these organizations and the appeal of their ideology can also be interpreted in the light of the ongoing competition for access to state resources and the dependence of citizens on political mediation. Given the degree to which the VHP and RSS are, just like the BJP, integrated into local patronage networks, we need to study how the strength of the patronage networks around Hindu-nationalist organizations and the popularity of their ideology go hand in hand. While a communal discourse about a 'Hindu *rasthra*' ('nation') serves to legitimize and strengthen the daily functioning of these patronage channels, the success of these channels in providing health care, education or government jobs also contributes to the popularity of Hindu-nationalist ideology. The dependence of citizens on political mediation generates an arena in which political actors employ a communal, exclusionist discourse to convey promises of access to state resources.

In this way I am adopting what, following Tilly (Tilly 2003, Bourdieu 1991, 1992, 1999, Elias 1978, 2000, Emirbayer 1997), might be called a relational approach to violence.[21] Violence should be studied in the light of the dynamics of everyday human interaction: the motives and drives of those who contribute to the violence, as well as their perception of the risks involved, can be seen as an outcome of the ever-changing web of social relations in which these individuals live their lives. If we study the structure of the interdependencies between individuals and groups in the various spheres of their daily lives we can develop an understanding of the interests, desires and perceptions behind the occurrence of violence. To understand the recurring outbursts of communal violence attention should not only be paid to the shifting relations between (religious) communities, but also to the pattern of interactions between the political elites, their supporters and local residents within a single community. We should look at the dynamics between different performers of violence—between those instigating violence through speeches and discussions, those organizing riots by taking care of logistics, and those taking the lead in a violent mob. We need to understand how the structure of the relations between these various actors generates incentives and perceptions that motivate them to contribute to the rioting. For that purpose a historical perspective is indispensable; in particular a focus on the state formation processes in Gujarat will be useful to understand how changing patterns of state-society interaction shaped the functioning of these present-day riot networks.

Research strategy: in the localities

This study is based on ethnographic fieldwork undertaken between January 2005 and March 2006 in three localities in Ahmedabad. With the conviction that the research method should follow the research questions—and not the other way around—I immersed myself in the political and social life of three localities in Gujarat's biggest city. This focus on the neighbourhood level served several purposes. Firstly, it enabled me to observe how broader historical processes that have affected Gujarat over the last decades—the liberalization of its economy and the collapse of the textile industry in Ahmedabad, as well as the increased popularity of Hindu-nationalist ideology—affect everyday interactions and shape the capacity of political actors to mobilize people for mass violence. Secondly, even though rioting mobs often move through different parts of the city, the mobilization and instigation take place in and around the localities in which people live their lives. Only in localities it is possible to document the processes of instigation and organization of communal violence, and at this neighbourhood level it is possible to study how the networks of actors who engage in the organization and instigation of violence are integrated into the social fabric of everyday life.

The choice for this focus on just three neighbourhoods was also prompted by the conviction that the more common practice of gathering data on local politics by interviewing a few politicians or informants in a number of different constituencies would not be adequate to reach meaningful conclusions about the functioning of the local networks around politicians. The reluctance of people to describe the violent events in 2002, as well as the inevitable amount of (false) rumours and secrecy that surrounds the functioning of local political networks, makes it impossible to study local politics through a few random interviews in different places. As there are many aspects of local politics that are not openly discussed—or at least not in a first interview—I needed to develop personal, trusting relations with a great number of informants who, in order to constantly crosscheck my information, needed to be from the same locality or part of interrelated networks of actors. For the same reason surveys and questionnaires are of limited use to penetrate these networks.

My understanding of the functioning of local political networks was gradually built up over the course of many mostly informal conversations, in which cups of *chai*, late-night discussions at street corners, off the cuff remarks, and friendships with local political workers played an important role. I gradually acquainted myself with a large group of social workers, government officials, local *goondas* ('criminals'), Hindu-nationalist activists, government officials, party workers and police officers; most of them, as it turned out, often interact with each other and with local politicians. In addition, I also conducted almost 200 more or less formal interviews with local actors as well as with outside observers (journalists, academics, senior bureaucrats etc.). For most of the 15-month research period I lived inside a *pol* (a small locality) bordering Maneknagar; the rest of the time I lived in a *chawl* (a small housing block) in Isanpur. In the process I struggled to remain an outside observer: like anyone involved in local politics, I unwittingly signalled support when I became close to someone—and my curiosity value as a foreign researcher sometimes even gave this impression of support certain weight. I have tried to balance my loyalties—I respectfully declined when Shailesh Macwana jokingly offered me a ticket to stand for elections, and I tried to avoid casting a 'bogus-vote' during the booth capturing that took place on election day—but throughout this book the reader will find some glimpses of how difficult it was to engage in a sustained study of local politics without becoming sometimes an actor in the local politicking.

I choose three localities for this study: Maneknagar, Isanpur and Raamrahimnagar. Maneknagar and Isanpur have seen repeated incidents of violence, while Raamrahimnagar has not seen riots for more than thirty years. Maneknagar is an old neighbourhood in the middle of the old city of Ahmedabad, where inhabitants live in streets that are a unique feature of the older cities of Gujarat. They live in *pol*s, small 'mini-localities' with often beautifully carved houses and narrow streets that, in order to protect the inhabitants, used to be closed off at night by a main gate. Previously, the inhabitants of a *pol* all belonged to the same caste or occupational group; nowadays, as people started to move to the more posh west side of Ahmedabad, the *pol*s house people from different castes. Apart from a small pocket of Muslim inhabitants, Maneknagar houses mainly upper-caste Hindus engaged in middle-class occupations; they are shop owners, traders, clerks, small factory owners, etc. I lived in one of the old *pol*s bordering Maneknagar.

Maneknagar had been at the centre of many of the outbursts of communal violence in the city; there have been many incidents of violence at the places where Maneknagar borders adjacent Muslim-dominated localities. Maneknagar's main politicians have often played an important role in this rioting: in 2002, the state minister Arun Pandya, who resides in Maneknagar, was seen leading an attack on a neighbouring Muslim locality while a sitting municipal councillor was engaged in a clash between two mobs in another part of the locality. The available reports argue that Arun Pandya (all the names in this book are changed) played a role in restraining the police from intervening while other local politicians were charged with, and later acquitted of, leading a rioting mob and the murder of a policeman during the 1985 riots. The BJP's rival, the Congress party, stands little chance in Maneknagar; the BJP and its predecessor, the Jan Sangh, have been winning elections in Maneknagar since the 1970s.

Isanpur used to be a neighbourhood of textile mill labourers: the families of the present-day inhabitants came from rural areas in the first half of the 20th century to work in the expanding textile industry. They lived in blocks made up of small houses and narrow lanes called *chawls*. There are still many textile mills in the area, although most of them are no longer operational. Many inhabitants lost their jobs as most of Ahmedabad's textile industry collapsed in the 1980s (see Breman 2003, 2004). Nowadays, there is a lot of unemployment in the area; inhabitants who do have a job work as rickshaw drivers, peddlers, labourers in factories, construction workers etc. Isanpur houses a mixed population of mainly Dalits and Muslims who live in separate *chawls*. As I described above, Isanpur was a hotbed of violence. Even in July 2002, when the rest of the city was calming down, there were still several incidents of violence. In December 2002, the BJP politician Shailesh Macwana won the seat in Gujarat's legislative assembly for this constituency in closely-contested elections.

Raamrahimnagar is very similar to Isanpur, except for one aspect: despite its mixed population of Muslims and Dalits the locality has not seen any riots since 1969. The locality is equally poor and many of Raamrahimnagar's elder residents also lost their jobs when the textile mills in their area closed down. There is a lot of unemployment among the youth; Raamrahimnagar's inhabitants mainly earn their livelihood through construction work, street vending, and cottage industries. When the locality managed to maintain peace once again in 2002, the press took notice of this neighbourhood with a name that combines a Hindu god and one of the names of Allah. Since then many dignitaries, police commissioners, politicians and inquiry committees have visited Raamrahimnagar to see what could account for the area's unusual peacefulness. In July 2002, Sonia Gandhi awarded the elders of Raamrahimnagar's neighbourhood committee the 'Indira Gandhi Award for National Integration' to highlight the locality's achievement. In this area of the city the Congress party is relatively strong; in the larger electoral ward Congress usually wins most of the seats in the municipal and state assembly elections. The three localities were chosen for their contrasts: the differences between these localities—in terms of income, composition and level of violence—allowed me to explore different aspects of the aforementioned questions. I will compare the different localities in various ways in the following chapters.

What is to come

The nature of the main arguments of this study compel me to focus first on the daily functioning of local political networks before returning to the violence that occurred in 2002. I will start, in Part Two, by discussing the historical developments that underlie the current dependence on various political intermediaries. As the Gujarat state gradually developed its capacities to provide various services to its citizens, the patterns of authority within cities changed. Older civic institutions became obsolete while politicians started to profit from their capacity to provide access to the state's expanding resources. Inhabitants gradually became more dependent on mediating politicians (Chapter 3). This dependence enabled Hindu-nationalist organizations to gain local support. The current polarization of Gujarati society along religious lines has been facilitated by the organizational weakness of political alternatives to the Hindu-nationalist movement, and the control that Hindu-nationalist organizations currently wield over the distribution of state resources (Chapter 4).

The third part of this book is an ethnographic study of the everyday functioning of the networks around local politicians. As ordinary citizens face various difficulties when dealing with state institutions, political actors need to develop their capacity to solve or bypass these difficulties. The municipal councillor I follow on his daily routine in Chapter 5 is engaged in a full-time effort to pressurize the bureaucracy to repair drainage lines, provide ration cards, solve disputes, arrange hospital beds, implement welfare schemes etc. The dependence of state institutions on political mediation is so entrenched in the policies, procedures and customs of state institutions that one can speak of a 'mediated state'.

The dependence of ordinary citizens on political mediation generates widespread networks of various intermediaries who profit from their capacity to access influential politicians and important bureaucrats. Poorer citizens in particular rely on these networks, because they lack the contacts and money to deal with state institutions without political interference. In poorer localities one can find numerous social workers and party workers as well as local *goondas* ('criminals') who all derive at least part of their livelihood from their contacts with politicians and bureaucrats (Chapter 6). Local state officials, politicians and local *goondas* need each other in a similar way to secure their livelihoods: the often perceived nexus between these different actors arises from a shared interest in manipulating the application of laws and regulations (Chapter 7).

In the fourth part of this book I relate this everyday mediation of the state to the violence that occurred in 2002. In Chapter 8 I discuss how the dependence of voters on political mediation stimulates politicians to invoke and emphasize social divisions among the electorate. In the context of a mediated state the various identity dimensions among the electorate—on the basis of caste, region or religion—are useful instruments to signal loyalty to a targeted segment of the electorate. In a political arena where identities are used to attract voters, violence is a useful instrument to manipulate the salience of these different identities. Chapter 9 discusses the mobilization and organization behind the rioting in Ahmedabad. In that chapter I will tie several strands in this book together by arguing that the cooperation and coordination of different individuals during riots can be seen as an extension of their more routine, daily interaction as intermediaries between citizens and state institutions.

But before further outlining this argument and the approach of this study I will review the available approaches to explain and understand India's communal violence. The next chapter will show that no single approach suffices to tackle this complex and multifaceted phenomenon—the arguments in this book can be read as an attempt to complement existing approaches.

2

EXPLAINING INDIA'S HINDU-MUSLIM VIOLENCE

The pogrom in Gujarat in 2002 was hardly the first instance of communal violence in India. There are many recorded instances of Hindu-Muslim rioting from even before the advent of the British *raj* (see Bayly 1985); the oldest recorded riot in Ahmedabad took place in 1714, when a fight broke out over the celebration of *holi*. During the reign of the British the number of riots increased dramatically; India's struggle for independence culminated in the apocalyptic bloodshed that took place during Partition in 1947, when an estimated one million people died and large masses of people crossed the new borders between India and Pakistan.[1] After a brief lull following independence communal rioting again regularly erupted, mainly in towns and cities,[2] throughout India from the 1960s onwards, with a severe outburst of violence in Ahmedabad in 1969. During the rise of the BJP, India's Hindu-nationalist party, India experienced increasing levels of communal violence, with particularly deadly outbursts in Moradabad (1980), Bhiwandi (1984), Bhagalpur (1989), Bombay (1992–93), Hyderabad (1990) and Coimbatore (1998).[3]

The term 'communal violence' is used in India[4] to refer to violence that takes place between not only religious but also caste and even language- or region-based communities. Not all communal rioting in India takes the form of Hindu-Muslim confrontations; apart from repeated bouts of caste violence, a severe outburst of communal violence took place in 1984 between Hindus and Sikhs. This was essentially an anti-Sikh pogrom instigated by Congress politicians after the murder of Indira Gandhi by a Sikh bodyguard. According to Wilkinson and Varshney (2002: 104), Ahmedabad holds the distinction of being India's second most riot-prone city, after Mumbai:[5] the city has seen earlier episodes of rioting in 1941, 1942, 1946, 1956, 1958, 1964, 1969, 1974,

1981, 1985–86, 1990 and 1992–93 (Spodek 1989, Shah 1984). Wilkinson and Varshney counted the overly precise number of 7,173 deaths due to communal violence in India in the period between 1950 and 1995, of which about one seventh is attributed to rioting in Ahmedabad.

There was, nonetheless, something exceptional about the violence that took place in Gujarat from 28 February up to July 2002. The first outstanding aspect was the scale of the violence. Not just in terms of deaths, even though the official death toll—1,044 casualties, a very conservative estimate—ranks the violence among the most deadly episodes in post-independence India. After the train coach was burned in Godhra, the violence spread throughout the state, affecting 154 out of 182 electoral districts, and not only 151 towns but also remote villages (991 in total), even in Gujarat's tribal areas.[6] Large mobs of up to fifteen thousand people thronged the streets, looting and burning especially the isolated localities and settlements of Muslims. The mobs left a trail of bloodshed and grief as they killed, raped and maimed at least 3,500 people, and probably much more.[7] The rioters were generally well equipped; they carried swords, *trishuls* (tridents), kerosene, petrol bombs and even gas cylinders on their campaigns. They often had voters' lists and sales tax details at their disposal to mark out Muslim houses and Muslim-owned establishments; much of the violence seemed targeted at hitting the livelihoods of Muslims, as factories, prominent restaurants, rickshaws, shops, textile looms, bore wells and even crops in the fields were destroyed throughout Gujarat. In addition, 230 shrines and mosques were demolished.[8] The Gujarat Chamber of Commerce and Industry put the total economic loss due to the riots at 110 billion rupees, or 1.96 billion euros.[9] More than one hundred thousand people have been displaced as a result of the violence (Mander 2006).

The violence was also extremely one-sided, compared to many other instances of communal rioting. Muslims bore the brunt of the attacks: there were three times as many deaths among Muslims, the religious sites destroyed were predominantly Muslim, and the burned houses and businesses belonged mainly to Muslims. There were instances of clashes between Hindu and Muslim mobs, as well as attacks by Muslims on isolated Hindu homes (see HRW 2002: 36–9), but generally the incidents amounted to a coordinated assault on the homes and property of Muslims. In these incidents members of Hindu-nationalist organizations such as the VHP, the Bajrang Dal (the VHP's youth wing) and the RSS played a prominent role; they often took the lead during the rioting, and they were often involved in the preparation for the attacks. There are indications that these organizations were organizing discussion-meetings, gathering information about Muslims and distributing weapons in the riot-affected areas before the outbreak of violence.[10]

The violence was also exceptional because of the open complicity of the state. State ministers were seen guiding mobs during attacks on Muslim localities, and there is some evidence that leading politicians also instructed the police not to intervene in the rioting.[11] State ministers spent several hours in the control room monitoring the actions of the police, while other leading politicians were in constant contact with police officers.[12] In some instances the police openly sided with the Hindu mobs, firing indiscriminately at Muslim localities and settlements. Where the police did not side with the rioters, they generally failed to take action to disperse the mobs and maintain order. When the victims approached the police for help they were often told that the police had orders not to intervene (HRW 2002, CCT 2002 81–96). Many of the rioters interviewed by the magazine *Tehelka* stated that 'the police were with us'.[13] After the incidents the police often refused to register the testimonies of Muslims, or the content was changed in such a way that it would be useless in court (see Amnesty 2005, HRW 2003).

Another exceptional aspect was the extreme cruelty of the perpetrated acts of violence. Whole families were electrocuted; people were burned alive and often tortured in extremely cruel ways. In one instance a small boy who had asked for water was forced to drink kerosene; a match was thrown into his mouth and his head exploded.[14] The sexual violence against women was widespread; the gang rape of women seemed a recurrent feature of the incidents of rioting. Foetuses were ripped out of women's bellies, metal rods and pins were inserted into their vaginas, and women were burned alive after being covered in wax.[15]

After the riots many commentators noted the absence of remorse in Gujarat's society. It was a widely held opinion that Muslims 'had it coming' and that they 'needed to be taught a lesson'. There was little indignation about the role of Gujarat's government during the rioting; ten months after the violence the ruling political party won a handsome victory in the state elections. Very few of the individuals and the police officers named in various investigate reports or in the more than four thousand FIRs submitted (a police case is filed with a 'first information report') have been punished. Despite the persistent and (given the risks) brave pressure from riot victims and various activists, the courts in Gujarat have been very reluctant to sentence riot perpetrators. Only after India's Supreme Court appointed a Special Investigation Team (SIT) was one state minister—Maya Kodnani—finally jailed in 2009 for leading a violent mob. It seems that riot cases are still only adequately pursued once they are moved to courts outside Gujarat.[16] Similarly the official inquiries into the post-Godhra violence—the Supreme Court's Special Investigation and the state-appointed Nanavati Commission—are being pressured by petitions from riot victims since, at the time of writing (more then eight years after the violence), no report has been finished and their independence is in doubt.[17] In the meantime many riot victims have not been able to return to their houses: in 2004 there were still about ten thousand people living in 81 relief camps throughout the state, in often appalling conditions.[18]

How to make sense of such gruesome violence? What to make of the scale of the rioting and the cruelty of the violence? How to understand the role of politicians in the rioting or the inaction of the police? A great number of different answers to these questions can be found in the relatively large body of literature on India's communal violence. In this chapter I will give an overview of the different ways of understanding and explaining the occurrence of communal violence in India, with a special focus on the explanations that have been offered for the violence in Gujarat. I will argue that the broad range of analyses and arguments in the literature basically reflect six distinctive approaches to the study of communal violence. I will distinguish a primordialist approach, an ideological approach, an instrumentalist approach, a constructivist approach, a social psychological approach and a relational approach. I will discuss these different approaches in turn. I will discuss the relative strengths and weaknesses of these approaches without, however, attempting to establish a 'hierarchy' of explanations (cf. Jaffrelot 1992). The many-sidedness of the phenomenon calls for a diversity of approaches; the different perspectives discussed below complement one another more than that they refute each other. The approach of this study—outlined again briefly at the end of this chapter—should be read as an attempt to complement existing approaches.

A primordialist approach

Primordialist approaches to the study of violence focus on the capacity of ethnicity to shape one's perception of the world and of one's place in that world. Primordial attachments, such as those based on caste or religion, are a basic, essential part of what it means to be a human because these attachments provide us with an orientation on which we can base our opinions and actions. These attachments are a 'given' and this 'givenness (...) stems from being born into a particular religious community, speaking a particular language, or even a dialect of a language, and following particular social practices. These congruities of blood, speech, custom, and so on, are seen to have an ineffable, and at times overpowering, coerciveness in and of themselves' (Geertz 1963: 109). In India, Robinson (2005) in particular called attention to how membership of cultural groupings induced individuals to perceive their social world in terms of the signs and symbols that came with this attachment. Identity, these theorists argue (see also Kakar 1996: 149–52), is an unconscious and important element of daily life that gives meaning to our actions and guides us in our choices.

Primordialists are sometimes seen as 'essentialists': since the primordial attachments are such an intrinsic part of human nature, they constitute basic, unchanging differences between human beings. Since this sense of belonging is such an essential part of our life, we will be inclined to associate with people who share our cultural background ('us'), and perceive an antagonism with people with a different cultural background ('them'). In this way cultural differences have the tendency to spill over into conflict and violence: communal violence can be seen as a more or less unavoidable consequence of existing religious (or caste-based) differences within a society.

On the basis of such arguments about the overpowering nature of primordial attachments, primordialist writers try to understand contemporary violence by relating these present-day tensions to past outbursts of violence and 'ancient hatreds': these earlier instances of conflict, it is argued, feed into present-day tensions between different cultural groups. Gaborieau (1985: 9), for example, argued that we can understand communal violence by appreciating how Hindus and Muslims have 'traditionally nurtured sentiments of hostility', while Gill and Deol (1995: 66) argue that 'riots in India mainly spring from inter-religious cleavages and rivalries which are deeply rooted in the past'. There is indeed much in India's history that can be marshalled as proof of a long-standing conflict between Hindus and Muslims. From the often bloody invasions of Muslim conquerors, like Mahmud of Ghazni—'the sword of Islam'—in the 11th century, to the ill-treatment of Hindus during the rule of the Mughal Emperor Aurangzeb or the repeated razing of Hindu temples: many such episodes have been taken up as proof that the two civilizations have always been fundamentally at odds. The Muslim League leader Muhammad Ali Jinnah used this 'two-nation theory' to demand the formation of Pakistan.

But such a reading of history is highly contested. Historians have criticized it by pointing to numerous instances of peaceful co-existence and cooperation, to various forms of syncreticism in art, architecture as well as religious ritual, and they have argued that the boundaries between communities were relatively blurred: people were only dimly aware of their religious affiliation as they practiced highly syncretic forms for religion until well into the 20th century. This points to a central weakness of primordialist explanations of communal conflict: by taking cultural identities (and accompanying antagonisms with other groups) as a given and unchangeable fact of human nature, they pay too little attention to the capacity of politics and societal structures to shape these identities. In this way, primordialist explanations for communal strife can serve as justification for more violence. Arguments about fundamental differences between communities can be used to heighten tensions and create prejudices, and can obscure the forces that have contributed to these tensions.

An ideological approach

A second approach sees the pervasiveness of a communal ideology within society as an explanation for the occurrence of communal violence. Bipan Chandra (1987: 5), for example, sees riots as a 'bitter and virulent manifestation and consequence' of a communal ideology, and Jaffrelot (2003a: 2) argues that 'riots largely originate from a distorted idea—ideology—of the "other"'. The ideology that both writers refer to has in India often been captured under the term 'communalism', which refers to the conviction that people who share certain cultural traits (such as caste or religion) have (political) interests in common that need to be defended against people not sharing these traits. The term Hindu-nationalist is generally used for Hindu communalists. I would summarize their ideology, often referred to as *Hindutva*, as follows:

> India belongs to those people whose religion has originated in India (Hindus, Jains, Buddhists); for too long have outsiders—i.e. Muslims and Christians—ruled over India, which has drained the wealth and resources of India's original inhabitants. Now that India has finally been freed from these oppressors the country should become a 'Hindu Rashtra': the values and concerns of the Hindu majority should guide the functioning of the Indian state. Unfortunately political parties like the Congress party have appeased the Muslim minorities to get their votes; under the banner of 'secularism' these parties have in fact pampered the Muslims at the expense of the Hindu community. As a result the violent and criminal nature of Muslims continues to be a threat for peace-loving Hindus. This has to be stopped; if Muslims want to live in India they have to submit to the rule of the Hindu majority.[19]

The ideas of communalists among Muslims—sometimes referred to as 'Islamists' (Ahmad 2009)—in many respects mirror this ideology; these ideas can be traced back to the chronicler Al-Biruni, who wrote in the 11th century: 'They totally differ from us in religion, as we believe in nothing in which they believe, and vice versa. (...) Any connection with them [is] quite impossible' (1030; cited in Smith, 2003: 51-2). The Muslim League under Jinnah emphasized the incompatibility of Hindus and Muslims and the dangers that Muslims would face in a country ruled by a Hindu majority. Later, organizations like SIMI or the Jamaat-e-Islami aimed at establishing a state based on the principles and teachings of Islam; according to the Jamaat-e-Islami's founder Maududi, India was to be transformed into dar al-Islam, a 'house of Islam'. As a recent study shows (Ahmad 2009), the radicalization of these organizations proceeded largely as a reaction to the capture of state power by Hindu-nationalist organizations.

The present-day Hindu-nationalist movement in India dates back to 1925, when the Rashtriya Swayamsevak Sangh (National Volunteer Corps, RSS) was founded. Its call for a revival of Hinduism combined with a fervent nationalist pride proved to be popular and the organization grew rapidly, creating new affiliated organizations in its rise. Today one speaks of a family of Hindu-nationalist organizations (the Sangh Parivar), all committed to turning India into a '*Hindu Rashtra*', a society and polity based on Hindu values. The RSS came to be seen as the 'social' wing of the family (because it runs more than 5,000 schools, hospitals and does charity work), the VHP (World Hindu Council) as the religious wing (as it aims to promote Hinduism in India as well abroad) and the political party BJP as the political wing. The VHP again generated several organizations; most notable are its youth wing, called Bajrang Dal, and its women's wing Durga Vahini. These are just the most prominent Hindu-nationalist organizations, as there are a great number of other organizations—from student unions, peasant groups and trade unions to tribal welfare organizations—in the Sangh Parivar. Although formally independent organizations, these different 'family members' maintain very close ties because its supporters and leaders are often active in several organizations (Noorani 2000, Jaffrelot 1996 and 2005, Kanungo 2002, Katju 2003).

This movement has grown tremendously over the last 25 years, especially in northern India. Since the 1980s these organizations have launched a number of successful campaigns, which dominated Indian politics for a long time. Their campaigns centred on a mosque in the North-Indian town Ayodhya, the Babri Masjid. According to Hindu-nationalists this mosque stood on the exact location where Hindu-god Rama was born; they argued that the mosque had been build on the foundations of a temple that had previously marked Ram's birthplace until it was destroyed in the 16th century by the army of the Mughal Emperor Babur. Throughout various campaigns—ranging from the collection of bricks for the construction of a new temple and several *yatras* (nationwide processions) to several manifestations at the disputed site—the VHP and the BJP used the Babri Masjid as a symbol of the injustices that Hindus had suffered at the hands of Muslims. These agitations culminated in the demolition of the mosque on 6 December 1992 by thousands of Hindu-nationalist activists (*karsevaks*), which led to widespread rioting across India and Pakistan. The issue brought the Hindu-nationalist organizations electoral success: the BJP won the parliamentary elections in 1996 after obtaining only four parliamentary seats in 1980. The BJP ruled India from 1998 until 2004 with its leader, A.B. Vajpayee, as Prime Minister. These electoral successes have enabled the BJP to change the textbooks used in schools in several states, so that they now lay much more stress on strife and differences between Hindus and Muslims.[20]

Commentators have often pointed to the popularity of these Hindu-nationalist organizations and their ideas as an explanation for the 2002 violence. Gujarat is considered to be a 'laboratory of Hindutva' because of the entrenchment of organizations like the VHP and the RSS in Gujarat's society, in politics and in state institutions. Girish Patel (2002: 4836), for example, argued that 'the Gujarat catastrophe was the successful outcome of the Hindu-communalisation of civil society and capture of the state and its Hinduisation at the service of the RSS and its affiliates'. Prejudices against Muslims are indeed widespread, and organizations like the RSS and the VHP are held in high esteem throughout Gujarat. At the time of the rioting various cabinet ministers maintained very close relations with these organizations, including Chief Minister Narendra Modi who used to be an RSS *pracharak* ('organizer'). Many high-level bureaucrats and police officers openly nurture relations with these Hindu-nationalist groups.

The patterns of rioting in Gujarat bear out the impact of these Hindu-nationalist organizations on communal relations in the state. Throughout the state, activists of the VHP, Bajrang Dal, Durga Vahini, and RSS were seen in the forefront of the rioting, and often played an important role in the organization and mobilization for the violence. Their links with government institutions have often been advanced as an explanation for the unprecedented involvement of government institutions in the perpetration of the violence.

The status and popularity of these organizations clearly contributed to their capacity to create tensions and instigate violence.

At the same time the popularity of Hindu-nationalist organizations and their ideology is, in itself, an unsatisfying explanation for the occurrence of violence. They are obviously related, but the two issues should not be conflated since this would obscure important questions: what societal developments led to the popularity of communalist ideologies, and how can we explain how perceptions of communal differences spilled over into a widespread acceptance of the use of violence? Such questions are the centre of the instrumentalist approach to the study of violence.

An instrumentalist approach

The instrumentalist approach sees communal violence as a political strategy that serves the interests of (political) elites. Communal sentiments are an instrument in the hands of economic and political leaders, which they employ to defend their electoral or economic interests. Exponents of this approach stress that (political) elites are involved in the instigation and organization of violence. Using various means—giving inflammatory speeches, organizing religious processions (Jaffrelot 1998) or distributing money and liquor—these elites are capable of mobilizing large mobs for full-scale rioting. Riots are 'willed' and 'purposeful' (Basu 2005: 374): to explain the occurrence of communal violence, one has to look at how politicians and economic entrepreneurs benefit from the violence. Engineer (1989, 1984: 34) writes, for example, that 'Communal tension arises as a result of the skilful manipulation of the religious sentiments and cultural ethos of a people by its elite which aims to realise its political, economic and cultural aspirations by identifying these aspirations as those of the entire community'.

Hence instrumentalist authors have paid specific attention to how specific events ('triggers') are converted into large scale rioting (see for example the articles in Engineer 1989 and 1984). In his book *The Production of Hindu-Muslim violence in Contemporary India* Brass (2003, see also Brass 1996, 1997 and 2004) focuses particularly on what he calls 'institutionalised riot systems', 'a perpetually operative network of roles whose functions are to maintain communal hostilities, (...) mobilise crowds (...), recruit criminals for violent action and (...) to let loose widespread violence' (2003: 58). During his extensive fieldwork in Aligarh, Brass identified several 'riot specialists', 'fire-tenders' and 'conversion specialists'. With these terms Brass aimed to emphasize the different roles of individuals within 'institutionalised riot systems'; these roles amounted to the organization of the perpetration violence, the creation and maintenance of communal tensions, and conversion of the meaning of a triggering incident, in such a way as to give the incident a communal overtone. These observations led Brass to conclude that riots are 'a continuation of politics by other means' (2003: 231): they are 'dramatic productions' and 'street theatre performances' that serve the interests of (especially) politicians.

Both Brass and Wilkinson (2004) argue for a close relation between elections and the occurrence of violence. Wilkinson used an extensive dataset on incidences of rioting throughout India to point out that riots occur significantly more often in the six months before or after elections. Both Brass and Wilkinson note that politicians use riots to divide their electorate on communal lines. Riots, they argue, serve to solidify communal identities: they polarize the electorate in such a way that the electoral competition is turned into a competition between Hindus and Muslims. Other issues and electoral divisions recede to the background as individual voters rally behind the candidate who is seen as a representative of 'their' community. Wilkinson built on this argument; he argued that the occurrence or absence of communal violence is best understood by looking at the electoral incentives that state governments are facing. On the basis of extensive statistical analysis he argued that riots are more likely to occur in states with a limited number of effective parties (that is, the number of parties that receive a considerable share of the votes) at a time when the state government does not rely on Muslim votes. This 'electoral incentives theory' argues that when ruling politicians do depend on the votes of minorities for their (re-)election, or when there are a considerable number of political parties competing for power, ruling politicians will have an important incentive to use state machinery to prevent or stop violence. If, on the other hand, the ruling party does not depend on the electoral support from minorities, it will be less inclined to order the police and the army to stop the rioting.

In a similar instrumentalist vein, commentators have argued that political parties make use of Hindu-Muslim tensions to deflect increasing tensions within the Hindu community, between Dalits and other backwards castes (OBCs) on the one hand and upper castes on the other. As Dalits and OBC's have been increasingly upwardly mobile, some writers (for example Punyani 2004) have argued that communal riots serve the upper castes to protect existing caste hierarchies against challenges from increasingly vocal lower castes: the antagonism between Hindus and Muslims serves to draw attention away from tensions between upper castes and lower castes. Discussing a 'dynamic of inclusion and exclusion' Breman (1999, 2003) as well as Shani (2005 and 2007) and Shah (2002) argued that riots between Hindus and Muslims in Gujarat have served to deflect the growing tensions between Dalits and upper castes.

The events in Gujarat in 2002 illustrate in several ways the value of these instrumentalist arguments. First, the numerous reports on the violence provide ample evidence of the involvement of politicians and their supporters in the instigation and perpetration of the rioting. On the whole, the available accounts of Gujarat's violence underpin instrumentalist arguments that political and economic elites are capable of triggering large-scale rioting. Other empirical support for instrumentalist arguments lies in the observation that the violence indeed seems to have served the electoral interests of the BJP. Not long before the rioting, the BJP had lost local elections by a landslide, as well as two by-elections for seats in the state assembly. But when in December 2002—ten months after the outbreak of violence—state elections were held, the BJP won a majority of the votes and increased its tally of seats in the state assembly to 127 (out of 182). Statistical analyses of the election results show that the BJP had done particularly well in the districts where riots had occurred: in riot affected areas the percentage of BJP voters increased on average by 10 per cent, while the BJP's share in the votes in riot-free districts fell by 3 per cent (Kumar 2003, Prakash 2003).

Because of such observations commentators often discuss the violence in Gujarat in instrumentalist terms. Engineer (2002: 8) argued for example that the riots were an attempt by the BJP to win back votes: 'The only trick up its [the BJP's] sleeve was polarization of Hindus and Muslims and thus to consolidate the Hindutva forces. The easiest way to do it was to organize communal riots'. Several commentators related the violence to a strategy of Hindu-nationalist organizations to increase their popularity among tribals (*adivasis*, see Devy 2002, Lobo 2006) and Dalits (Namishray 2002, Shah 2006) as the violence seemed to have served to cement the BJP's popularity among these traditionally Congress-voting groups.

But, despite its obvious relevance, the instrumentalist approach has two important weaknesses. Firstly, the arguments discussed here lack a convincing account of how and why political leaders (and their 'riots specialists' and 'fire tenders') are capable of inciting large mobs of people to participate in violence. Instrumentalist arguments too easily take the capacity of political leaders and their organizations to foment violence for granted; the instigated are depicted as docile followers, easily swayed by the conflict mongering of their leaders.[21] Hence there is little attention paid to the agency of individual rioters; the (attractive) impression is created that the large mass of rioters are merely innocent victims of the scheming of political elites (see Pandey 1992a: 41 and Kakar 1996: 149–52). As a result instrumentalist accounts often take the unsatisfying garb of a conspiracy theory as they reduce violent outbursts to a 'production' that came out of the scheming and manipulation of a powerful few. This raises the question, if the analyst is able to see through the ruses of politicians, why then is the ordinary man repeatedly duped?

Some answers to this question might be found by focusing on the concerns that drive people to participate in the violence; in the following sections I discuss some of the theories that focus on those. But these answers would also be incomplete if we do not take into account how political leaders make use of these concerns. We need, in other words, to link the motivations of the instigators with the motivations and interests of the instigated in order to understand why and how the instigators succeed in mobilizing the instigated. That will be a central concern of this study: as I will argue in the last section of this chapter, to understand the capacity of interested elites to spread communal tensions and instigate violence we need to look at the dynamic of the daily interactions and cooperation between (political) leaders and their followers, and how the nature of the relations between the followers and the followed creates incentives for non-politicians to contribute to the rioting.

Secondly, we need to understand better how and why political parties derive electoral benefits from outbursts of violence. It has been repeatedly observed that those groups involved in the instigation and organization of rioting are later rewarded at the time of elections. As mentioned above, this electoral success is often explained by pointing to the electoral polarization that riots provoke: as a result of the riots, it is argued, the voters tend to vote along religious lines, that is, for parties that claim to represent their religious community. Such arguments require attention to the way communal identities are shaped and manipulated over time (see the constructivist arguments below), but also to how and why the nature of the game of politics in Gujarat rewards such manipulation: why is the manipulation of the importance that the voter attaches to his or her religious identity (through instigation of rioting, for example) such a useful political strategy? Why does (religious) identity seem to be a more successful instrument for political mobilization than, for example, ideological or socio-economic differences among the electorate? Such questions require us to probe into the motivations of the voter, and his (or her) relation with political parties and politicians. I will argue that the need for politicians to polarize the electorate on the basis of religious differences should be understood in the light of the role of politicians as intermediaries between state institutions and voters.

A social-constructivist approach

This approach criticizes the first three approaches for obscuring or neglecting that communal identities are social constructs. Social identities are not unchangeable, fixed characteristics of human beings; constructivist writers argue that we should look at how the content of what it means to be a 'Hindu' or a 'Muslim' changes over time, and how the importance one attaches to this aspect of one's identity is contingent on historical and political developments. As our faith is just one aspect of our identity as textile labourer, father, Gujarati, Dalit (etc.), the relative importance of these different identities can be manipulated and changed over time. In this way constructivist writers draw attention to the contingent and flexible nature of communal identities and communal conflict: in opposition to primordialists they argue that the perception of a communal antagonism has formed over time through a complex interaction of government (colonial) policies, political machinations and socio-economic developments.

Writers such as Hansen (2001: 10) and Pandey (1992b) discuss how discursive practices of important individuals or groups—their public speeches, writing, and public rituals as well as the formulation of government policies—construct collective identities, and how in this way the perception of a threatening 'other' is created and maintained. These writers hold that identities 'only exist as collective identities when they are named in public rituals, organized and reproduced through performative practices as groups and categories for themselves'. In this fashion Pandey (1992b: 6) sees communalism 'as a form of colonialist knowledge'. He described how the British, in an attempt to understand Indian society, created and used simplified categories of caste and religion. As these simplified categories informed their policies and activities (as in the adoption of separate electoral constituencies for Hindus and Muslims) they became self-fulfilling prophecies: while caste and religion used to be flexible social categories, the British increased the importance and consciousness of these categories within daily life.

A second strand of constructivist arguments focuses on the broader discursive frameworks that underlie perceptions of 'us' and 'them': such writers (see for example Van der Veer 1994) focus on how available terminology, rituals, symbols and gestures shape our perceptions and the categorizations through which we approach and evaluate society. These 'discursive frameworks' or cultural interpretative systems underpin our perceptions of communal boundaries, and our perceptions of differences between 'us' and 'them'. For example, in her many-layered analysis of a Hindu-Muslim riot that broke out over an unruly cow in a village in what was to become Bangladesh, Roy (1996) focused on how the perception of what it means to be a member of a religious community was shaped by both the lived experience and everyday grievances of village life and the way a new and expanding state changed the power relations in the village. Some authors extended this approach to the study of violence itself: Veena Das (1990) called for attention to the cultural repertoire that sustains and shapes the (legitimation of) violence: the symbols and cultural practices that acts of violence draw on, and the meaning and interpretation attached to acts of violence. Her call was heeded by Ghassem-Fashandi (2006); in an impressive encyclopaedic thesis he related Gujarat's communal violence to the practices of sacrifice within Hinduism; he sees a 'sacrificial logic' and, paradoxically, the notion of *ahimsa* (non-violence) and related practices of vegetarianism as three central elements of a cultural repertoire that sustained the legitimation and perpetration of violence in 2002.

The major contribution of the constructivist approach lies in its capacity to provide a historical 'genealogy' of categories of perception and interpretation that underlie us-them categorizations and acts of violence. In doing so, this approach can help to develop an insider's perspective of how violence is perceived and legitimized. This approach is weak, however, when one questions why certain cultural practices and categories of perception have become dominant: why, for example, a militant version of Hinduism that was on display during the 2002 riots has become so popular in Gujarat (and why the once popular Bhakti and Sufi movements with their emphasis on devotion and tolerance have faded). Why are certain elements of a rich cultural heritage promoted and other elements forgotten or neglected?

Such questions of selection cannot be answered without taking into account political and societal developments; a focus on prevalent discursive frameworks within society needs to be supplemented, particularly, with a focus on changing forms of political and societal competition, in order to understand how particular discourses serve to maintain or create power differentials within society. I will argue in later chapters that a focus on the nature of political competition, and in particular on the intricacies of the kind of state-society mediation that political actors are engaged in, can help understand how processes of identity formation and the development of state capacities feed on each other.

A second weakness is that constructivist arguments, too, do not clearly distinguish between communal tension and communal violence (Varshney 2002: 3–23). Arguments about the formation of Hindu-Muslim divisions are presented as explanations for the occurrence of Hindu-Muslim violence, without descriptions of mechanisms linking the two phenomena. In fact, as recent reviewers of constructivist literature on communal conflict conclude, there are as yet no clear theoretical or empirical underpinnings of a relation between the social construction of communal identities and the occurrence of violence (Fearon and Laitin 2000: 847). Why and how do socially constructed perceptions of Hindu-Muslim divisions lead to violence?

A social-psychological approach

Some answers to this question might be found in the social-psychological explanations for India's communal violence. This very diverse set of explanations focuses on the motivation and drive of those who participate in the violence. This approach uses psychological insights to discuss the gratification that participants get out of the rioting; the writers one can group under this heading advance the argument that riots occur because such violence serves various psychological needs. I will discuss three different arguments that have been advanced to interpret the nature of Gujarat's communal violence.

First, there are those writers who argue that violence serves to establish or maintain a longed-for feeling of superiority. One's self esteem, these writers argue, is closely tied up with one's membership of an ethnic group; by establishing the group's superiority over another group through violence we can boost our feelings of self-worth. Such arguments go back to Freud, who wrote that 'it is precisely the minor differences in people who are otherwise alike that form the basis of feelings of strangeness and hostility between them (....) it would be tempting to derive from this 'narcissism of minor differences' the hostility which in every human relation we see fighting against feelings of fellowship and overpowering the commandment that all men should love one another' (1917, cited in Ignatieff, 1999:20). Freud believes that out of this self-love people are inclined to draw a dividing line between groups, between 'us' and 'them'. On the basis of little differences people construct different identities, which serve, through the glorification of one's own group, to boost one's self esteem. In other words, the perception and evaluation of the self are closely bound up with ideas about 'the other'. Blok

(2000, see also Ignatieff 1999) took up this 'narcissism of minor differences' to argue that violence is especially likely when differences and power-differentials between groups are small or in flux: in such a context violence serves to overcome the uncertainty and ambiguity of one's social status: violence helps to 'put them in their place'.[22]

Using such insights, Kakar (1996: 20) describes India's Hindu-Muslim violence as a 'narcissistic rage'. He notes how often communal organizations refer to 'Hindu pride' or 'Muslim honour' and he argues that 'to me the Hindu-Muslim rift appears as much the consequence of a collision between two collective narcissisms, between two equally grandiose group selves (...) as of differences in matters of faith'. In this fashion communal violence is related to slights and threats to these grandiose group selves: violence can be seen as the result of an 'inferiority complex' (Jaffrelot 2003b) of people who, because of centuries of foreign subjugation and perceptions of economic under-development, have developed an insecurity about their own self-worth. Violence then serves to rebuild the injured self-esteem by physically asserting one's superiority over others.

Such arguments have been used to acquire some perspective on the especially horrific treatment meted out to women during the riots. Not only were women repeatedly gang-raped during the rioting, in many instances they were also mutilated in extremely brutal ways. Tanika Sarkar (2002: 2875) argued that the sexual violence against women was an effective way of claiming one's superiority over the other community. The control over and abuse of the bodies of women is a way to establish the power of one's own group, since this act is the ultimate way of shaming the men: 'the same patriarchal order that designates the female body as the symbol of lineage and community purity, would designate the entire collectivity as impure and polluted, once their woman is raped by an outsider'. She relates this violence to anxieties among (Hindu) men about their own virility and masculinity: 'Violence, for the Sangh [Parivar], is both source and proof of maleness'.

Secondly, there are commentators who relate communal riots to the anxieties caused by the rapid processes of modernization that India is experiencing. The rapid changes in society have undermined cherished certainties: through urbanization, social mobility and an increased communication with outside cultures the established worldviews and patterns of thought are being severely challenged. As people experience a loss of meaning and identity, they look for ways to protect or re-establish the values and convictions that could offer guidance in an increasingly confusing world. This argument is often used to explain the popularity of Hindu-nationalist groups or Muslim fundamentalism; Hansen (1999) has argued in his study about the rising popularity of Hindu-nationalism that feelings of insecurity about one's cultural identities and accompanying ways of life have contributed the formation and popularity of organizations such as the RSS and the VHP.[23] Yagnik and Seth (2002, 2005) argued that this argument holds especially for the expanding middle classes in Gujarat, for whom *Hindutva* served as a beacon in their rapidly changing world: through this ideology, the new middle classes could protect and validate their new social status.

A third line of reasoning sees the violence as a result of a psychological need to project the suppressed and shameful aspects of oneself onto an anonymous other. In this way the 'other' serves as a 'container for one's disavowed aspects' (Kakar 1990): the aspects of one's life that give cause for shame and self-hatred are externalized and attributed to others. Violence, then, is in effect an act of purging oneself of these impurities within: it is 'a substitute for expelling or annihilating the enemy one harbours within oneself, which may account for the overdetermined brutality against and guiltless obliteration of the 'other'' (Tambiah 1996: 276, see also Ghosh and Kumar 2005).

In her analysis of Gujarat's violence Martha Nussbaum singles out the difficult relationship with our bodies as a cause for such violent manifestations of shame and self-hatred. She argues that anxieties about the impurities (its mortality, its fluids, smells etc.) and the sexual nature of the body give rise to violent attempts to establish the desired purity: 'The sense that one fails to have some desired characteristic, often some kind of control or mastery, seems ubiquitous in human beings' relationship to their own bodies, and to the many areas of need and uncontrol that characterize a human life. [This] self-hatred can all too easily turn outward, as symbolic acts of violence seek to remake a world, a longed-for pure and spotless world, in which the once-helpless are in total control, no longer threatened by the vicissitudes of mere human limbs and desires' (Nussbaum 2007: 189). In this way violence can be seen as the result of the rift between the desires and emotions we experience and our internalized social norms and values about these desires and emotions. As we fail to live up to the ideal that society imposes on us, the resulting feelings of helplessness and inadequateness can spill over into aggressive attempts to alleviate these tensions (see also Kakar 1990). In this way there is undeniably an element of fun, of enjoyment, in the perpetration of violence (Verkaaik 2003). Violence provides an occasion for release, for catharsis: the frustrations that have been penned up inside find a release, as the anger about numerous aspects of one's daily life can be acted out, and concentrated on a legitimate target. 'The roots of what happened in Gujarat lie in every mind and heart, because human life is very difficult and our psyches, wounded by mortality and finitude, seek to heal that wound by discreditable means' (Nussbaum 2007: 336).

One could criticize the speculative nature of these theories, and decry the difficulties of verifying and testing them. One could also deride their arguments as 'blame displacement', since these more general arguments about human nature diffuse the responsibility for the violence, and take attention away from the impact of specific acts of individuals who plan and organize it (Brass 2003). Indeed a focus on individual motives alone would miss the relation between these psychological drives and the interactions and power differentials between and within (communal) groups. Nonetheless these theories make an important contribution as they provide us with an avenue to understand the extreme cruelty of the violence that took place. None of the other approaches discussed above—nor any of the arguments developed in this book—are of any help to understand why the outbursts of violence in 2002 were accompanied by such extremely brutal forms of torture and rape. The psychological arguments discussed here are the closest we can get to an understanding of these darkest aspects of the violence.

A relational approach

A last category of attempts to understand India's communal violence could be described, following Tilly (2003), as relational approaches to violence: this approach focuses on the changing patterns of social interaction between and, less commonly, within conflicting communities to explain the repeated incidents of Hindu-Muslim violence. This approach stresses the relational mechanisms behind the occurrence of violence, as it sees violence as a product of the web of relations that bind and divide human beings. By studying the changing patterns of these relations we can gain an understanding of how perceptions of conflict arise and how and why certain individuals feel violence to be legitimate or desirable: by looking at the structure of relations between human beings in different spheres of life we can gain an understanding of the formation of the motives and perceptions underlying violence. The literature on India's communal violence contains quite a number of arguments that, implicitly or explicitly, follow such an approach. I will discuss economic explanations, institutional arguments, and civil society arguments, in that order, before briefly outlining comparatively the approach of this study.

Communal riots have regularly been interpreted in the light of the evolving economic relations between communities. Quite often economic competition between communities has been advanced as an explanation for communal violence. In this fashion the first major outburst of communal violence after independence, in Jabalpur, was attributed to competition between Hindu and Muslim *bidi* (cigarette) manufacturers (Engineer 1995: 31). Shifting patterns of economic competition are a particularly powerful drive behind communal violence: Kumar (2003) describes for example how, as Muslim craftsmen in Mau began to compete with Hindus, communal violence served to drive these new competitors out of business. In a similar fashion riots have been attributed to conflicts over land, as riots could be used to chase away inhabitants from valuable land (e.g. Agnes 1996, Das 2003). Some of the outbursts of violence in 2002 in rural Gujarat have been attributed to a conflict of interests between Muslim moneylenders and indebted farmers (Devy 2002). In this vein, I argued earlier that the overlap of religious and class divisions is a particularly fertile background for communal violence (Berenschot 2005).

Others advance the informalization of Gujarat's economy as an important backdrop for Gujarat's violence. As India's economy opened up to global market forces, Gujarat's working class has lost many regular employment opportunities, which, some argued, strained Hindu-Muslim relations and made large sections of the population more vulnerable to instigation by political actors and communal organizations. As Gujarat's textile mills closed down and neo-liberal policies curtailed the regulation of labour standards and wages, many inhabitants of localities like Isanpur and Raamrahimnagar had to fall back on daily-wage labour in construction sites or small workshops. As the retrenched labourers had to compete fiercely amongst themselves for scarce employment opportunities, ethnic divisions became more pronounced and easier to exploit (Mahadevia 2002, Shah 2004b). For these reasons Breman (2002, 2004: 288) argued that Gujarat's violence could be seen as an outcome of a 'resurgence of Social Darwinism': 'The high tide of communalism is engineered by the promotion of a political economy which seeks to keep the working classes fragmented and in a state of dependency in order to reduce the price of their labour to the lowest possible level'.

A few authors have related the occurrence of violence and ethnic conflict to the 'deinstitutionalization' of the Indian state. With this term Basu and Kohli (1998, see also Kohli 1990) referred especially to the demise of the Congress party since the 1970s and the weakening of the civil bureaucracy in the face of political interference. The changes in the 'organisational pillars' of the Indian state, these authors argue, have spawned new forms of politics and changed local patterns of authority. As more groups were mobilized by new political actors the demands on the state intensified, and the competition for state resources increasingly strained the relations between ethnic groups as their differences were being used for political mobilization. D'Souza (2002) related the violence in Gujarat explicitly to the growing power of politicians over the bureaucracy, as this limited state officials' capacity to stop the rioting. The arguments in this book have some affinity with these institutional arguments; I will return to the relation between the politicization of the bureaucracy and communal violence in the next chapters.

In his book *Ethnic Conflict and Civic Life* Varshney (2002) proposed that changes in the civic life of a city can account for the occurrence or absence of violence. On the basis of a comparison of six violent and relatively peaceful cities he argued that in cities with strong and active civic associations violence is less likely than in cities with little civic engagement. According to Varshney, inter-ethnic engagement—in organizations in which Hindus and Muslims cooperate—can prevent communal violence, because such organizations prevent 'exogenous shocks' (like a major political event, a dispute etc.) from creating local tensions: by countering rumours and keeping small skirmishes in check, such organizations can forestall hostilities. In addition the cooperation within such organizations create incentives for their members to maintain communal harmony.

Varshney's book draws attention to the relation between the pattern of interactions between Hindus and Muslims and the capacity of inhabitants to resist or prevent the instigation of violence. This is a relevant point; as I hope to show in the coming chapters, associational activity does affect the capacity of interested actors to instigate violence (although I will emphasize the importance of both intracommunal as well as intercommunal civic activity). But Varshney has overstated his case by presenting the absence of interethnic associational activity as the proximate cause of violence. By doing so he obscures the political context that requires civic bodies to counter rumours and prevent hostilities in the first place: with his focus on associational activity he obscures the fact that various actors are at work who have an interest in creating and maintaining communal tensions. To revert to a well-worn metaphor, it is as if we would explain the occurrence of fire by looking at the presence or absence of a fire extinguisher, without looking at how or why the fire was lit in the first place. What is needed is a more inclusive approach: attention also needs to be paid to how the structure of relations between communities (including associational life) as well as relations within a community creates incentives and opportunities to organize and instigate violence.

This is one reason why this study will focus on the evolving social and political life within localities. To understand the recurring outbursts of communal violence, attention needs to be paid not only to the shifting relations between communities, but also to how the pattern of interactions between the political elites, their supporters and local residents of a single community change over time because, for example, of the development of state institutions, economic shifts or political developments. Violence arises out of the dynamics of everyday human interaction: the motives and drives of those who contribute to the violence, as well as their perception of the risks involved, can be seen as an outcome of the web of relations in which these individuals are embedded. The goals that individuals set themselves and the strategies they devise to reach these goals, as well as the perceptions and appreciations that underlie these goals and strategies, are shaped by the social reality in which individuals live their lives. In this way I will focus on the relational mechanisms behind the violence: by studying changing patterns of interdependencies we can gain an understanding of how the interests, desires and perceptions behind the occurrence of violence are generated. I thus aim to go beyond merely positing the political interests behind communal violence (as instrumentalists do) by showing how historical and social processes generate these interests.

In this way this study derives inspiration from the work of Norbert Elias (1978, 1994, 2000, 2001) and Pierre Bourdieu (1977, 1991, 1992, 1999, see also Emirbayer 1997), and from various authors who have applied their work to the study of violence in different contexts (Zwaan 2001; Blok 1974, 2001; De Swaan 1997, 2001, 2003, 2007). The work of Elias and Bourdieu is, I think, highly compatible and deserving of a wider application to the study of state-society dynamics in South Asia. Both Elias and Bourdieu draw attention to the relation between the patterns of interdependencies between individuals and the behaviour they display. Their work goes a long way in surmounting the opposition between structure and agency[24] that has marred so much of social science, as these authors help to envisage a dialectic between social structures and individual strategies. The goals and desires that motivate individuals, as well as the strategies that individuals employ, are shaped by the social reality—be it the web of interdependencies (Elias) or the structure of relations within specific fields (Bourdieu)—in which individuals live their lives, while at the same time these goals and strategies produce and reproduce that social reality. Elias in particular (2000: 366) emphasized how this dialectic between individual actions and the broader social fabric can lead to results that nobody envisaged:

> [The] basic tissue resulting from many single plans and actions of people can give rise to changes and patterns that no individual person has planned or created. From this interdependence of people arises an order *sui generis*, an order more compelling and stronger than the will and reason of the individual people composing it. It is this order of interweaving human impulses and strivings, this social order, which determines the course of historical change.

Even though I will not always make it explicit, the influence of work of Bourdieu and Elias will be apparent in several chapters of this book. I will emphasize, for example, the dialectic between the gradual development of the Gujarati state and the particular nature of local politics. As Bourdieu (1999: 58) argued, 'the construction of the state proceeds apace with the construction of *a field of power*, defined as the space of play within which the holders of capital (of different species) struggle *in particular* for power of the state'. This 'field of power' is at the centre of the coming chapters, as I will pay much attention to how the nature of this competition for control over the resources of the state shapes the interdependencies between various actors. The various strategies that individuals employ to develop this control can be seen as a product of (their perception of) the structure of the competition in this field, as well as a product of the specific resources that they have at their disposal: 'the strategies of agents depends on their position in the field, that is, in the distribution of the specific capital, and on the perception that they have of the field depending on the point of view they take *on* the field as a view taken from a point *in* the field' (Bourdieu and Wacquant 1992: 101, see esp. Bourdieu 1991: ch. 8). Bourdieu distinguished several forms of capital (social, cultural, symbolic, and economic) to capture power differentials within a field; in the following chapters I will identify several specific forms of capital that play a role in the interactions between the social workers, politicians, bureaucrats, and others in the localities I have studied: I will discuss how influential contacts, local support (from voters), money, control over musclemen, and a record of favours performed in the past are all useful assets that can help individuals to extend their control over the resources of the Gujarat state.

The 'ground-structure' of this 'field of power' is shaped by the particular development of the capacities of Gujarat's state institution to provide services and uphold legislation. The dependence of citizens on politicians to deal with state institutions structures the competition and cooperation between political actors, and this dependence shapes the possible strategies that political actors can employ to gain support and win elections. As voters rely on politicians to deal with the state, they have an important incentive to judge politicians on their capacity to facilitate this interaction with the state; competing politicians need to cooperate with a large group of different actors to develop this capacity to help citizens deal with state institutions. In such a political field, proposals for policies or new legislation are largely irrelevant if they do not serve directly to improve the access of prospective voters to government resources: political contests are won by developing a control over the distribution of government resources and by using symbolic means to convey promises about the distribution of these resources, not by developing a distinctive position within the 'economy of stances'[25] of policy-debates. Kitschelt and Wilkinson (2007) proposed to use the terms 'programmatic' and 'clientelistic' to capture these two forms of linkages between politicians and citizens.

Such an approach can help to understand the motives and perceptions of those involved in the instigation of violence. Violence can indeed be perceived, as it is by instrumentalists, as a strategy to gain power, and the salience of communal identities can, as social constructivists have stressed, be seen as a result of the repeated confirmation of these identities through various discursive practices; but we need to place such arguments in the context of the political game that engendered such practices. We need to understand how the nature of the competition that political actors are involved in stimulates and rewards such manipulation of inter-communal relations. In this way, the observation that conniving politicians are behind the violence can be given some perspective by studying the role and position of local politicians in the daily life within riot affected localities: a focus on the changing interdependencies between the various contributors to the violence can help to understand political actors' capacity to tap into the fears and desires of the different bystanders and participants in the violence, and to understand how the nature of the political contest in which these actors compete, stimulates them to foment violence.

This is why I will focus on the daily routine of local politicians and their followers before returning to the incidents of violence in Gujarat. I will start out by discussing the emergence of these political networks during the last century, and the historical developments that facilitated their rise. Not too long ago the governance of Ahmedabad was in the hands of old civic institutions like neighbourhood committees (the *pol panch*) and guilds (the *mahajan*). In the next chapter I will discuss how their authority was gradually undermined as a new institution, the municipality, took over their functions.

PART TWO

SHIFTING PATTERNS OF STATE-SOCIETY INTERACTION

3

THE COMING OF THE CHAMCHAS AND THE POLITICIZATION OF GUJARAT'S NEIGHBOURHOODS

'There were not so many party workers before. People were honouring each other. There was much immediate contact. People were looking after each other to help each other. Then the *chamchas* came in the picture, the [political] party people. They are the nuisance people. We use party workers, but we do not honour them. They are selfish people'. Bipinbhai Jhaveri sits every evening at the little square outside his house, where the conversation with his neighbours often turns to the many changes he has witnessed in his neighbourhood.

Bipinbhai lives in one of the oldest localities of Ahmedabad, where the unique design of the houses and the streets reflects the city's tumultuous history. Inhabitants refer to these localities as *pols*. The *pols* are a unique feature of the urban layout of the main cities of Gujarat.[1] Derived from the Sanskrit word *pratoli*—meaning 'enclosed area'—a *pol* is a gathering of houses grouped around one main street delimited by (the remnants of) a main entrance gate that used to be closed at night to protect the inhabitants from outsiders. Inside the *pol* the main street often bifurcates into small lanes (*khanchos*) and little squares (*chowks*). Until recently each *pol* was inhabited by people from the same caste, religion or occupation. The old city of Ahmedabad still consists of approximately 500 *pols* (AMC 2001). Bipinbhai is one of the oldest inhabitants of the jewellers' *pol*. When he arrived here more than fifty years ago, his neighbours were all Jains and all employed in the jewellery business. Nowadays the *pol* has become more heterogeneous since many Hindus, mostly from the Soni ('gold- and silversmiths') caste, have moved in. Bipinbhai's neighbour Hemantbhai is a *Rabari*, traditionally a cattle-rearing caste. 'Hemantbhai, what do you think?', challenges Bipinbhai. 'Don't you agree that party workers are acting as if they are working for the community, but actually they are working for themselves only. I never honour them, I just use them to get some work done. They are bogus people. They honour the party more than their family. Who do you honour more, the family or the party?'

Hemantbhai smiles, he does not seem to mind Bipinbhai's gentle mocking. He is a good-humoured man with a trademark belly that seems to symbolize his material success. His family used to live off the five buffalos that they keep next to their house, but Hemantbhai's connections have enabled him to take up a new profession. He now works in 'real estate': through his political connections he facilitates the sale, renovation or acquisition of houses. He does not often sit out in the evening with Bipinbhai; he maintains a much wider social network throughout the city, and he boasts of many influential friends. These political friendships have prompted Bipinbhai to challenge him: what is Hemantbhai willing to sacrifice for his political contacts?

Bipinbhai has been influential as well. He used to be the president of the *pol panch*, a neighbourhood committee. Bipinbhai had just spoken enthusiastically about the *pol panch*: 'People gave the *panch* great respect. It was providing the basic requirements for living and we kept control over the sale of houses. People had to pay a tax to the *panch*. If you did not pay the tax nobody would keep relations with you'. Bipinbhai's activities have now been reduced to the administration of the nearby temple, but the surroundings still remind him of a more glorious past. Opposite Bipinbhai's house is a latched well which used to be the source of water for the *pol*'s inhabitants. After the municipality started to provide water in the *pol* the *pol panch* closed the well, and turned it into a reading place with newspapers. Nowadays the place is only used for drying laundry. On the other side a huge tree grows out of the foundation of a house. The tree marks the spot were a *haveli* (mansion) with some of the city's most intricate woodcarvings once stood, a prime example of the unique architecture of the *pol* houses. The inhabitants had wanted to move to the more posh western part of Ahmedabad and, unable to sell the house, they had opted for removing and selling the stones and the woodwork. Hemantbhai's buffalos now graze at the foot of that tree.

Hemantbhai takes up Bipinbhai's challenge. 'It is like I told you', he says, turning to the foreign researcher, 'money is like a god. The first god is in the sky, but money is the second god. Money does make people happy. We do everything for the stomach. We do some good things for the stomach, and we do some bad things for the stomach also. We have to maintain relations. But for me my family comes first, then the community, and then Pravinbhai [the local municipal councillor, WB]. For some people Pravinbhai comes first. They have no sense of duty, they only care about money'.

Chamchas literally means 'spoons', but in daily usage the word refers to sycophants or 'yes-men': the numerous men that associate themselves with local and state-level politicians. These 'party workers' are indispensable for these political leaders as organizers of rallies, as campaigners during election times, and as intermediaries who help political parties to maintain local support and gather funds. In return for these valuable services party workers can profit from preferential access to politicians and bureaucrats. This access can be turned into a source of revenue—when party workers sell their services as brokers—and it can help to build a local reputation, which a party worker can use to launch a political career of his own.[2] In this way Hemantbhai has proved himself to be a valuable intermediary for local builders and other businessmen, which brought him an income unprecedented in his family. His skilful maintenance of various contacts has enabled him to launch a (unsuccessful) bid a few years ago to become a municipal councillor. Because of their usefulness, party workers like Hemantbhai occupy a prominent place in their localities: they are approached when a street light needs repair, when somebody needs treatment at a municipal hospital, when a license needs to be arranged, etc.

In this chapter I will discuss how these networks of local intermediaries have come to occupy such a prominent position in many localities in Gujarat's cities. I will argue that this process is largely a result of the development of the Indian state's capacities. Borrowing a concept from Michael Mann, I will propose that the development over the last two centuries of the state's infrastructural power in Gujarat—'the capacity of the state actually to penetrate civil society, and to implement logistically political decisions throughout the realm' (Mann 1986: 112)[3]—has led to the demise of Gujarat's civic institutions. Institutions like the *pol panch*es as well the local trade guilds, the *mahajans*, occupied a central position within Gujarat's civil society until at least the beginning of the 20th century. The *mahajans* were influential guilds that regulated not only the occupational life of many of Gujarat's traders and artisans, but also played an important role in the administration of Gujarat's cities. Together these two institutions performed many of the functions that have since been taken up by Gujarat's state institutions.[4] This process has undermined their local authority and their capacity to discipline members. As different state institutions started offering more services to citizens—from sanitation or street lighting to hearing cases in court—they undermined the functionality of the *pol panch*es and the *mahajans*.

Then the *chamcha*s took over: the development of the state's infrastructural power has led at the same time to a growth of networks of local politicians and their supporters, who became increasingly useful to gain access to the growing resources of the state. The state's infrastructural power has not developed to such an extent that the newly developed services are easily accessible. This development of the state's infrastructural power—its strengthening as well as its limitations—has led to replacement of the elder dignitaries of the older civic institutions by local politicians and their *chamcha*s as the most influential figures in Gujarat's neighbourhood life.[5] As I will show in later chapters, this coming of the *chamcha*s has engendered local political networks that, in 2002, could be used to mobilize people for violence.

A protection plan

Most sources[6] see the development of the *pol* in its present form[7] as a response to the disorder that engulfed Gujarat during and after the gradual collapse of Mughal rule in the 17th and 18th centuries. Ahmedabad was repeatedly captured and plundered by different armies, and the nominal Maratha rulers had to seize the city several times to gain and regain control. In between most of Gujarat's major cities suffered from repeated raids by roving bands of Bhils and Kolis. As a commercial city Ahmedabad was especially attractive to raiders; because of its vibrant trade in, among other things, textiles, opium, silk and indigo[8] many valuables were stocked inside Ahmedabad's crumbling city walls. Outside travellers noted that merchants were outwardly leading a very frugal life, since an open display of wealth risked drawing unwanted attention from thieves or greedy officials.[9]

The communal life inside the *pol*s could give inhabitants some protection against these ongoing attacks and raids. The pattern of housing as well as the tight social control within the *pol* enhanced the security of the inhabitants. The main entrance gate at the beginning of the *pol* was closed every night, until as late as 1953 (Doshi 1974: 77). At times of rioting or in case of outside attacks, the doors could be closed in daytime as well. Most of the *pol*s employed a watchman, called *polio*, to close these doors and to keep a watch over who entered the *pol*. The *polio* often lived in a little house that was built above the entrance gate of the *pol*. In the 18th century defensive considerations played such an important role in the construction of the houses that no windows or even ventilation holes were built in the outside walls of the *pol*s. The most coveted area was the most interior part of the *pol*, where the houses were safest from outside attacks. A chronicler of the city's history noted that 'for the foreigner it was difficult to know where the city's doors and houses were, and what type they were, and they were going back with a strange idea about the city' (Ratnamanirao 1929: 322).

In one of the few available insider accounts of life in the *pol*s the local politician and writer Jayanti Dalal writes the following about the formation of the *pol*s:

> Like rulers who build a wall around the city to arrange the defence, similarly the *sheri* [street, *pol*] imitated this to protect itself against natural and manmade disasters. The setup of the *pol* was such that there was enough space for the [incorporation of] the old panchayat system. So this protection plan was not only taking care of the protection of one's life and property, but its scope expanded to include the welfare and prosperity of the people living in the collectivity. (...) There was an intensity of the social relations with each other, so the burden of the collective welfare and prosperity fell on the whole *pol*. That was the peak of the glory of the city's pol. The social fibre of the *pol* was then at its strongest. In the *mahajan* this network was much respected. Its voice, although it had limited strength, even reached the courts of the king.(...) The elders of the *pol* were implementing new experiments of democracy. And even some novel experiments in equality, disturbing for some, were also being carried out. The decisions that the pols democratic system had taken were put into

practice by using methods of pressurization that are incomparable to other methods (Dalal 1990 (1948): 12).[10]

As Dalal's description indicates, a form of organization developed that started to perform various functions related to many different aspects of daily life inside the *pols*. Probably established for the administration of the *pol*'s temples (Dalal 1990: 147–8), the *pol panch* acquired a central role in social life.

All house owners could become members of the *pol panch*; they elected among themselves a number of inhabitants to perform the different tasks of the *panch*. As the name suggests (meaning 'five'), the *pol panch*es often had five main working members, including a president, a treasurer and a secretary. The leadership of the *pol panch* was usually taken up by the elderly members of the community, who commanded respect in the *pol* because of their professional accomplishments, wealth or family background (Doshi 1974). A major task of the *pol panch* was the upholding (and sometimes revising) of its rules regarding the renting and sale of houses in the *pol*. These rules until recently were instrumental in maintaining the homogeneity of each *pol*, by prohibiting or restricting the sale and lease of the houses to people from other communities. Sale, as well as renting out of every house needed to be approved by the *pol panch*, and every new house owner was obliged to become a member of the *pol panch* by paying a tax to the *panch*, a percentage (up to 10 per cent) of the value of the newly bought house. This *pol*-tax entitled the house owner to take part in the meetings of the *pol panch* and to make use of the facilities that the *pol panch* provided. Tenants were excluded from the decision-making in the council, but they could also become a member of the panch by paying a fixed amount to the *pol panch*.

Another important function of the *pol panch* was the provision of various amenities (Doshi 1974: ch. 8). The *pol panch* arranged the maintenance of the local well, it built and maintained the common latrines, provided and arranged streetlights, and organized the cleaning of the *pol*'s streets. In many cases the *pol panch* administered the *pol's* temple affairs. In the richer *pols* the *panch* also provided medical equipment, cooking utensils and even a library for inhabitants. The *pol panch* itself also organized several communal and mostly religious celebrations, a task that is now mostly taken over by the *yuvak mandals*, the youth groups. In spring a *havan* is still organized in many Hindu dominated *pols*: a day-long religious rite in which several gods are invoked for the wellbeing of all *pol* residents. On this day, an earthen pot and a coconut—a *gagar bandhyu*—are hung above the entrance of the *pol* to ensure the wellbeing of its inhabitants, as a still visible outward sign of the organization and cooperation within the *pols*. Some of the costs of these activities could be met because of the *panch*'s administration of common property of the *pol*. Many *pol panch*es could collect rent from the *pol* houses that it owned.

Another task of the *pol panch* was the upholding and enforcing of certain norms of behaviour. The interference of the *pol panch* could extend to many facets of the daily life of *pol* residents. Residents were expected to obey the rules regarding the lease and sale of houses, and they were obliged to assist at times of death or marriage of *pol* members. Because of the uniformity of caste within a *pol* the *pol panch* often functioned like a caste *panchayat*:[11] the elders of the *panch* could sanction the residents' behaviour in areas like marriage, work or even travel,[12] and they were often consulted to settle disputes between residents or even between family members. There is a Gujarati saying that still conveys the importance of the *panch* in settling disputes and maintaining harmonious relations between residents: '*panch tya parmeshvar*', where there is a *panch*, there is God.

The *pol panch* could make use of an elaborate system of sanctions to enforce its rules. For minor offences a fine was imposed. Inhabitants had to pay, for instance, a small amount to the *panch* if they had failed to attend the funeral of one of their *pol*-neighbours. Some walls next to the *pol*-gate still have a small box or hole where inhabitants were supposed to deposit their fines.[13] In the case of grave offences whole families could be excommunicated: the *pol panch* could direct its members to cut off all communication with families who, for instance, refused to pay the *pol* tax or whose behaviour was considered to be a serious offence. This social boycott was often accompanied by a ban on the use of the *pol* amenities, which could seriously hamper the excommunicated family in its daily life. As Doshi remarks, the capacity of the *pol panch* to impose its rules was closely related to its provision of several indispensable facilities:

> In the past when there were common latrines and common well and other such public utilities managed by the pol-council, the families so excommunicated were not allowed to make use of these amenities whereby their daily life in the pol became very difficult. This treatment was extended up to the level that no family in the pol could supply them a spark of fire to light the hearth and lamp. This was locally called 'Deevo-Devata-bandh'. (…) The Jain and the Patel *Pols* being located in interior part of the city, were far from the open-fields which could be used in absences of latrines, therefore, no family could afford to ignore the importance of this amenity provided by the *pol* and that made every family conform to the requirements of the *pol*. (Doshi 1974: 60 and 121)

To understand the social control within a *pol*, another typical feature of the *pol* needs to be discussed: the *otla*. Since the entrances of the houses in the *pol*s are slightly raised, people can sit on the stone platforms next to the entrances of the houses. These raised platforms are called *otla* and they play an important role in the social life of the *pol*. Hemantbhai and Bipinbhai were talking on such an *otla*: especially in the evenings residents (mostly men) gather there to enjoy friendly conversations or heated debates. Dalal lamented the way in which such gatherings influenced the life in the *pol*s:

> The *otla* plays a very important role in the life of the community. (…) Much abuse and hatred is digested by the *otla*, and there is no need to feel sorry if you can't hear a single word of selfless praise. To find out minute faults in the behaviour of others, and to advise others on how to behave, these are the true characteristics of the *otla*. The elderly authority that the *otla* gives plays an extraordinary role in the life of people liv-

ing in the pol. (...) It is the basis of the community life of the city and sometimes it might be the parliament of the city's people. Today, lacking a sense of responsibility, this democratic community life is worn out and has become a Vaghri [a Dalit caste considered to be undisciplined and chaotic] panch (Dalal 1990: 108 and 110).

Before discussing Dalal's analysis of the changing community life in the *pols*, I will discuss another civic institution that Gujarat could once boast of, the *mahajans*.

Guilds as an 'inner domain'

As Ratnamanirao (1929: 548) noted with some pride, the trade guilds of Gujarat, and especially Ahmedabad, were more active and stronger than those in other parts of the country:

There are no organisations like this in India. They have lived up to their name till now. They are here since ancient times, and they have bloomed more in Gujarat than in any other part. In comparison with other regions, whatever culture and characteristics are important in Gujarat, it is there because of the *mahajans*. They have sustained trade and kept foreigners out.

The *mahajan* is a very old institution[14] that until recently played a central role in the administration of Gujarat's major cities as well as many of its villages.[15] They are guilds that regulate occupational life, and to a certain extent also the social life of members. There were *mahajans* for all major trades in the region: for instance a *mahajan* for the cloth markets, a cotton-dealers' *mahajan*, a share-market *mahajan*, a silk-traders' *mahajan*, a jewellers' *mahajan* etc. The most prominent guild was the *sharaf mahajan*, the guild of the bankers. The guilds of the artisans, like potters, carpenters, tile-makers and blacksmiths, were referred to as *panch*, which reflected a lesser status of these guilds, as well as the fact that their members were mostly from a single caste: the guild and the caste *panchayat* were often just one institution (Mehta 1988: 1977). In most of the trades that the *mahajans* regulated merchants from different communities were active. The head of the *mahajan* was called *Sheth*, a title that was in many cases hereditary or conferred to persons of (families of) extraordinary prestige. The Sheth was often advised by a council of influential elderly men (Mehta 1984: 177).

The primary task of the *mahajan* was to regulate trade. Each *mahajan* had elaborate rules that stipulated the wages, the price of its products,[16] when the holidays were to be observed, and what the working hours were. In the absence of legal contracts, traders often relied on *mahajans* to ensure that their oral agreements would be honoured: when dealers failed to live up to these agreements the aggrieved party could have recourse to the *mahajan* to pressurize the defaulting dealer. At the same time the *mahajan* checked production to maintain quality standards, and kept control over who could enter the profession. With these rules the *mahajans* prevented internal competition and protected the sector in times of falling demand. Their constraints on production discouraged people from working harder than others, since the guilds' regulations prevented them from benefiting from their extra work. The British author of the *Ahmedabad Gazetteer* referred in 1879 to this aspect of the functioning of the *mahajans* as 'bigoted communism' (Ratnamirao 1929: 553).

The head of the most prominent *mahajan*—for a long time the bankers' *mahajan*—was called the *nagarsheth*. As the most prominent citizen of the city, his position was the equivalent to the present-day mayor. He was excluded from paying taxes, and lived in a big mansion in the centre of the walled city. The *nagarsheth* was active in the administration of the city, and he arbitrated and negotiated when disputes between different *mahajans* arose. There were frequent conflicts between *mahajans* and the artisan' guilds over the prices of the artisans' products; through their trade guilds the lower castes could deal with upper castes on a more equal footing (Misra 1981: 89), which enabled them occasionally to get a better price for their products. And cooperation within the trade guild could occasionally prevent exploitation by upper caste clients, because the artisans could decide to boycott a client who had maltreated one of their members (Mehta 1984: 179). But generally the guild system served to preserve the status quo: through alliances between different powerful *mahajans* it was difficult for lower caste guilds to win a dispute.[17]

The larger *mahajans* collected money through the various fines and fees that they imposed on their members, and they could also derive income from the purchases of members on which they imposed a small tax. Hopkins describes how, for example, from every cart of grain that enters the city, a few handfuls were taken out and thrown on a heap next to the city gate (1901: 90).[18] The money thus collected was mostly used for charity: money was spent on temples, but also on the city's infrastructure, like water tanks, shade-trees, fountains and *dharamshalas* (accommodation for pilgrims). The *mahajans* were also an important contributor to the *panjra pols*, the accommodation for sick and decrepit animals.

Apart from the regulation of trade the *mahajans* played a prominent role in the settlement of disputes, which added to their leaders' local standing. Especially in small towns the *mahajan* was the accepted referee up to the late 19th century, while in bigger cities the courts often referred cases to the *mahajan* for settlement. When conflicts arose between members of different guilds, the disputants appealed to a bigger *mahajan* or to the *nagarsheth*, or a committee was formed to settle the dispute. The arbitration of such disputes was based on custom, not on legislation; but, according to Hopkins, 'there is seldom a complaint of injustice' (Hopkins 1901: 198).

The lack of complaints could be due to the heavy price that an individual had to pay for going against the *mahajan*. For smaller offences the *mahajan* could impose a fine, for example when somebody had worked more hours than the *mahajan* had stipulated. But when a person refused to abide by its rules or verdicts the *mahajan* could ostracize someone from the guild. The result of such outcasting was severe, as Hopkins writes in 1901: 'In the country, such an outlaw is debarred from all social recognition. No man will work with him or for him, nor will any one employ him. In the cities, no dealer will serve him, no broker will act for him, no servant will remain in his house. The (...) lowest of the lowly refuse to take his orders, deliver goods to him, or perform any service for him at any price'. This excommunication could be aggravated if the caste *panchayat* decided to enforce the outcasting as well; then the offender 'becomes a social pariah, more wretched than a village dog' (Hopkins 1901: 193).

In carrying out their verdicts the trade guilds and caste associations often functioned in unison. In theory the *mahajan* was only concerned with the regulation of trade, while the caste *panchayat* regulated personal conduct and settled non-trade related disputes between caste members. But since a guild often consisted of members of a single caste the functions of the caste *panch* and those of the guild overlapped considerably; in the case of many artisan castes they were one single organization. Even when the *mahajan* consisted of members of different castes, it cooperated with the caste *panch* in punishing erring individuals.[19]

At least from the Mughal time onwards, Gujarat's rulers and their officials relied on the *mahajans* to deal with the local population. They often needed the consent of the *mahajans* to raise taxes, and sometimes even used them to collect the tax (Mehta 1984). The *mahajans* were also the channel through which local grievances and requests were transmitted to the court; Hasan (2004) emphasizes how, especially from the 17th century, the *mahajan* acquired a more active political role beyond its older commercial and social functions.[20] In this fashion state officials and the *mahajans* helped each other to preserve their power: the *mahajan* also occasionally sought the help of state officials to punish a person who had disobeyed its rules (Hopkins 1901: 203). The *sheth* functioned as a spokesperson for the whole *mahajan*, and the officials dealt with the *mahajan* only through the *sheth*. This enabled the merchants to restrict the interference of rulers and state officials in their businesses; to a certain extent Gujarat's rulers administered the state only indirectly, through the institutions of the *mahajan* and especially through the *nagarsheth*.[21]

Gujarat's rulers did have local representatives to enforce their rulings; under the Sultans and Mughal viceroys each city had at least one *kotwal* ('police officer') who headed a limited police force, as well as a *kazi*, a judge. Both were entrusted with the task of maintaining law and order, but their authority was limited and decreased as the Mughal Empire faded.[22] Since state institutions lacked the capacity to enforce regulation or laws independently of the cooperation and mediation of the *mahajans*, the role of the state in the administration of the cities was limited. For a long time these institutions effectively prevented the state from establishing and exercising its full authority in urban Gujarat; the social control in Gujarat's cities was highly fragmented,[23] as a diverse set of local bodies as well as state officials could claim some authority over the daily lives of inhabitants. As a result sovereignty in these areas was effectively shared: the institution of the *mahajan* (and the *pol panch*) constituted an 'inner domain' within Gujarat's cities on which the consecutive Mughal, Maratha and British rulers had little grip (Haynes 1992: ch. 4). But when from the 19th century onwards the role of the state in the administration of Gujarat's cities increased, the 'inner domain' of the *mahajans* and the *pol panch* was gradually encroached upon, and their local authority was slowly undermined.

The tracks of a snake that has passed

In 1948 Jayanti Dalal wrote the following about the *pol panch*:

> The panch might have shown tremendous organizational power in the past, but nowadays the panch is no more than, as they say, the tracks of a snake that has passed. (...) Once upon a time, it had full strength to punish any offender of its rules, nowadays the people of the *pol* tolerate the *panch* out of respect. The authority of the panch is now negligible. (...) The connecting threat of the *pol* residents—be it mutual protection, community life, or relations of love or fear—have broken completely. The warmth of the relations has gone (Dalal 1990 (1948): 147–9).

More than fifty years later one can add that the tracks of the snake are fading away as well. A recent survey of the Ahmedabad Municipal Corporation (AMC 2004a) found that only in 39 per cent of the Ahmedabad's *pol*s could some local administrative body be found, of which 75 per cent were, according to inhabitants, inactive or hardly active.[24] And even the *pol panch*es that are active no longer play a central role in the organization and regulation of neighbourhood life: their role is mostly restricted to the organization of religious functions or community dinners. The *panch* rules regarding the sale and lease of houses are no longer upheld; houses are rented out and sold to people from other castes or even other religious communities. Most informants attributed this change to the fact that inhabitants wanted a better price for their houses, which they could get if they sold to buyers from other communities. The *pol panch*es who have not sold their property often have difficulties collecting the rent from inhabitants who live in the houses belonging to the *panch*. In only one *pol* in the old city of Ahmedabad is the *panch* still regulating the sale and lease of houses.[25] Virtually no *pol panch* is still endeavouring to provide amenities to residents.

A similar story can be told about the mahajan. Hopkins noted already in 1901 that the authority of the *mahajan*'s *sheth* and its council had eroded, and in 1929 Ratnamanirao wrote that:

> Before it was considered very important to be a member of a *mahajan*, and to an extent even now. Now the courts power is supreme, because of that the importance of the members of the *mahajan* have decreased a bit. Before the *mahajans* had an influence on the courts and the officials, so their opinion was valued. Because the authority declined, whatever rights and protection of trading [of the *mahajan*] also went away. Because of that the respect for the *mahajan* was more before.

At present there are still many *mahajans* active in Gujarat,[26] but they no longer regulate the transactions or productions of a trade, nor are they enforcing rules that limit competition. Most trade related disputes are settled in court. Apart from offering some social security to its members, they function mostly as a lobby group with the aim of influencing government policy regarding trade tariffs or tax. And they mediate with the police in case of theft. As the secretary of one of the now many diamond associations remarked: 'Most *mahajans* are strong when some member feels a problem, after that they go to sleep. The generation has changed. People are more selfish now, so the *mahajans* are not so strong anymore'.

How did this happen? How did institutions that dominated the civic life of Gujarat's cities for centuries lose their prominence to such extent? One could relate their demise to the many developments that, often grouped under the heading of 'modernization', have taken place in India over the last century. In the case of the *mahajans* one could point to economic exigencies that came with India's increased integration into a global economy, to the growth of new industries, or to the loosening of occupational patterns. In the case of the *pol panch* one can point to growth of the western side of Ahmedabad: many *pol* residents moved out of the congested and noisy old city to the more alluring apartment buildings on the other side of Ahmedabad's main river. The *pols* of Ahmedabad are being left behind: the number of inhabitants in the old city has dropped by more than 20 per cent since 1971 while the city's total population more than doubled over the same period (AMC 2004b: 14). The large-scale shift of people out of the old part of the city, and the loss of status of this part of the city, might have contributed to a loosening of the *panch* rules regarding sale and rent of the houses: people belonging to different communities have moved in who did not want to participate in the *pol panch*. Since the *pol panch* is still associated with management of the temple and religious activities of the erstwhile dominant community, it is difficult to integrate members of different communities—who worship in different temples and in different ways—into the *pol panch*. Jayanti Dalal (1990: 12) already commented on this process in 1948: 'The group of people of one blood more or less diminished or with various reasons has spread over the earth and the *pol* has become the residential area of people with different occupations (...). The discord with the newly arrived people is still unsolved'.

A major reason behind the demise of the *mahajan* and the *pol panch* was that various state institutions, especially Gujarat's municipalities, acquired the capacity to provide basic services to citizens. As the municipalities gradually expanded their operations, and started to offer more services to inhabitants, they undermined the position and status of the *pol panches* and the *mahajans*. The development of Gujarat's municipalities undermined these civic institutions in two ways. It undermined both the functionality of *panches* and *mahajans* and their capacity to discipline their members: the *panches* and the *mahajans* lost the stick as well as the carrot through which they had inspired support and obedience in the past. A short excursion into the history of Ahmedabad's Municipal Corporation can illustrate this point.

Ahmedabad's municipality came into being as a response to the same problem that had shaped the *pols*, the city's vulnerability to outside attacks.[27] After the British had taken control of the city in 1817, they received several requests to rebuild the city walls that had fallen into ruins. A small 'town wall committee' with, among others, the *nagarseth* as a member was formed on 22 April 1831 to collect funds to restore the city walls. The committee resolved to impose a small tax on the import into the city of several products, such as silk, ghee (clarified butter) and opium. With the funds that the tax generated the repair works were started. This work, as well as the general improvement in the security of Gujarat's cities through stricter policing, contributed to an early popularity of the British rulers (as compared to other parts of the country). When the walls were finished in 1842, the five-member committee received several requests to continue its work and to use its funds to provide amenities to improve the very unhygienic living conditions in the city. This committee was to become Ahmedabad's municipality: the enactment of several municipal acts by the British rulers gradually expanded its responsibilities and changed its name. The town wall committee was reconstituted as the 'Municipal Commission' in 1858, which became 'Ahmedabad Municipality' in 1874. It started to water the otherwise dusty roads, schools were set up, water-tanks were put in place and poles for street lighting were installed (Boman-Behram 1937).

At that time the administration of the municipality was still dominated by British officers. As the activities of the municipality expanded, its popularity declined, and its intrusions into the city were increasingly regarded with suspicion. In 1873, at a large public meeting, a petition was adopted to protest against the strictness of the municipal rules and the invasion of privacy by municipal inspectors. The petition read: 'In their zeal to carry out favourite schemes of sanitation and reform, the municipal authorities utterly set at nought [sic] the feelings, the ability, and the circumstances of the people'. (Gillion 1968: 121)

After 1885 the municipality managed to overcome this opposition and enacted several schemes to enlarge its—at that time very limited—provision of amenities, although the increase in taxes that accompanied this expansion was still bitterly criticized. After some failed attempts, and after considerable local protest, a first water tank became operational in 1891; water was pumped into the city through water pipes. In Maneknagar a beginning was made with an underground drainage system, which from 1903 onwards was expanded to other parts of the city. Gradually the municipality employed more sweepers to assume responsibility for the cleaning of the city (Gillion 1968: ch. 4). From 1915 onwards an electricity plant supplied electricity, a bus service was put in place and gradually more and more *pol* streets were paved. A health department was set up, and with the financial support of a textile baron a municipal hospital was opened. A grid of water pipes and gutter lines was laid throughout the city, which was greatly enlarged between 1924 and 1928 when Vallabhbhai Patel was the president of the municipal council. These facilities were gradually expanded throughout the city; Doshi describes how water connections were provided in the *pol*s until as late as 1937, while many private and common latrines were not connected to the municipal drainage system until 1952 (Doshi 1974: 70 and 120).

This increased presence of the municipality in the city slowly changed the nature of its politics. Consecutive electoral reforms slowly enlarged the electoral franchise as well as the number of elected representatives on the Municipal Board, which allowed a new urban elite to gain ascendance. In the 19th century the most prominent representatives were local notables and leaders of the *mahajan*s, whose authority was based on their wealth, professional success and the prestige of their family. From the late 19th century onwards a new elite emerged who came from a 'lesser' family background and were less wealthy. They were well educated in the new educational institutions and they had acquired considerable professional skills as lawyers or doctors, which they could use to deal with the evolving government institutions. Their knowledge of the English language and their ability to deal with the new and foreign government institutions made them indispensable as an interface between the government and the population.[28]

These new urban leaders adopted a more oppositional attitude towards the British rulers than the often deferential notables. This opposition served them well: they could make use of local resistance to the government's controversial town planning schemes, such as the removal of Ahmedabad's now obsolete city wall, to gain prominence. Furthermore, they started to use their influence in the municipality to woo the leaders in the *pol*s. The still prevalent practices of patronage evolved in this period: the new urban leaders around the famous Congress politician Vallabhbhai 'Sardar' Patel started to build up support by selectively delivering public amenities to leaders of industries or *pol* leaders. Through their dominance in, especially, the municipality's sanitary and public works committees they acquired control over the provision of municipal amenities in the city. In exchange for the provision of amenities these political leaders ensured the allegiance of local leaders (Raychaudhuri 2001). These new patronage networks integrated local authority structures in the *pol*s into a larger political sphere.

This short history of Ahmedabad's municipality is the story not only of the rise of the *chamcha*s, but also of a gradual substitution of the traditional functions of the *pol panch*es and the *mahajan*s. From its early improvements of the city's defence to, later on, its water supply, sweeping, street lighting, drainage etc.: gradually the municipality started performing the same functions that the *pol panch*es and the *mahajan*s were performing. These services were already considered superior in 1929 (Ratnamirao 1929: 375): 'Just about every work of the *pol* the municipality is doing now, was earlier done by the panch (...) so in our society we found a similar element like the municipality, but it was not well organized, and not universal'. At the same time the development of local courts and the implementation of extensive government regulations undermined the role of the *mahajan*s as arbitrators of disputes. Furthermore, the *mahajan*s lost their role as an interface between the city's rulers and its population to the new educated urban leaders who filled the official positions within the municipality. As we will see below, this role was later monopolized by professional politicians and their numerous local supporters.

In his study of life in Ahmedabad's *pol*s, Doshi (1974) expressed the hope that the *pol panch*es could evolve to perform other valuable services. This did not happen, because the development of the municipality had also undermined the instruments that the *panch*es, as well as the *mahajan*s, could use to discipline their members. In the past the *panch*es and the *mahajan*s could exercise strict control because they could threaten their members with outcasting. This threat could inspire obedience: the life of an excommunicated member could be made very difficult since such a person could no longer go to the common latrines, use the well, obtain a spark to light a fire etc. Even a person's livelihood could be endangered. Since the municipality started providing the same services to every inhabitant—irrespective of his or her standing in the local community—the *pol panch*es and the *mahajan*s lost a stick to wield to command obedience. Deprived of this stick, they could no longer make inhabitants conform to their once extensive regulation. However, the particular development of the municipal institutions provided new sticks and carrots to another, new group of actors: to politicians and their *chamcha*s.

A new generation

There are enough reasons not to feel nostalgic about the demise of the *pol panch* and the *mahajan*. The social control that these institutions exercised could be oppressive, their handling of disputes often served to keep social inequalities in place, and the basic amenities that they provided were—compared to the present municipal services—clearly inadequate. Yet the growing irrelevance of the *pol panch* and *mahajan*s has created new inequalities as well. New patterns of authority and new power differentials have taken shape as local politicians and their *chamcha*s have become more prominent.

The word *chamcha* can refer to quite a diverse group of people, who are unlikely to use that word for themselves: some would call themselves party workers, some social workers, and occasionally someone might refer to himself as a *dalal*, a 'broker'. *Chamcha*s have in common that they all play a mediating role to help inhabitants deal with various government institutions. Their services are especially useful for those who need help to deal with those institutions: they can be found especially in poorer areas of the city, where, as they lack resources and useful contacts, inhabitants are more dependent on political actors to arrange health care, water provision, welfare benefits, etc. *Chamcha*s profit from the obstacles that ordinary—that is, politically unconnected—citizens face when dealing with government institutions. Their current local status and the development of the state's infrastructural power are thus related: the development of the various state services and the expansion of the state's capacity to uphold regulation have produced a demand for intermediaries who can help to gain access to these resources. This demand is premised on the capacities as well as the limitations of Gujarat's state institutions: intermediaries are needed because the state has services to offer and because these services are not easily accessible to everyone.

These two aspects—the extended scope but limited strength (Fukuyama 2005)[29] of the state's capacities—underlie the current dependence of citizens on the mediation of political actors and their *chamchas*. On the one hand the expanded scope of Ahmedabad's municipality (as well as Gujarat's state institutions) stimulated its inhabitants to turn to the state (and away from the *pol panch* and the *mahajans*) to make use of the municipality's expanding range of services, while on the other hand the limited capacity to meet the demand for these services engenders a dependence on those intermediaries who can provide access to the limited resources of the state, and can manipulate the application of policies and laws. The limited capacity of state agents to enforce legislation and to provide basic services underlie the current dependence of citizens on political mediators, as these limitations make it difficult for ordinary citizens to deal with state institutions without recourse to influential intermediaries.[30]

This has changed the patterns of authority within localities. The demise of the *pol panches* and the *mahajans* and the development of municipal institutions is not an inconsequential change from one organizational form to another; that process of change has had an impact on local power relations and has increased the capacity of supra-local political actors to manipulate political and communal sentiments. The increased dependence of inhabitants on political networks has made the poorer neighbourhoods in particular more vulnerable to political instigation as these neighbourhoods have become politicized through the proliferation of networks of *chamchas*. In this way, the development of the state's infrastructural power and the weakening of the *pol panches* and *mahajans* have made the poorer neighbourhoods more vulnerable to political instigation and manipulation.

We will turn to the functioning of these political networks in the next chapters, but let me, by way of summary, mention three important changes in the local patterns of authority. Firstly, localities have become politicized as they have become gradually integrated into wider political networks. Before, both the city's neighbourhood life—through the institution of the *pol panch* (and the caste *panchayat*)—and the cities' trade, through the *mahajans*, were essentially self-administered and functioned largely independent of state power. The rules and regulations that guided these institutions were based on local customs and caste-rules. This ensured that cities consisted of relatively autonomous 'enclaves' where outside authorities had very little influence. But when municipalities began to offer basic amenities and developed their capacity to draft and uphold various rules and regulations, a new urban elite gained prominence by using these increased capacities to enlist local support. This spurred the development of extensive patronage networks, and *chamchas* became active in the remotest localities. In this process, political parties achieved an active presence throughout Gujarat. As I will show in the later chapters of this book, it was this active presence in poor neighbourhoods that provided the infrastructure for the organization of communal violence.

A second consequence of the gradual development of Gujarat's state institutions is that the provision of basic services, especially to poorer citizens—from school admissions to street paving or a licence extension, etc.—is now to a certain extent premised on (electoral) support for politicians. To get influential politicians to help them deal successfully with the (municipal) bureaucracy, party workers have to offer unconditional support in return—hence the use of the word *chamchas*, 'yes-men', to refer to party workers. In order to maintain their access to politicians, these party workers have to canvass during elections, help collect funds for the elections, and show their capacity to mobilize crowds for protests and agitations. In return for their assistance during the elections, the party worker can expect some cooperation at a later stage.

Thirdly, the sources of local authority have changed. Before the coming of the *chamchas* the most prominent inhabitants of the *pol*—often members of the *pol panch*—were respected because of several non-political considerations, such as their wealth, their age, their professional success or the prestige of their family. As Haynes (1992) describes, the upholding of the family's *abru* ('honour' or 'prestige') was a central concern in the conducting of one's business as well as in one's social life. These sources of authority have slowly lost their value, and a new source of authority has become more important: access to influential politicians and bureaucrats. Since the people with political clout now hold sway over the provision of amenities or the application of rules and regulations—as the *pol panch* and the *mahajans* did before—they have gained in local status and authority. Their status in the neighbourhood is based not only on relations with their neighbours, but is also based on their prestige in larger, citywide networks. The outside contacts shape one's position inside the *pol*.

One can observe this change during evening discussions at the *otlas*. A person like Hemantbhai is respected and liked among different groups of inhabitants. Hemantbhai dominates most of the discussions on whichever *otla* he sits. He invariably sits in the middle of the *otla*, and on many occasions he entertains his neighbours with extravagant tales of the latest exploits of municipal councillors or party leaders across the city. He was never seriously taken to task—at least not when I was around—about the practical implications of his earlier remark that 'money is the second god'.

There might be resentment, at least among inhabitants like Bipinbhai. The former president of the *pol panch* only sits at the *otla* next to his house and, although he is always treated with respect, his reflections on the changes in the city are not always taken seriously. By way of responding to Hemantbhai's remarks, he turns with an apologetic gesture to the researcher and confides: 'It is this generation. The people born after seventy-five, those are the mischievous people'. By that time Hemantbhai had already taken his scooter to move to another *otla*, in another part of the city.

4

CHANGING PATRONAGE CHANNELS AND THE RISE OF HINDU-NATIONALISM IN GUJARAT

Close to the old mosques, city gates and old fort in Ahmedabad's city centre there is a big, if somewhat run-down, villa called 'Gandhi Majoor Sevalaya' ('Gandhi's workers welfare'). The building houses Gujarat's famous Textile Labour Association, the Majoor Mahajan Sangh or TLA. This trade union was founded in 1920 under the guidance of Mahatma Gandhi to mediate between the labourers and the owners of Gujarat's expanding textile industry. The TLA was able to unite a large section of the textile labourers and in negotiations with the mills owners, the trade union managed to secure modest but important improvements in living standards and wages. Its large membership—the TLA had over 100,000 members in the 1960s—made the union an important player in Gujarat's politics.

Today the big villa that houses the TLA stands quietly beside Ahmedabad's busy bus terminal. Inside, middle-aged men sit behind old wooden desks, shuffling through big piles of paper while seemingly whiling away their time. The woodwork and the brown, stained paint on the walls create a damp and heavy atmosphere, which adds to the lethargy that the officials exude. Now and then, a visitor drops in to ask something or to drop something off, but even for Javerbhai Desai, one of the TLA's 'officers-in-charge', few people seem to be queuing up. He is in charge of the 'Latta Khatu', the TLA's 'area department' which helps people solve all sorts of everyday problems. Desai says: 'For any problem people may come here. For problems with the municipality, tax problems, a fight with the neighbours, people come here to present their complaints. Usually they come through the representatives. They know the people, and they take their problem here'. Desai claims that he can help solve these problems because he can pressurize government officials: 'government workers listen to us because we have a good image and we have much credit because, once, even a prime minister came from here'. Desai refers to Gulzarilal Nanda who was the TLA's general secretary before becoming India's Prime Minister for short periods in 1964 and 1966.

Some of the people hanging around Desai's office are introduced as 'representatives'. The representatives are the TLA's main contacts in the working-class areas in and around Ahmedabad, as they relay requests and problems to the TLA's main office. In its heyday the TLA had 5,000 active representatives in Ahmedabad alone, but nowadays there seem to be only a handful in the city. Jhaverbhai Desai sighs when I tell him that I have not encountered many representatives in the localities where the textile workers used to live. 'There was a time that we had a hold all over Ahmedabad. Thirty years ago the prime minister came from here. Then it was decided in this building who became minister of which department. Now the political leaders are not listening to us as much as before'. While the TLA earlier represented a large section of Gujarat's total workforce, nowadays the organization is little more than a relic of the past.

In the last chapter, I discussed how the development of state institutions made people dependent on local patronage channels. In this chapter I will discuss how, over the last forty years, the patronage channels through which people gain access to the state have changed considerably. While in the first decades after India's independence these channels were centred around organizations and institutions that mobilized supporters on the basis of class and caste, since the early 1980s access to state institutions became increasingly controlled by the Sangh Parivar, the 'family' of Hindu-nationalist organizations like the BJP, the RSS and the VHP. To a large extent, this shift is the result of changes in Gujarat's economy and the collapse of the once strong local Congress networks. I will argue in this chapter that this particular historical development of the channels that provide access to the state can help explain why Gujarat has been relatively more riot-prone and more polarized on communal lines than most other Indian states. While in other Indian states political organizations and social institutions that jostle for access to state resources are still using a discourse of class and (low vs. high) caste (and region), in Gujarat this kind of political mobilization has since the 1980s gradually withered away because of an erosion of the patronage networks around Congress and organizations like the TLA. By discussing the rise of Hindu-nationalism in Gujarat this chapter will provide a brief[1] historical background to the analyses of the coming chapters, in which I will discuss how the channels that provide access to the state are currently operating.

The patronage of a trade union

At the time of the Textile Labour Association's foundation the textile labourers' living conditions were abysmal. The wages they earned at the mills were often insufficient to sustain their families and they were housed in small, overcrowded and unhygienic hutments with no sanitation. They were still often better off than their family members in Gujarat's villages: in the first decades of the 20th century, many lower-caste villagers moved to Gujarat's cities to work in the expanding textile industry in order to escape the destitution and caste discrimination they faced in their native villages.

The owners of the textile mills were generally unconcerned about the textile labourers' plight. They hardly responded to calls for better living conditions or higher wages, until two of Ahmedabad's most famous residents, Anusuyaben Sarabhai and Mahatma Gandhi, started to mediate on behalf of the workers in 1918. Their success in securing slightly higher wages inspired the founding of the Textile Labour Association to improve the living conditions of the textile labourers, 35 years after the mill owners had organized themselves in the Ahmedabad Mill Owners Association (AMA).

Despite setbacks the TLA managed to attract a very large membership. In the early 1980s the TLA could boast a membership of 135,000 workers, almost 90 per cent of the total workforce in the textile mills. This large membership enabled the union to provide various services to improve the living conditions of the workers: in its heyday in the 1950s and 1960s the TLA provided its members with childcare centres, clubs for physical exercise, reading rooms for papers and magazines, libraries where books could be read or borrowed, youth clubs, literacy courses for adults, sewing and embroidery classes, primary health care centres, maternity homes and even a co-operative bank where loans could be obtained. The TLA set up various local ward committees to organize and oversee all these activities (Breman 2004: 124). Through these various services the TLA had a big impact on the social life in the textile-mill localities.[2] The TLA had, however, relatively few Muslim members: as Muslims were generally employed in different departments in the textile mills, they felt more at ease in their own, separate trade union (Breman 2004: 75).

The prominence of the trade union in these localities was also due to its close relations with the ruling Congress party. Through the TLA the workers found a channel to pressurize the municipality to improve the facilities in their neighbourhood. As early as 1924 the Congress party agreed to put up a TLA member for election in the municipal council, who was duly elected. At that time the working-class areas had largely been neglected by the municipal authorities, and the grid of electricity, water and gutter connections had not been expanded beyond the walls of Ahmedabad's old city. The labourers began to notice that, through the TLA, they could gain access to the expanding municipal services. As one member remembered: 'With Kacharbhai in the Municipality it became easy to take up the work of providing the necessary facilities in the workers' neighbourhoods. The attention of both the congress party and the municipal officers was called to the various needs for roads, lights, water, toilets, and other facilities, and efforts were made to provide whatever improvements were possible' (Spodek n.d.: 217).

In 1937, a quarter of all members of Ahmedabad's municipal council were put forward by the TLA.

Because of its contacts within Congress and the municipal council, the TLA could help its members by taking up various public and private problems. The TLA set up an 'area department', the *latta khatu*, to relay various problems and requests to the relevant authorities. People could come to report disputes with the management of the mill, problems with basic amenities, police harassment, paperwork requests, etc. The TLA tried to solve these issues using its contacts with leading Congress politicians and influential officials within government departments. In this process the TLA's representatives—*pratinidhi* in Gujarati—played an important role, as it was their task to communicate the complaints and requests in their area to the main office.

The TLA was for the Congress party a useful vehicle to capture the votes of the working classes while, through the Congress party, it acquired useful contacts to help their members deal with the expanding municipal institutions. The TLA and Congress set up 'worker-voter associations' with both Hindus and Muslims as members. During elections these committees actively campaigned for the Congress candidates, and after elections the committees lobbied for the improvement of the facilities in their localities (Spodek n.d.: 217). TLA leaders began to campaign actively for Congress during elections. This is one speech from a TLA leader in 1961:

> You have built an organization to find solutions to industrial questions. The TLA looks after these questions on a daily basis. But just solving questions of pay, inflation, bonus, and working conditions alone does not bring satisfaction to the workers (...) there must be clean water to drink and adequate water for cleaning and bathing; there must be arrangements for children's education. There must be adequate health education and also arrangements for nursing people who fall sick (...) the municipality is responsible for all these tasks and therefore it is of the utmost importance that the members we have chosen participate in the administration of the municipality. (Spodek n.d.: 34)

In this particular election, Congress put up 31 TLA candidates, 29 of whom won seats on the municipal council. This exchange of favours served Congress well: 'working class votes had become the basis of the Congress' electoral power in Ahmedabad' (Spodek n.d.: 34).

However, at the same time one can argue that the TLA's policies and collusion with Congress prevented the emergence of real class-based political mobilization in Gujarat. The often upper-caste leaders of the TLA adopted a peculiar view on labour relations, which helped to neutralize more progressive notions of social justice. Throughout the TLA's history, the textile workers were not admitted to leadership positions and day-to-day affairs were in the hands of upper-caste outsiders. This resulted in a very patronizing attitude towards textile workers and a very accommodating stance towards the mill owners. After 1923, the TLA never called for a strike and generally avoided confrontation; under Gandhi's guidance the labour union advocated restraint and favoured arbitration to settle labour disputes. At the same time the union's leaders believed that the textile labourers' miserable living conditions were due not so much to exploitation and oppression, but rather to the inferior character of the labourers. This line of reasoning stimulated the TLA to play an active role in disciplining the work force by discouraging drinking and gambling, promoting personal hygiene, and calling for work discipline. As Breman (2004: 50–4) argued, at times the TLA was more engaged in 'taming the work force' than in defending the workers' interests vis-à-vis the very wealthy textile-mill owners.

The TLA's accommodating stance vis-à-vis the mill owners did not, however, lead to lasting support among the workers for more radical trade unions. Some alternative trade unions were set up, but they never managed to gain a foothold in Gujarat. The TLA could use its contacts with Congress and the mill owners to fend off such competition. The mill owners actively promoted the TLA by refusing negotiations with other unions, and the close relations between the TLA leadership and Congress ensured that the TLA simply had more to offer than other unions. In this light it becomes clear why the TLA received active support from the mill owners, as the TLA served as a bulwark against more progressive class-based political mobilization. As Sujata Patel (2002: 111) has argued: '[the close relations between the TLA and the mill owners] pushed back the political growth of class-based alliances. The growth of such class-based alliances would have created a repertoire of cultural practices that would have, in turn, served as resources for the reformulation of further political collectivities. It is unfortunate that these practices have been lost as a result of the capitalist incorporation of the workers'. The weakness of class-based alliances became all the more apparent when the TLA went into decline in the 1970s: as no progressive trade union had managed to organize the working classes in Gujarat, class-based political mobilization gradually became a less viable strategy to win elections.

An authority vacuum

In the first decades after India's independence the electoral power of the Congress party in Gujarat was unassailable. Rival parties like the PSP, the Swatantra party and the predecessor of the BJP, the Jan Sangh, did not really challenge Congress' hegemony until 1977, even if big protests in 1956 (the Maha Gujarat movement) and 1973 (the Navnirman movement) did damage its popularity. Congress' repeated electoral successes were, to a large extent, due to its unmatched grass-roots network and its capacity to exchange votes for access to (state) services. The party was, according to Spodek (1989: 766 and 774), 'a parallel government' which functioned as a 'service delivery system for famine relief, an alternate educational system, tools for cottage industries, and campaigns for Hindu-Muslim cooperation, all through an organizational structure which, in Ahmedabad, reached into each neighbourhood'.

Up until the late 1960s the Congress party controlled the main structures that mediated between state institutions and citizens: it had control over state resources as well as the most important local network of mediators, sometimes in cooperation with organizations like the TLA. The TLA helped Congress to win elections and in return could use the elected Congress politicians to gain access to the state. These mediating channels were organized around loyalties based on class and caste, not religion: organizations like the TLA invoked a class-based solidarity, and even though the TLA had relatively few Muslim members it actively campaigned for Hindu-Muslim unity. The union actively used its grassroots network to suppress communal tensions and prevent riots. As a TLA leader remarked in 1948, when he looked back on the communal riots in Ahmedabad in 1942 and 1946: 'The [TLA's] broader outlook and its practice in day-to-day activity is responsible to a very large extent for keeping peace among the working class when communal sentiments are running very high throughout the country' (quoted in Varshney 2002: 236). If there was a social cleavage that dominated politics at the time, then it was the division between upper caste elites and lower caste workers, as organizations like the TLA based their demands for government support on claims about poverty and class-based grievances.

The patronage channels around Congress and the TLA gradually began to change in the 1960s and 1970s. The decline of Congress can be traced back to 1956, when Congress' opposition to demand of the 'Maha Gujarat' movement for the creation of a Gujarat State separate from Bombay greatly damaged the party's popularity. The leader of the movement, Indulal Yagnik, had since long opposed Congress for failing to address the structural inequalities in Gujarat's society, and in 1956 he managed to whip up such opposition to the Congress party that even the wearing of a Gandhi-cap (associated with Congress) could invite public hostility. When Congress ultimately acceded to the demand for a separate Gujarat State, the party had lost much local support. The local cadre was losing the commitment it had shown during the struggle for independence: as the Congress cadre became more accustomed to the spoils of political offices, the commitment to support and maintain a grassroots presence gradually declined. As early as 1957, a Congress committee noted that 'the craze (...) for power [has vitiated] the atmosphere' and 'Congress workers at the base have lost contact with the people (...) their discipline has become loose' (quoted in Varshney 2002: 268).

This organizational decline was further accelerated by political developments outside Gujarat. A rift between Indira Gandhi and the national leadership of Congress led to a break-up of the party in 1969: Indira Gandhi broke away to lead a faction called Congress (R), while many of the older bosses in the party led a faction called Congress (O). This split had important repercussions for Gujarat's politics, as some of the main leaders of Congress (O) were important Gujarati politicians. Under the leadership of Morarji Desai especially, most of Gujarat's main Congress politicians sided with Congress (O). The TLA, keen on maintaining good relations with these important leaders, followed suit. But in 1971 it looked as if it had bet on the wrong horse, as Indira Gandhi won a resounding all-India victory at the polls with her slogan '*Garibi Hatao*' ('abolish poverty'). Morarji Desai's Congress (O) was beaten again in the state assembly elections of 1972, when his party won only 16 seats while Congress (R) won 140 seats (Shah 1976). As Indira's Congress party ultimately gained the upper hand in Gujarat, the already crumbling grassroots network of the party began to fall apart under conflicting loyalties. As a Congress worker in Maneknagar recalled: 'At that time, the old Congress workers stopped being active, they could not decide whom to join, so they quit'.

The Congress party in Gujarat never really recovered from this break-up. Protest movements against Congress, like the 1973 Navnirman protests against rising costs of basic commodities, further weakened the party and no real effort was made to revive the party's local base. Under Indira Gandhi, the Congress party was led in a more centralized manner, as local politicians were increasingly promoted on the basis of their loyalty to the party's central command. This further undermined the attention that Congress politicians paid to building the party's local networks (Khilnani 2003: 40–55). It was during this period that Hindu-Muslim tensions resurfaced. Ahmedabad had been peaceful since India's independence, but in 1969 large-scale Hindu-Muslim riots broke out which cost at least 630 lives. At the time of the yearly *Rath Yatra* procession, a fight broke out between a few *sadhus* (holy men) and Muslims over the behaviour of one of the *sadhu*'s cows. When newspapers carried the story the incident sparked retaliatory attacks on Muslim shops and houses, which spread from Ahmedabad to other parts of the state. In contrast to earlier outbursts of violence TLA workers and Congress politicians did little to stop the violence (Shah 1984: 197).

This gradual decline of the Congress party's local base was highlighted by Kohli (1990), who in the late 1980s re-studied the way the Congress party operated in a Gujarati district (Kheda) thirty years after his mentor, Myron Weiner, had studied the same district (Weiner 1969). While Weiner encountered a strong Congress party with a large number of dedicated party workers in the 1960s, Kohli could not even find an open party office in the late 1980s and concluded that the party's base was largely defunct. He attributed this change to Indira's decision to split the party, as well as to the growing tension between competing castes. Factionalist struggles had greatly damaged the local base of the Congress party: 'It is clear that political prominence has increasingly become a function of association with those higher up, rather than building an independent local power base. The result is that those who occupy political offices do not readily command respect; there is a growing authority vacuum at the local level' (Kohli 1990: 55).

Gradually the Congress party became a party of careerist politicians who could attain political success by nurturing good contacts within the party's leadership. No longer could Congress' politicians rely on the local support of a committed cadre. Consequently, the party had to change its strategies to win elections. Increasingly the party began to rely on the support of local (caste) leaders and local criminals outside the party to win elections (Spodek 1989:

769). It had to rely much more on its capacity to dispense state resources to make up for its lack of committed local workers (Sud 2007b: 14). Because of the increased importance of the state in daily life, this still proved to be a successful way of securing votes, at least for a while. As one official of the then still ruling Congress party remarked in 1986: 'If you are not with the ruling party today (…) life will be difficult. The state is everywhere. Life chances are influenced by the state. If you don't have access to the state, life is difficult' (quoted in Kohli 1990: 266).

However, around these local leaders the support for Congress began to wane. As the Congress organization withered away, the TLA also lost its political clout. After Indira Gandhi's political successes in the early 1970s the TLA's leaders realized that they had supported the wrong Congress party, since they had damaged their relationship with important elected politicians. As they received less favourable responses from these politicians—who had not relied on their support to win the elections—they even tried to launch their own political party. This attempt failed and the TLA had to forge new ties with Indira Gandhi's Congress. It had lost its pivotal role in Gujarat's politics.

In this period, the TLA started to lose its members and stopped providing many of its neighbourhood services. The weakening of the union was largely due to the gradual collapse of the textile industry in Gujarat. From the late 1970s fifty-two of Ahmedabad's sixty textile mills closed down. Owing to a mix of mismanagement, changing government policies, and the increased integration of Gujarat into the world economy, these mills had become less competitive, and some owners reasoned that it would be more profitable to organize their production in smaller units—which enabled them to pay their workers lower wages. By the end of the 1990s only eight mills were still operational, employing around 25,000 people. As a result the economic prospects of the poorest sections of society deteriorated. The available jobs for these workers have increasingly been informalized; those who lost their regular jobs at the textile mills had to settle for lower daily-wage jobs that are, generally, unregistered and unregulated (Mahadevia 2002, see also Breman 2004).[3] Ahmedabad now displays stark contrasts between rich and poor: while the generally well-educated inhabitants on the western side of Ahmedabad have profited from the opportunities that the deregulation of India's economy has brought, the much poorer residents on the eastern side have generally suffered from these economic developments.

The informalization of Gujarat's economy limited the scope for class-based political mobilization: not only did the increasing number of self-employed workers erode the membership of the TLA, the uncertain legal status of these workers also precluded a successful political mobilization on the basis of this shared economic status. As people could no longer use their work-related networks to defend their interests, they became more dependent on their caste networks and the networks based in and around their place of residence. As localities are generally highly segregated on the basis of religion, caste and regional background (see Chapter 8), the informalization of Gujarat's economy propelled an identity-based political mobilisation.[4]

As the number of textile workers dropped as a result of the closure of the mills, the TLA's membership also went into a rapid decline. This was accelerated by the failure of both the TLA and Congress to represent the mill workers' interests during this difficult period. The TLA's upper-caste leadership was perceived to be siding with mill owners as the organization grew more and more lethargic. The decline of the TLA deprived a large section of Ahmedabad's population of an effective channel to get access to the resources of the state. As Jan Breman (2004: 211) writes, 'having lost their mediated access to the municipal corporation and other state agencies as members of a powerful trade union, the former mill workers are now dependent on slumlords for the representation of their interests. To that extent the collapse of the textile industry has been a major cause in the criminalization of local level politics'.

The gradual demise of Congress' and the TLA's grassroots networks created opportunities for a new kind of politics. Hindu-nationalist organizations gradually managed to fill the vacuum created by the demise of these older networks: in the absence of powerful caste- or class-based alternatives, the BJP and its affiliated organizations could gradually develop a considerable control over the resources of the state. As these Hindu-nationalist organizations developed their own patronage channels, they managed to change the course and the tone of Gujarat's politics.

Hindu-nationalists take over

In the mid-1970s the Congress party changed its electoral strategy. As the party was gradually losing its grassroots network, Congress began to rely more explicitly on caste loyalties to win the support of voters. Caste had always played an important role, and caste associations had become important instruments to exchange votes for access to state resources (Shah 1975). But from the mid 1970s the Congress party openly started to appeal to caste to forge a new support base. Under its leader Madhavsinh Solanki, Congress forged a coalition of different groups of voters that came to be known as KHAM, an acronym of Kshatriya, Harijan (Dalit), Adivasi (tribals) and Muslim. Its patronage, its policy proposals and the selection of party officials and candidates were geared towards these four groups. Middle and upper caste members—Banias, Patels, Brahmins—were gradually excluded from the party's ranks.

With this KHAM coalition, Congress targeted poorer sections of society that were numerous enough to secure large electoral victories. With this 'pro-poor' coalition Congress won 141 seats in the state parliament in 1980, and a record high of 149 seats (out of 182) in 1985. The BJP won just nine seats in 1980, and 11 in 1985. But the upper caste groups who had also become economically dominant (Rutten 1995) were not going to accept their exclusion from political power with their hands down. They started agitations and campaigns that would gradually break the KHAM coalition and restore the upper caste dominance in Gujarat's politics. In 1981 and 1985 riots broke out between upper castes and lower castes over the issue of reservations in colleges. Congress had supported plans to extend the reservation of government jobs for lower castes and places in colleges, which led to vigorous protests from middle class urban youth who saw their chances of advancement frustrated. The Gujarat middle class, feeling threatened, started to join the BJP in large numbers, while the mostly upper-caste bureaucrats in government offices became more supportive of Hindu-nationalist organizations (Sud 2007b, Shani 2007).

At the same time the BJP and its affiliates, the VHP, RSS and the Bajrang Dal, started to adopt strategies to gain the support of Dalits. These organizations realized that they would not be able to win elections and ward off the threat to upper-caste dominance without winning Dalit support. Not only did these organizations make efforts to proclaim that they were fully committed to ending caste discrimination, they actively recruited lower caste leaders into their fold (Nandy *et al.* 1995). Gradually, lower-caste communities were included in the evolving patronage networks of Hindu-nationalist organizations. As the Congress party was increasingly incapable of responding to requests and demands from these communities, many lower caste leaders responded to the flirtations from the BJP and its affiliates.

The 1985 riots dramatically illustrated how successful the Sangh Parivar had become in wooing the Dalit population. The violence that started out as clashes between upper-caste and lower-caste youths gradually shifted in focus. This time the local network of Hindu-nationalist organizations had become sufficiently strong to manipulate the local dynamics of the violence. At the beginning of 1986, the violence had turned into a fight between lower and upper-caste members on one side and Muslims on the other (see Shani 2005 and 2007, Dave 1990). The 1985 riots marked the end of Congress' dominance in Gujarat: since 1985 Congress has never won more than 40 per cent of the vote in either state or national elections, while the BJP steadily increased its tally from 14 per cent in 1980 to 42 per cent in 1995. Since that year the BJP has been Gujarat's biggest party. The rise of the BJP was accompanied by increasing Hindu-Muslim tensions, culminating in Hindu-Muslim riots in 1990, 1991, 1992 and 2002.

The success of the Sangh Parivar in breaking the KHAM coalition cannot be seen in isolation from the broader 'saffron wave' (Hansen 1999) that swept through India in the late 1980s and early 1990s. The Babri Masjid in Ayodhya (Uttar Pradesh) served as a focal point for a feverish campaign of big rallies, brick collections, and chariot tours that culminated in the destruction of the Mosque on 6 December 1992. Through this campaign the BJP, the RSS and especially the VHP managed to gain national prominence, while raising tensions and provoking riots between Hindus and Muslims throughout India. Hindu-nationalist organizations in Gujarat managed to keep the campaign around the Babri Masjid at a high pitch, which helped to bring religious divisions to the forefront of Gujarat's politics.

However, at the same time Gujarat could not have become the 'laboratory of Hindutva' (Spodek 2008) had it not been for the capacity of Hindu-nationalist organizations to develop a firm grip on Gujarat's state institutions. As the local Congress networks and affiliated organizations like the TLA gradually collapsed, people became more dependent on the new patronage structures that developed around the BJP, the RSS and the VHP. These organizations were well placed to fill the vacuum that Congress left behind. Through its local branches, called *shakhas*, the RSS was organizing daily training and discussion sessions throughout Gujarat, and the VHP and its youth wing Bajrang Dal gradually managed to expand their activities to the remotest localities. In cooperation with the Jan Sangh and, later on, the BJP these organizations offered the infrastructure to link grassroots workers to influential state-level leaders; the wide-ranging networks around these organizations offered people new channels to gain access to the state.

From the 1960s these organizations gradually managed to put their members in the government institutions, local *panchayats* and municipal councils as well as the broad range of parastatal organizations that play an important role in everyday life: they gradually developed a hold over co-operative banks, educational institutions, credit societies, milk cooperatives and agriculture produce market committees (Sheth 1998: 28). The RSS, the VHP and the BJP, and their many affiliates, have become entrenched in Gujarat's most important institutions—universities, farmer cooperatives, government institutions, the press etc.—as well as in Gujarat's social life. Membership of the VHP or the RSS is now very useful to secure a new job posting, arrange a licence, solve a tax dispute etc., since through these organizations influential people at various levels of government may be contacted.

Using the increased access to state resources the VHP, the RSS and the BJP were able to further develop their impressive (overlapping) grassroots network of workers capable of reaching the remotest villages. Not only have these networks been capable of providing often neglected communities with access to state resources, but Hindu-nationalist organizations have also been able to set up their own schools and health care facilities in the countryside as well as in cities. In many areas the VHP and the RSS provide the most important link with the outside world, as there are few other organizations that people can turn to for help to deal with the police, secure a new water tap, arrange education, etc. The changes in these local patronage networks were dramatically illustrated in the aftermath of the earthquake that struck Gujarat in 2001: while decades earlier Congress workers were those involved in relief work, in 2001 much of the relief and rehabilitation work was taken up by Hindu-nationalist organizations who explicitly targeted Hindus (Simpson 2005). As Sud (2007b) has argued, the hold of Hindu-nationalist organizations over the state has become more and more visible in recent decades, as the pronouncements and actions of state institutions gradually became more pro-Hindu.

The popularity of the BJP, the VHP or the RSS cannot just be attributed to the attractiveness of their ideology—even if, as Yagnik and Sheth (2005) have argued, this ideology served the expanding middle class well to legitimize and stabilize their changing status in Gujarat's society. The strength of the Hindu-nationalist patronage networks and the popularity of their ideology go hand in hand: while the Sangh Parivar's vision of a 'Hindu *rasthra*' serves to legitimize and promote the daily functioning of its patronage channels, the success of these channels in providing health care, education or government jobs also contributes to the popularity of Hindu-nationalist ideology. The BJP and VHP have gained a large following among Dalits and tribals—traditionally staunch Congress voters—not because these groups were attracted to the socially conservative worldview that the Sangh Parivar promoted, but because they offer useful patronage channels at the time when the older patronage channels around Congress and the TLA were collapsing. As local leaders realized they had a better chance of accessing state resources and developing a political career through Hindu-nationalist outfits, they gradually drew their communities into the *Hindutva* fold. The communal violence of 2002 once again illustrated how successful this strategy has been: Dalits and tribals played, by comparison with earlier outbursts of violence, a central role in the actual perpetration of the violence.

The violence of 2002 further cemented the strength of the Sangh Parivar in Gujarat. Before the violence, the BJP had lost a few local elections which had led to the dismissal of the BJP Chief Minister Keshubhai Patel in October 2001. He was replaced by the *Hindutva* hardliner Narendra Modi, who took the BJP's popularity to new heights. The former RSS worker seized on the violence as an occasion to boost the party's appeal: the attack on the train in Godhra, in which 58 Hindus were killed, was actively taken up as proof of the threat that Muslims were posing, while criticism of the way the post-Godhra violence had been handled was construed as an 'offence' to Gujarat's 'pride'. Modi clearly realized that the violence could serve to rally the Hindus behind him: in an obvious move to benefit from the communal tensions he tried to advance the date of the state elections, which the BJP won handsomely in December 2002.

Since then Narendra Modi has blended a Hindu-nationalist ideology with a neo-liberal developmental discourse. In 2007, Modi attempted to distract attention from the 2002 mayhem by portraying himself as the harbinger of economic prosperity. Modi could boast of a growth rate of more than 8 per cent in recent years, and the increase in posh high-rise buildings, fast highways and foreign investment suggests that Gujarat is changing fast. This development, however, is extremely one-sided: with low taxes, a focus on infrastructure and a minimum of attention for welfare, basic amenities or the enforcement of labour rights, Gujarat has adopted an economic model that mainly serves big business (see Sud 2009) and Gujarat's expanding middle class. The poorer sections of society have hardly been able to benefit from these developments: the conditions and wages of unskilled labour have deteriorated, while the poor lack the skills and education to benefit from the high-skilled jobs that are opening up.

Nonetheless, the increasing gap between rich and poor has not undermined the support for the BJP, despite considerable factional struggles within the BJP. The combination of Modi's larger-than-life image, his promises of economic prosperity and a skilled invocation of 'Gujarat Pride' and anti-Muslim prejudice has led to another impressive victory in the state elections of December 2007, when the BJP won 117 out of 182 seats and Congress won only 59 seats (Shah *et al.* 2008). The BJP looks set for a long period of prominence in Gujarat, as at present alternative parties lack the necessary grassroots network and mass appeal to challenge its hegemony.

Conclusion

The days when Gujarat's labour association supplied state ministers, even a prime minister, are long past. Now many of Gujarat's cabinet ministers have a background in the VHP—in 2002 four ministers were prominent VHP leaders—while Chief Minister Narendra Modi used to be an organizer (*pracharak*) for the RSS. Many of the members of Gujarat's legislative assembly, as well as lower-level politicians, started their careers as workers for the VHP or the RSS.

The fact that ministers are now coming from different organizations reflects an underlying change in the channels that provide access to the state. Economic developments—in particular the informalization of labour due to the liberalization of Gujarat's economy—and the institutional collapse of the Congress party conspired to weaken the earlier patronage channels organized around the TLA. This gradual collapse enabled Hindu-nationalist organizations like the RSS, VHP and BJP to gain a firm hold over the functioning of the state, which subsequently laid the ground for the prominence of a Hindu-nationalist discourse in Gujarat's public debate. This can help explain why Gujarat has seen so much communal violence in recent decades. As Gujarat's economic development generated increasingly precarious working conditions for the underclass, this section of society remained very dependent on the limited security and income that local political networks could provide. Furthermore, in contrast to other Indian states, a class or lower-caste movement failed to maintain mass support in Gujarat after the patronage channels around the TLA withered away. The paternalist nature of the labour movement in Gujarat has precluded the development of a more permanent and more progressive class-based political movement. Over the last twenty years there has not been a caste-based organization or political party capable of successfully mobilizing supporters on the basis of divisions between higher and lower castes. Alternative political movements could have changed the tone and content of the political discourse, and they could have undermined the capacity of Hindu-nationalist organizations to develop support through their capacity to access state resources.

The control of Hindu-nationalist organizations over the distribution of state resources, and their capacity to help people gain access to the state, have greatly contributed to the polarization of Gujarat's society along religious lines. I will further explore the relation between the nature of patronage channels and the prevalence of communal tensions in society in the next chapters, but I will make two preliminary remarks here.

Firstly, the grassroots activities of Hindu-nationalist organizations, and their capacity to solve all sorts of daily problems, make people more susceptible to the anti-Muslim rhetoric of Hindu-nationalists. The patronage that Hindu-nationalist organizations can dispense, and their capacity to solve life's daily problems, contribute to the legitimacy of Hindu-nationalist ideology. In many areas in Gujarat there are simply no other political organizations with a sustained presence and a comparable capacity to deal with state institutions. As in other states the BJP and its affiliated organizations mobilized their followers and voters by appealing to the common interests of Hindus and emphasizing the dangers that Muslims are posing, but this Hindu-nationalist rhetoric was able to gain popularity in Gujarat because such speeches could, indeed, be backed up by increased access to state resources. As organizations like the RSS or the VHP are now useful channels to secure a government job or a loan, many supporters are not attracted to these organizations out of ideological fervour, but simply because they offer an attractive opportunity to secure access to state resources or to develop a political career.

Secondly, as Hindu-nationalist organizations gained control over the distribution of resources, they could change the content of the political discourse and bring Hindu-Muslim divisions to the fore. Through their political campaigns Hindu-nationalist organizations have associated the right to access to state resources with one's religious background. While in earlier decades the Congress and the TLA could mobilize support of Hindus and Muslims with a political discourse based on class (and caste), now the BJP and its affiliates attempt to portray the political contest as a competition between Hindus and Muslims—with the BJP on the side of Hindus and Congress on the side of Muslims. In their speeches, banners and slogans, Hindu-nationalist leaders associate promises about the distribution of state resources with the need to defend Hindus against Muslims: the rhetoric about the need to 'end the privileging of Muslims' or slogans like 'he who speaks about Hindu interests should rule' creates the impression that someone's chances of securing a government job, college admission, a license etc. are firmly tied up with one's religious identity. This is dangerous: when political rhetoric and the structure of patronage channels create such a strong association between one's religious identity and one's chances of securing important benefits from the state, then members of another community may come to be seen as a more or less personal threat to one's chances of advancing in life. I will further explore this relation between the capacity of politicians to provide access to state resources and their use of a communal discourse in Chapter 8.

I will return to the capacity of Hindu-nationalist organizations to mobilize supporters in the following chapters, where I will delve into the functioning of the present-day political networks that mediate between state institutions and citizens. The everyday mediation of the state goes on from morning till evening on street corners, in tea-stalls and in private late-night meetings, and this mediation involves a great number of different people. In the following chapters I will further explore how the control of politicians over the resources of the state engenders complex networks of various local supporters, who expect to benefit from the services they provide to their political leaders.

PART THREE

THE EVERYDAY MEDIATION OF THE STATE

5

THE EVERYDAY MEDIATION OF A MUNICIPAL COUNCILLOR

The city is getting ready for another day when Pravin Dalal arrives at a small bicycle shop on one of Maneknagar's main roads. The municipal councillor and BJP politician looks sharp, even at this early hour: his small spectacles and expensive clothing give Pravin Dalal a man-of-the-world-like appearance, which is further accentuated by his purposeful gestures. He enters the bicycle shop to pick up the necessary materials for his work: a little piece of cloth to sit on, a pen, a stamp and stamp cushion, the diary with the phone numbers of all the municipal officials, and—most important—his letter pad with the logo of the municipality. With this equipment he installs himself on a raised stone platform—an *otla*—on the other side of the road. His regular helpers arrange themselves around this *otla* on plastic chairs.

Often they have not even ordered *chai* from the *kitli* (tea-stall) on the corner as the first people needing help present themselves. With a friendly but curt '*bolo*' ('speak') or '*shun chhe?*' ('what is it?') Pravin Dalal welcomes them and starts his work. Soon a small queue is forming. Young and old, men as well as women, approach Pravin Dalal with complaints and requests that in one way or another involve governmental bureaucracies. Pravin Dalal listens to them, nods, says something or writes the complaint down on his letter pad, and then gestures to the next person in line to come forward. His answers are always concise, and he can come across as somewhat impatient as he limits his responses to one or two sentences: 'bring me the papers tomorrow', 'meet me at the hospital' or 'I will talk to the principal of the school about it'. There is one sentence that all visitors are hoping for: '*tamaru kam thai jaashe*' ('your work will be done').

Pravin Dalal is known for his capacity to get a lot of work done; on a regular day, he manages to deal with the questions and requests of around 30 to

40 people in less than two hours. In the busy first weeks of June, when parents are trying to arrange school admissions for their children, there might be twice as many people. There are many other municipal councillors who sit out on street corners like Pravin Dalal, but few are said to be so efficient. Dalal's supporters say this has contributed in no small measure to his electoral successes: Pravin Dalal has been elected to represent Maneknagar in Ahmedabad's municipal council four consecutive times. His career mirrors the rise of the Hindu-nationalist BJP in Gujarat: he was made a BJP candidate after the 1985/86 communal violence that greatly undermined the popularity of Congress in Gujarat. Pravin Dalal became a prominent local leader during the 1985/86 riots and has since then adhered to his image as a 'defender of Hindus', which, as we shall see, has a big impact on the way he allocates state resources. Since then he has done well for himself: while coming from a family of lower-middle class Brahmins he now owns a relatively lavishly decorated flat in the middle of Maneknagar.

Table 1: At the roadside with Pravin Dalal

The issues brought before municipal councillor Pravin Dalal on a Tuesday morning (8:30—10:15) in March 2005	
Gutter and water problems	9
Road paving and street lights	4
Hospital admission and fees	5
Governmental support schemes	6
Request to arrange marriage hall	1
Signing official papers	4
School admission	1
(Reduction of) Tax bill	3
Settling of disputes	2
Total:	35

As the inset table shows, people come to Pravin Dalal with very diverse requests. The list summarizes the issues brought before Pravin Dalal on a normal Tuesday morning in March. Complaints about drainage and inadequate water provision are most common. Every day people line up to tell Pravin Dalal about a clogged gutter, a leaking drainage line or a lack of pressure in the water pipe. When only maintenance is required to solve the problem, Pravin Dalal takes his letter pad and jots down the details of the complaint. He puts his stamp on it, and passes the paper on to one of his helpers. At the end of every morning a sizeable amount of such slips of paper have accumulated; they are passed on to the municipal departments with some admonitions to make sure the work gets done. By writing down these complaints on his official letter pad, Pravin Dalal gives the request some extra weight and status: both the visitors to Pravin Dalal's roadside office as well as governmental officials generally believe that complaints coming from politicians are acted upon more quickly than when they come directly from a local inhabitant.

Most of the letters go to the zonal office nearby, where the officials responsible for the sanitation, paving, and street lights in the area have their office. Other letters go to the various offices in the main municipality building. Often the officials themselves come to Pravin Dalal's *otla* in the morning to pick up the slips of paper: they come to ask Pravin Dalal if there is any repair work to be done, and they inform their municipal councillor about the progress of the work they are carrying out. The sanitation official of the nearby zonal office had urged inhabitants to take their problems to the municipal councillors first: 'We put an advertisement in the newspaper to tell people to go to the councillor so that the work would be done efficiently. Councillors have a direct connection with representatives of the *pols*. Because they live near the people, they know the problems and they are closer to them'. Officials often said the intervention of a councillor reassured them that the complaint was genuine and really merited action on their part.

Pravin Dalal can count on several party workers to check whether government officials are acting on the complaints. During the morning several party workers drop by, and there are five regular workers who come every day to assist Pravin Dalal. Some specialization has evolved among these five workers: one worker regularly stamps the official papers, the second deals especially with requests that involve welfare schemes such as widow pensions, a third passes the complaints about sanitation and basic amenities to the concerned officials, while a fourth helps with filling out official forms. The fifth, Himansubhai, deserves special mention: he is Pravin Dalal's PA, his personal assistant. He maintains contact with the councillor throughout the day and is instrumental in passing on (and scrutinizing) various other requests that reach him from people who could not or did not want to come to Pravin Dalal's seat on the roadside. Every morning Himansubhai spends quite some time on the phone, and often passes on information to Pravin Dalal in such a whispering tone that the ever-curious researcher cannot make out what they are saying.

Social science terminology is often of limited use to capture the complex embeddedness of the Indian state in society (Kaviraj 2001, Gupta 1995, Chatterjee 1998, 2001, 2004). The (Western) connotations that come with terms like 'civil society', 'political party', 'citizenship' or 'bureaucracy'—terms that originated from Western experiences of state formation—do little to clarify the actual interactions that take place between the state and India's citizens. The associations that such terms evoke can blur our perspective on the Indian state, as much of this terminology evokes a 'Weberian' ideal-type of the state: a goal-oriented, unitary institution discrete from society, with an undisputed sovereignty in its spheres of jurisdiction (Migdal 2001:13–15), and with a clear separation of powers between judiciary, legislature and executive branches of government.

In practice the control of politicians over the bureaucracy fragments the authority of the state (Hansen 2005); it distorts the outcome of government policies according to local (political) needs, and it undermines a straightforward application of the law. The hold of politicians over the daily operation of the bureaucracy makes it difficult to see the state as an actor discrete from society, since through these political mediators societal elements can manipulate the functioning of the state. This makes it difficult to see the 'state' and 'society' as two separable entities as they are demarcated by a 'blurred boundary' (Gupta 1995) or a 'spongiform interface' (Nugent 1994, Harriss-White 1997). This awareness of the interpenetration of state and society has led a number of authors to call for more ethnographies on the everyday appearances of the state (Fuller and Harris 2001, Hansen and Stepputat 2001, Barkey and Parikh 1991, Das and Poole 2004).

This chapter aims to offer such an ethnography of what goes on at this 'interface', by discussing the daily routine of Pravin Dalal, a BJP municipal councillor from Maneknagar. This examination of Pravin's daily activities has two related aims. First, I aim to show that the mediating activities of politicians like Pravin Dalal cannot be seen as an aberration or an intrusion into the 'normal' operations of the state. On the contrary, I argue that political intermediaries—mediating between bureaucrats, citizens and service providers—are a constitutive part of the state in Gujarat. Political mediation is so deeply entrenched in the procedures, policies and habits that guide the daily functioning of state institutions that we can speak of a 'mediated state': the state is embedded in society in such a way that its interaction with citizens is, to a large extent, monopolized by political networks whose political (and also often financial) success depends on their capacity to manipulate the implementation of the state's policies and legislation.

Secondly, this chapter proposes a mechanism to understand the centrality of political mediation in the daily operations of the state. I will suggest that the institutionalization of political mediation should be seen as the outcome of an interplay between the limited capacity of the Gujarat state to provide public services and the strategies that local politicians employ to win elections. Taking inspiration from Pierre Bourdieu's (see especially 1991; 1999; Bourdieu and Wacquant 1992) and Joel Migdal's work (2001) I will argue that the limited capacity of the state to provide basic services generates a political field in which control over the distribution of state resources is an important prerequisite for electoral success. This reproduces the dependence of both citizens and state institutions on political mediation: the strategies that political actors adopt to win support make it more difficult for state agents and citizens to deal with each other without the mediation of political actors. To win elections politicians like Pravin Dalal need to monopolize the interaction between state institutions and citizens, which in turn reinforces the limited capacity of the state to provide basic services.

This dependence on political mediation will serve to understand the capacity of politicians to instigate communal violence: as we will see, the everyday mediation of the state generates incentives for various local actors to contribute to communal violence.

Political mediation as a response to ineffective bureaucracies?

The 'roadside offices' of Pravin Dalal and other municipal councillors (and MLAs) are daily, visible indications of how ordinary citizens depend on politicians to facilitate their interaction with state institutions. 'Roadside offices' of municipal and state-level politicians can be found throughout Gujarat, although they are much more common in poorer localities than in posh areas: as richer citizens use more influential contacts and monetary resources, they have the means to deal with (or circumvent) the state without political intervention, while for poorer citizens political mediation is often the only option.

Their attendance at Pravin Dalal's roadside office might be seen as a response to both the strengths and the weaknesses of state institutions in Gujarat. Compared to a number of states like Bihar and Uttar Pradesh, Gujarat is relatively successful in providing a wide range of services to its citizens; in a comparison of the fifteen largest Indian states the relatively wealthy state of Gujarat hovers around sixth place in terms of the provision of various services, after more successful states like Kerala, Karnataka and Punjab (Hirway and Mahadevia 2005). It is this relative success in offering various services that makes access to the state valuable: as citizens have come to rely on services that the state provides, politicians are judged on the basis of their capacity to provide access to these services, and less—as Mooij (1999) observed in Bihar—on their capacity to provide (monetary) alternatives to these resources. At the same time the roadside offices are also a response to the inability of the state to make public services universally available. Governmental institutions in Gujarat are often overburdened and the growth of the population is adding to this pressure on the limited resources of the state (D'Costa 2002; Kundu 2002, Kundu and Mahadevia 2002). Various legislative bodies have enacted a wide range of legislation, but state institutions lack the capacity to implement this legislation fully, and the courts are generally overburdened (SK 2000). The state in Gujarat is 'omnipresent, but feeble' (cf. Kohli 1990: 6).

Both Pravin Dalal and the Maneknagar residents who come to see him described the functionality of the roadside office in terms of the weaknesses of the state: people come to Pravin Dalal because the bureaucrats are incapable of dealing directly with all the requests and demands. As Pravin Dalal said of his work:

> When people inform me that there is a problem, I immediately start to solve the problem. The official procedure is too long, it takes too much time. If people go by themselves, the offices might refuse to do the work. Here they can easily meet me and I can solve the problem. I inform the involved authorities and I take complaints to the municipal cooperation.

Pravin Dalal could genuinely see his work at the roadside as charity, while at the same time being acutely aware of the electoral and financial benefits of his morning activities. A similar awareness made residents take a pragmatic stance towards Pravin Dalal's work:

> People know he is making money in this way. But at the same time he is helping them. He helps many people with problems. So people still go to him, because they know that he will solve their problems. So people accept that he is also doing these things. Even I go to him, I know that he will get my work done. If I would go to the office myself, they would not listen to me, so I go to Pravin Dalal and get it done much faster.

Maneknagar residents often used the expression *'dhakka khaavadave chhe'* to describe their experiences with the bureaucracy. That could be translated as 'getting pushed around': you have to visit the officials involved again and again without any result. The visitors to Pravin Dalal's roadside office regularly complained about the arrogance of governmental officials who seemed unwilling to listen to them. There are often long queues, the procedures are complicated, the officers involved demand 'speed-money' to process a request, and you are often told to come back tomorrow: for an ordinary citizen lacking influential contacts or money for bribes, the obstacles in the way of obtaining a business license or getting a police case registered can appear insurmountable. Such difficulties propel especially poorer residents—who lack the necessary contacts and money to deal with the bureaucracy independently—to deal with state institutions through political networks. This can be observed—albeit in differing intensity—throughout India (see for example De Wit 1996, Jeffrey and Lerche 2001, Ruud 2001, Veron *et al.* 2003).

But the difficulties that citizens face when dealing with governmental bureaucracies are not just the cause of their reliance on political mediators, these difficulties are also the result of the political dynamic that this reliance on political mediation generates. This is what a local bureaucrat said of the political interference in his work:

> Some people come here directly. But if they go to the elected people their request gets status. He [the politician] wants to win the elections, so he wants to create the impression that he is doing their work. If they go through politicians, we do their work quicker, if they come here directly it will take 3–4 days. This is a democracy, so we have to do what politicians tell us to do.

Political actors have institutionalized their mediating role in such a way as to undermine the capacity of state institutions to respond to demands articulated by citizens directly. The mediated nature of the state can be seen as the outcome of a dialectic between the historical development of the state and the strategies that politicians adopted to gain access to the expanding resources of the state. As I discussed in Chapter 3, the emergence of a class of political intermediaries coincided with the gradual expansion of the capacities of the state. The expanding scope of the services that the state was providing, as well as its increased capacity to regulate daily life through various laws and regulations, created a need for intermediaries who could provide access to these services and could manipulate the implementation of these laws and regulations. People turned away from older institutions like the *pol panch* and the *mahajans* as they began to rely more on the state. But, as the expanding state institutions lacked the resources and the information to make services easily available to all, poorer residents in particular came to depend on political actors to facilitate their interaction with the state. This shaped the nature of the competition between different political intermediaries after a majoritarian democratic system was enacted:[1] political success came to be premised not on a programmatic appeal but on a capacity to distribute state resources and manipulate the implementation of laws and regulations (cf. Kitschelt and Wilkinson 2007). To win elections aspiring politicians need to develop some control over the operations of the state, and they need to use this control efficiently and instrumentally; that is, they need to distribute state resources to groups of voters who can deliver a maximum number of votes (Keefer and Vlaicu 2008). These attempts to develop and maintain control over the distribution of resources reinforce the dependency of ordinary citizens on political mediation.

I will illustrate this dialectic between the character of the state and political strategizing in the remainder of this chapter, when I will show that different aspects of political mediation that Pravin Dalal engages in can be seen as both a response to and a cause of the limited capacity of state institutions to deal with citizens directly. I will distinguish three different aspects of the political mediation that Pravin Dalal engages in: (a) brokerage—the facilitation of the flow of information between state institutions and citizens; (b) patronage—the practice of exchanging access to state resources for political support; and (c) particularization—the practice of undermining the uniform application of laws and legislation to the advantage of private interests.

Political mediation as brokerage

Much of the work that Pravin Dalal does at his roadside office amounts to facilitating the communication between citizens and state officials: he puts complaints and requests from citizens on paper and passes them on, and he helps government officials to verify the veracity of these complaints and requests. Every day quite a number of people line up at that roadside office with plastic bags full of (copies of) official papers, such as death certificates, income proofs or university results. They want Pravin Dalal to turn these papers into a 'true-copy': with his signature and stamp on them the papers stand a better change of being accepted at the various governmental offices. Other paperwork requests are the direct result of governmental policies. Many people ask Pravin Dalal, for example, for a proof of residence or an income certificate because various governmental schemes require such intervention from a politician: a signed letter from Pravin Dalal can help a resident to get a ration card (a card entitling the owner to a subsidized discount on various products), discounted treatment at the hospital, a widow pension or a governmental loan. The municipal library even requires new members to get an endorsement from local politicians and other prominent citizens, so that it can turn to these politicians to recover the costs when books are not returned to the library.

In these different ways, Pravin Dalal supplies the bureaucracy with the information needed to implement governmental policies, which gives him in effect a certain discretionary power to decide who is eligible to benefit from various governmental services. This discretionary power is partly due to the limited 'legibility' of Indian society. Indian state institutions often lack reliable information about citizens: various instruments that could enable the state to 'see' (cf. Scott 1998) its society—such as a population registry or a landed property register—have not been uniformly well developed, and the informality of the employment of many citizens limits the capacity of state institutions to acquire reliable information about citizens' actual income.[2]

This limited capacity of the Indian state to 'read' society increases the dependence of state institutions on political actors: since the available official registries are not available or are faulty, government officials are often forced to rely on political actors to provide the information needed to uphold the law and implement various schemes and policies. Welfare departments rely on Pravin Dalal to determine who qualifies for support, police officials rely on him for solving police cases, libraries rely on him to make sure they get their books back and, as we will see below, hospitals rely on him to determine whether patients deserve discounts on their hospital bills.

But these departments do not just rely on political intermediaries because political actors make it easier to implement governmental policies; they also rely on them precisely because these policies stipulate that political actors can be relied upon to provide vital information. Various schemes or procedures in the field of health care, welfare or identity proof stipulate that political actors can be relied upon to obtain or verify the necessary information. These schemes have been adopted by political actors who know that it is politically profitable to control the flow of information between state institutions and citizens. Pravin Dalal can use his capacity to provide municipal departments with vital information to extract money (occasionally) and to take the credit for the execution of governmental policies. After supplying officials with the information necessary to execute government policies, politicians can portray themselves as benefactors to those who approached them for, for example, a repair of a clogged gutter or a broken street light. For this reason politicians like Pravin Dalal have no reason to improve citizen or land registration: the more clouded the glasses through which the Indian state sees society, the more opportunities for political actors to make money and gain supporters.

From the budget of the municipal councillor: political mediation as patronage

Not all complaints that people bring to the roadside office can be solved with a piece of paper from Pravin Dalal's letter pad. Solutions for the recurrent water and drainage problems in the area often require sizeable investments; often requests are made for the replacement of a drainage pipe or the installation of a new water pipe. For such requests Pravin Dalal makes use of the budget that the municipality has allocated to him. Under various 'Local Area Development Schemes', money is allocated to the Members of Parliament, the MLAs and the municipal councillors to spend on development work in their constituencies. The provisions for these budgets are vague; they are intended for 'all works to meet the locally felt community infrastructure and development needs',[3] which encompasses drinking water, education, public health, sanitation and roads. At the time of writing every MP has a budget of two crore (approx. 350,000 euros), an MLA has seventy lakh (125,000 euros) and each individual councillor gets nine lakh (16,000 euros) for work in his or her electoral ward.[4] The Ahmedabad Municipal Corporation also has a general budget for the improvement of local infrastructure, but generally this budget is used for public works on or around the main public roads, while the politicians' budgets are more commonly used for the improvement of facilities inside residential areas.

It is because of this budget that many inhabitants make their requests directly to Pravin Dalal: every day one or two people—often already known to the councillor—come to demand things like the installation of new water piping to overcome water shortages, or extra street lights. They often come repeatedly over a period of months to influence Pravin Dalal's use of his limited budget. Pravin Dalal often uses his budget to reward loyal supporters and localities: the road might be paved in the locality of a loyal worker, or the water supply might be improved in localities that have been very supportive during elections. These budgetary provisions have very visible effects on the urban landscape: throughout Ahmedabad one may find public benches with words like 'from the budget of Municipal Councillor Pravin Dalal' painted on them to remind residents of how supportive local politicians have been.

Clientelism or political patronage[5] is a central feature of India's democracy; commentators have described elections in India as an 'auction' (Chandra 2004a) because of the persistent practice of exchanging (promises of) government resources for electoral support (Kohli 1990, Bardhan 1984, Brass 1997, Rudolph and Rudolph 1989, Wilkinson 2007). Politicians direct not only water connections or drainage lines, but also government jobs, roads, electricity connections, irrigation, government contracts etc. to those groups of voters who are considered to be useful in securing successful (re-)election. This may take, as Weiner (1967: 195–6) describes, the form of a negotiated deal when villagers offer their votes to the politician who pledges to deliver maximum benefits. Chandra (2004b: 116) therefore describes India as a 'patronage democracy', because 'the essential element influencing voting behaviour in India is not simply the dominance of the state, but the ability of those who control the state to exercise discretion in the implementation of state policy'. In this context, a policy-oriented party has little chances of success, since voters tend to look to politicians more for a favourable implementation of policies than for innovative visions or ideas for new policies (Wade 1982: 486, Chandra 2004b, Kitschelt and Wilkinson 2007).

In such a patronage democracy, access to government resources is often traded for votes in a more indirect fashion: politicians engage in practices of rent-seeking, which enables them to gather the necessary financial resources to launch expensive (re-) election campaigns. Politicians may use their discretionary power over the bureaucracy to demand kick-backs in return for awarding government contracts (often referred to as the 'tender system') or they may ask for 'contributions' from applicants in return for smoothing over their dealings with the bureaucracy. The money thus gained comes in handy at election time when expendable finance is needed to enlist supporters, and money is not the only incentive: politicians may oblige local leaders in their constituencies by doing them certain favours. These favours—building a new road, tolerating certain illegal practices, arranging a government job for a family member etc.—can be cashed in at election time when the local leaders are obliged to return the favour by mobilizing voters.

As we will see in the next chapter, this system of patronage depends on local leaders or 'big men' (Mines 1996): politicians use local leaders to deliver the votes of a community, while the community depends on these brokers to pressurize politicians and bureaucrats to deliver government services[6] (see Bailey 1970, Mitra 1991, Brass 1984 and Jeffrey 2002). These local leaders can convert their social contacts within political parties to sources of power and wealth (see Michaelson 1976, Rosenthal 1974), while political parties use such leaders to target their patronage efficiently to those communities who could deliver a majority of the votes;[7] the term 'vote-bank politics' is regularly used to describe the often blatant attempts of politicians to woo whole communities by supplying these communities with extra government resources and favourable policies.

These practices of patronage may be seen as a response to pressures arising from the specific political arena in which people like Pravin Dalal operate. Political patronage is sometimes related to certain cultural traits or to a lack of experience with democratic institutions. But such arguments fail to see the relation between political patronage and the demands of a political arena structured by citizens' difficulties in gaining access to state resources. As poorer citizens in particular can hardly get an electricity connection, a new water supply, a government job etc. without the intervention of political actors, they have a strong incentive to judge politicians on their capacity to help them gain access to these resources. This shapes the strategies that politicians employ: in order to win elections, politicians need to develop some control over the distribution of state resources, and to exchange the access to these resources for votes. In this sense the practice of patronage is a product of the limited capacity of state institutions to make state services equally available to everyone: as this limited capacity structures the nature of the competition for political power, it generates incentives to trade government resources for votes.

At the same, time the strategies that politicians employ to gain control over the distribution of state resources reinforce the limited capacity of state institutions to provide equal access to their services. The 'local area development schemes', for example, has served politicians to institutionalize the capacity of politicians to distribute state resources: such policies give politicians great freedom in determining where and how governmental budgets should be spent, and these policies enable them to use governmental resources to build up local support. Political actors like Pravin Dalal have no interest in adopting clearly worded policies that can be executed without political intervention: the nature of the competition they are engaged in stimulates them to adopt legislation and policies that are vaguely worded or stipulate their involvement in the implementation. Such policies make state officials and citizens even more dependent on the cooperation of politicians, and thus institutionalize political mediation in the heart of the daily operations of the state.

In this context it is not surprising that politicians like Pravin Dalal spend little of their time in meetings to discuss or draft new policy proposals. The strengthening of governmental institutions through the enactment of such proposals is simply no priority: local politicians have little interest in drafting general policies to enhance the provision of services such as water or education, they can benefit much more from a targeted distribution of scarce governmental resources. Unambiguously worded policies could diminish the capacity of municipal councillors or MLAs to influence the distribution of government resources by enabling administrators to provide services without the interference of politicians. Policies that stipulate the involvement of politicians are much more attractive: policies such as the local area development schemes offer politicians a powerful instrument to develop and maintain support in their constituencies, since these schemes allow politicians to decide how money should be spent.

Mediating hospital beds

Around 10:30, Pravin Dalal tells the people before him to come back the next day. While Himansubhai and the others return the chairs, stamps and letter pad to the bicycle shop, Pravin Dalal jumps on the back of another party worker's scooter. They drive to one of the city's main municipal hospitals. There Pravin Dalal has a real office: right next to the entrance of the main hospital building, a clean white room with two desks is reserved for four municipal councillors. Pravin Dalal is entitled to a seat behind these desks because he is a member of the hospital's Board of Trustees. This position is an important political asset: it has helped him to earn the gratitude of many voters of his constituency, since membership of the Board gives him considerable influence over the daily affairs at the hospital.

This influence is very valuable in an overcrowded hospital, whose *paan* stained corridors are filled with long queues of people who wait for hours for their turn to be diagnosed with the aid of the hospital's modern equipment.

As there are often not enough hospital beds, some patients have to squat on mattresses on the floors of the wards or in the corridors of the hospital. The doctors and nurses have to move purposefully through such wards, as they are besieged with questions and requests. Many patients and their family members also direct their requests to men without uniform who move around holding big piles of paper. They are party workers: many municipal councillors have a few supporters doing daily rounds at the hospital.

Vinodbhai is one of Pravin Dalal's party workers in the hospital. He arrives there early in the morning, and spends a lot of time talking to the nurses and doctors. Vinodbhai is a typical 'fixer' (Manor 2000), he uses his proximity to Pravin Dalal as a means to help people who, one day, might help him to launch a political career of his own. He says of his work: 'I keep a list of all the patients from Maneknagar [Pravin Dalal's electoral ward]. I check on their status and communicate this to the families and we make sure that they are treated. Pravin Dalal is on the board of trustees of the hospital, so when I go to a doctor, the doctor makes sure the patient is treated well'. As Vinodbhai showed me around the hospital, he pointed at the many people sitting or lying down in the corridors: 'There are so many people that come; the doctors cannot treat them all. We can just make sure that the doctors treat some patients. There are so many people that cannot be helped. If he would go to the doctor [points to a scruffy-looking man on the floor], the doctor would not talk to him. So we go for him, and get him to the doctor'.

These party workers, however, do not help everybody. Their work seems to be reserved for those groups that will be helpful during elections. Since control over the hospital's resources is an important instrument to gain electoral support, the political competition outside the hospital shapes the daily struggle for hospital beds and cheap treatment. As another (BJP) party worker related: 'Hindus do not get as much help in VS hospital. The Muslim *corporators* [municipal councillors, a word derived from the term for a big city municipality, Municipal Corporation] prevent this, so we only help Hindus. We only take care of Hindus. Eighty per cent of the patients in this hospital are Muslims, they get all the benefit. For Hindus, only Pravin Dalal and Shaivalbhai [another municipal councillor] and some boys are there. Muslims have all these [charitable] trusts to help people and the Congress councillors are there all the time to help them. This is a very sensitive area; if we would help a Muslim, the Hindus would reproach us, they would complain to us, so we cannot help them'.

Such remarks illustrate the selective nature of the mediation that actors like Pravin Dalal engage in: their daily mediating activities—and thus the provision of state resources—are guided by a keen awareness of the kind of support that needs to be nurtured in order to win the next elections. India's majoritarian voting system ensures that politicians can benefit more from a targeted provision of state resources than from a more universal distribution: the budgets that local politicians control are generally used to reward loyal supporters and nurture the support of those sections of the electorate that can guarantee a majority of the votes. As I will explore more fully in Chapter 8, religious, caste and regional identities are used to identify such winning majorities

The big piles of papers that people like Vinodbhai walk around with are hospital bills. The patients or their family members approach the party workers to get the amounts on the bills reduced. Compared to the fancy private hospitals in the city, the cost of treatment in this municipal hospital is not very high, but it is still insurmountable for many patients. As Vinodbhai related, 'The doctors think that people should pay for their medicines, so we intervene and we fight for them to get the reduction. We make sure the people get less expensive bills. And often this is not enough, people become indebted to pay their hospital bills. Especially the CTI scan is expensive, and it is needed at the beginning of the treatment'. Generally, the reduction amounts to about 30 per cent of the total bill. In special cases the municipal councillors use their charitable trusts, often set up by the local MLAs or MPs, to cover the whole bill.

Vinodbhai takes the pile of hospital bills to Pravin Dalal with an attached income certificate. When the municipal councillors arrive in their offices, several party workers like Vinodbhai crowd the room to get their papers signed; some senior workers may sign the income certificates themselves, while others approach the municipal councillors for a signature. With the income certificate the patient can 'prove' that he or she cannot afford to pay the full hospital bill. The hospital administration relies on these declarations signed by politicians and their workers to make the actual decision about reduction of the bill; after the addition of the income certificate, the papers go to the administrative officer of the hospital, who clears the bill. This procedure requires some daily compromising: while the hospital wants to get the cost of the treatment covered, the politicians and their helpers are keen to do a favour to their supporters and friends. Given the amounts of hospital bills that go around every day, it seems that the municipal councillors have the upper hand.

Pravin Dalal spends almost two hours at the hospital. During this time he arranges treatment for some patients, checks on others, signs various papers and attends the occasional meeting of the Board of Management. After lunch and some rest he arrives at 3:30 at the main office of Ahmedabad's Municipal Corporation. Since he is not a member of any of the municipality committees (such as the Town Planning Committee or the Water Supply and Sewage Committee), Pravin Dalal does not have a separate office; he proceeds to the general office of the BJP councillors on the municipal council.

The way this room is furnished suggests that the councillors use this office to receive visitors rather than to hold meetings. A row of tables is placed parallel to the wall with chairs for the councillors behind them. In front of the tables there are lines of chairs for visitors; when Pravin Dalal is behind his desk several people occupy these chairs to await their turn. Each desk is empty apart from a phone. This phone is used feverishly. As in the morning, several people approach Pravin Dalal for help to deal with the municipal institutions. But in the afternoon, there are more individual requests involving city-level departments; many people come with tax bills and requests for licences. Pravin Dalal often uses the phone to contact a municipal department to alert the officers to a particular request. His efficiency is again impressive: he can shift quickly between conversations about topics as disparate as tax regulations and municipal policies on hawkers; often he juggles a mobile phone in one hand and the office phone in the other while simultaneously holding a conversation with the people in front of him. When Pravin Dalal gets the relevant officer on the phone, a few sentences may be enough: later, when the supplicant arrives at this department to get his work done, the phone call has generally served to ensure the cooperation of the administrators.

Pravin Dalal often said that he tried to maintain friendly relations with these officials, convinced that this would speed up his work: 'I have good relations with the officers, so they do the work quickly. You have to do those people favours, in order to keep up relations'. Not all local politicians adopted such an approach. The MLA Shailesh Macwana in particular could make quite a show out of scolding low-ranking bureaucrats when some work was not done. He would take the phone and lash out: 'I've decided that after the 20th we will do *todfod* ('breaking') in your office everyday. The public may beat up your officials. There are two women standing here, otherwise I would explain it to you in your own language'. In this particular instance, the officials involved arrived in Shailesh Macwana's office only ten minutes later.

Pravin Dalal does not spend the whole afternoon behind the desk; like the other municipal councillors in the room, he comes and goes. There are always people to meet or offices to visit, and often party workers demand his attention to discuss political developments or the progress of their local affairs. At least once a week there is a meeting to attend, though these are rare: Pravin Dalal spends only about three hours a week in meetings at the municipality, and for two hours a week he attends a meeting of the hospital management board. This excludes meetings with other politicians and party officials for political strategizing, which generally take place once a week in the evening.

Political mediation as particularization

The involvement of politicians in manipulating the implementation of policies and law is a recurring element in the available ethnographies on the functioning of local politicians (Church 1973, Hansen 2005, Oldenburg 1976, Rosenthal 1970, 1974 and Michaelson 1976). Unsurprisingly, the involvement of political mediators can greatly distort the actual outcome of various policies of the state (see Mooij 1999, Benjamin and Bhuvaneshwari 2001, Oldenburg 1987), since at the implementation stage a great number of local interests can, depending on their bargaining power or hold over the bureaucracy, influence the application of legislation. The municipal rules and regulations about, for example, the allocation of hospital beds or the reduction of hospital bills are selectively applied according to considerations unrelated to the purpose of these rules and regulations. This constant interference, by political actors in particular, undermines a universal application of the state's rules and regulations.

Political interference is part of the normal daily routine of bureaucrats, in the sense that the political hold over the daily operations of the bureaucracy is supported by much regulation and policies that institutionalize political mediation as a routine element of the functioning of state institutions. In a study on the functioning of Indian bureaucracy, Das (2001: 19) concludes that 'from the evidence available, it is clear that the present bureaucracy in India is used as the personal instrument of ruling politicians'. Benjamin and Bhuvaneshwari (2001) use the term 'porous bureaucracy' to capture the political hold over the bureaucracy that they witnessed in Bangalore. Harriss-White (2003: 72–103) used the term 'shadow state' to describe these mediating networks of people who generate their livelihood by influencing the state's daily operations. These networks, she argues, should be seen as part of the actually existing state.[8] Her 'shadow state' seems to be very close to what Chatterjee (1998, 2001 and 2004) calls 'political society', a concept I will discuss more extensively in the next chapter.

This political influence over administrators is institutionalized through what has been called a 'transfer system'. Indian government officials are generally appointed for life but they are regularly assigned different postings in different departments or districts. These transfers are intended, officially, to create obstacles to corruption by limiting the development of personal relations between officials and locals. But as both De Zwart (1994) and Wade (1982, 1985) discuss in great detail, the transfer system is also an effective instrument for politicians to ensure the cooperation of bureaucrats. De Zwart's informants estimate that every year 20 to 80 thousand transfers take place in Gujarat alone; on average the highest-ranking officials are transferred within 20 months (De Zwart 1994: 52–5). Bureaucrats often pay visits to influential politicians to obtain a better posting or to prevent a transfer to a lesser posting. De Zwart (1994: 76) cites a Gujarati police officer saying, 'the [Gujarati] police force (...) has been ruined due to heavy politicization. Every transfer used to take place at the behest of politicians (...) while we are not here to take directions from politicians'. Harriss-White (2003: 97) used the term 'spinning state' to capture the speed at which government officers are transferred because of political interference.

Politicians benefit in two ways from their hold over the transfer of state officials: it allows them to manipulate the activities of the administrators, and to make money. They can manipulate the activities of administrators by (threat of) transferring out an uncooperative official, and their capacity to direct transfers may also be used as a means to create personal obligations among the bureaucracy. In return for a favourable transfer, an administrator can be called upon later to get something done. As De Zwart describes, the transfer of bureaucrats also plays a role in the struggle between different political factions or parties. Both sides in such a struggle attempt to get 'our man' in and 'their man' out, since such manoeuvring can weaken opponents' capacity to get things done. The manipulation of transfers is therefore essential for electoral success; the resulting influence over the administration can be used to attract supporters and to direct government resources to voters.

The political manipulation of bureaucratic transfers also yields money that can be used to pay for election campaigns. The transfer system has created a 'market for public office' (Wade 1985), as state officials can purchase lucrative postings by passing on sufficient amounts of money to influential politicians. Government officials are willing to pay large amounts of money—up to several million rupees—for a lucrative post. This is, of course, an investment: the highest prices are offered for posts that offer the highest returns. Posts where many government contracts are handed out and posts where a lot of (illegal) business activities have to be 'regulated' are especially interesting: these are lucrative postings since they offer ample opportunities for collecting bribes. The money that government officials spend to 'purchase' such a post is very useful for politicians who need sizeable budgets to buy or induce voters. For this reason Wade (1985: 479) argues for a relation between the costs of an election campaign and the rent-seeking that bureaucrats engage in: the more money politicians need for their election campaign, the more money they need to demand for sanctioning transfers, which in turn stimulates bureaucrats to collect more bribes in order to make good on their 'investment'. In this sense the strategies of politicians to increase their hold over the bureaucracy reinforces the difficulties of citizens in dealing independently with state officials, since the operation of the transfer system impels officials to collect bribes from citizens.

This need to collect bribes constitutes another instrument for politicians to control the bureaucracy. The practice of many bureaucrats to demand small bribes for processing requests requires some co-operation from politicians: these administrators are vulnerable to complaints about their behaviour from influential politicians. They are aware that everybody who is close to these politicians could use this proximity to lodge a complaint and create difficulties; this forces rent-seeking bureaucrats to be extra attentive to requests from party workers or other individuals known to be 'close' to a politician. Those bureaucrats who maintain good relations with politicians and their workers may be rewarded when there are government contracts to award: as I will discuss below, if bureaucrats and politicians co-operate they can jointly demand kick-backs from contractors or suppliers in return for awarding a contract. Such deals can be a topic of discussion during the more private meetings that take place at Pravin Dalal's house in the evening.

Evening compromises

When there are no meetings of his party to attend, Pravin Dalal spends the evenings at home. There the work continues, as the evenings are the moment to approach the municipal councillor for more sensitive matters. The visitors seem to prefer the privacy of Pravin Dalal's home, either because people do not want their problems to become public knowledge, or because the councillor's involvement should remain relatively invisible. To discuss this less visible aspect of Pravin Dalal's daily routine, let us take one evening in December as an example, when two different visitors dropped in during an interview.

The first visitor was a slightly agitated woman. She wanted to become the sole owner of her house; currently an unrelated man owned a part of the house. She had approached this man to buy this part from him, but they could not agree on a price. She asked Pravin Dalal to contact the man on her behalf to settle the issue. Pravin Dalal agreed to look into the matter. The settlement of disputes is a lucrative activity; not only politicians but also local social workers and *goonda*s ('criminals') spend much time brokering compromises between neighbours, family members or business partners. Through Pravin Dalal's mediation a problem can be solved much quicker and easier than through the courts. The large backlog of court cases, and the large amount of bribes needed to carry a case through the courts make people turn to local politicians to solve their problems. Politicians dispose of their own enforcement mechanisms: even though such harsh methods are seldom necessary, the involvement of a politician does convey an implicit threat. A politician can harass one of the disputing parties by creating difficulties with the police or bureaucracy, or by sending local musclemen to threaten a disputant. These methods of pressurization are especially useful to settle disputes involving real estate. Builders, contractors or house owners often face difficulties evicting unwilling (but legally well protected) tenants or illegal squatters from their property. Local politicians and *goonda*s can make a handsome profit if they help to 'solve' such disputes by harassing people.

According to Pravin Dalal people come to him every day to settle family issues. They come to help convince parents to agree to a marriage: 'I know many people, so I can check about the person. I tell them that the boy or girl is good and I promise that if there will be problems, I will help to solve them'. And, indeed, politicians like Pravin Dalal also help in solving marital problems: (the parents of) bickering couples approach him to try to improve their marriage and prevent divorce. I have attended one such session in which an Isanpur politician managed to convince an angry and suicidal wife to return home by instructing the husband to find work and save money. This is another indication of the increased prominence of politicians: the settlement of such disputes used to be the domain of the *pol panch*es and the caste *panchayat*s. The involvement of a politician in such disputes does not, however, necessarily lead to a satisfactory solution. As one older inhabitant of Maneknagar reminisces: 'People are suffering, there is no system like a *panch* or a *maha-*

jan to provide relief [to settle disputes]. People go to politicians even if they distrust them: just to add more weight to their case they go to politicians. Politicians know who is more important [of the persons involved in the dispute], so according to importance they will use their influence. Like he is my [political] party-man so I will listen to him'.

The second person to interrupt the interview on that evening in December was a well-dressed businessman. He was a representative of a company that supplies buses. He asked Pravin Dalal about a tender that the Ahmedabad's municipal corporation was about to issue: the Ahmedabad municipal bus service needed new buses to strengthen its fleet. The man referred to his closeness to an influential state-level politician and requested Pravin Dalal to help him secure the contract.

The involvement of politicians in the allocation of government contracts has created a 'tender system': politicians and bureaucrats often demand kickbacks and support in return for awarding a government contract. This requires close contact and a certain level of trust, because the businessman involved should be reliable: he has to be trusted to discreetly hand over a certain agreed percentage of the total budget of the contract (usually around 10 per cent). In particular, contractors maintain very close relations with influential politicians to increase their chances of landing a government contract. These contractors often become associated with a political party, and often help to mobilize support for a party during elections (for example by influencing the voting behaviour of their labourers) to curry favour with the party's politicians. By mobilizing voters and by contributing money to an electoral campaign, contractors may oblige politicians: this much-needed support forces politicians to return the favour when there are government contracts to be rewarded. For contractors, election results are therefore of vital importance: if they bet on the wrong party they stand little chance to secure lucrative government contracts.

The 'tender system' is another illustration of the interaction between state capacities and political strategies. The need to organize expensive election campaigns stimulates local politicians to trade government contracts for electoral and financial support which does not necessarily lead to the most efficient use of state funds: contractors often use the cheapest materials in order to save the necessary money to pay the politicians involved. The tender system thus increases the cost and limits the effectiveness of government projects.

Conclusion

Throughout this chapter I have discussed several examples of the dialectic between the capacities of state institutions to provide various services and the strategies that politicians employ to gain and maintain power. On the one hand, the difficulties that ordinary citizens face when dealing with state institutions are an important reason why politicians like Pravin Dalal are deeply involved in the manipulation of state officials' daily work while, on the other hand, this involvement of politicians in the day-to-day administration is also a cause of these difficulties. The involvement of politicians in the daily affairs of the hospital, for example, does help individual patients to secure treatment or reduce their bills but does not necessarily increase the efficiency or capacity of the hospital since, by their involvement, politicians limit recovery of the costs of treatment. Similarly, the difficulties citizens encounter in arranging (repair of) basic amenities stimulate politicians to engage in constant manipulation of the implementation of various government policies, which undermines the bureaucracy's capacity to use the budget reserved for provision of basic amenities in an efficient manner.

In these different ways, the dependence of citizens and state institutions on mediating politicians is constantly reinforced. The difficulties inhabitants face in dealing with the state's bureaucracy generates a field in which political actors' financial and electoral success depends on their capacity to mediate successfully between citizens and the state. As voters expect politicians to help solve bureaucratic hassles and to provide access to government resources, electoral success depends on their capacity to get things done for voters. This need to get things done is an important incentive for politicians to increase their hold over the bureaucracy and their influence over the implementation of policies: if they can strengthen their position as mediators between state and society, they increase their capacity to gain the support of voters. The practice of patronage and the political interference in the transfer of bureaucrats, as well as the constant meddling of politicians in the execution of policies, may therefore be seen as a response to citizens' difficulties in dealing with state institutions, while these different elements of the daily routine of politicians also reinforce those difficulties: this dialectic engenders a mediated state.

The institutionalization of political mediation challenges the common view that sees it as an intrusion into the 'normal' functioning of the state. The activities of politicians like Pravin Dalal cannot be seen as a deviation from (and a sign of not yet having achieved) a 'normal' state—that is, the Weberian ideal of a rule-bound unitary state with a clear separation of powers, in which politicians operate as policy makers who merely oversee the provision of public services. I have suggested in this chapter that political mediation is not an aberration or a deviation, but rather is already at the heart of the state—in this case a state which, as the institutionalization of political mediation progresses, is on the path to becoming a different kind of state, a mediated state. For most of the citizens of Gujarat, the elements that constitute a state—its employees, its numerous laws and rules—are only experienced through the intervention of political intermediaries, and are thoroughly shaped by the operations of these intermediaries.

However, the mediated nature of Gujarat's state institutions not only shapes the daily routine of politicians. In the next chapters I will show how the dependence of citizens on political mediation generates large, widespread networks of various local intermediaries who derive their standing, as well as their livelihoods, from their capacity to access influential politicians and important bureaucrats. Much of the dynamic and complexity of neighbourhood politics is a product of the constant exchange of favours through which these local intermediaries improve their access to state resources.

6

NEIGHBOURHOOD WORKERS AND THE POLITICS OF EXCHANGING FAVOURS

At first sight nothing distinguishes Raamrahimnagar from the many other settlements built around Ahmedabad's now largely defunct textile mills. The locality is a matured slum: no longer are the houses made of wooden boards and corrugated iron as they must have been in the 1960s. Now all the houses are *pacca*—they are all made of bricks and cement and some of them are up to four storeys high. But you can still see that this locality was once an illegal settlement of migrants who had come to the city looking for a better future. The odd angles of the lanes, the loose wiring that connects the houses, and the fact that many houses stand around one of the main outlets of the city's sewer—these are present-day reminders of the unplanned and chaotic manner in which the slum grew and took shape. Close to twenty thousand people have found a place to live here; inhabitants say that 40 per cent of them are Muslims, the rest are Hindus from lower castes.

Right in the middle of this locality's main road stands a small building with the words 'Raam Rahim Nagar Jhupadavasi Mandal' (RJM) painted on its façade, together with an Aum symbol, a crescent moon and a cross. This office houses a neighbourhood committee; since 1973 the RJM has represented the interests of inhabitants to the outside world. According to Nathwarlal, its current president, the *mandal* has played an important role in the development of the locality: 'We are popular because we are *jagrut* (awakened, knowledgeable) and we have the best facilities here which we managed to get. We managed to maintain unity here because slowly we got more facilities'. The older members of the RJM, like Nathwarlal, can still recount the history of these developments:

There used to be only public taps, people were waiting in line for water. Then we approached the municipality. We brought the [municipal] *corporator* here and then

20–25 taps were made, in 1972. After that, the Mandal was formed. We thought, 'if we get organized we can get facilities'. After 1980 we gave water connections to each house. We also made latrines. When they got dirty we filled forms for each individual to get individual gutter connections. Now there are streetlights, water, gutter and all the houses have private toilets. A doctor comes to our office every week.

The members of the *mandal* call themselves social workers. They play an important role in the resolution of all sorts of local problems: they help inhabitants get ration cards or a widow pension and they play a role in the settlement of local disputes. Because of their local standing the members of the *mandal* can impose a solution without involving the troublesome police: 'When we go to the police, they harass both sides and take bribes. We give a better solution, we form a small group and sit down with the people involved. In this way we will solve the problem. People respect us, that is why they listen to us'. People approach the *mandal* to deal with the recurring breakdowns of basic amenities: frequently the gutters get clogged and they overflow into the narrow lanes. Rats eat holes in the pipelines, which sometimes causes the gutter to leak into the water pipelines below. During one of my walks through the locality with the RJM's vice-president Kapadiabhai we were given a bottle of tap water with little animals in it: the vice-president was pressed to solve this as soon as possible.

For such matters the vice-president goes to a street corner at the end of Raamrahimnagar, where the local municipal councillors from the Congress party sit together every morning. These councillors help to arrange the necessary budget, and they can direct the officials to repair the leaking pipes. As one local councillor explained: 'We help them solve their problems. The administrators do not do the work; they just say 'yes yes'. So people come to us because we get the work done. When a worker [of the RJM] goes he will be successful, because I tell the administrator that he is my worker so you get his work done'. The members of the *mandal* do not have to approach the councillor for everything, as the councillor has delegated some responsibilities to them: the councillor has given them a stack of papers from his own letter pad, which the RJM members use to provide inhabitants with a proof of residence or an income certificate.

The support of the municipal councillors is not just *seva* ('service'): in return for their cooperation the councillors expect help during elections. As Kapadiabhai explained: 'During elections they need us. We are educated so we can make people understand. We can tell people what to vote. We make people understand that if you vote for this person you will get facilities. If this persons wins we will get the budget [to improve facilities]. If we give support, they also give support, it is *haras paras* ('give and take'): we get them votes so they do work for us'.

The dependency of citizens on political mediation—discussed in the last chapter—generates large networks around politicians of various actors who help common citizens to ensure the cooperation of politicians and, by extension, the bureaucracy. A person like Nathwarlal and Kapadiabhai can be found in almost every *chawl* (housing block) or slum: these ubiquitous 'workers' earn local standing (and often also money) by using their closeness to politicians to extract benefits from the state for their clients. In this chapter and the next I will delve into the complexities of the networks around politicians: we will see how besides politicians there are various other actors who make at least a part of their living by performing distinctive roles in the daily facilitation of interaction between state institutions and citizens.

In the context of a mediated state one should be hesitant about using the term 'civil society' for organizations like RJM. In a series of publications Partha Chatterjee proposed to use the term 'political society' as well as 'civil society' to capture the different forms of cooperation and association that take place in the realm between the state and the household. The actual civil society in India, Chatterjee (2004: 66) argues, is 'demographically limited' because 'the poor who mobilise to claim the benefits of various government programs do not do so as members of civil society (...) they must succeed in applying the right pressure at the right places in the government machinery [through] the bending and stretching of rules'.[1] The practices and forms of mobilization of poorer citizens are inconsistent with the practices usually associated with 'civil society'—based on principles of equality, autonomy, freedom of entry and exit, recognized duties of members, voluntariness, respect for procedures (Cohen 1992: 131)—because these forms of association are not open to people who stand in an uncertain and dependent relation to the institutions of the state. This dependence is, as Chatterjee argues (2004: 40), related to the limited capacities of state institutions: 'The state agencies recognize that these population groups do have some claim on the welfare programs of the governments, but those claims could not be regarded as justifiable rights since the state did not have the means to deliver those benefits to the entire population of the country. (...) What happens then is a negotiation of these claims on a political terrain'.

This chapter and the next explore this realm of 'political society'. In this chapter I focus on the role that large groups of middlemen—men but also, to a lesser extent, women—play in the everyday mediation of the state. Earlier papers on this group of 'fixers' described them as 'lubricants' (Reddy and Haragopal 1985: 1154) and 'enablers' of the democratic process (Manor 2000: 817, see also Krishna 2007) as they facilitate the communication between political leaders and local communities. In this chapter I will build on their work to explore the interdependencies between these local fixers and elected politicians. I will focus on local neighbourhood workers here. Similar intermediaries could also be identified at higher levels of government, infiltrating ministries and courts on behalf of their private clients, but their lucrative and even shadier dealings follow a different dynamic and fall outside the scope of my local fieldwork (but see de Zwart 1994).

To describe their interactions I will distinguish two types of fixers: social workers and party workers. Party workers are open supporters of political parties who develop their preferential access to political leaders by performing all sorts of organizational tasks for them. Social workers (also sometimes referred to as neighbourhood leaders (*stanik neta*), when they are accorded local leadership)[2] maintain some independence from politicians. Social workers' access to politicians is largely based on their capacity to rally voters at the time of elections. These various intermediaries and elected politicians are engaged in a constant exchange of favours: the actors that operate in the realm between state institutions and citizens need each other and compete with each other to develop a profitable capacity to deal with government institutions. The pervasiveness of these workers should be seen as an indication that their exchange of favours is relatively lucrative compared to the scarce alternative sources of income in the studied neighbourhoods. In this exchange of favours women are generally disadvantaged, which undermines their capacity to develop a political career.

In the next chapter I will focus on two other types of actors that play a role in the mediation between state institutions and citizens: local criminals ('*goondas*') and state officials. Such a five-fold categorization of the different actors that play a role in the mediation of the state—social workers, party workers, *goondas*, politicians and state officials—has its drawbacks. Individuals do not always correspond neatly to the generalized stereotypes discussed below, and in practice these categories are also not as neatly separable as the labels suggest: a party worker might function like a *goonda*, a social worker can become a politician, and so on. But the distinction among these five groups is a very real one for inhabitants in the studied neighbourhoods. As some of the quotations below show, the *goondas*, social workers and party workers figure regularly in the way local inhabitants talk about local politics. Moreover, a categorization of different local political actors makes it possible to go beyond mere anecdotal descriptions, and this categorization enables me to tease out some more general conclusions. If we keep in mind that they are generalized stereotypes, this categorization can be a useful instrument to describe the complex realm of neighbourhood politics.[3]

Poverty and the dependence on political mediation

During my research I had occasion to live in three very different parts of Ahmedabad. Initially I lived in the posh western part of the city; then I moved to the old walled city on the eastern side of the Sabermati, and in the last phase of my fieldwork I shared a small house inside one of Isanpur's *chawls*. I spent many evenings outside, talking to my neighbours on a bench or an *otla* close to my house. Generally these conversations were similar wherever I lived, but when the conversation turned to politics there were marked differences between the three localities. If the inhabitants of my posh housing society in western Ahmedabad talked about politics at all, then they discussed national and state level politics. Few of my neighbours there knew the names of the municipal councillors who represented them. But in Maneknagar and especially Isanpur and Raamrahimnagar inhabitants could spend a whole evening talking about the activities of their municipal councillors. Much time was devoted to an analysis of who was close to whom: inhabitants were keenly aware of who had access to the local police inspector, who had befriended the municipal councillor, who had good contacts within political parties, etc. It seemed to me that the conversations in Isanpur and Raamrahimnagar had even greater detail: there people would know exactly which social worker was close to what police officer, they joked about which politician supported which small-time criminal, how the campaigning funds were gathered, and so on.

These different conversations reflect the differing importance of politics in the daily life of these localities. Whereas inhabitants of Maneknagar and especially Isanpur and Raamrahimnagar often rely on the mediation of politicians and their workers to deal with government institutions, the relatively well-off residents can by and large do without the interference of political actors. In the context of a mediated state, the unequal distribution of social, cultural and economic capital in society is translated into an unequal access to government services. While citizens of poorer localities have to rely on their votes and collective strength as instruments to deal with state institutions, richer inhabitants dispose of more individual means to influence the state's bureaucracy, which reduces their dependence on the many party workers and social workers that abound in localities like Isanpur and Maneknagar. Their privileged position within society advantages their access to government institutions in at least three different ways.

The first obvious advantage is money. The greater financial resources of the privileged reduce their dependence on state services: well-off citizens can afford to buy the services that the state is providing inadequately or not at all. In the posh housing societies of western Ahmedabad one can find tube-wells, electricity generators, privately hired watchmen and sweepers, all of which makes inhabitants relatively independent of the municipal services. Around these localities one can find high-standard private hospitals and prestigious private schools that charge high fees but guarantee successful careers; as a result government departments only serve those who cannot afford better services. And when these more privileged citizens do need to approach government officials, they have the money to buy their cooperation. The common practices of rent-seeking by bureaucrats and the police favour the rich: well-off inhabitants can pay for the services of officials, while less privileged citizens do not have the income to influence the operations of the bureaucracy in this manner.

The second advantage lies in the social networks in which the more privileged inhabitants are embedded. Middle-class residents move in the same social circles as senior government officials, which greatly facilitates their access to state institutions. Even if there are no direct contacts, a family member, an influential neighbour, a befriended businessman or a college-friend can be relied upon to contact a senior bureaucrat or police officer; in these exchanges references to common friends, to a shared past, or to an old friendship can be very useful. In the context of a mediated state this social capital is of immense value to get government institutions to act favourably. Most inhabitants of the slums and *chawls* of Ahmedabad do not have this kind of social capital: their contacts are hardly sufficient to enlist the support of class four bureaucrats—the peons—which leaves these inhabitants few other options than to approach political actors for help.

The exchange of favours within these more privileged social circles ensures that someone who needs, for example, a license for a business or a passport can find a contact to whom the relevant bureaucrat or officer has some obligation. That constitutes a third advantage: well-off residents have more to offer in exchange for a favourable intervention by a bureaucrat or police officer. Their jobs offer more opportunities to engage in a lucrative exchange of favours since such jobs often come with some control over valuable resources as well as opportunities to establish influential contacts. These resources and contacts can be used to ensure the cooperation of government officials: bureaucrats might be persuaded to help because, for example, the supplicant owns a hotel where a cooperative bureaucrat might stay at a concessional rate, or because the supplicant is an influential journalist who might write a damaging article, or because he or she runs a business that could offer a lucrative job to family members. The professions of residents in Isanpur and Raamrahimnagar generally do not allow them to engage in such an exchange of favours, and so they have to find other ways to pressurize the bureaucracy.

These advantages of well-off citizens are reflected in a different attitude towards politics, of which the differing evening discussions are just one expression. It has often been commented that during elections the turnout among the poor is much higher than among the rich. This higher turnout is not because poorer citizens are more enthusiastic about their civic duty. It should be seen in light of the above: since poorer residents have fewer alternative means to get access to government resources, they depend more on the mediation that political networks engage in. Since residents in Maneknagar and especially Isanpur and Raamrahimnagar have few other options, they need to use their votes as leverage over these political networks. As one inhabitant of a nice apartment building in western Ahmedabad put it, referring to the poorer eastern side of Ahmedabad: 'Here we have to solve our problems individually, there it is done collectively. Here the individual contacts somebody to solve the matter, there collective pressure is used. When the municipal councillor does not pay attention to an issue he just loses an individual here, [but] there he loses a whole area'.

Furthermore, while poorer residents are disadvantaged in these three ways when dealing with state institutions, at the same time they have a more pressing need to gain access to state resources. As I discussed in Chapter 4, both the lack of secure alternative livelihoods (particularly after the demise of the textile industry) and the discrimination that Dalits experience when searching for private sector jobs make governmental jobs and resources very sought after. The limited (and often precarious) sources of income and the relative importance of state resources for local livelihoods have thus contributed to the politicization of neighbourhoods. In this way, the gradual liberalization of Gujarat's economy has contributed to the pervasiveness of various 'fixers', since the relentless pressure to reduce labour costs has boosted the dependence on the state as a more stable and more lucrative source of income. Complex networks of municipal councillors, party workers, neighbourhood associations, social workers etc. have come into being in areas where access to the state is valuable. These networks are ubiquitous in eastern Ahmedabad, while they are relatively absent in the more posh localities in the western part of the city: this unequal dependence on political intermediaries forms the backdrop for this chapter's exploration of the functioning of local political networks in poorer localities.

Canvassing as investment

When the date for the 2005 municipal elections was finally announced, the RJM members geared into action. One of their former presidents, Aaljibhai, was contesting one of the three seats in the municipal council, and RJM members reasoned that it would increase their prospects to have Aaljibhai as a municipal corporator. They went around the neighbourhood on their bicycles and motorbikes, and told people that Aaljibhai would work very hard for the people in the locality. They organized several election meetings to instruct their neighbours about whom to vote for. In their speeches they presented the elections as a chance to solve some of the pressing problems of the neighbourhood. As one RJM worker related: 'When people came [to us] with problems, like with the gutter, or household problems, we told the people that when our candidates are elected we can demand all this [work] from the candidate'.

On the day of the election Nathwarlal and other members had placed a table in front of the RJM office. From there they distributed 'election-slips': these are little pieces of paper with a name and registration number on it, which voters use to identify themselves at the polling booth. Other workers helped their candidates by taking up positions inside the polling booths. They sat on plastic chairs with large lists of voters, partly to oversee the voting and partly to observe who came out to vote. In some areas these workers were instrumental in capturing the booths: with the use of some muscled supporters, and by bribing the election officer, it was possible to add several votes of dead or absent voters in the last hour of polling. I was present at one occasion of 'bogus voting' in a booth that was completely controlled by the party workers of one party. They had apparently bought the election officers, and the supporters of the other party were so far outnumbered that they could do little. When the police officers on duty left, the doors of the booth were closed and a great number of votes were added ('now the dead people will vote', a befriended party worker told me before he closed the doors). Afterwards the party workers were boasting about the number of times they voted; in their somewhat festive mood they had even asked me to vote. The RJM members were, as far as I know, not engaged in such activities: they spent polling day touring the neighbourhood, instructing inhabitants about the importance of voting, and, if necessary, accompanying them to the booth.

To stand a chance of winning the elections, candidates need these forms of support from social workers like the RJM members. The authority that the RJM's leaders have in Raamrahimnagar enables them to sway a large number of votes, which forces candidates to court their support. This dependence underlies the implicit (and often explicit) exchange between candidates and neighbourhood leaders like the members of the RJM: in return for support during the elections these local workers can count on the cooperation of the candidate once he or she is elected.

This dependence allows influential local workers or neighbourhood committees like the RJM to strike a deal with a candidate: they can exchange their support (and thus a large number of votes in their locality) for promises that, once the candidate is elected, budget funds will be reserved to improve the drainage, change the street paving, provide electricity connections, etc. For this reason the RJM's usefulness to local residents lies for a large part in its capacity to pool their votes: through the RJM, individual voters can increase their leverage over politicians (and thus over the bureaucracy as well), not unlike the many 'election clubs' that played the levers of the 'political machines' in America's cities in the early 20th century.[4] This reasoning informs Nathwarlal's remark that 'if we get organised, we get facilities': the RJM can deliver a big number of votes in return for improvements of local facilities. Without an influential local organization, or without local representatives that can be trusted to enforce such a 'deal', politicians have no guarantee that their support will translate into votes. Nathwarlal put it as follows: 'Some areas are so backward, they cannot use the budget. All that budget is wasted'. This vote-pooling is not always aimed at improving access to government services: in some localities local leaders help candidates to buy the votes of residents by distributing the candidate's money and by pressurizing residents to ensure that this investment translates into votes.

Because of such 'deals' candidates study the actual patterns of voting with great interest. Candidates need to know if their investments have paid off, and if local leaders actually did deliver the votes they had promised. If not, an elected candidate would not feel an obligation to act on their demands.[5] As I noted before, the RJM has been very successful in these exchanges. During successive elections they could pressurize politicians to improve the facilities in their localities. This was possible because for many consecutive years the RJM had supported winning candidates. If their preferred candidates had lost, their efforts during the elections would have yielded no benefits and the votes of Raamrahimnagar's residents would have been, as people often put it, 'lost'. That is the calculation that local leaders need to make before pledging their support: if they support a candidate with limited chances of winning the elections, they risk wasting the opportunity to improve their access to the state. The importance of supporting a winning candidate could make even drinking a cup of *chai* at the *karyalay* in the evening a sensitive issue, since by sitting at the election office of a particular candidate, you signalled your support. One can imagine that this was a sensitivity that even this researcher had to keep in mind when stopping by for an interview: when a local leader chooses to drink his tea only at the *karyalay* of one candidate, he risks straining his contacts with other candidates.

This time the RJM was less fortunate. Its candidate, Aaljibhai, lost by just 26 votes. He had received many votes in Raamrahimnagar, but too little support from inhabitants in other localities. This changed the RJM's capacity to get things done: since the elected *corporators* had not relied on the RJM's work, they were not expected to react as speedily to its requests. As local social worker Taajubanu commented after the elections: 'now the *mandal* [the RJM] is less strong, which creates problems for the public. The people that won do not live here, so our work is a bit blocked now'. After the elections RJM members said they preferred to approach the local member of the state assembly to solve their issues.

Becoming a neighbourhood leader

People like Nathwarlal and Kapadiabhai help residents to understand the functioning of state institutions and act as brokers between local residents, politicians and government officials. These local workers often display an impressive knowledge of the intricacies of the Indian Penal Code, which comes in handy when they deal with the police on behalf of their neighbours. They have regular interactions with the local bureaucrats, as they press them for ration cards, licenses, loans, hospital treatment etc., and they play an important role in securing the limited developmental budgets for the establishment or improvement of basic amenities in the area.

All this work would not be possible without at least tacit support from politicians. The backing of a politician increases the capacity of a social worker to deal with government officials: social workers can use the influence of politicians over the bureaucracy to further their own agenda. They use this influence directly and indirectly: social workers ask local politicians to deal with uncooperative government officials or to secure the budget for the improvement of local amenities, but social workers might also deal with bureaucrats themselves by using the name of the politician ('I am close to so and so') to pressurize local bureaucrats. As I discussed in Chapter 5, mentioning this association with an influential politician is an implicit threat: if you do not cooperate fully, I might get you transferred or I might arrange some complaints against you.

A social worker's capacity to solve local problems earns him respect and lends him authority. He becomes a neighbourhood leader as he gradually extends his hold over his area by demonstrating a capacity to solve local problems. This is the crux of the daily exchanges between social workers and politicians: by supporting a social worker, a politician can boost the local status of that social worker, which in turn gives social workers such an authority that they can influence their neighbours' voting. The mechanism of this exchange is reflected in the commonly used expression 'to have a hold' ('*prabhav chhe*'), as used in these remarks of two inhabitants about the work of social workers: 'You get a hold if you are forthcoming, if you organize religious events et cetera. (...) If he can solve problems with water, or when the gutter is overflowing, then he becomes a leader. So people start to think that what this person says is true. So they follow the opinion of this person'. The expression 'to have a hold' refers to the authority of a person, and to the power to condone or sanction inhabitants' behaviour. Having a hold also suggests political importance, since this 'hold' implies the capacity to influence a sizeable number of voters. Neighbourhood leaders, *goonda*s and politicians can all be said to have a hold over their neighbourhood.

The 'hold' that the leaders of RJM currently exercise over Raamrahimnagar's residents is a product of the area's particular history. After people started to build their hutments in this slum in the late 1960s, they were forced to pay rent to a local slumlord. Residents soon found out that this slumlord had no claim over the land—which was government property—but at first they felt helpless against the threat of (and sometimes use of) force by the slumlord and his gang. After some time a group of residents—both Muslims and Dalits—decided to fight this slumlord. Among them were the then still youthful Kapadiabhai, Aaljibhai and Natwarlal. After a few pitched battles with the slumlord's gang the dispute reached a local court, which decided that from then on the residents only had to pay a (lower) rent to the municipality. This victory led to the establishment of the RJM and the adoption of the name 'Raamrahimnagar' for the area: the Muslims and Dalits who had jointly fought the slumlord wanted to adopt a name that reflected their unity. And they wanted to build on the status that their victory had brought them: after their heroic victory over the slumlord the founders of the RJM had established themselves as the leaders of the local community. This leadership subsequently enabled them to deal successfully with local politicians, which further cemented their leadership over the following decades. Aaljibhai, Kapadiabhai and Nathwarlal—now in their sixties and seventies—remained highly respected leaders and they formed the backbone of their neighbourhood association, the RJM.

The RJM's history illustrates how local leadership is often a product of both a proven capacity to 'get things done' and the patronage of a useful political leader. A politician can, to a certain extent, 'make' a local leader: he can decide to boost the status of a local social worker by opening his channels of patronage, by helping this person whenever there is a problem to be solved. The local social worker is introduced to local bureaucrats, with words like 'he is my worker'. Such support can increase the status of the social worker in the area and turn him into a neighbourhood leader: with the support of the politician he or she will be much more successful in dealing with the issues that people need help with. This success leads to greater status, and a greater following in the neighbourhood: through these successes the social worker slowly acquires a hold over his community.

But a politician would be wise to support someone who already has some local standing. The social worker needs to help in the election campaign, and he is expected to use his or her local status to influence the voting in the area. The 'hold' that the social worker has developed can help the political patron to win elections because it enables the social worker to influence the voting of large groups of people. This is what made the RJM's leaders such attractive partners for campaigning politicians: the RJM's local standing reassured them that promises for basic amenities would really result in a large number of votes. The hold that the neighbourhood leader or *goonda* has over the locality reassures the politician that the money he or she spends actually translates into votes. At the same time the proven ability of a neighbourhood leader to get things done—like getting rid of a slumlord—reassures residents that heeding this leader's voting advice will really translate into improved access to state resources. Once a social worker has established some local standing, his relation with his political patron becomes more symmetrical since this politician also needs the local leader to deliver the votes. Neighbourhood leaders can then decide to switch allegiance if they are unhappy with the support offered by a politician.

This capacity of local leaders to influence the voting of localities is, however, not the result of simple obedience of residents to the wishes of a local leader. There is an element of calculation: residents have an interest in following the advice of their prominent neighbour, since this allows the neighbourhood to pool their votes. The pooling of votes is a smart way to extract maximum resources from a politician: a strong social worker can 'trade' the votes of a whole neighbourhood in exchange for the promise to, for example, improve the provision of water or electricity. Sometimes vote-pooling is just a way to make money: a politician can give a social worker (or a *goonda*) an amount of money to buy the votes of the locality.

In this way, establishing a local 'hold' is often the first step in a political career. Having acquired the support of an influential politician, a new neighbourhood leader can slowly build up a name for himself or herself by solving all sorts of issues for the people around him. In the process people become obliged to return the favour, so that after some time the local leader may be able to drum up enough local support to convince a political party to offer a ticket for the elections. At this time all the favours these aspirant politicians performed for others are like 'credit slips' (Coleman 2000: 300–306) that can be 'cashed in': through a history of accumulated favours a local worker can develop the necessary local goodwill and support to actually win the elections and become a municipal councillor himself. That is what, unsuccessfully, Aaljibhai tried to achieve.

Such a promotion depends on a skilful maintenance of contacts. Before reaching this stage, the aspiring social worker needs to develop good relations with leading politicians by mustering the necessary support for their election. He (and sometimes she, see below) also needs to maintain good relations with police officers and administrators by showing willingness to compromise with them. By cooperating with these administrators, and by performing favours for local as well as higher level politicians, the aspiring social worker can build up obligations that can be used to boost his own status and position. An ambitious social worker needs to engage, therefore, in a constant exchange of favours: he can ensure the cooperation of influential politicians and bureaucrats—and thus increase his capacity to get things done—by offering them (electoral) support or by performing all sorts of services. A successful career depends on a calculated exchange of favours: a social worker can build up his local status by supporting those people that are most likely and most able to return the favour.

But until the aspiring social worker has established a number of useful contacts on his (or her) own, his prospects are closely tied to the electoral success of the political patron. When this politician loses, other politicians cannot be expected to be very helpful, since the social worker is already associated with a competitor: this is why the work of the RJM members got a bit 'blocked' when their candidate Aaljibhai lost. In this context, there is little for scope for political ideologies since strong political convictions can only hinder the development of useful political contacts. Many of the social workers I met had changed their political allegiance, while very few seemed to be motivated by coherent political ideas: most of them simply said they were supporting politicians because the politicians could help them to help others. As I will explore more fully in Chapter 9, this is a reason why the expression of support for communal and exclusionist ideologies is often an indication of the structure of local patronage channels rather than deeply held beliefs.

Your seat is our seat

Let me further illustrate this exchange between social workers and politicians through the career of another social worker, Rajubhai. Despite only being in his mid-twenties, he is already a prominent man in Isanpur. He holds office in a little house on one of Isanpur's main roads, where he receives a steady stream of local supplicants as well as party workers and social workers from different parts of the city. Recently he became the district president of the Bajrang Dal, the youth wing of the VHP, which further boosted his status. The young boys from his area always seem willing to go on errands for him, although some of them occasionally voice their surprise about Raju's steady rise: 'He became big because of the riots. Before that he was just a person, during the riots he went with the VHP and became big. He became a leader because he started to solve the problems of the people. During the riots he was active, he helped people to get out of jail, and he became a member of the VHP. They choose him as a leader. That is how he became popular'.

The VHP is, in name, a religious organization concerned with the promotion and protection of Hinduism. The organization and its youth wing, the Bajrang Dal, played a prominent role during the 2002 riots. In areas like Isanpur the religious goals of the VHP have taken a back seat behind its local political goals: the organization is seamlessly woven into local patronage channels and operates in tandem with the BJP. During the riots local leaders noticed Raju's efficiency in distributing food and his skills in rallying people. The district president made Raju a local secretary, and told him to call whenever there was some problem. This contact was essential in establishing Raju's local fame; he used this contact to solve all sorts of problems which helped him develop his skills and fame as a social worker. As he became more experienced, and acquired more contacts, he no longer needed to rely on this leader:

> First when I was new-new, then if there was a small problem [and I would call to the district secretary] then it would get solved immediately. But then I felt that for small problems I should not call. [I believe] that one should personally be strong [i.e. solve the problem independently]. So I stopped calling, and police- or whatever work was there, I used to do it myself only. I did not tell anyone. By doing that work my confidence opened up. [I learned] how to talk and with whom.

As Raju's fame spread, more BJP politicians started to offer their support. Raju started to campaign for the VHP leader and BJP candidate Shailesh Macwana, who became a close contact. When Shailesh Macwana captured a seat in Gujarat's legislative assembly in December 2002, Rajubhai had firmly established his image as an influential local leader. His flair and charm appealed to many people, which helped him develop useful contacts. For a feeling of Raju's flair in presenting himself, let us turn to a story that Rajubhai told his neighbours and me numerous times. In the early days of his career, Rajubhai went to see an officer in the social welfare department, Mr Damor, with a straightforward question:

> 'Forgive me sir I came in without permission. Sir, the caste certificate that you give. How much do you charge for that? And when you charge for it, do you give a receipt?' He said 'No, no, that is wrong. We do not take any charge'. So I became angry with him: 'if you do not take money then for why do you take the 50 rs. for the caste certificate'.
>
> He told me 'where have you come from? We will have to call the police for you'. I said 'Sure sir. Why not? You do not need to call the police, I will call the police. I can prove it to you that you have issued false certificates from here. I have proofs. So Mr Damor, the seat where you are sitting, is our seat. You are our servant. You are my community's servant. Understand? Not your father's seat. This is not your *baap*'s seat. Understand? You are also servant of government of Gujarat. Ok? You can call the police and I can call a press reporter. So tomorrow you can read about it in the paper'. So Damor is very cool. And afraid. I told him, 'I have heard that you like wine and girls'. He said, 'It is wrong, it is wrong'. 'Then you see what I do. Damor, you won't be here any more. You will not be sitting at your desk any more. You will not be able to do a job. Understand?'

After that, he called all his staff. He called all the staff inside and he shouted at all of them. 'Because of you I have to listen to all this! What is this man saying! You take 50 rs. for the caste certificate!' He got angry with everyone. Then Damor said 'I am sorry if there has been some mistake because of the staff. But if you do not mind, anywhere and anytime come to my office. Even if you are not able to come and if you call then also your work will get done'. So whenever I go the work gets done.

We can trust Rajubhai to have grossly exaggerated his tale, but the story does illustrate a common practice of social workers to use the threat of exposing corruption to ensure cooperation from bureaucrats. It is clear why Rajubhai likes to tell this story: he comes across as a staunch defender of Dalits who by sheer audacity and bluff (he ends the story by saying that he did not have any proof) managed to get the better of the bureaucracy. His neighbours really enjoy the story, not least because of Rajubhai's capacity to imitate Mr Damor. Rajubhai has a useful gift for imitation; his imitation of my botched Gujarati was also, I admit, quite funny.

Raju's story also reflects the performative aspect of being a social worker: a social worker's local hold also depends on a capacity of 'knowing how to talk' to people, to make people laugh, and to engage in a constant attempt to present oneself as powerful and influential. Social workers indeed need to be very social: they need to sit and 'do *cha-nasto*' (to have tea with snacks) with a wide range of people in order to develop their contacts. To be seen, for example, 'doing *cha-nasto*' with an influential politician or police officer can boost one's local status, since these cups of tea suggests the social worker is close to important people—and thus influential. Such meetings might be used later for exaggerated stories about how many powerful people the social worker knows, and how supportive these people have been.

Inhabitants were not always swayed by such performances. They regularly pointed out that there was much self-interest behind social workers' talk about 'service (*seva*) for the community': 'They say they are working to help people, but in reality they are helping themselves. They are acting to help people, but in reality they are just becoming a bigger man. By helping their name gets bigger. They help out of self-interest. Then they get a ticket for the elections'. And another: 'Social work is only social in name. I can see that in social work it is mostly *goondas*. He says he is a social worker but he has expectations of getting money. There are very few people who work completely free of charge. There are 5 per cent people who are good'.

This cynicism about the *seva* of social workers is not very surprising, given the often rather open ways through which they make money. Small-time social workers in Isanpur have several ways of exploiting their contacts with politicians and bureaucrats for financial gain. Very common is the demand for a fee for arranging bureaucratic paperwork: many social workers seem to demand a fee for arranging someone's ration-card, a government loan, widow pension etc. Isanpur residents often cannot avoid paying this fee, since they need the social worker's useful contacts to arrange the matter. Another way to make money is through 'legal extortion': a social worker can approach businessmen (factory owners, builders, alcohol traders etc) and point to certain illegal aspects of their business. By threatening to create difficulties for a business that, for example, pollutes the environment or does not pay minimal wages to workers, the social worker can demand money from the owner in return for smoothing over any problems with the police and with politicians. The elections offer a third avenue for making money. In poorer neighbourhoods like Isanpur vote-buying is still common. Social workers and *goonda*s play an essential role in these practices. A candidate supplies them with money and liquor to distribute among their neighbours. Of this money the social workers and *goonda*s keep a percentage for themselves. A fourth way of making money has already been mentioned: often social workers earn money from their involvement in the settlement of disputes. For helping to 'do a settling' social workers regularly get a small percentage of the fee that was agreed upon to settle the issue.

These different options are profitable enough to provide many social workers with a livelihood. Since there are not many alternative ways to earn a living for Isanpur residents, many social workers spend their days in tea-stalls and on street corners, settling small issues and developing their contacts. Good contacts are essential for everything: as I tried to show with the examples in this section, social workers need to maintain a very broad network of contacts with police officers, politicians, local *goonda*s, etc., since all these contacts can increase a social worker's capacity to get things done. This capacity, in the end, depends on a skilful exchange of favours: for social workers it is vital to make good judgments about whom to support and whom not to support. Since these choices can undermine or strengthen one's capacity to develop a 'hold', the scope for considerations about 'good' or 'bad' is limited. Rajubhai seems to be aware of this dilemma: 'If there is any good work to be done then I go and do it. Sometimes I also go for the wrong things. So I am like a *dalal* [broker]. So may the right person come and may the wrong person also come. Police-wallahs come to us and the people who run alcohol businesses also come. Whom to listen to, whose work to do that is my subject matter. That is the matter of the heart'.

The 'loose character' of female workers

In these local exchanges of favours female social workers face a number of disadvantages. In recent years the prospects for women in local politics have improved: in 1992 India's national parliament passed a constitutional amendment that greatly expanded the scope for women to participate in municipal politics. The 74th constitutional amendment stipulated that one-third of the seats in every municipal council (and *panchayat*) should be reserved for women. This provision enabled many female social workers and party workers to capture seats in the municipal council—every electoral ward in Ahmedabad now elects at least one woman—and it has increased the prominence and influence of women in local politics.

But that influence is still limited. The social workers and party workers I met were mostly men, although there are many female workers as well. Especially in Isanpur, one can find many women like Saamaben, a local social worker who combines the task of representing the needs of their neighbourhood to authorities with a role as a marriage counsellor. In their locality such female social workers often distinguish themselves by solving disputes and by facilitating discussions between quarrelling couples. But those women who become social workers or party workers often run the risk of being stigmatized; female party or social workers who operate in the same manner as their male counterparts are often considered to have a 'loose character'. This is how Saamaben described her difficulties as a social worker:

> Men do not see women as equal. I had to face a lot of mental difficulties. I was educated, I studied law so I wanted to use this for the community. But women themselves did not accept my behaviour. They said 'she sits with boys, this is not acceptable'. At first my family members did not understand me either, but then they started to support me. The people of the community started defaming me; they said that my character was bad. They defamed me because I sat with men, and because I spoke out. In our community your character is your jewel, your most priced possession. It is very important if you want to live in society. At that time, in spite of being courageous, I thought of committing suicide. The very women I wanted to tell not to be exploited went against me. Their family-members said to me 'You may not want to marry, but we want our women to marry, so leave them alone'. In our society women could not even speak in front of fathers. Now this has changed. The women have become educated and they realized my courage, they say that I went before them.

Saamaben had decided not to marry; according to her, it would have been impossible for her to combine social work with marriage: 'I would not have been able to this kind of work. If he says stand up, you'd have to stand up. If he says 'go there' you have to go there. I do not like that. And if you are married you cannot go and talk with other men'.

Female political workers face a number of extra difficulties that undermine their capacity to develop (electoral) support and operate effectively. The field of local politics is structured in such a way that the discrimination against women within the private realm of the house spills over into the public realm of local politics: the obligations and restrictions imposed on women in the private sphere also hinder the capacity of women to participate fully in the exchange of favours that is so central for the development of a political career. The obligations of women in the household and the restrictions on their movement leave female workers often less free to take up personal issues and solve local problems.

This sheds some light on the observation found in studies of female politicians that, while India boasts of numerous prominent female politicians at the elite level (from Indira Gandhi to Mayawati and Sonia Gandhi), local female politicians often find it difficult to get re-elected (see Katzenstein 1978 and Chattopadhyay and Duflo 2004). Above, I discussed how social workers build their local fame by taking up all sorts of local problems and developing a useful network of influential contacts. In localities and among communities where the personal life of women is severely circumscribed, female political workers are not as free to engage in such activities as their male counterparts. In Isanpur, for example, women are not expected to be sitting out on street corners talking until late at night, and they are not supposed to be seen talking with all sorts of different men. They cannot always visit influential politicians or bureaucrats for a courtesy call, and even doing *cha-nasto* with a police constable could be frowned upon. Yet all these social activities all contribute to the capacity of a social worker or a party worker to 'get things done'. Because of the restrictions imposed on their daily activities, women are seriously impaired when it comes to developing influence over bureaucrats and politicians.

These obstacles do not prevent a woman from becoming a social worker or a party worker—in Maneknagar and Isanpur one can find many more workers like Saamaben—but because of restrictions, female political workers cannot as easily develop the kind of support needed to launch a political career. Their capacity to develop a network of influential contacts is limited, and they face more difficulties building up an independent support-base by performing favours for others. Consequently, the effectiveness of elected women in municipal (as well as state) politics is limited. The women who are elected to the municipal council are often considered to be subservient to male political patrons, and it is not uncommon that a female municipal councillor functions as a proxy for her unelected husband. Few female councillors manage to be re-elected: after four years they rarely get their party's support for another term. Some women do manage to become prominent politicians—an example from Gujarat is Maya Kodnani, who could use her eloquence and her status as a physician to become an MLA and state minister[6]—but without the support from a powerful patron (or family ties) they face more difficulties in developing a powerbase of their own. At the state level, where there is as yet no reservation of seats for women,[7] only eleven out of the 182 MLAs in Gujarat's 2002–7 state assembly were women.

Party workers: dealers in proximity

Some workers smilingly talked about a '*chotla parishad*', a meeting of pony tails: at least two hundred women have assembled in the courtyard of one of Maneknagar's oldest schools. They are sitting in front of a table decorated with BJP flags. Behind the table are five men draped with saffron BJP scarves. The women are expecting money: after the function they will get their widow pension, 10,000 rupees. Their husbands have died many years ago, but today the BJP politicians can finally announce that they have arranged the money.

All the important local politicians have their say: the BJP ward-president congratulates the women, and Pravin Dalal dwells on the efforts that have gone into arranging the widow pensions. State minister Arun Pandya has the longest speech; he tries to console the widows with sentences like 'there was sadness, there is sadness, but you have to remove the sadness'. He admonishes them to use the money wisely ('be productive') and he discusses different examples of people who became rich by making good use of ten thousand rupees. After his speech the politicians get more saffron scarves and garlands draped around their necks, and then the women can move to a classroom to pick up their cheques.

The seating arrangement, the speeches and the garlands all transmitted a very clear message to the audience: it was thanks to the BJP politicians that the women had got their money. In this way the difficulty, if not impossibility, for the widows to arrange their widow pensions independently allowed politicians to take the credit for what on paper is just the execution of state policy. This political success was made possible by the efforts of a party worker. Mahendrabhai Desai sat silently behind the table throughout the speeches of the politicians, but after the meeting he related how he had arranged the money: 'It took three years for these women to get the money. I went for two months everyday to the office of the welfare officer in Gandhinagar [the state capital]. We were given only 25 *lakh* before, not enough for everybody. So I told him that we had much more widows. So he called Delhi, and they send people to Maneknagar to check, and we got 1.5 *crore* now. With this money this function is being held'. He added that it had taken such a long time because the administrator wanted a bribe to arrange the pensions, 'but they cannot ask me for money, because they know I am a party worker. They know I have Pravin Dalal and Arun Pandya behind me'.

Mahendrabhai Desai belongs to the quite large group of BJP supporters in Maneknagar. Others refer to such party workers with the derogating terms *chamcha* ('sycophant') or *tapori*: the supporters of prominent politicians like Pravin Dalal and Arun Pandya seem to be at their beck and call to perform whatever service they require. The party workers themselves generally present their activities as a way of contributing to the development of the city: they point out how they help politicians to be more effective, and help inhabitants by alerting politicians to their complaints. They do indeed increase their political leaders' capacity to get things done. In the name of the municipal councillor or the MLA they can take up various local problems, which generally reflects positively on the status of their political leader. They facilitate the contact between their political leader and the electorate, by passing on complaints and requests and by spreading the word about the work their political leader has done.

In this sense there is a thin line separating a party worker from a social worker or neighbourhood leader, as they all function as brokers; all help ordinary inhabitants contact politicians as well as bureaucrats. Both the party worker and the neighbourhood leader take up issues, complaints, problems of people around them (and often also of members of their caste) to politicians and state officials, and both make use of their political backing to deal with the bureaucracy. The party worker, just like the neighbourhood leader, uses his proximity to a politician to pressurize the bureaucracy. In this way, the support of politicians lends both party workers and social workers status and authority in their neighbourhoods. In that sense the distinction between the party worker and the neighbourhood leader is just a difference in presentation. A neighbourhood leader presents himself or herself as more or less independent of politics, as somebody primarily interested in the wellbeing of the people of the area, while party workers associate themselves more openly with a political party.

The main difference between a neighbourhood leader and a party worker lies in the kind of support they are expected to offer to politicians. A party worker is expected to attend various party functions and to perform all sorts of organizational tasks, while politicians only call upon social workers for support at election time. While a neighbourhood leader can make use of political channels because of his (future) capacity to deliver votes, the party worker develops his proximity to political leaders through his willingness to perform all sorts of organizational services for the party.

A party worker generally starts his association with a party by signing up as a member of the party for a small fee of five rupees. In the course of time a party worker might become a *sakriya sabya*, an active member, and even later this might translate into a '1,000 rs. membership'; a membership for life. As the general secretary of the BJP in Maneknagar explains, the rise within the party depends upon the activity of the worker: 'we see the work the new members are doing and slowly they get more responsibilities. Attendance is important. It is important to be present at the different functions. Whoever comes, the BJP writes down, [to decide] who is an active member'.

I mentioned some of the services that party workers perform for politicians in Chapter 5: some were helping in the hospital, while others were sitting with Pravin Dalal at his roadside office and still others were maintaining contacts with local bureaucrats to check on the progress of their work. Local party workers also help to manage the trusts that politicians have set up: a number of politicians have set up trusts to provide inhabitants of their constituency with cheaper medicines or with financial support, and party workers manage these trusts and use the budget to help local inhabitants. The money for these trusts often comes from businessmen who have profited from political support to solve a bureaucratic matter. This support from businessmen allows politicians and their party workers to engage in charitable work, as one BJP worker relates: 'When their work gets done the traders will get faith in [Pravin Dalal]. [He] will not take money directly, but if some poor person comes, he will send him to the trader, and tell the trader to help this guy out. When the earthquake happened [in 2001], the traders send us material that we distributed'.

Party workers are also useful to supply the crowds for protests and rallies. Their attendance at a rally helps to create the impression of popular support: the presence of a large contingent of party workers creates the suggestion that many people share the concerns and demands voiced during the rally. Their enthusiastic participation can help to create the idea that 'the public' is appalled or outraged by a political matter. But in reality many party workers attend such rallies not because they feel strongly about the issue at hand but because they know that their regular attendance is important to improve their prospects within the party. This is for example how a BJP worker described his participation in protests:

> They call and say, 'come at 4 o clock tomorrow', and we take all the workers, so some thousand people are there and we do whatever needs to be done. If some destructions need to be done, we do it, or if a complaint needs to made we do that. They might take us in at the police station, but this would only last for 15 minutes. Now the BJP runs the state, so they tell the police not to interfere in the *tod-fod* ('breaking of things').

Attendance and cooperation during elections are especially important. During elections party workers are indispensable to organize the recurring functions and rallies. During election time a large number of party workers make themselves useful by putting up banners, organizing meetings, convincing voters and managing the voting at pooling booths etc. At that time there is so much work to be done that a large contingent of loyal party workers is essential for an effective campaign.

By participating in the election campaign, the party workers not only help the candidate, they also help themselves. Through their efforts during the election campaign party workers can oblige an elected politician to return the favour: once elected the politician is expected to be responsive to the demands and requests from his or her supporters. By voluntarily performing all sorts of services for a politician, a party worker can get powerful politicians into a debt relation (cf. Boissevain 1974: 85), which can prove to be highly beneficial. As one party worker remarked about his support for a municipal councillor during election time: 'We have to participate. I do his work for two months, and then he does my work for five years'. As a real estate agent, this party worker is very much aware of the possible benefits of being close to an elected politician: in return for all the services that party workers perform for politicians, they get lucrative preferential access to the politician and, by extension, to the bureaucracy. As Pravin Dalal's personal assistant Himansubhai said: 'I get more respect, because I do the work and because I sit with him. People listen to me because I sit next to Pravin Dalal. Officials think of me as being next to Pravin Dalal so they listen to me'.

This perceived proximity could be turned into a source of income. Their contacts and accumulated favours enable party workers to sell their services as intermediaries. Local businessmen approach these workers to get their paperwork done in exchange for a fee, which is often shared with the politician. Builders especially are known to use these contacts to get the necessary paperwork for their building projects done. To take two local examples: in the changing old city of Ahmedabad it is very lucrative to convert residential houses to commercial establishments. Since residential buildings cannot officially be used for commercial purposes, party workers and politicians can make much money by forcing the bureaucracy to change the officially designated purpose of the building. Another example concerns the frequent flaunting of the regulation for new buildings, as apartment blocks often exceed the stipulated maximum height for a building. Through the mediation of party workers an 'impact fee' can be agreed upon to settle the issue. Everybody benefits from such arrangements, as the builder can build more profitably and the party worker and bureaucrat are duly compensated for their cooperation. Party workers are good contacts to settle such an issue, because they can take the matter to the politician. Direct contact risks exposing both builders and politicians to accusations of corruption.

There are more reasons for builders to enlist the help of politicians and their party workers. Builders are often faced with disputes about the ownership of the land they intend to build on. The land might be encroached upon by squatters, or in other cases the well protected tenants of houses might be unwilling to leave a house that the builders want to demolish. To solve these disputes, builders often make use of their political contacts and the *goonda*s behind them. Through these contacts the police might be convinced to clear the area, and if that does not work the local *goonda*s might be used to scare the inhabitants of the land. It is said that builders reserve 10 per cent of the total budget of a new project for the necessary bribing of political actors, bureaucrats and *goonda*s.

Another way to make money lies in the 'regularization' of illegal businesses like hawking, gambling or the alcohol trade. Through the mediation of party workers, owners of illegal businesses pay *hapta*, a weekly or monthly fee, to politicians and the police to avoid interference in their business. This can vary from the small fees that street vendors pay to the police to the very large sums of money that alcohol vendors and owners of gambling halls pay to keep the police out. In both Isanpur and Maneknagar the monthly collection from the gambling halls and alcohol dens run into millions of rupees. This money is shared by a large number of people, from the local constables to the police inspectors, and from the local party worker to the MLA. These monthly contributions are often essential for local politicians to win elections, which is why they cannot be very sincere in their efforts to stop gambling or the liquor business. Party workers generally collect the *hapta* for them.

These examples illustrate how the willingness of many inhabitants to become active party workers is related to control that politicians exert over the bureaucracy. The capacity of politicians to manipulate the daily operation of the local bureaucracy is an important asset to build up a dedicated group of followers, since this control over the bureaucracy is an important incentive for party workers to oblige these politicians by doing favours for them. By performing all sorts of services for their political leaders, party workers can get politicians to intercede in the bureaucracy.

But this help from politicians is not guaranteed and depends to a certain extent on the need of politicians to keep their local base happy. On the basis of more comparative research on the functioning of the political fixers, Manor

(2000) identifies, among other factors,the level of political competition, decentralization and the management style of ruling politicians as important factors shaping the prominence of fixers.[8] When politicians feel that their political future is more or less secure, or when they maintain a tight grip on resources, the efforts of party workers (and social workers) stand a smaller chance of being rewarded which leads to dwindling numbers of such workers. One can interpret in this light the complaints that could be heard from local VHP, RSS and BJP workers at the time of the 2007 state elections in Gujarat: it seemed that the strong position of Chief Minister Modi at that time (and the weak opposition from Congress) had made him less mindful of the numerous requests coming from local workers.

But such neglect of local supporters can boost opposition within the party's own ranks. Party workers can, like social workers, become prominent politicians themselves if they manage to gather enough support. By performing services for politicians as well as doing all sorts of favours for local residents and businessmen, party workers can develop their own support-base. A distinguished record of service for the party combined with such a large support-base can convince the party to make the party worker an official candidate for the elections. In the race for these 'tickets' for the elections, party workers need to compete as well as cooperate with each other: party members need to cooperate with each other in order to develop some fame and better access to the bureaucracy, but by performing such favours for each other, party workers and politicians also build up their own competition. The exchange of favours can boost the fame of fellow party members who might compete on the same ticket in the next elections. Thus the career of a party worker also requires a calculated exchange of favours: even though their obedience might earn them the derogating name '*chamcha*', the loyalty of party workers can serve them well to capture the seat of their political leaders in the future.

Conclusion

With a number of illustrations I have discussed in this chapter the different strategies that local actors around politicians employ to increase their political prospects and their incomes. I have discussed how these strategies are structured by their need to establish a certain degree of control over the functioning of government institutions. Even if the practices and exchanges that shape this 'political society' do not always conform to the (Western) normative models of civil society and democracy, that is no reason in itself to view its operations as negative. As Chatterjee emphasizes (2004: 67), through political society poorer citizens are able to mitigate harmful laws and policies, and by using their vote instrumentally they are able to build local coalitions that can go against the distribution of power in society as a whole. By doing so, 'they have expanded their freedoms by using means that are not available to them in civil society'.

But these smaller freedoms come at the expense of a larger freedom. For the sake of this negotiated capacity to bend the implementation of government laws and policies, the capacity to influence the shaping of these laws and policies is sacrificed. The dependence of poorer citizens on political actors to access state services has engendered forms of politics that, besides being violent (as we will explore in the following chapters), also severely limit the capacity of poorer citizens to affect the overall distribution of power within society (Kothari 2005). The dependence of poorer citizens on hierarchical patronage channels undermines their capacity to press for reforms that would go against the interests of political and economic elites. Most of the political energy is taken up in the struggle to gain access to basic services. If any energy is left to fight for substantial reforms—for, say, adequate budgets for basic services, implementation of minimal wage regulations or the development of a welfare state—then such demands can hardly be effectively voiced because poorer citizens cannot risk upsetting the relationships with political patrons that are so central to their security and livelihoods.

In such a context it is misleading to attribute the political strategies of India's poorer inhabitants to a limited incorporation of democratic values or associational skills.[9] Such arguments fail to perceive how the political practices of the less privileged sections of society are shaped by their dependence on various (political) intermediaries. The political attitudes that poorer citizens might display—such as the 'tendency to rally around strong men' (Ruud 2001: 132), the respect for masculine, violent behaviour, or admiration for those who manage to bend the law to their advantage—are not the result of a limited experience or knowledge about the functioning of democratic institutions. On the contrary, these attitudes are consistent with a daily experience of the functioning of state institutions that are generally unresponsive to the needs and demands of citizens who lack influential contacts or money. In that context the strategies of local political actors are shaped by the need to develop some control over the distribution of state resources. The importance of establishing a 'hold', the necessity of developing influential contacts, or—as we will see in the next chapter—the need to develop a violent, '*mathabare*' image: such strategies are all responses to the limited capacity of the state to provide impersonal access to its resources.

7

MONEYPOWER AND MUSCLEPOWER

ON THE NEXUS BETWEEN POLITICIANS, STATE OFFICIALS AND *GOONDAS*

The police officials sensed an opportunity when they arrested a ten-year-old Muslim boy for stealing silver ornaments from his neighbours. As the boy quickly confessed his crime, the police officials thought that they could make some money by offering his family their help in settling the issue. The police officials approached the boy's grandmother and they asked her for 25,000 rupees; in return they would prevent the boy from being sentenced. At first the old woman agreed, but then she changed her mind just before the case was scheduled to be heard in court. The police officers, frustrated with this change of heart, furiously beat the old women with a stick until they broke several bones. They beat her so badly that her injuries could not be concealed. This presented the high-handed police officers with a problem: they had to present the old woman in court to settle her grandson's case.

After deliberation at the police station the officers decided to keep the grandmother in their police van. To prevent the judge from noticing her injuries, they used another old woman as a stand-in in court. Apparently this other old woman played her role well, because the judge did not notice the mix-up. After the court case was conveniently settled, they took the little thief's grandmother to the hospital to get her treated. There they left her with the words, 'If you do [tell] anything we will shoot you'. That was the moment municipal councillor Ahmed Faraz got involved in the case, who relayed this story to me. The old woman was a relative of a local *goonda* ('criminal'), Sirajbhai, who felt he had no other option but to ask Ahmed Faraz for help: 'With clear dislike Siraj called me, the first time he called me, three years after the elections. During elections he had taken down our banners and he created disturbances. He said, 'I want to meet you urgently, come to me to LG hospital'. I went there and saw a *maji* (old woman) with fractures'.

Such stories are quite common in Isanpur. Involving the police can be costly and dangerous. This is still worse for Muslims, as they have to deal with a police force that is often prejudiced against them. Because of such harassment inhabitants use social workers and politicians to prevent the worst forms of extortion and intimidation: these local leaders at least have the capacity and contacts to prevent harassment and, if need be, expose police officers.

Ahmed Faraz did his job. He talked to the doctors, and he made sure the *maji* got proper treatment at the hospital. Then he went to the police station to file a complaint. At first the police officers tried to protect their colleagues by refusing to register the case. But when Ahmed Faraz called the DCP (deputy commissioner of police) a case was finally filed against the involved police sub inspector (PSI). The press got hold of this story, and the PSI got into a lot of trouble: 'The press people came. Photos were printed and copies were distributed in the area. The PSI was about to be suspended, [but] the PSI knew the home minister so he was saved, but transferred immediately. He used *lagvag* ('influence') and went in to crime [department]'. The *maji* became well and she was discharged. Everything was over.

Or at least that was what Ahmed Faraz then thought. But as it turned out, the accused PSI had managed to make use of the competition between different Congress politicians. Months later Ahmed Faraz went to the airport to meet Sonia Gandhi. There Faraz met the same PSI again: 'He asked me "do you know me or not?" I said no. [He said] "I know you very well. You were running around to get me suspended"'. When Ahmed realized who was before him, he defended himself very politely: 'I said: listen *bhai*, *maji* had come to me. I am a Muslim representative, so if a Muslim *maji* comes to me with this then I have to do *rajuaat* [present her problem], no?' Then the PSI made a remark that kept returning to the municipal councillor for quite some time: 'It is good that Bhanuben [another local Congress politician] and Sirajbhai [the local *goonda*] made the compromise'.

This made Ahmed Faraz realize how the PSI had managed to avert his suspension: apparently the PSI had struck a deal behind his back with the local *goonda* and another Congress leader. Through this compromise, and probably the payment of a considerable sum of money, the PSI could make sure the charges against him were dropped. Ahmed Faraz felt betrayed as he was left out of the deal: 'I had helped in the entire case: I got her admitted, I took her to the press, and I complained to the DCP. When she was discharged [from the hospital] then I got her fee reduced, I arranged everything. So they both got together and went to the *maji* and made the compromise, so that he [the PSI] did not get suspended, he only got transferred. I did not even know that. Now that we found out that they did the compromise then, I would get really mad, no? Some of these public people here are really *nalayak* ('messing around') people'.

Ahmed Faraz's story illustrates the complex patterns of cooperation and competition that typifies the relations between state officials, local criminals and politicians. The *goonda* Sirajbhai, the Congress politician Bhanuben and the municipal corporator Ahmed Faraz needed each other to help the injured old lady, but they are also competing over the money and status involved in the resolution of such issues. Often they need to set aside their grudges against each other in order to cooperate to get something done. But the competition for money and status also ensures that these coalitions are never really stable. In this case the PSI could benefit from these local power struggles.

This ambivalent cooperation between local criminals ('*goondas*'), politicians and local state officials is the topic of this chapter. The 'criminalization of politics' is, I will argue, not so much a sign of moral decay among politicians as another consequence of the difficulties faced by (poorer) citizens in dealing with state institutions. The nexus between state officials, politicians and *goondas* can be seen as the outcome of the political dynamic that a mediated state engenders: in the context of a political field structured by the need to manipulate the implementation of state policies, politicians, state officials and *goondas* need to cooperate with each other to secure their jobs and their sources of income. For local politicians, good relations with local state officials as well as *goondas* are essential to gain local support and win elections since their support lends local politicians the necessary leverage to arbitrate disputes, intimidate rivals and gather a campaigning budget. As local inhabitants put it, the cooperation with *goondas* and state officials provides politicians with the necessary moneypower and musclepower to win elections.

From their end, both local state officials and *goondas* need to maintain relations with local or higher-level politicians in order to protect their legal and illegal sources of income. Not only can local state officials and politicians make much money by allowing illegal activities—'number two' work: alcohol trade, extortion practices, gambling, etc.—to continue, but the control of politicians over the posting of state officials also discourages the police from stopping these activities. In return for their moneypower and musclepower, politicians are forced to safeguard the illegal businesses of *goondas* from police interference. As politicians can influence the posting of police officers, police officers risk damaging their career prospects by arresting a *goonda* who enjoys such political protection. The relations between state officials, *goondas* and politicians are never stable: the constant political competition to improve one's access to state resources ensures that these coalitions are constantly shifting according to the need of the moment. To substantiate these arguments, I will discuss the interaction between local *goondas* and politicians. In the second part of this chapter I will discuss their interaction with local state officials.

Goondas: *The various uses of moneypower and musclepower*

They are probably the most common characters in Bollywood films: the materialistic and violent criminals, often depicted with a hairy chest and a menacing look, drinking lots of alcohol and sporting big golden chains. They are almost invariably a threat to the heroes of the film: the *dada*s ('grandfather'). *Dons*, or *goonda*s are the prototypical bad guys who threaten and intrigue others by flaunting all social and legal norms. The *goonda* is at once frightening and appealing: the supposedly immense power and extravagant lifestyles of famous *goonda*s like Dawood Ibrahim, Chotta Rajan or Arun Gawli are discussed throughout India; a constant stream of newspaper articles bemoans their power while simultaneously catering to the widespread fascination with these larger-than-life characters.

The power and lifestyle of the small-time local *goonda*s in Isanpur and Maneknagar are not comparable to the famous *dons* who own property throughout the world and manage their global drugs trade and extortion rackets by phone. The *goonda*s that we will encounter here are small-time extortionists and liquor traders, whose area of work hardly extends beyond the borders of their neighbourhood. There is, however, one thing that these small-time *goonda*s have in common with their famous *dons*: their status and income are boosted by maintaining good contacts with politicians. This is a common theme in the stories about Indian *goonda*s: in films (like *Saatya* or *Sarkar*), in investigative reporting (like *Maximum City* by S. Metha) or in novels (like *Sacred Games* by Vikram Chandra) the cooperation between *goonda*s and politicians is a recurring topic. In this section we will see small-scale examples of this cooperation.

The career of Pradeepbhai can provide us with a starting point. Pradeepbhai used to be an alcohol supplier in Isanpur, an illegal occupation in Gujarat. In the following (abridged) excerpt of an interview he speaks about his relationship with Shailesh Macwana, the MLA (member of Gujarat's legislative assembly) of the area.

In the 2002 elections [for the State Assembly] I had captured a [polling] booth, I told people to move away, and I enjoyed it. I gave full votes to Shaileshbhai. I had given Shaileshbhai 25,00rs. for propaganda, because if he would win he would help me in my business. So I captured the booth for him. I came with my gang, and I fought with a police officer, I made him go away.

Booth capturing is especially done at the last hour and the beginning hours [of the voting]. I told the staff of the booth 'I will frequently add some votes'. If I would add 500 votes every hour people would doubt it, so I infrequently put down some votes. My gang was there with me all day, with their hockey sticks. To accept the votes, I gave the staff some money, and they easily accepted it.

Shaileshbhai had come to me before the elections. He said 'Pradeepbhai, I will appear in the next elections. If I win I will help you. So if you help me first to win the elections, then I will help you later'.

And he did help me. Once some of my liquor was caught in a big quantity by the police. He came immediately and he told the police officer in the den not to start any legal procedure against me. And the last time, when I stopped that business, plenty of my liquor was caught. I surely would be sent to jail for one year. So during two months I was in hiding. I called Shaileshbhai, I asked him to help me. He said 'don't worry, come with me to the police and nothing will happen to you'. So I went to the police station, and the police dropped the case.

WB: So the money you spent on Shaileshbhai's election was a good investment?

It was a very good investment. If I had not helped him, I would have been in jail for one year. Shaileshbhai wants to be re-elected, so he knows he must help me. If he had not helped me, I would not have helped him again [in the next elections].

WB: Why did the police officer listen to Shaileshbhai?

If he would not listen, Shaileshbhai would have him transferred, and this is a good place for corruption. He had offered much money to Shaileshbhai to be transferred to this place.

*Goonda*s like Pradeepbhai are individuals who, sometimes unintentionally or unexpectedly, acquire an image of heavy handedness in their neighbourhood, which make people fear them. The word that Pradeepbhai uses to describe himself is *matabhare*, literally 'heavyheaded', which implies he is headstrong and prone to fighting. This image as a *matabhare* man makes the *goonda* useful for politicians, during as well as after elections. *Matabhare* people can have an impact on the results of the elections because of the 'muscle power' that they add to electoral campaigns. Their local standing enables them to influence voters, and their violent image makes *matabhare* men like Pradeepbhai useful to capture election booths or to protect candidates during the elections. They can prevent election meetings from being disturbed by *goonda*s from opposing candidates, and can prevent such *goonda*s from harassing their candidate.

The need for *goonda*s to perform these services is such that informants deemed it near impossible to win elections without the support of musclepower. A candidate for the 2005 municipal elections in Isanpur confided: 'Every *chawl* has 2-3 anti-social elements. They threaten the person that opposes their candidate. And on the day of the elections, they started stamping ballots, or they do not let other people vote. I would also need those elements, even if I do not want it. I need them to stop opposite elements; otherwise they can disturb my meetings'. This candidate seemed genuinely opposed to cooperation between politicians and *goonda*s, but he saw no other option but to employ them, and ended by concluding that 'the system has gotten worse'.

*Goonda*s are also indispensable for the money that they bring in; Pradeepbhai mentioned how he contributed to Shailesh Macwana's campaigning budget. In a locality like Isanpur, where thriving businesses are scarce, there are few alternative sources of money. The budget for contesting elections in these neighbourhoods necessarily comes, in no small part, from the liquor traders and from the owners of gambling dens. A large part of this budget is collected throughout the year in form of *hapta*, the regular payments that owners of illegal businesses pay to the police and politicians to prevent arrest or harassment. Although the collected money also helps to support the lifestyles of politicians, this money is essential to finance their campaigning during elections.

After the elections politicians have several reasons to call on local *goondas*. As I have already mentioned in passing, a *goonda* can help to solve a dispute by pressurizing one of the disputants, for which both he and the politician might receive a fee from the other disputant. A *goonda* can also help to deal with issues that need muscle power to solve, for example, the clearance of encroached land for a building project, the intimidation of businessmen who want to start a new business in the area (and who are unwilling to go along with the 'legal extortion' of party workers), and the collection of *hapta* from hawkers (sometimes as an intermediary between these hawkers and the police).

In the real estate business, especially, the services of *matabhare* people can be valuable to settle disputes. By intimidating tenants or owners of buildings, they can put pressure on inhabitants to vacate their premises. This can help to speed up new building projects by 'settling' ownership issues that would otherwise linger in the courts for years. Similarly, *matabhare* people can be used to vacate land that is encroached upon by squatters. This is how an Ahmedabadi real-estate builder deals with encroachments:

> The first way, which we prefer, is that we try to free the land by giving money to the people on the land, we try to give them cash so that they will leave. If that does not work we sometimes go to court to free the land. But this takes a long time and it is expensive. The third way is that we employ *goondas* to pressurize the residents. He tortures them, threatens them so that they want to leave by themselves. (...) Sometimes we do not want to engage him [a *goonda*], but he intervenes. He will hear about our plans through the slumholders and then he approaches us. He comes to us and he makes threats that he will make the work difficult or he says 'they will not free the land without my help'. Then we sit at the table and decide how to work on the problem. He will take some money from us and sometimes he is used to clear the land.

There is an expression that is often used in Gujarat to describe these methods to solve such problems: *Saam, daam, danda, bhed*—such problems are solved 'by convincing, by offering money, by force or by dividing people' ('by hook or by crook').

In this sense *goondas* are the product of the difficulties that people face when dealing with Gujarat's state institutions: they can operate relatively openly and undisturbed because they help people overcome the difficulties of dealing with government institutions and regulations. Their political contacts as well as their local support are for a large part premised on the way they help others deal with the limited capacity of government institutions to provide basic services and uphold laws and regulations. One can discern both a direct and an indirect relation between the local standing of *goondas* and the difficulties of dealing with state institutions. A direct relation lies in the capacity of *matabhare* people to provide an alternative for the overburdened courts and uncooperative police. *Goondas* profit from the fact that court cases take very long to reach a conclusion: for that reason, and because both police officers and the courts require considerable bribes to register and deal with a case, it is profitable to involve a local *goonda* to recover money, settle a dispute or vacate occupied land.[1]

An indirect relation lies in the need for local politicians to employ *goondas* to increase their capacity to deal with the demands of residents in their constituency. As electoral success in localities like Isanpur is largely premised on a capacity to provide access to (and alternatives for) state services, politicians can make good use of the cooperation of *matabhare* people to maintain their authority and improve their capacity to solve local issues: *goondas* can help politicians to settle a dispute by threatening one (or both) of the disputants, and a *goonda* can help with 'policing' a locality and can uphold the authority of local politicians. In this way the political usefulness of a *goonda* is related to the need for local politicians to develop a capacity to provide alternative avenues for dispute-settlement. Since inhabitants with a *matabhare* image can help politicians to get things done, local politicians can profit from their relations with them.

Violence as performance

In order to effectively perform these various services for political leaders, *goondas* need to develop a certain public image of themselves: they need to be recognized as *matabhare* people. This is why it would not be completely correct to translate the word '*goonda*' as 'criminal': while a criminal is commonly assumed to be as secretive as possible about his or her illegal activities, the success of a small-time local *goonda* depends to a great extent on the openness of his involvement in criminal activities. A *goonda* needs to be perceived as a *goonda* because the necessary political support depends on this public image. Furthermore, his activities, be it as an extortionist, a liquor-trader or an owner of a gambling den, need to be relatively well-known to the public in order to be successful. Because of this unavoidable openness, only a 'violent' public image and some political backing can restrain the police and the broader public from interfering in their illegal activities. Consider in this light the following story, told by the social worker Akashbhai:

> One Mr Gupta, a doctor, was approached by a *goonda* called Shaidev who had been arrested for rape and extortion. Shaidev went into his office, and emptied a gun on his table. He put the six bullets on the table and asked 'which one do you want in your head?', and he demanded 50,000 Rs. Dr Gupta came to me, but he did not want to involve the police, he was afraid for his security, and that of his children. I said, 'if you as a doctor will not do anything, then who could'. I made clear that I was willing to lose my life for this, and that I had some friends who would also help. That gave some confidence to the doctor. Then I went to Shailesh Macwana to talk about it, who just told me, 'he is a very *mathabare* person, I know him from the jail, he is also in the VHP'. Then I went to another *goonda* called Samir, and since he saw I was with Mr Gupta he said 'OK let us do some compromising'. Samir told me Shaidev had also asked and gotten money from the owner of Milind theatre, and from some oil trader, he got 5 to 10 thousand every month from them. Then I went to people from my organization [Akashbhai was involved with a local trade union], and asked them about Shaidev. They said he was a *mathabare* person, but not for them. So they gathered 25 people and went for him. After that he fled and only after a month the police caught him.

A large part of Akashbhai's strategy consisted of checking how strong people considered Shaidev to be. He checked with the MLA Shailesh Macwana, who indicated his unwillingness to tackle Shaidev, suggesting that he had political backing (from the VHP). This made it difficult to lodge a police complaint: Shaidev would find his way out. It was only when Akashbhai found enough muscle power himself that he could tackle Shaidev. Akashbhai's strategy illustrates how important political support is for a *goonda*'s local standing and career. Many of the activities that *goonda*s are involved in, like gambling or the sale of alcohol (banned in the dry state Gujarat), need to be sufficiently known in order to attract clients. For this reason a *goonda* needs protection from local politicians: since the police are generally well aware of their activities it would be more difficult (and require more *hapta*) to prevent arrest by the police without political support. Once an understanding has been reached with an influential politician, the business can flourish: the local alcohol trader can import liquor with limited risk of getting caught, and the owner of a gambling den can come to an understanding with the police about the *hapta* that needs to be paid to keep his place open.

This political support depends on the image that the *goonda* has in his area. The image of being a heavy-handed, dangerous ('*mathabare*') person gives the *goonda* a certain hold over the inhabitants in his area, which makes him interesting for politicians. And such a violent image is also needed to engage successfully in extortion, or the settlement of disputes. Pradeepbhai described one such instance when he used violence to protect his business:

> There is a person here called [Rajesh]. He started saying to people 'I am a social worker'. He did some things, like getting a loan, and then he forced people to give a commission. He does not have many political contacts, but people are afraid of him. He once went up to me. He told me 'give me 1,000 rupees every month, otherwise I will complain against you'. He wanted *hapta*. I slapped him right there, and I kicked him, in front of a lot of people. 'I will sell liquor at your home', I told him.

Such violence not only aims to teach a small competitor a lesson, it also serves to impress the audience. Pradeepbhai also wanted to teach the audience a lesson: you had better listen to me or you will be treated in the same manner. The psychoanalyst Sudhir Kakar (1996: 81) psychoanalyzed four notorious Hyderabadi gangsters, who all had a history of violence during Hindu-Muslim riots. The result was an impressive mix of psychology and ethnography, with vivid descriptions of the communal ideologies of the four men as well as some general conclusions about their psyche:

> There is also a notable depressive tendency in their underlying mood, a threatened depression against which various defences are employed. (...) Perhaps the need to defend against an emptying and fragmenting self, the inner experience of depression, contributed to the building up of a defensive hyperactivity wherein the cohesiveness of the self is restored and most immediately experienced through an explosion in violent action. The excitement of violence becomes the biggest confirmation that one is psychically still alive, a confirmation of one's very existence.

This conclusion over-emphasizes the pathological character of the four *goonda*s and their violent behaviour. By doing this, we risk losing sight of the very rational and calculating side of their violent behaviour, which is grounded in the political context in which these *goonda*s operate. In that context, violence is also a means to establish a very useful image. Akashbhai, the social worker who helped to settle the dispute about the wall, used to be a small-time alcohol seller before he devoted himself to social work. This is how he describes the career of a *goonda*:

> First you need to fight a lot. You should be ready to be beaten, and to go to jail. Then you develop a certain image. Then you can start a business, then you meet influential people, and politicians. With these contacts you can get smaller *goonda*s to do things, and you can start different businesses. So there are three levels. I was only at the first level, when good friends gave me that book and I gave up all on it [Akashbhai was given a novel about social justice which inspired him to take up social work]. [Before that] I beat up and was beaten up 2–3 times a day. I had no respect for ladies.

The violence of a *goonda* is a performative act: its main target is not just the victim of the beatings, but also the audience that watches the spectacle. The *goonda*'s violence serves to make future violence unnecessary, as it helps to command the obedience of the audience. The violence instils fear in the audience, which allows a *goonda* to develop a certain hold over his neighbourhood. This image based on violence is captured by the Gujarati word '*dhaak*', which can be translated as 'fear' as well as 'awe'. The word denotes an authority based on intimidation. In the words of the social worker Jagdishbhai: 'They always pick up fights. This is in order to get *dhaak*, to create fear, that is why they fight. They get *dhaak* through fighting and contacts with the police. So people stay away, they are afraid of the *matabhare* people. People are afraid to be beaten up, so we cannot do anything'. This image can be accidental; some of the *goonda*s I met did not start out their careers with the intention of becoming *goonda*s. An accidental local dispute, or a fight over a sister's illicit relationship, might establish a violent image, which can be the beginning of a career in 'number two work'.

Once a person has instilled this *dhaak* in other people the threat of violence can be enough to settle a dispute; a simple command might be enough to pressurize a neighbourhood into voting for the preferred candidate. The threat of violence suffices. Such a local *goonda* might gather a group of boys around him who can intimidate anybody who opposes their leader. In this sense *goonda*s also have a 'hold' over inhabitants, just like social workers. While a social worker's hold is mostly based in his or her capacity to get things done, *goonda*s can also rely on the threat of the use of force to exert authority. This makes them important political actors: in areas like Isanpur, local people with a *matabhare* image are expected, like social workers, to sway a large number of voters.

With their money and their political contacts *goonda*s can be as helpful as social workers to solve local problems. Although the *goonda*s are often referred to as 'anti-social elements', the people of the area where they live often consider them to be very social: they help them solve problems, offer opportunities to earn money, and arrange improvements of basic facilities. As one informant said: 'Many people are not interfering in the activities of *matabhare* persons. The *matabhare* person is unharmful in his own area. The mentality of people is this: (...) 'he is not harmful to us, that is enough, so why protest against him?' It is because the *matabhare* person is helpful to people in his area'. This local usefulness contributes to the 'hold' that *goonda*s can exert over entire neighbourhoods: this local influence is not based just on fear or intimidation, but also on their capacity to do favours for people.

Goonda*s as politicians*

Through this local hold, *goonda*s can alter the balance of power between themselves and their political contacts. When a *goonda* has developed some local fame, politicians cannot easily forego their support. The following quotation can illustrate this uneasy interdependence. This is how Ahmed Faraz, the municipal councillor who helped the injured grandmother, spoke about his difficult relation with local *goonda*s like Sirajbhai:

> I will explain to you the *majburi* (difficulty) of the political people and social workers. I am a Corporator [municipal councillor]. I know that Ashokbhai is in alcohol business, that Ashokbhai is doing 'number two work' [meaning illegal work]. My difficulty is this: if Ashokbhai is taken away by the police and if his brothers come to me, then I know that Ashokbhai is wrong. Still I need to go to the police station in his favour. Because it is politics. If I want to go to Ashokbhai's *chawl* and if he comes along then people would vote for me. Then they will respect me. It is such a mentality. If I don't go [to the police station] for Ashokbhai or if I tell his brother clearly that your brother is doing wrong and I will not come, then they will create disturbances during elections and do *nalayaki* [mess around]. Then the good people who should stand by me would not stand by me. The times are very bad. In the beginning I used to say no but I looked wrong to people. I saw that [people] are doing *wah wah* ('praising') in the favour of all the 'number two people' [people engaged in illegal activities].

This local hold of 'number two' people makes policing against them difficult: because of their local support and the backing of politicians, the police can be easily prevented from intervening. As the quotation illustrates, the local hold of *goonda*s forces local politicians to intervene on their behalf. In this way *goonda*s can become popular politicians themselves; they can use their local authority and the money gained through their businesses to launch a successful electoral campaign. In the 1980s the infamous *don* Latif managed to get elected from three of Ahmedabad's municipal constituencies simultaneously while he was in jail. In this way there is a constantly shifting balance of power between politicians and *goonda*s: in some areas and some periods politicians are very dependent on local *goonda*s for local support, moneypower and musclepower, while on other occasions local politicians can develop their own power-base, forcing local *goonda*s into a more subservient role. Several informants have commented to me that over the last decade this balance of power in the neighbourhoods studied has shifted in favour of local politicians: according to them the local hold of *goondas* seems to have diminished, and politicians are rumoured to feel less obliged to intervene with the police on behalf of 'their' *goondas*, so that there has been an increasing number of arrests. It is a common perception that nowadays there are no more 'big' *goondas* (like Don Latif) in the city. It is difficult to ascertain the truthfulness of these claims: they might also be inspired by politically motivated propaganda, intended to boost the image of the ruling party.

The past prominence of a *don* like Latif illustrates how *goondas* can benefit from the need of politicians to develop local support: the money-power and muscle-power that they provide are very useful to win elections. As we shall see below, in return for their support during elections *goondas* can benefit from the close relations between bureaucrats and politicians.

The politics of local state officials

Shailesh Parmar seems to be enjoying my visit, and he takes time to introduce me to the people working in his sub-zonal office. The people in the office deal with maintenance of the municipal services in the area, like road paving, drainage, and sanitation. Shaileshbhai himself is an assistant engineer, and in charge of repairs to the drainage system in the area. I had met him one evening during the elections at the *karyalay*, the 'election office', of the BJP at Isanpur where he was sitting 'to support some old friends'. He had been working for 15 years at a zonal office in Isanpur, but just one week ago he was promoted to his present post at the Rakhial zonal office, close to Isanpur. 'It has just been fixed. Before the elections transfers were not allowed, otherwise officials might misuse their *laagvag* (influence)'.

During our conversation an elderly man walks in and complains about a gutter in his locality that still has not been repaired. He shows a pink slip to prove that he has complained before. Shailesh Parmar looks at the paper and writes something on the back of the paper, saying reassuringly 'It will be done'. 'It has been a week', the man complains on his way out. As if to show me how they deal with such complaints, Shailesh Parmar takes out a big brown book. This is a 'complaint-book': the officials in this zonal office write down whatever problems people come to report. With carbon-paper three copies are made, one for the book, one for the department involved, and one for the complainant: that was the pink slip the old man was carrying. The white slips in the book record a long history of broken pipelines, flooded gutters and water shortages.

At that moment, a broad shouldered man with a big smile enters the office and introduces himself as Haresh. He greets Shailesh very warmly and sits next to him at his desk. He says he is a personal assistant of Shailesh Macwana, the local MLA. 'I come here to pass on the complaints, when people have a problem and they tell Shaileshbhai, I come to tell them [the people in this office]. When some work does not get done, we make a list and we go with that list to the officials. To do check up, to follow up on these problems. So we make sure that the work gets done. And sometimes people come here, they are sometimes angry when their work does not get done, then we find a solution together for the problem'. Today Vinod has come to talk about the local development budget that every MLA has for the improvement of facilities in his or her constituency (see Chapter 5), he wants to talk with Shailesh about how this budget can be used in the coming months.

I ask Shailesh how he knows whether the people who come to his office are really party workers, but Hareshbhai has taken over the conversation: 'The MLA lets the people know that we belong to him, that we are his assistants. And sometimes we use his visiting card. But we have very good relations; we are friends so we solve all matters very cooperatively'.

Neighbourhood workers and politicians regularly deal with various officers and engineers in the zonal offices, with the constables and inspectors in the police stations, and with different officials in the municipal departments and schools. Given this varied group of contacts, any general conclusions about the functioning of these officials are bound to have important limitations. Nonetheless, I will try to tease out a few general observations about the relations between local bureaucrats and local politicians.

The encounter in Shailesh Parmar's office can illustrate some of the pressures that shape the functioning of these local state agents. These pressures force them to compromise between their own interests and the laws, regulations and policies that they are supposed to implement. This capacity of politicians to influence the application of rules and policies cannot simply be attributed to a general disregard for or lack of commitment to laws and policies (cf. Myrdal 1970). The 'particularized' implementation of laws and policies is the result of the various pressures that politicians can exert on local bureaucrats. One form of pressure surfaced repeatedly in the last chapter: the control of politicians over the transfer of bureaucrats. It seems safe to conclude that Shailesh's promotion and his presence during the BJP's election campaign were not entirely accidental: he seems to have made good use of his political contacts to arrive at his present post. Now Shaileshbhai's assistant Haresh can benefit from this promotion: Haresh acquired a good contact within the bureaucracy, which stands obliged to return the favour extended to him.

As I discussed in Chapter 5, the transfer system is a very important instrument for politicians to control the bureaucracy, even at the neighbourhood level. This is how Isanpur's PI (police inspector) described the influence of politicians over his work: 'In 10–15 per cent of the cases we have to listen to the will of politicians. In these cases we cannot decide independently what to do. These politicians decide our postings and our transfers, so we are dependent on them; we are in their hand. So we have to listen to their wishes. Sometimes this hurts my heart, when we cannot do something that is justice'.

Few local state officials can contact a Home Minister to prevent a transfer. Most of the officials in the zonal offices do not have enough personal contacts to withstand demands for a transfer, which makes it very difficult for these officials to resist political demands, even if they are illegal. My various interviews with low-level as well as high-level bureaucrats suggest that the capacity and willingness of departments to withstand demands for transfers is low. This is what a retired police commissioner remarked: 'We are at the mercy of the government. If we do not listen, we are transferred. If a police officer does not do the work [of a politician], he would be send to Bhuj, or Kuchch [remote areas in Gujarat]. The police commissioner has to be loyal to the politicians, otherwise he cannot work. He has to maintain relations'.[2]

As well as brandishing the threat of such 'punishment postings', local politicians can also secure the cooperation of state officials by exchanging favours: the cooperation of local bureaucrats might be helpful in the long run, for example to arrange a loan or secure a job for a son or daughter in a municipal department. Local lower-level staff without influential contacts can be especially tempted with such promises. This is how Himanshubhai, Pravin Dalal's assistant, said he arranged admissions in local schools: 'All the trustees in the school have some problem, so when they need help they come to us. So when we ask them for admission for somebody they help us'.

A third incentive for local bureaucrats to cooperate with local politicians is the possibility to earn money. I have touched upon many such practices, from the joint collection of *hapta* from illegal business, the arrangement of paperwork for all sorts of business activities (in particular for builders), to all sorts of petty bribery involved in the arrangement of a loan, a ration card, widow pension etc. In Chapter 5 I touched upon the 'tender system', which allows politicians and bureaucrats to make large sums of money: if they cooperate politicians and bureaucrats can demand a high commission from contractors in return for handing out government contracts.

In particular, the collection of *hapta* from liquor-traders and owners of gambling-halls serves to cement the relations between politicians and the police: the amount of money involved is such that both police and politicians would risk losing a substantial part of their income if they failed to cooperate. According to informants, a medium-sized *addha* (alcohol-den) has to pay at least one lakh rupees per month; with around 50 *addhas* in Isanpur the total collection of *hapta* from liquor-traders alone would run to at least 5 million rupees per month. For this reason the post of police inspectors is highly valued; rumours have it that police inspectors (PI's) have to pay 25 lakh for a posting in Isanpur. This money is an investment, and a newly appointed police inspector can hardly risk the returns on this investment by souring relations with influential local politicians: the amount of money involved is such that police officers have a strong incentive to cooperate with these politicians. In this sense Gujarat's ban on alcohol contributes to the inability of local police officers to withstand political pressures.

The fear of exposure of corruption and malpractice also provides politicians with a useful instrument to manipulate the functioning of the local bureaucracy. For example, stories about the difficulties that Ahmed Faraz created for the high-handed PSI can stimulate other state officials to remain in the good books of this politician. The fear of complaints about their petty corruption or their performance can help to cajole local bureaucrats to cooperate. To this list of different pressures I should add the fact that the implementation of various policies requires bureaucrats to maintain close contacts with politicians: the 'local area development' schemes that Hareshbhai came to discuss, as well as various welfare schemes, give politicians considerable leeway in deciding how the associated budgets should be spent.

These different pressures—the threat of being transferred, the benefits of exchanging favours, the need to make money, the threat of being exposed, the involvement of politicians in the implementation of policies—all stimulate local state officials to pay heed to the wishes of politicians. As a result politicians and local bureaucrats—especially the police—are considered to be hand in glove: inhabitants regularly complain about how they 'eat' the money together, and how politicians allow incompetent and corrupt bureaucrats to remain in office. They engage in a constant exchange of favours: the help of a police officer to keep *goonda*s with political backing out of jail might be traded for a lucrative posting in the future, and a bureaucrat's willingness to supply a politician's friend with a business license might be reciprocated with help to suppress a complaint about corruption.[3] In most cases such an exchange of favours can appear innocuous, and form an almost unnoticeable part of the daily operations of state institutions: the repair of a gutter or the paving of a road may be done quicker if the officials involved feel that the work can get them into a politician's good books.

These different pressures contribute to the inability of the local administration to draft and implement policies. At the higher level in the municipal bureaucracy, this inability can lead to frustrations among those bureaucrats who aim to formulate and execute policies. According to a retired deputy commissioner of Urban Planning: 'The municipal commissioner is always saying 'be tactful, do not raise issues', if you want to discuss a complaint. The [politicians] are not trained to give a destination to the ship, to formulate some policy. At all levels the politicians are always talking about elections, not about policy. And the professionals are doing extreme window-dressing, to make their superiors happy'. Similarly, according to a retired municipal commissioner: 'The professional aspect [of the work of bureaucrats] is distorted. The politicians tell the bureaucrats 'you do this', and he thinks of electoral benefit, not about the reasonableness of the plans. I sometimes think that if democracy was not there it would do some good, we could make better use of technical expertise and we would get more done'.

At the local level there seems to be little scope for such concerns. Many of the local administrators interviewed seemed to consider, like Shailesh Parmar above, that political interference in their work—if legal—was on the whole legitimate. The position of these lower ranking bureaucrats is different. The position and contacts of higher-level bureaucrats (they can generally be transferred only by state ministers) allow the higher level bureaucrats at least some independence vis-à-vis local politicians, while the local police officers and the administrators at the zonal offices find it very difficult to go against the wishes of these politicians: they risk their careers as well as, in many cases, a good portion of their income.[4]

That is, unless these state officials have contacts with higher-level politicians. The police sub-inspector who had harassed the old lady could make use of his contacts with the Home Minister, which made him less vulnerable to the allegations of the local municipal councillor, Ahmed Faraz. Such contacts with 'higher-ups' in the party or bureaucratic hierarchy have a large impact on local power relations: these contacts can greatly contribute to the capacity of local political actors and bureaucrats to get things done, and hence to their local status. Those who have good contacts with city or state-level politicians or bureaucrats, and those who have put these people into 'debt' by performing favours for them, command an important resource to boost their own status and career. Ahmed Faraz used several of these contacts to get the police case registered, and the accused PSI on his side seems to have used his *laagvag* ('influence') with the Home Minister (for whom he might have done favours in the past) to limit the damage done by the articles about him in the newspapers.

Conclusion

The daily cooperation between politicians, state officials and *goonda*s should be interpreted in the light of the limited capacity of state institutions to uphold laws and regulations. The limited capacity of the police and the courts to dispense justice creates incentives for local politicians to make use of *goonda*s as alternative enforcers of authority, which again poses obstacles for the police and the judiciary in upholding government laws and regulations. On the one hand the forms of social control that exist in localities like Isanpur limit the capacity of state institutions to expand their local authority, while on the other hand the operations of state institutions—the laws as well as the availability of various state resources—also shape these local patterns of authority. In the context of a state that on the one hand has enough authority to brand certain activities as illegal, but on the other hand does not have the capacity to fully implement such injunctions, politicians, state officials and *goonda*s rely on each other to establish their local authority as well as their livelihoods.

In this sense the daily cooperation between *goonda*s, state officials and politicians is a product of the particular pressures and incentives that a mediated state generates. The intermediary role that local politicians fulfil—as mediators between citizens and state institutions—forces them to maintain close relations with both local *goonda*s and state officials. The electoral (and financial) success of politicians is largely premised on their capacity to provide access to state resources and also to provide alternative resources: developing a capacity to get things done is an essential precondition for electoral success. In that context, the control over the use of force that *goonda*s provide is an important instrument for politicians to increase their capacity to get things done, since it gives local politicians the necessary leverage to solve local problems, arbitrate disputes, intimidate rivals, and gather a campaigning budget, among other things. In poorer localities a nexus between *goonda*s, politicians and state officials is thus inevitable: these relations are central to the daily exchange of favours that characterizes local politics.

This chapter concludes the discussion of how local political networks mediate between state institutions and citizens. The following chapters will focus on the relation between the functioning of these mediating networks and the communal violence that took place in 2002. In the next chapter I will discuss how the dependence of ordinary citizens on these mediating networks feeds a politics of identity. Using the election campaign for the 2005 municipal elections as a starting point, I will discuss how and why politicians make use of the various social divisions among their electorate.

PART FOUR

POLITICAL MEDIATION AND COMMUNAL VIOLENCE

8

POLITICAL MEDIATION AND THE POLITICS OF IDENTITY

Rajubhai is ordering people around with his usual flair and energy. He tells the boys in his chawl to arrange the plastic white chairs in the narrow streets between their houses, while he spreads a blanket on the floor. This is an important evening for Rajubhai: the local MLA Shailesh Macwana and the Member of Parliament Vikram Brambhatt are coming to his chawl to endorse the BJP candidates for the municipal elections. It is the evening before the municipal elections when, officially, campaigning is not allowed, but that does not deter Rajubhai. He is visibly proud that he will be bringing such important men to his own locality. The Brahmin and senior politician Vikram Brambhatt will walk in the small lanes where usually only Dalits come.

Rameshbhai is not showing much enthusiasm. As Rajubhai attaches a light to a tree in the middle of the chawl, the elderly neighbour mumbles, 'they are all tied to the mud. They want a lotus [the BJP's symbol] to come up out of the mud, but this is not possible. They make all these promises, but it never happens'. He plans to confront Vikram Brambhatt today. During the riots his son was killed; a handmade bomb exploded in his face. Vikram Brambhatt promised to support the family; indeed he sent 5,000 rupees directly after the riots, and for the next seven months the family received a small allowance from Vikram Brambhatt's trust. But after that the six-member family had to live on the small salary that Rameshbhai earns as a chowkidar (watchman). Will this meeting convince him to vote for the BJP candidates? 'I vote for a person if I think he is my person, that he will do my work in the future, like for water matters or when there is a problem with the police. That is the only important thing'.

Vikram Brambhatt's visit to Isanpur provides an occasion to probe into the various ways politicians make use of the social identities of their voters. The elections for Ahmedabad's municipal council took place three years after the Hindu-Muslim rioting in 2002. When some of Gujarat's most important politicians came to Rajubhai's chawl, the violence between Hindus and Muslims still hung like a dark cloud over the election campaign. But at the same time there were other social divisions at play: the politicians who competed for a seat in Ahmedabad's municipal council invoked various identity dimensions among their electorate.

Discussions about Indian politics are often dominated by observations about how politicians invoked social divisions for political gain. These discussions yielded roughly four different approaches to identity politics. The 'modernist' approach to identity politics sees the prevalence of caste and religious identity in Indian politics as the result of 'pre-modern' primordial attachments that formed central elements of a traditional society before the advent of modern state institutions. Adherents of this approach see the daily outpourings of religious sentiment as an age-old feature of Indian society. This traditional inheritance, it was expected, would gradually wither away as the Indian economy developed and modern democratic state institutions became more firmly established. This line of reasoning sees identity politics simultaneously as a sign of and as the result of a lack of development: with the advent of modern democratic institutions these 'parochial' interests will give way to a more 'modern' identification with the Indian nation state.

The second approach sees the advent of democracy not as the antidote to identity politics; on the contrary, it advances the democratization process in India as the cause of identity politics. Scholars noted how since independence the role of caste and religion, instead of diminishing, seemed to become more and more prominent in Indian politics. They focused their writing on the adaptability of caste to the needs of democratic mass politics. Describing a 'politicization of caste' (Kothari 1970) or a 'democratic incarnation of caste' (Rudolph 1965 and 1960), these writers pointed out that caste turned out to be a valuable instrument for political parties to mobilize support with minimum effort (Bailey 1970), while caste institutions started to function as pressure groups to maximize the benefits that their members could extract in return for political support. The democratic contribution of caste was, it was argued, that caste could help integrate previously excluded groups into mainstream politics, which has led to a diversification and an expansion of the pressures on the Indian state (see also Shah 2004a). The decision, taken just after independence, to combat India's caste discrimination and social inequalities through reservation of places for Dalits (and later OBCs) in colleges and government bureaucracies further encouraged the political mobilization on the basis of caste. As Weiner (2001: 209) argued, the importance of this positive discrimination in contemporary politics has undermined calls to abolish caste: 'Caste, once an instrument for the maintenance of hierarchy, is, paradoxically, [now] seen as the vehicle for egalitarianism between castes'.

A third approach criticizes these authors for reducing politics to a struggle for power between different castes (Gupta 2000, Hansen 1999 and 2004); as the caste or religious identities that politicians invoke are 'always fragmented, imprecise and contested, and thus ultimately unattainable' (Nandy 1995, Hansen 2001: 10); religious and caste groups should not be taken as coherent blocs of voters. Attention needs to be paid not only to how politicians use these identities, but also to how both democratic processes as well as recent social and economic developments in India tend to reaffirm and strengthen the political salience of these identities. These authors argue, for example, that changing lifestyles and increased competition in India's economy have engendered uncertainties and anxieties about one's position in the world, which enabled political actors to use religious identities to offer a desired sense of stability and order: out of a 'need for an image of shared anchorage and a theory of collectivity' (Nandy et al. 1995: 112) people felt attracted to the promises of order and belonging that a politics of caste and religion had to offer (Hansen 1999). Kohli (1990) has argued that the organizational decline within the Congress party contributed to the political salience of caste and religion: that weakened political institutions have created an 'authority vacuum' in which political entrepreneurs could come to power by politicizing various social divisions.

A fourth approach can be found in Kanchan Chandra's *Why Ethnic Parties Succeed: Patronage and Ethnic Head Counts in India* (2004b). In this book she relates the predominance of identity symbols in Indian politics to the dominant role that elected officials play in the distribution of state resources. In the context of what she calls a 'patronage democracy'[1] she argues that ethnicity—she mainly focused on caste—is a useful political tool because the ethnic background of candidates gives voters some reassurance that an elected candidate will actually be of help after the elections. She argues that both voters and parties engage in head counting: the voter will choose a party on the basis of a count of the number of fellow caste-members in influential positions in the different parties, while ethnic parties will mobilize support around ethnic categories that, in order to be successful, represent a portion of the voters sizeable enough to win seats.

In this chapter I will build on especially Chandra's work to argue that the salience of, in particular, religion and caste in local politics is due to voters' need to use their votes as an instrument to improve—via politicians—their access to state institutions and its resources. Identity politics represents a powerful strategy for politicians to do what is essential to win elections in the context of a mediated state: convey a credible promise to the electorate that they will be more helpful to the voter than the opposing political party. In this context voters are stimulated to invoke their group identity as well: voters can use their group characteristics as an instrument to extract maximum promises from the politician in return for their votes. This is how a dependence on political intermediaries leads to the politicization of social divisions.

The success of such a strategic use of identity depends not only, as Chandra argues, on the size of the targeted ethnic group and the capacity of a political party to promote members of the targeted ethnic groups to influential positions within the party, but also on politicians' capacity to manipulate and balance other divisions among the electorate. Since the electorate consists of people with different, overlapping identities—based on, for example, caste, religion and region of origin—with different accompanying antagonisms, politicians have to engage in a skilful and subtle manipulation of these different characteristics of the electorate. Political success requires a capacity to increase the awareness of a targeted social division and a capacity to mitigate other social divisions. Communal violence serves this purpose: violence between Hindus and Muslims serves politicians to promote an awareness of one's religious identity while relegating other social divisions to the background.[2]

In effect, politicians are engaged in continuous attempts to influence the way their voters perceive the social world and their place in it, and this is what makes communal violence so useful for politicians: violence is a very powerful instrument to inculcate a politically advantageous perception of the social world. In this sense this chapter can be read as an illustration of Bourdieu's assertion that 'the production of ideas about the social world is always in fact subordinated to the logic of the conquest of power, which is the logic of the mobilisation of the greatest number' (Bourdieu 1991: 181). Or—which is more precise in a state with a majoritarian electoral system—the logic of the mobilization of a majority.[3]

Hindu unity

As soon as the car carrying the politicians arrives, the lane in the chawl fills up. Vikram Brambhatt slowly makes his way through the crowd, and takes his chair at the other end of the chawl. There is no room for a stage, so Vikram Brambhatt, MLA Shailesh Macwana and the candidates for the municipal elections sit down in a semi-circle while the inhabitants of the chawl crowd all around them. The earlier cynical atmosphere seems to have given way to a festive mood, induced by the sight of such an important person, and a Brahmin at that, in the street. Even Rameshbhai starts to look energetic, and he manages to get a few words across to Vikram Brambhatt before Rajubhai opens the meeting with three rallying cries, dutifully repeated by the audience: '*Mataki jai, Vande Materam, Babasaheb Ambedkar Amar Raho!*'[4] I am seated next to Vikram Brambhatt and on the spur of the moment I cannot think of an excuse to prevent this—which later got me into some trouble with Congress workers who saw my presence there as a sign of support.

Rajubhai does not savour the moment for long. He quickly passes the microphone to one of the BJP candidates in these municipal elections, Jayent Parmar. For a long time Mr Desai was considered to be the most important BJP politician in Isanpur, but after the riots Shailesh Macwana managed to get the BJP ticket for the 2002 state elections.[5] There is still bitterness between the two; Jayent Parmar accuses Shailesh Macwana of corruption, and Shailesh Macwana is thought to have campaigned actively against Jayent Parmar. Now Jayent Parmar has to stand next to his rival to deliver his speech. He stresses that Congress has done little for the people of Isanpur. He dwells on the fact that gutter and electricity problems in the area have not been solved, and he ends by arguing that Congress has an anti-Hindu bias: 'I want to give you figures and I want to show you to what extent Congress has spread its power in the [municipal] corporation. The Congress for whom we voted took away the ticket of 25 Hindu candidates ['giving a ticket' means naming a person as the official candidate of a party]. None of the Muslim Corporators' tickets have been taken away. They took away the ticket of 25 Hindu candidates by saying that they are corrupt, but I ask aren't the Muslims also corrupt?'

Jayent Parmar joined the BJP in the 1980s. He was still in college when a BJP worker approached him. As Jayentbhai later recalled, the worker said to him 'Our party believes in nationalism. You are a Hindu although you are a SC [Scheduled Caste]. From now on there will be no more untouchability. We will help you'. Before 1985 the BJP in Gujarat was largely an upper caste party that mobilized voters around the issue of reservations for scheduled caste members in government and educational institutions. This made it difficult to capture Dalit voters: there are still stories told in Isanpur of how the MP Vikram Brambhatt and the MLA Arun Pandya garlanded an Ambedkar statue with shoes during such an anti-positive-discrimination rally. But in the mid 1980s the BJP seems to have shifted its strategy as it attempted to gain support among Dalits. In 1985 the VHP asked its youth members to dedicate themselves to the abolition of untouchability (Nandy et al. 1995: 103). The riots of 1985 and 1986 illustrate this shift dramatically: while the fighting during the first days was between upper castes and Dalits, in the latter phase of the rioting Dalits and upper caste groups fought together against Muslims (Shani 2005 and 2007).[6]

An important element of this new strategy to gain the support of Dalits was the opening of patronage channels to influential members within the Dalit-community. This is how Jayent Parmar described the beginning of his political career in an interview:

> They [the BJP] thought that if we are to come to power we need to have the support of these low castes. So they took more interest in this area. They started contacting people, the educated persons who know the political situation. They told me 'we will help you if you join' and then they did help. Even Vikram Brambhatt I could call in the middle of the night. I remember I called him at 1:30 in the night once and he immediately helped me to get blood for a patient in the hospital. At that time BJP took interest in educating people, and it slowly became popular in Isanpur. We told the people 'BJP will help you', that was the strategy. For five years [after that] they did work for us. Then the communal problems started and this led to more support. Now they do not respond as much to our requests.

The promise of support from such important politicians as Vikram Brambhatt could easily sway young Dalits as they realized this support could help solve local problems and boost their political careers. Nowadays one can find many BJP workers in Isanpur who benefited from this opening of BJP patronage channels in the late 1980s and early 90s. Most of them described the start of their involvement with the BJP in opportunistic terms. Harjivan, one of the oldest BJP workers, stated for example: 'As an ordinary person we had to face this difficulty from different state departments. That is why it seemed to me that if I do not want to suffer all these difficulties and if I want to do the work of the people properly, (...) why should we not do the work of whichever party that is coming to power? So that if that party comes into power then our work will get done'. Another local BJP worker who joined around that time added, 'The elders were with the Congress. The BJP was a new party, and there was more chance for progress, there were better prospects. There were already many workers with Congress'.

Voting for access

The words of these BJP workers illustrate how a party with an upper-caste image could become successful in lower caste neighbourhoods like Isanpur: the channels the party offered to gain access to state resources meant much more for the daily life of its inhabitants than the BJP's upper-caste background. The expansion of the patronage network through people like Jayent Parmar or Harjivan increased the inhabitants' prospects of getting benefits from the state. These benefits are more tangible and more important for people's daily life than the casteist ideology of many upper-caste leaders of the BJP.

For inhabitants dependent on the mediation of political actors, concrete offers to help solve daily problems are more alluring than a political ideology. Jayentbhai did not mention any policy proposals in his speech, nor a description of a programme or innovative general solutions for societal ills. It makes little sense for local politicians to advance policy proposals or grand visions in electoral speeches because their voters do not choose them on the basis of the ideas that they hold. In the context of a mediated state the consideration in the minds of most voters is simple: when I need help, who will help me the most? Which candidate will be most beneficial to me?

This concern was of prime importance to those who were listening to Jayent Parmar's speech, sitting on the blanket that Rajubhai had spread out for them. Not only Rameshbhai believed that votes should be given 'for my person', 'who would do my work'. One of Rameshbhai's neighbours reasoned as follows about his vote: 'I vote for the active worker, and the person who understands people and somebody who solves problems for people, who can pass on the problem to top level people and solve it for them. It does not matter which party [the candidate belongs to]'. Another resident said: 'Ideally you should vote for the person who does the work. If that person is clean [not corrupt], there is always the question if he will do the work or not. For example, if there is some problem in the street, like if the pavement is broken, then he [a 'clean' person] will say "I will send someone", but what is the use of voting for someone if he does not do your work. A corrupted person will send someone and that person will do work for 50 Rs. and show work of 200 Rs. But in the end our work will be done, no?'

These considerations make sense in the light of the difficulties that people face when dealing with the state. As I discussed in Chapter 6, especially in poorer neighbourhoods like Isanpur most inhabitants depend on the support of political networks to improve their access to the resources of the state. This relation shapes the strategies that politicians employ in their bid for power and has an impact on the instruments politicians can use to mobilize a maximum number of voters. When, in poorer neighbourhoods like Isanpur, voters depend on political networks, a political party's electoral victory is not just the result of a positive response by voters to politicians' stances on political issues. The votes of a large section of the electorate—the section that needs politicians to deal with government institutions—depend also on whether a political party has credibly conveyed the message 'We will help you most'. This means that the politician has to make promises that appear credible (Keefer and Khemani 2004, Keefer and Vlaicu 2008), and he has to find ways to assure the voter that after elections he will really be accessible to listen to voters' demands, and willing to act on these demands.

This makes identities, as personal attributes of both the voter and the candidate, useful political instruments: identities can be used and manipulated to convey the central message 'I will help you most' to the voter. When Jayentbhai handed over the microphone to Shailesh Macwana, the local MLA stood up to address his public with a speech that could illustrate this point:

> Congress is not caring for Dalits. Mithiben's ticket was cut down [the sitting Congress councillor who resides close to the chawl where the meeting is being held], but not the tickets of upper-caste candidates.
>
> Vikram Brambhatt is a very popular Dalit helper, he is a superb Dalit. He is of great importance to Dalits. His driver is a Valmiki [a Dalit caste] and his cook is also a Dalit. Vikram Brambhatt has adopted Rameshbhai's sons and has paid for their education expenses.
>
> It is very difficult to practice what you preach. I will tell you why you should vote for BJP and not Congress. When from '95 to 2001 I was elected we tried to improve the roads. We had tried, we did not finish all the things, but we had made things better. Congress has three corporators right now, and they have not made a single road or footpath. If you show me one thing I will resign as an MLA.

Such speeches serve to tell the voter that, as Rameshbhai had put it, I am 'your man'. The reference to a shared identity as Dalits suggests something in common between the voter and the candidate, a shared experience and outlook, which can help to inspire trust and credibility (Bailey (2001) used the term 'fraternal identification'). The implied message is that 'I will help you because I am the same as you'. Given the voters' need to find assurances that they will be helped, such a symbolic appeal to their identity is like a proof of loyalty, to prove that the promises made are not just words. Such appeals can be made explicitly ('Vikram Brambhatt is a superb Dalit') but this association can also be made in more symbolic ways. It can be through dress, by wearing clothing that is considered typical for the audience to be addressed. Or by invoking cultural traits that the audience has in common, like the rallying cry '*Babasaheb Ambedkar Amar Raho!*' (referring to the famous Dalit leader). As we will see below, Vikram Brambhatt greets the audience with '*Jay Bhim!*' (Ambedkar's first name and a Hindu god), while such a greeting would be unlikely before an upper caste audience. Another effective way of associating oneself with a religious community is to support religious ceremonies, which politicians do throughout the year.[7]

Such strategic use of identity symbols is not limited to local arenas: similar considerations might help understand the dominance of symbolic issues in India's public debate. Such issues—for example, the issue of whether the supposedly anti-Muslim song Vande Materam should be sung in school, the debate about Ram Sethu (a proposed canal that would damage the 'bridge' that Lord Ram used to reach Sri Lanka), or the symbolic issue of the last twenty years, the building of a temple in Ayodhya—have often dominated the public debate, more than policy oriented debates related to pressing social problems. The reason for the salience of these more symbolic issues is not just that the attention to them deflects the attention from the failures of consecutive governments to deal with poverty or to provide basic facilities. These identity-related issues are also an opportunity for politicians to prove their loyalty and to associate themselves with the targeted group of voters.

The need for social divisions

Such proof of loyalty, however, requires an antagonism. The message 'I am your man' can be made more convincing with an accompanying 'and I am not their man'. By invoking an 'us' and a 'them' a candidate can give his voters ('us') the impression that they would benefit disproportionately from his election to office. As Shailesh Macwana continues his speech, we can see how a threatening 'them' serves to convince voters of the usefulness of the BJP:

> During curfew Ahmed Faraz and Vinodbhai [two Congress candidates and sitting corporators, a Muslim and a Dalit] were feeding Biryani [a luxurious rice dish] [to their people] when people here weren't even getting milk [from Congress]. Even [Ahmed Faraz's] name is there in a case for murdering someone. RSS, VHP and BJP have helped Dalits with oil, milk and clothes.
>
> (...) What did Congress do? For example when there is the month of Ramzan [Ramadan] then in the mosques they give water for free. If anyone asks for water for the temples then they will not give any water. OK? And if Muslims do daban [selling things illegally on the roads] then they can do it anywhere (...) [but when] Hindus they do it at Ashram road then the municipality removes it. If you go to Jamalpur [a Muslim dominated locality], no one takes permission to do construction work. They take water connections there for free too. They take gutter connections for free too.

The electoral usefulness of such speeches and slogans lies only partly in tapping into emotions of fear, insecurity or hatred towards the Muslim community. The constant focus on the perceived privileges of Muslims, and on conflicting interests between Hindus and Muslims, should be related to the opportunity such campaigning brings to politicians to convince the electorate of their usefulness after the elections. It is again in the light of the politician's intermediary role between the state and citizens, and the general scarcity of state resources, that these speeches should be understood: a divisive discourse raises the credibility of the candidate's promises to voters, who are looking for avenues to maximize their access to state institutions. In order to convince the voter that he or she will be most useful in dealing with state institutions, a candidate cannot easily escape from an us-them discourse, because that would rob him or her of an important instrument to convince voters.

In these speeches the suggestion of a conflict of interest between Hindus and Muslims serves two important purposes: it conveys a sense of loyalty, and, in the context of a scarcity of government resources, it serves the politician to convince the voter that he will be more useful in delivering public goods or in dealing with the government machinery. In that context, one would not be so inclined to vote for a politician who promises an equal distribution of government resources to all: one would be inclined to vote for a politician who promises you an extra large part of the government resources (or, similarly, for a politician who promises to end the perceived advantages of others). The Muslims in the above speeches feature as an instrument to make that promise: 'I will make sure you get more because I will not give anything to them' or, in the same vein, 'I will stop them from getting an uneven share'.

This focus on a Hindu-Muslim divide is not restricted to speeches only. The table below shows how Shailesh Macwana used the budget that was allotted to him through the 'Local Area Development Scheme' in 2003 and 2004. This scheme allows MLAs to spend up to seventy *lakh* rupees per annum on developmental work in their constituencies, like the installation of new water pipes, street paving, a new water tank, etc. The table is a comparison of the different projects that Shailesh Macwana financed under this scheme, and the settlement pattern in Isanpur. Most of the financed projects mentioned in this list took place within, or in the vicinity of, particular chawls. Since Muslims and Dalits live in different chawls we can use this list to assess to what extent Shailesh Macwana distributed his budget evenly between these two communities.[8]

Table 1: The use of MLA Shailesh Macwana's budget in Isanpur

Budget used in or around locality mainly populated by					
	Dalits	*Muslims*	*Hindu/ Muslim*	*Outside area*[9]	*Unable to locate*
2003–2004	24	0	4	28	6
2004–2005	24	1	2	12	6
Total	48	1	6	40	12
	87%	2%	11%		

As the table shows, Shailesh Macwana financed just one project in a Muslim dominated chawl in two years, while Muslims constitute roughly 40 per cent of Isanpur's population. But Shailesh Macwana did use his budget in line with the way he presented himself at the election meeting: as a Hindu candidate. In the light of Shailesh Macwana's speech we can see how the uneven use of his budget makes electoral sense: his use of the budget underpins the allusions in his speeches to Hindu-Muslim divisions. Not only did he promise that Hindus would benefit most from his election, he also made sure that they in fact got a larger share of the state's resources. Since gaining access to state resources is a prime consideration for voters, Shailesh Macwana could strengthen his support among Hindus by making them profit from his election as an MLA. And by responding to the requests to improve their amenities, he could ensure that, in return, local leaders among the targeted voters would be obliged to mobilize support for him at the time of elections.[10]

By targeting a Hindu-Muslim division through speeches as well as through the use of resources, Shailesh Macwana could increase the credibility of his promises to the Hindu electorate: these voters could expect that, with him in office, a bigger part of the resources of the state would be directed to them. Such a 'dynamic of inclusion and exclusion' (Breman 2003, 2004) is an important element of local politics in a majoritarian electoral system where voters depend on political mediation: as voters look for ways to improve their access to state resources, political candidates can hardly win the confidence of voters by targeting—through speeches as well as patronage—all the voters. It is a smarter electoral strategy to focus all their efforts on a target group big enough to win a majority of the votes, and limit the attention and resources spent on other groups.

This dynamic of inclusion and exclusion is fuelled by the fact that a Hindu-Muslim division is not the only social division that can be used for political mobilisation. As we return to the election meeting where Vikram Brambhatt was about to speak, we will see that the successful invocation of Hindu-Muslim tensions requires the manipulation of other possible divisions as well.

A superb Dalit

Vikram Brambhatt's experience as an orator shows as he takes the microphone. Even in the narrow and overcrowded lane of the chawl he manages to create the impression that he is addressing each and every person personally. It does not take long before the audience is enthralled by his speech (here abridged):

> I fought and won the parliamentary election for the sixth time. I have been working hard here. I do not differentiate between Brahmins and Dalits. I fought Ambedkar's fight in my own house, because my father was a staunch Pandit. It was not his fault; it was the way he was brought up. He did not even allow Patels and Vanya's [more upper-caste groups] in the house, so how would he allow Dalits? Our elders misrepresented

things, we have to change that. In the last 25 years my father has changed. My mission is complete. Now Jayenti, the Dalit worker in my house, he pours water and milk on Shiva when my father was not longer able.

Even if I get votes or not, it is my mission to help the people in this area, even if I do not get a single vote. I remember there was a scene when riots broke out and Dalits were hospitalized. I spend 20,000 rupees on fees for them. I was sitting in the hospital with a stack of notes. The society went with the flow [at that time], but it will change. Let us hope that the wrong doing people change themselves. Get Congress out, they make Muslims and upper castes fight, that is what they have been doing since the last 50 years. For example, Congress has put in a reservation [for government jobs] for Muslims in Andra Pradesh. It was a maximum reservation of 50 per cent. Because of that the percentage of Dalits will decrease.

(...) BJP has more Dalits than Congress, because the misunderstanding has been cleared between the Dalits and the upper castes.

If there is any work, you can call me in the middle of the night, I will be there. JAY BHIM!

It would not be an exaggeration to say that the audience was shining after this speech. There were smiles all around, and throughout the speech the audience erupted in various bouts of laughter. Even Rameshbhai looked as if a big favour was bestowed upon him when he reported, 'He said he would look into my request'.

The enthusiastic reaction of the crowd around Vikram Brambhatt is not only testimony to his eloquence, it is also an indication of the capacity of these political meetings to shape the audience's perception of society, and to impose social categories to define one's own position in society. In these speeches the audience is addressed in terms of their Dalit and Hindu identity. They are offered an idea of who they are and, simultaneously, an idea of who they are not. Such meetings create and maintain an increased awareness of one's membership of a social group, as well as a heightened sense of antagonism between oneself and an 'other': these meetings convey a sense of the content of the social category the audience belongs to and, simultaneously, a sense of enmity with Muslims.

In this way the repeated speeches, the symbolic posturing and performances by politicians constantly reinforce a perception of a Dalit-Muslim conflict. Such appeals to the identity of the electorate can have the effect of strengthening the importance the audience attributes to the addressed aspects of their identity. With their speeches politicians suggest that one's identity as a Dalit has something to do with their right of access to government facilities. The authority that the speakers exude, as well as the power they have to provide access to state resources, gives their speeches the strength to boost the awareness of an 'us-them' boundary between Dalits and Muslims. They 'speak the group into existence' (Hansen 2001: 26).

Vikram Brambhatt's speech also illustrates the complexities of such an electoral strategy. The fact that Vikram Brambhatt is a Brahmin brought another, competing, antagonism to the fore. He spend considerable time in his speech—as Shailesh Macwana did before him—defusing the suspicion that he, as a Brahmin, would not empathize with the needs and desires of Dalits. In their speeches one can see that the successful invocation of a Dalit-Muslim antagonism depends on the suppression or 'softening' of other possible us-them categorizations: the speakers argued for a common interest and for a unity between Dalits and upper castes under the banner of the common denominator 'Hindu'.

As it turned out, there were more us-them categorizations that the BJP politicians needed to suppress in order to consolidate this 'Hindu vote'.

A change in the panel

One week after the municipal elections I drank a cup of tea with a visibly disappointed Jayent Parmar. The BJP won Ahmedabad's municipal elections, but not in Isanpur. While the BJP managed to win 99 out of 129 seats in the municipal council in the 2005 elections, all the three Isanpur seats went to Congress. Jayent Parmar says he saw it coming: not because he or the other candidates weren't popular enough, but because 'the panel' (the three candidates for the three available seats in a municipal ward) did not have the required caste and regional background. He believed his campaign was doomed from the start:

> The main reason [for our defeat] was a change in our panel. The first panel was with me, Lilaben Patel and Rohit Vaghela. This panel was perfect in terms of caste and region. They decided to change the panel because of pressure from the MLA [Shailesh Macwana] and from party workers. Then Mumabhai came in the panel, who is a Gujarati like me. Rohit was a Chamar [a caste] from Saurashtra, and now the perfect mix was broken. Here there are Gujarati and Saurashtran voters. If one party gives a ticket to one region, then the voters of that region are attracted to that party, because the voters are attracted to candidates from their own region. So all the Chamar's and people from Saurashtra went against us, while Congress had a candidate, Bhanuben, who is from Saurashtra. Congress used this, they went around saying BJP is neglecting Chamars and they are against people from Saurashtra.

The 'Gujaratis' Jayentbhai speaks about are people from the northern districts of Gujarat; people in Isanpur use the word 'Gujarati' to contrast them with people who are originally from Saurashtra, a peninsular and south-eastern part of Gujarat. Chamars and Vankars are the biggest caste groups in Isanpur, and both are considered to be Dalits. These categories overlap: there are Vankars from northern Gujarat as well as from Saurashtra. In Jayentbhai's reasoning, different us-them boundaries come to the fore: the voters did not rally strongly around a Dalit-Muslim antagonism, because other competing identities of region and of caste caused the Dalit vote to split. The fact that for each electoral ward three candidates are chosen allows parties to make a panel of candidates with different backgrounds. According to Jayentbhai the best mix for the BJP in Isanpur should contain the two biggest caste groups in

Isanpur (Chamars and Vankars), upper castes (there is a small upper-caste pocket in Isanpur), people from Gujarat's Saurashtra peninsula and people from northern Gujarat.

To illustrate why his panel was so bad Jayentbhai repeated his calculations for me: according to him there are 20 thousand Muslim voters in Isanpur, about 32 thousand Dalits and 10 thousand voters from upper castes and other smaller communities. About one fourth of the Dalits are Chamar, and there are about 10 thousand Dalit voters from Saurashtra. Most of the upper castes, Jayentbhai reasoned, would vote for BJP and all Muslims would vote for Congress. That left the Dalit voters as the most important group to win over: if Chamars and people from Saurashtra—two overlapping groups—would vote in large numbers for Congress, the BJP would not stand a chance. For this reason Jayentbhai was looking for three candidates who would represent the different groups among Dalits. His preferred mix of candidates would target all Hindus and exclude Muslims. To succeed, such an electoral strategy should not only unite people in opposition against Muslims, Congress should also be prevented from dividing its electorate by appealing to other 'us-them' categorizations.

Jayentbhai reasoned that voters want somebody from their own caste as well as their regional group elected because they expect such candidates to be more useful after the elections. According to him, 'The impression is there, that if you have an elected politician from your community your work will be done more, so the voters united and they gave the vote to a person from their community'. His assessment resonates with the way people spoke to me about their votes: especially during more private conversations, people indicated that they believed that a candidate from their own region or caste would be more helpful after the elections. One of Rajubhai's neighbours, who attended Vikram Brambhatt's speech in their chawl, argued thus: 'We want our man to be elected. For example, in our own area there are Chamar and Vankars. If they would come together, we could rule the city. But each community wants their own people to be elected. So there is competition, and everybody thinks; 'if a person from my community will be elected, my work will be done'.

Chandra (2004b) argues that the limited information available to voters is the most important reason why ethnic categorizations are more prevalent in Indian politics than non-ethnic categorizations (based on, for example, income, education, rural-urban differences, etc). The ethnic characteristics of a candidate are easier to discern (through his or her dress, last name or manner of speaking, for example). Since other characteristics of candidates involve a more intensive background check, a candidate's ethnic background is the easiest indication of the candidate's loyalties: it forms the clearest indication to the voter of whether the candidate will help him/her or not. This, the argument goes, will induce voters to favour ethnicity at the expense of other distinctions.

The role of caste and regional networks in daily life, however, is also an important factor in such a calculation. It is not just because of visibility that people consider a common caste, religious or regional background (more than a common class, educational or ideological background) as a better indication of the reliability of a candidate; the existence of networks based on caste, region or religion can also convince the voter that a candidate from the same caste or region, once elected, will be more accessible. To put the strategizing of these voters and Jayent Parmar into perspective, a short excursion into the history of Isanpur is needed. The role that caste and regional, as well as religious identities play in Isanpur's daily life can help to understand why these different identity dimensions play such a dominant role in the strategizing of voters and politicians.

The urban fabric of identities

The families of most present-day inhabitants in Isanpur arrived in the first half of the 20th century. Attracted by the burgeoning textile industry in the area, they established themselves in squalid huts around the newly built factories. These settlements were gradually legalized and converted into the present-day chawls with more or less uniform houses and small but straight streets (as compared to a slum). The families mostly came from villages in Gujarat, although there are also groups from other states like Andhra Pradesh, Rajasthan and Uttar Pradesh. The textile industry offered a way out of the oppression and destitution that they faced in their villages, where most Vankars worked as weavers, while Chamars were traditionally engaged in the skinning of the hides of dead animals. The Muslims that settled in Isanpur came from similar backgrounds, though from more diverse occupations often related to the weaving and printing of cloth.

The migration of all these people was facilitated through networks that linked people from the same region: when there were new job opportunities in the factories, people sent word to their ancestral villages to bring over more people, whom they then often helped to house in their own chawl. Today one can still see the effects of this migration pattern: many chawls still consist of families that originally came from the same region. One can today divide large parts of Isanpur between chawls with inhabitants from northern Gujarat (who are referred to as 'Gujaratis') and inhabitants from Gujarat's peninsula, Saurashtra. Because of this migration pattern there was originally much less segregation of caste or religious groups: Chamars, Vankars and Muslims with the same regional background were living together in the same chawl.

This seventy year old migration pattern remains an important part of daily life in these localities. Isanpur residents are still well aware of the settlement pattern in their locality. To draw the map below, I asked a number of informants about what people were living in the different chawls in Isanpur. I mentioned a great number of different chawls, and each time my informants could

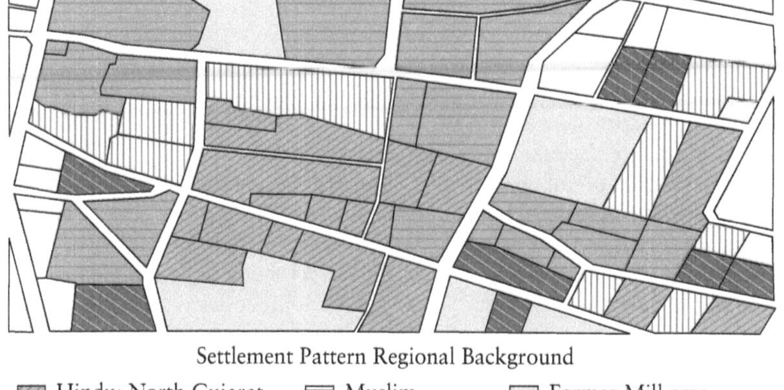

Settlement Pattern Regional Background

Hindu: North Gujarat | Muslim | Former Mill area
Hindu: Saurasthra | Hindu: Mixed | Other/Public Building

name, without much doubt and without much disagreement, the caste and regional background of the residents living there.

The settlement pattern of a neighbourhood has an impact on the mobilization capacity of various 'us-them' categorizations, because people living in the same chawl or street have many interests in common. Many of the pressing reasons to contact a politician are related to issues that concern the whole neighbourhood: installation of a street light, a new water pipe, overflowing of drains, etc. This pits the interest of one chawl against those of another chawl: since the funds available to a municipal councillor or MLA are limited, he has to choose where to spend his budget. Thus a voter's electoral considerations will to a certain extent follow the settlement pattern. This makes both the regional as well as the religious background of a candidate an important factor in elections: people in a Gujarati-dominated chawl feel that by electing a Gujarati candidate they stand a better change of getting the funds for a new water pipe, more public toilets, a water tap etc. Similarly, as Muslims now live in different chawls, they have fewer interests in common with the Dalit population in their area and might feel a Muslim candidate could be more useful.

The present segregation between Muslim and Dalit chawls is to a large extent the result of the communal riots that regularly took place in Gujarat. After each round of Hindu-Muslim riots the communal segregation of Isanpur increased as Muslims, for reasons of safety, moved away from their regional neighbours to Muslim-dominated areas and Hindus moved to Hindu dominated areas. This movement itself strengthened religious identity: since Hindus and Muslims were no longer living in the same chawl they had fewer and fewer interests in common. The competition to secure a budget to improve the street paving or the water supply, for example, was no longer only a competition between Gujarati and Saurashtran neighbourhoods, but also between Muslim and Dalit areas.

The importance of caste and region during elections also lies in the fact that people draw on caste and regional networks to solve various problems in their daily lives. One's caste background provides people with a whole network of contacts that can be drawn upon in times of need. A shared caste background enables people to invoke a feeling of solidarity which could be used to get help to find a job, borrow money, arrange a wedding etc.[11]

Caste is also a useful instrument to find one's way in the myriad networks that lead to access to state institutions. One's membership of a caste is in itself an instrument to ensure the cooperation of politicians and influential party workers. When a gnati bhai is elected to office, there is a greater expectation that you might know somebody, who knows somebody (who knows somebody, etc.), to whom a politician has an obligation. The elaborate caste networks provide people with the necessary contacts to approach a politician.[12] As a Congress official involved in the selection of candidates argued, 'People believe that people from the same caste are easy to approach and people feel that there is an internal discipline; there is a check from caste leaders. After elections the elected leaders are only accountable to their own caste'.

Caste and regional (and religious) identities are also used for the purpose of pooling votes: group identities are useful to pool voters to extract maximum promises from politicians. By promising to vote en bloc a chawl or community is in a stronger position to extract promises from candidates to improve facilities. For example, a social worker can claim to represent a group of voters, which gives them a certain leverage vis-à-vis politicians. When presenting a request for, say, new street paving or drainage repair, brokers can implicitly or explicitly offer to deliver votes in return for the delivered services. The success of their request depends to a certain extent on whether they can be expected to deliver these votes: whether they have, as I discussed in the previous chapters, 'a hold'. Such brokers can strengthen their credibility by claiming to represent a certain community: their claim to represent a group—be it Chamars or Muslims or people from Saurashtra—strengthens their promise to deliver votes in return for the budget for street paving or drainage repair. In this sense their identity is an important instrument to boost their careers: the more voters they can claim to represent, the more they can 'get done', which in turn can strengthen their hold.

Along the same lines, one can understand how, in the context of a mediated state, voters have an interest in pooling their votes along caste, regional or religious lines. They stand a better change of actually getting the street paving or drainage repair if they can offer a large number of voters in return for these services. This vote-pooling is what neighbourhood leaders can arrange: they strengthen the leverage of individual voters with politicians, while they offer some reassurance to politicians that a delivery of services will actually yield votes. Through the representation of a local leader people can increase their pressure on politicians and, by extension, on the bureaucracy. A common caste or regional (or religious) background makes it easier to pool votes, since along these lines the networks and the leadership are available to coordinate this vote-pooling and to make the promise of a group-vote appear credible to politicians.

The importance of caste, region and religion in local politics is to certain extent a self-fulfilling prophecy: since voters have the impression that their work gets done if someone of their group—be it a religious, regional or caste group—is elected, political parties feel a need to select candidates, set up patronage networks and campaign on the basis of these identities, which in turn reinforces the impression among voters that they would benefit most from a candidate from their own community. The importance of different identity dimensions in people's lives is thus constantly reinforced: not only do politicians address them in identity-related terms, the residents themselves also use these identities and the identity-based networks to acquire the necessary help to deal with state institutions.

Praantvad, Jaatvad, Komvat

Much of the complexity of local politics results from the fact that people can invoke various different identity dimensions to drum up support. As the religious, caste and regional identity of voters influenced their voting, politicians were required to balance these different identity-dimensions in their campaign. This is how Jagdishbhai, who was in charge of the campaign of one of the Congress-candidates, spoke about the BJP's 'mistake':

> We told people and social workers from Saurashtra that 'who will do your work if your man is not there in the municipality?' They [the BJP] made a mistake with their panel, and we made use of it. Because we have Bhanuben [in our panel for the municipal elections], who is from Saurashtra. If in some area the majority of the people is from Saurashtra, they want a person from Saurashtra to be elected to get their work done. They want a person from their region in the municipality, because if somebody from their region is not elected, how will they get the work done?

As I argued above, it makes little electoral sense to aim to please all the voters: in the context of a mediated state, politicians gain support by targeting one group of voters at the expense of another group. The targeted group differs: in this case the BJP's campaign focused on a Hindu-Muslim divide, while Congress attempted to bring a regional divide to the fore. Congress could win votes, as Jayentbhai stated above, by pointing out that it had a candidate from Saurashtra while the BJP did not. Political parties need to be very selective in their choice of candidates: the selection needs to reflect the targeted social division—by excluding Muslim candidates, in the case of the BJP—and at the same time needs to balance other relevant identity dimensions in order to prevent other parties from exploiting these divisions.

To select the right candidates political parties make use of detailed information about the people in the different constituencies. All the politicians in Isanpur could give the percentages of the number of Muslims, Saurashtrans, Vankar, Chamars etc. in their constituencies; one evening a municipal councillor even showed me a computer program that he used to count the different voters. Politicians need to engage in such headcounts because they need to select candidates able to represent the biggest caste, regional or religious groups in the constituencies. As a candidate can be expected to receive many votes from his or her own community, people from small communities stand less chance of securing a ticket: as parties try to maximize the number of possible voters they need to select candidates who represent big communities.

When the Congress worker Jagdishbhai admitted that they had tried to gain votes by exploiting a regional divide, I asked why this was a successful strategy during the municipal elections, while it had not worked in 2002 when the BJP's Shailesh Macwana became the local MLA. After a long pause, he answered:

> What matters is the majority. This time they were thinking and talking of region, because both the panels did not have Chamar candidates, and only Congress had a candidate from Saurashtra, so people were thinking about praant [region]. If the candidates are from different castes, then jaatvat [casteism] comes, and if the difference is in region then praantvat [regionalism] comes. In 2002 religious thinking, komvat [communalism] was more important because then there was only one seat to win. Politicians must think about the people in their ward, and they must try to balance everything, the prant, the caste and the religion. Otherwise he [the politician] will lose.

Jagdishbhai's and Jayentbhai's remarks show how a political contest is to some extent a contest over which party can most successfully engrain the social divide it targets in the public imagination. Through their speeches, their slogans, their patronage as well as the selection of candidates, political parties strengthen one social division. But at the same their exploitation of one social division needs to be accompanied by attempts to relegate other social divisions—those divisions that other parties are targeting—to the background. Since voters can see different aspects of their identity (as a Vankar, a Gujarati, a Hindu, etc.) as an instrument to gain leverage over politicians and bureaucrats—and thus base their voting on these different aspects of their identity—politicians need to engage in an ongoing manipulation of the subjective importance of all these possible divisions. The targeted division has to resonate in the public imagination: a group that feels its interests need defending against another group will be more inclined to support politicians who proclaim that they will offer that defence. Political success thus depends on choosing an us-them division that could yield a majority of the votes in the constituency, and finding ways to make that us-them division more central to the self-perception of voters than other social divisions.

The ongoing competition between politicians and the flexible nature of the patronage networks that support them ensure that the political salience of different us-them categories is in a constant flux. The contemporary history of Gujarati politics can be read as a constant struggle between political actors to take advantage of different social antagonisms (Nandy et al. 1995, Seth 1998, Sud 2007b). The present Hindu-Muslim enmity, as we saw it being used in the above speeches, was not always at the forefront of Gujarati politics. As I discussed in Chapter 4, different social divisions served as a basis for political mobilization in Gujarat: while Congress adopted a 'pro-poor' image in the 1960s, the party adopted caste-based electoral strategies that focused on Ksathriyas, Dalits, Tribals and Muslims in the late 1970s, after which Hindu-nationalist organizations managed to bring Hindu-Muslim divisions to the fore. The collapse of the trade union-based patronage networks and economic changes (in particular the informalization of labour due notably to the collapse of the textile industry) enabled the BJP and its associates to relegate the divisions that Congress was exploiting (divisions between upper castes and lower castes and between rich and poor) to the background, while managing to increase the saliency of Hindu-Muslim divisions. In this process communal riots have played an important role.

Rioting for unity

Jagdishbhai's choice of words—casteism 'comes' and communalism 'comes'—illustrates how the capacity of local politicians to manipulate public awareness of different social antagonisms is limited, as the parameters are set by events that take place outside their constituencies. Shocking political events, various state policies and national political campaigns have an impact on the mobilization capacity of different social divisions. Economic changes—such as the collapse of Ahmedabad's textile industry—can undermine the mobilization capacity of class and caste. And national events—terrorist attacks, caste violence in Bihar or a war against Pakistan—offer local politicians an occasion to strengthen us-them divisions. Similarly, the speeches and campaigns of state-level and national politicians, and the us-them divisions that they succeed in invoking, set the parameters within which local politicians have to operate.

But within such parameters local politicians have various means at their disposal to manipulate the salience of different social divisions. Apart from their speeches, the organization of their patronage channels and their targeted distribution of state resources, local politicians in Isanpur can use another instrument to engrain social antagonism in the public imagination: communal violence. In a political arena where politicians need to invoke different social antagonisms to attract voters, communal violence is a powerful tool to weaken the mobilization capacity of the social divisions that competing politicians are targeting.

Riots can heighten the awareness of one dimension of one's social identity. The real or imagined threat to life, the fear of being killed or of losing one's property, can contribute like nothing else to strengthening of a social identity, and to the perception of enmity with another group. Such a perception serves those political actors who claim to represent the interests of one group in the conflict. Political leaders who attempt to bridge that division (who are targeting another division) stand to lose from such violence: in an atmosphere of fear and hatred other social divisions can be bridged.

In March 2002, Shailesh Macwana was leading mobs on violent raids throughout Isanpur. He encouraged mobs to attack Muslim localities, he set fire to several houses, and some residents say that he personally killed a few Muslims. He gave speeches in several chawls about the dangers that Muslims were posing, and he intimidated those appealing for peace. At the same time Shailesh Macwana and his supporters were providing relief to the Dalit and upper-caste residents of Isanpur. At that time whole families were deprived of income since it was more difficult to go to work. The long curfew hours, and the danger of venturing out into the streets made it difficult for people to obtain even the most basic food items. In addition, people were living in a general atmosphere of fear, a widespread feeling of being under threat, all of which increased the need for outside help that people felt. Shailesh Macwana and his supporters provided this support: they distributed food packages, helped people move after curfew, brought injured people to the hospital and secured the release of arrested rioters.

Shailesh Macwana was arrested after the first, most intense weeks of rioting; the police charged him with murder and rioting. The arrest provoked widespread protest and the police, thus pressurized, decided after three months that the BJP politician should be released. At that time Shailesh Macwana held no official position: two years before he had lost the municipal elections. But when he was released he had become a local hero. The BJP supported his candidature for the state elections and ten months later he won a seat in what many considered to be a Congress constituency.

Without the riots, Shailesh Macwana would not have been elected. Without the riots he would not have had the necessary local stature to get a ticket for the state elections, and without the riots he would not been able to overcome the caste and regional divisions among the electorate. As informants related, 'After the riots there were elections. At that time Vankars and Charmars had become Hindus, so they voted for a Hindu. So the Hindu won. The riots were over. Then they stopped being Hindus and again became Vankars and Chamars'. A local VHP leader said: 'After Godhra [the burning of a train coach, allegedly by Muslims, when 58 Hindu activists died] Shailesh Macwana won. He won because of feelings that came out after Godhra. Everybody was united against the Muslims'.

Shailesh Macwana himself attributes his victory to his activities during the riots: 'My name came forward as a Hindu representative. I had helped people without caring about my own life. So there were feelings for me, since other MLAs had not done this work'. The riots had provided him with an occasion to prove his loyalty to voters; in the election meetings in 2005 Shailesh Macwana and Vikram Brambhatt referred to their work during the riots. One can hardly underestimate the effect of relief work that takes place during the riots on the political attitudes of people after the riots: at these times politicians can prove their worth and show that their promises were not hollow words. Since their relief work coincides with a heightened perception of conflict with 'the other', the symbolic impact of such work can be quite strong.

The relief work done during riots leads people to perceive the providers of help as 'our party'. The feeling that 'the BJP and the VHP have given us food, while Congress was feeding them biriyani' can inspire loyalty towards the BJP, while the relief that Congress workers provided to affected Muslim families can create the impression that Congress only supports Muslims.

The riots thus strengthened the Hindu-Muslim division at the expense of other us-them divisions. Shailesh Macwana could benefit from this increased polarization between Hindus and Muslims, because the violence helped him (as a Chamar and as somebody from Saurashtra) to win over the Vankar and Gujarati vote. His opponent in these elections was a Vankar. In usual circumstances these difference could have divided the Dalit vote along caste lines. But casteism, *jaatvat*, did not prevail because of 'the feelings that came out after Godhra': the riots thickened some lines among the electorate, while temporarily erasing other lines.

Conclusion

In this chapter I have tried to show the coherence between identity politics, political mediation, and communal violence. The dependence of voters on political intermediaries creates a political arena in which politicians can hardly avoid exploiting different cleavages among the electorate. Voters who depend on politicians to facilitate their interaction with state institutions have little reason to value politicians for their ideas or their policy proposals. They need to base their vote on perceptions of who will be most helpful in securing access to state resources. As a result, an election campaign revolves around promising voters that they will benefit from a candidate's election. The social background of both the candidate and the voters serves this purpose: the different identity dimensions among the electorate are instruments for politicians to make these promises more convincing. Through the use of different identity symbols, and through the invocation of antagonisms among voters, politicians can convey their most important message: after the elections I will be more helpful to you than other candidates. Identity politics can thus be seen as a product of citizens' difficulties in dealing with a mediated state: the identity politics that both voters and candidates engage in is shaped by the overriding needs of voters to elect politicians who will help them deal with government institutions.

The election meeting in Rajubhai's chawl has provided an occasion to illustrate the different forms that such identity politics can take. In passing I have discussed (1) the use of identity symbols to address a targeted group of voters; (2) the use of divisive political discourse that links political struggles with existing or created social antagonisms; (3) the development and maintenance of a patronage network considered as trustworthy and capable of solving problems by voters of (especially) the target group(s), and (4) a selective use of state resources, targeting especially those groups considered capable of delivering a majority of the votes. These different ways of putting social divisions to political use all serve the same purpose: they enable politicians to convince voters that, once elected, they will be more helpful than other candidates in securing access to state resources.

Much of the complexity of local politics lies in the fact that different social antagonisms can be used for such strategies. BJP politicians in Isanpur focused on a religious division among the electorate, while Congress politicians tried to undermine BJP support among Dalits by exploiting caste and regional divisions. In such an electoral contest competing politicians need to find ways to manipulate the importance that people attach to these divisions: they need to find ways to engrain the targeted social division more firmly in the public imagination than other social divisions. Communal violence serves that purpose. When there are multiple, competing identity-dimensions at play, an outburst of violence serves politicians to heighten the awareness of one social antagonism at the expense of other divisions. Riots provide politicians with an occasion to prove their usefulness to prospective voters, and riots help politicians to unite the targeted group of voters.

9

THE INFRASTRUCTURE FOR VIOLENCE

RIOTING AS MAINTAINING RELATIONS

Salatnagar was a small slum on Isanpur's outskirts, built in and around a compound of a demolished textile mill. Its 1,500 inhabitants—mainly Muslims but also Hindus—had recently arrived from the countryside, and had used corrugated iron, metal sheets and bricks to set up their new houses. On 1 March 2002 a mob of around two thousand people assembled in front of the settlement. There were prominent VHP and RSS activists, local youths as well as local criminals among the crowd. Some of them were wearing saffron headbands, and they carried swords, *trishul*s (tridents), and plastic bottles filled with petrol. As the mob advanced menacingly towards the settlement, a police sub-inspector arrived in his police jeep. He had no intention of stopping the mob; on the contrary, to the dismay of Salatnagar's inhabitants he filled the plastic bottles of the rioters with the petrol from his own jeep. After that the residents could no longer repulse their attackers. The locality was burned to the ground and its residents had to flee to a nearby relief camp.

After the incident a local social worker managed, after several foiled attempts, to lodge a FIR—a 'first information report'—about the incident at a police station. In his report he named the police sub-inspector who distributed the petrol, and his recorded statement concluded with the words 'It looked preplanned and it pains to say that the police has not arrested anybody from the mob, while the police did arrest 12–15 poor people from the settlement'. According to this social worker the mob had been encouraged by the local MLA, Shailesh Macwana: 'Shailesh Macwana helped to distribute the petrol, and he encouraged the violence. He is against Salatnagar; he is not getting votes from here and he wanted to build a new colony at this place five years ago. He has good connections with builders, they give him money during elections'.

At a distance of less than three miles from Salatnagar lies Raamrahimnagar, a much bigger slum locality that also has a mixed Hindu-Muslim population. In Raamrahimnagar local youths were engaged in round-the-clock patrolling of the main entrances of the neighbourhood. The elder members of Raamrahimnagar's neighbourhood committee had instructed them to prevent all outsiders from entering their locality. In the tense first months of March and April 2002 these elder neighbourhood leaders—both Hindus and Muslims—stayed up all night to quell any disturbances, while throughout the day they toured the neighbourhood to convince the Hindu and Muslim residents that they did not need to fear each other. They were successful; the most important violence in this locality occurred when VHP workers came to Raamrahimnagar to protest against the cowardice of its Hindu residents; they were severely beaten up by the young men at the entrance of the locality.

What to make of this contrast? Isanpur and Raamrahimnagar are similar in terms of income levels, unemployment and composition, so why did Isanpur see so much violence—the incident above was just one of many—while Raamrahimnagar remained peaceful throughout these tense months? In this chapter I will take up this contrast between Isanpur and Raamrahimnagar to probe into the dynamics underlying the mobilization and instigation of communal violence. I will focus on the roles that local political workers, Hindu-nationalist activists, and local *goonda*s as well as the police played during the riots, on how and why they contributed to the organization and perpetration of communal violence. I will argue that the contributions of these local (political) actors to the rioting can be understood by looking at the way they function within the patronage networks that provide access to state resources.

This focus on the relation between the way in which political patronage networks function and the instigation of violence can help to bridge the division between different approaches to communal violence: those that stress the political machinations behind the rioting, and those that advance the nature of civil society as an explanation for the occurrence of violence. On the one hand there are authors like Engineer (1989, 1995), Wilkinson (2004) and Paul Brass, who see riots as 'productions', engineered by political networks that gain electoral benefits from the violence. Behind this production of violence are 'institutionalised riot systems': 'a perpetually operative network of roles whose functions are to maintain communal hostilities, (...) mobilise crowds (...), recruit criminals for violent action and (...) to let loose widespread violence' (Brass 1996 and 2003: 258). On the other hand there are authors like Varshney who, in an influential book (Varshney 2002), compared three violent and three relatively peaceful cities, which led him to the argument that in cities with strong and active civic associations violence is less likely to occur than in cities with little civic engagement. According to Varshney, inter-ethnic engagement—in organizations in which Hindus and Muslims cooperate—can prevent communal violence, because such organizations can counter rumours and keep small skirmishes in check. Such civic activity also generates incentives for their members to maintain communal harmony. While Brass criticizes Varshney for obscuring the role that political actors play in the instigation of violence, Varshney counters that his approach is more successful in explaining why violence happens in some places and not in others.[1]

In this chapter I will show that an 'institutional riot system' of riot organizers, *agents provocateurs* and 'riot specialists' (see also Shah 2002a) can indeed be identified in Isanpur. However I shall argue that we can further our understanding of these networks' capacity to instigate violence by noting how their operations during riots are shaped by the more regular practices of political mediation that the networks are engaged in. In this chapter I use the preceding analysis of the everyday functioning of local intermediary networks to show how the outbursts of communal violence in Ahmedabad are an outcome of the difficulties that ordinary citizens experience when dealing with omnipresent but feeble state institutions. I shall argue that variation in the levels of communal violence within a city can be understood by looking at the composition and structure of the local patronage channels through which inhabitants gain access to state institutions. This will shed a different light on the role that civic engagement can play in preventing violence: intra as well as intercommunal engagement limits the capacity of politicians and their supporters to instigate violence because such civic activity can—under certain conditions—reduce the dependence of citizens on political patronage networks. In this way this chapter suggests that we need an analysis of the historical development of local patronage channels—as was attempted in Chapters 3 and 4—to understand why certain areas become riot-prone.

Getting rioting done

Newspaper articles about communal violence often stress the emotional state of a violent mob. In their descriptions of riots, journalists regularly speak of 'frenzied mobs', 'on a rampage' to 'vent their anger'. By offering the emotional state of the rioters as an explanation for the violence, journalists help to legitimize the violence, as such reporting often implies that anger and outrage about a particular incident can indeed be a cause for violence. Furthermore, the result of such reporting is that the organization and coordination that underlie this violent 'frenzy' remain underexposed.

Those who witnessed and participated in the rioting in Isanpur not only talk about the emotional state of the rioters, they also stress the organization and planning that facilitated the rioting. Rioting involves quite a bit of cooperation and coordination; if the riots are to be sustained over a longer period of time, it requires a fairly great number of individuals to perform a number of different organizational tasks. Not every rioter is involved in all of these tasks; one can discern a division of tasks and some coordination between the different people involved in rioting.

Residents recalled how local social workers organized meetings in their neighbourhood:

> There are some residential workers here; in their houses they used to make people sit down. The residents and the neighbours of that social worker are called for the meeting with the excuse of doing *cha-pani* [drinking tea together]. Then they say that in order to pressurize the police, our leaders are coming and they will help you out. [They say that] in our Hindustan our sisters and daughter are harassed [by Muslims], that they eat the meat of cows etc. They reside in Hindustan at our expense and are pressurising us. This is how the leaders will be present to instigate them.

Another inhabitant recalled these somewhat secretive meetings thus: 'People are made angry by speeches behind the curtain against Muslims. The leaders have twenty supporters to gather a mass and then they give their speeches'.

Such meetings create an atmosphere in which the actual mobilization for the violence becomes much easier. In such an atmosphere of fear and anger it takes very little to bring people out on the street, even if people only come 'to see what will happen'. But even in such an atmosphere this mobilization did not seem to have been completely spontaneous; quite a lot of energy and money was spent on mobilizing crowds and spurring them into action. This is how, according to one informant, the perpetrators of the violence were mustered: 'RSS, Bajrang Dal, Durga Vahini [VHP's women wing], they roam around in the area first, and they get hold of people, they find out the people who drink and who are in need of money. They contact such people through two different groups. One group does the work of giving money and the other group instigates them, this can be clearly seen during the riots'.

Some aspects of this instigation were very visible during the riots: witnesses throughout Gujarat reported seeing BJP politicians as well as VHP, RSS, Bajrang Dal and Shiv Sena workers directing and motivating the violent mobs. Politicians of varying stature—from state ministers to local party workers—were seen goading large mobs into action. And politicians did more than giving speeches. The rioters were also given money, alcohol, tobacco and weapons to motivate and de-sensitize them. Informants described to me how they saw political workers approaching local liquor dealers with big stacks of money; the dealers were instructed to provide people with large quantities of alcohol. The rioters thus 'recruited' were often transported by truck from one site to another.

These recruitment drives were not only limited to poor drunkards in need of money; it seems that local politicians made active efforts to get local residents known for their violent behaviour—the *'mathabare'* people, the local *goondas*—to lead the mobs. Many inhabitants felt that politicians used such *goondas* to trigger riots: 'They have one person killed, then the other community becomes angry. Then they give their communal talk, which makes the Muslims angry and they counterattack'. This is what a social worker from Isanpur observed about the cooperation between politicians and *goondas*:

> Shaileshbhai [MLA Shailesh Macwana] would call some *matabhare* person [a person with a violent image] and tell him to kill two Muslims. He would say 'just kill and

then move'. Then four Hindus would be killed, and this is how the riots would start. Shaileshbhai has good contacts with anti-social elements. He uses them during elections. They are paid for, generally they get boys from outside to do it, and then they help to get them released. They use business people to get them, and they tell them to kill four Muslims, for example. They would say 'come at different times, and each time kill one Muslim, shoot them, or use your knife'. If someone gets caught, it depends on the party in power if this person is used to fix the blame. And it will be used to release political anger, as a way to frame your opponent in politics.

Many commentators have noted that local *goondas* play a pivotal role during riots (e.g. Brass 2003: 168), which has made some observers argue that 'without a nexus between politicians and criminals, big riots are highly improbable' (Varshney 2002: 47). Such local criminals often play a prominent role during the actual rioting; they are generally among the small group within a mob that commits most of the actual physical violence. Most people in a mob are just there to watch; they may be attracted by the spectacle of it or may be just curious to find out what is happening. As this informant observed: 'Ordinary people cannot use weapons. But when antisocial elements step in their strength [of ordinary people] increases. The impression that the public has of him [the 'antisocial element', *goonda*] is that he is not afraid of dying. So the public is right behind him and the *dadas* [gangsters, *goondas*] lead'.

Another boost for the morale of the rioters was the tacit—and sometimes very open—support that the Hindu mobs received from the police. As the slogan ran at that time: '*Andar ki bat hai, police hamare saath hai*' ('this is insider's information, the police is with us') (HRW 2002:22). The police force played a dubious role throughout Gujarat,[2] but in Isanpur it provided especially active support to riotous mobs. The Isanpur police not only failed to stop the attacks on Muslim localities, they often participated in those attacks in unison with Hindu mobs, by shooting at Muslim localities, providing petrol to the mobs and arresting Muslim residents at random. Several witnesses reported that the police fired indiscriminately at Muslim residents, with the aim to kill.[3] Several informants complained about the many arbitrary arrests that the police made after incidents of rioting. Under pressure from politicians, the police officers were unwilling or unable to arrest the most prominent rioters; instead police randomly arrested young boys from nearby *chawls*, making sure that they arrested equal numbers of Hindus and Muslims.[4] During as well as after the riots, local VHP and RSS activists and political workers constantly approached the police to press for the release of those arrested.

This pressure on the police to release rioters is an important element of the organization of riots. If the police cannot be convinced to release the rioters, others can feel discouraged from participating. In fact, the promises of judicial and financial help for those arrested were an important element of the mobilization drive that preceded the rioting: 'At that time some Hindus—some BJP and VHP leaders—were instigating in our *chawl* [locality]. [They were saying] 'Our Hindus are lawyers, they can get you released. They will not charge fees from you and until they release you from jail, we will provide you with food. Every month we will pay your family 3,000 rs'.

By promising food and financial support, the VHP tried to take away some of the hesitation of those participating in the riots. They were promised that, should anything happen to them, their families would receive food parcels and financial support. For those who could not be released, the VHP provided lawyers;[5] it has been observed repeatedly how VHP members as well as BJP politicians attempted to manipulate the course of justice by pressurizing the judiciary, the police and witnesses to prevent the sentencing of those involved in the riots.[6]

Their liaising with the police and the judiciary was a small part of the various forms of relief work that VHP, RSS and BJP workers were engaged in. Some workers were distributing food parcels to those who could not go to the shops or to their work in affected areas; some provided temporary shelters, while others were engaged in full-time efforts to secure medical treatment for those injured during the riots—some party workers spent long days at the hospital for that purpose. As in more peaceful days, these party workers cooperated with local politicians to arrange medical treatment. As one party worker recalled: 'When Godhra happened, I was at the hospital from nine until one o'clock at night, I had a curfew pass. Vinodbhai [a municipal councillor] was in the area, and he called me about some stabbing, when someone was injured. At that time I arranged treatment for 107 cases'.

Others went around distributing food parcels to the many day-labourers who had no income during the riots. Many of the local workers could carry out the relief work because of their curfew passes, which allowed them to move around in the evenings when curfew had been declared. The police—often acting on suggestions from politicians—presented prominent social workers, party workers and members of the local 'peace committee' with such passes. Because of the influence of politicians over the distribution of these passes, they were often misused for the rioting itself: those involved in the (instigation of) rioting often also managed to secure a curfew pass. This relief work had a communal colouring; the VHP, RSS and BJP workers targeted their efforts at the affected populations of Hindus and Dalits, while Congress workers seem to have had difficulties entering these areas and often concentrated on affected Muslim neighbourhoods. This relief work was in itself an important contribution to the continuation of the rioting, since it helped to keep morale high, and helped boost the credibility and status of the organizations and people involved in the rioting.

With these observations from Isanpur residents I have aimed to sketch the contours of a fairly big and fairly differentiated network of people involved in the planning, instigation and perpetration of violence. The observations above suggest that a fairly closely-knit network of VHP and RSS activists, municipal councillors, MLAs, the police, party workers and local social workers facilitated the organization and perpetration of the violence. The MLA

Shailesh Macwana was a central figure in this network, as he coordinated and communicated with a range of different contributors to the riots.

Such descriptions suggest the existence of what Brass (1997, 1998, 2003, 2004) called an 'institutionalized riot system'. The descriptions above corroborate Brass' observations about specialization within such networks: among the different actors who contributed to the rioting in Isanpur, one can identify certain 'fire tenders' who spread rumours and maintained a certain level of communal tension in the area, while neighbourhood leaders functioned as 'conversion specialists' who, by using their authority to provide interpretations of preceding triggers of unrest and of the rioting itself, helped to legitimize the violence. Similarly, the *goonda*s whom politicians recruited for the violence could be labelled 'riot specialists' or 'riot captains' whose specialized role lay in provoking mobs into committing acts of violence. Above I also tried to emphasize, like Brass, the established communication links that facilitated the operation of this 'riot system'.

We would, however, misinterpret the nature of these networks if we saw them as having only 'two persisting purposes [...namely] to keep the members of the rival community cowed' and to 'keep the members of one's own community always ready and alert for mobilisation, for crowd action, and for violence' (Brass 1996: 13). We can increase our understanding of these networks if we see their operations during riots in the light of the functions that these same networks perform when there are no riots. These networks are not just 'riot systems' and they do not come into being with the sole purpose of fomenting violence. They are, in fact, versatile patronage networks that provide a livelihood for their members by mediating the interactions between state institutions and citizens. As I discussed in previous chapters, the links between *goonda*s, politicians, the police and local 'fire-tenders' did not come about because of a shared interest in fomenting violence; they came about because of a shared need to cooperate in order to develop a profitable hold over the distribution of state resources and the implementation of state policies. For these actors communal violence is a beneficial strategy within a larger game of capturing (state) resources, gaining support and winning elections. So this chapter will tie together several observations made in earlier chapters about the ways in which political networks mediate between citizens and state institutions: the networks of actors that instigate, organize and perpetrate communal violence cannot be distinguished from the networks we have discussed in earlier chapters, the networks of intermediaries between state institutions and citizens. The structure of the interdependencies between these different intermediaries generates incentives to contribute to the violence, while their capacity to access state resources lends these actors the necessary local status and authority to instigate violence.

This interpretation of the nature of 'riot systems' will help to understand the way they work during riots. In the remainder of this chapter I will discuss how four different groups of actors identified above—local neighbourhood leaders, Hindu nationalist activists (VHP, Bajrang Dal, RSS, BJP), local *goonda*s and the police—contributed to the rioting, and I will try to show the relation between the different ways in which these actors contribute to the violence and the observations made in earlier chapters about the way local patronage networks operate. I will start by discussing the speeches and rumours that generally precede the rioting: in the following section I will show how the capacity of local leaders and politicians to both instigate and prevent violence is related to their capacity to provide access to state services. There were riot-mongers as well as peace-mongers in the studied neighbourhoods; whether the arguments and rumours of the riot-mongers gain the upper hand depends to a large extent on who has better access to state institutions.

'He who has power can make his talk heard'

Mahendra Vaghela's grey hair and thoughtful speech make him a charismatic appearance. Mahendrabhai was one of the first inhabitants in Isanpur to benefit from the quota for Dalits at the municipality. More than four decades ago he got a coveted job at one of the municipal departments, which lent him local status as well as financial security. While working at the municipality he had been active at the municipal trade union and earned a respectable reputation as a prominent local leader. He has not been active in any political party since the Communist Party in Ahmedabad withered away in the 1980s, but his interest in politics is still alive; now that he is retired he spends many hours discussing the latest events with friends.

Because of this commitment Mahendrabhai felt obliged to attend the meeting that the police had organized behind his house on 3 March 2002. The rioting had been intense during the days prior to the meeting; right in front of Mahendrabhai's house inhabitants from two adjacent localities had clashed. The police had assembled all prominent local leaders—Hindus as well as Muslims—to talk about ways to end the violence in Isanpur. Two hundred people were present, but apart from the police only two people spoke. One of them was Mahendrabhai; he gave a passionate speech about the need for communal harmony. 'I told them that we should maintain peace, because we are poor and we will lose our income because of the riots. Because of the riots we will not be able to go out for work, and we will suffer from hunger'.

The next day a crowd of hundreds of people gathered in front of Mahendra's house, shouting 'Mahendra *hai hai*' ('down with Mahendra'). 'They were Shaileshbhai [Macwana]'s people and misguided people from my neighbourhood. The BJP and VHP people [had said] that Mahendrabhai was also there [at the meeting], let's go to his house. The people were misguided. They were not given the correct information about the speech in the meeting. They were misguided and brought to my house'. The first stones were coming down on his roof when Mahendra mustered the courage to face the people in front of his house. He brought out a plastic chair; he climbed on this chair and delivered another speech to the angry mob about the need to prevent violence. According to Mahendra, his speech had a great effect: 'There was shouting in the beginning. When I came out there was a lot of shouting. But I stood on a stool and started speaking very loudly. So slowly, slowly those people became quiet. Some of the people looked at me and said that 'we were not supposed to come here'. Then slowly, slowly they dispersed'.

But his speech did not have any lasting impact, as the violence continued unabated during the following weeks. Mahendra had not been the only target of this mob; before gathering in front of Mahendra's house the mob had also shouted slogans against Tikesh Macwana, a local Dalit activist who had published a newspaper article accusing Shailesh Macwana and several others of instigating violence. People seemed to have been more irritated than influenced by the actions of the two men; even three years later people criticized both Mahendra Vaghela and Tikesh Macwana for their actions during those violent weeks in 2002. As one of Mahendra's neighbours said: 'Mahendra Vaghela is useless, he is not doing anything for the community. He has a good job at the municipality, he had the chance to arrange jobs for youths but he didn't. It was a meaningless speech. At that time Muslims were attacking, stabbing, they were killing people, so how can people be motivated for peace in such an atmosphere. It was useless. If we are friends with Muslims then they will kill us'. And this is what a fellow Dalit activist with little sympathy for the BJP said of Tikesh's articles: 'He angered the community against him. I am against an ideology, not against people. We should attack this BJP ideology, not our personal enemies. Shaileshbhai is from my caste, and whenever I have some work to be done, he is the first person to help me. He wrote about Shaileshbhai with all the details, he wrote everything he had done. That is why people went against him, his whole family came out and protested against Tikeshbhai'.

Tikeshbhai and Mahendra failed to get the crowds behind them, whereas local politicians like Shailesh Macwana and his VHP and RSS activists were seen leading mobs of thousands of people. They too had been making speeches throughout Isanpur. Shailesh Macwana had given numerous speeches inside Isanpur's *chawl*s, and as the quotes above indicate, there were many neighbourhood leaders who organized similar meetings; during these meetings the events in Godhra were presented as another example of how Muslims are always 'harassing and pressurizing us' while 'living here at our expense'.

Such speeches are an important element of the lead-up to rioting. By the spreading of rumours about perpetrated or imminent attacks, or more general talk about the dangers that a perceived enemy is posing, the occurrence of communal violence is preceded by intense, discursive activity; a wildfire of rumours and accusations, true or false, about the target population. Many observers of communal violence in South Asia have pointed to this important role of rumours; Horowitz (2001: 75), for example, argued that 'rumours narrow the options that seem available to those who join crowds and commit them to a line of action. They mobilise ordinary people to do what they would not ordinarily do'.

The burning of the train coach in Godhra and the resulting death of the Hindu-nationalist activists can be interpreted in many different ways: the burning might be seen as a Pakistani plot to weaken India, it could have been an unfortunate explosion of a cooking stove, it could have been a local fight between passengers and tea vendors, etc. What makes these speeches of local leaders such an essential element of the lead-up to rioting is that during these speeches a triggering incident—such as the events in Godhra—acquires an interpretation that can serve to legitimize violence against a local target group; the triggering incident is interpreted in such a way that it becomes an illustration of locally felt tensions and grievances. For a shocking incident to become an occasion for violence, the event needs to be perceived as an expression of broader us-them divisions prevalent in the political discourse at that moment, and the incident needs to be interpreted as an illustration of purported negative character traits of a *local* target group (generally people who had nothing to do with the triggering incident). While the relentless invocation of Hindu-Muslim divisions over the years by Hindu-nationalist organizations—see Chapter 4—created a political atmosphere in Gujarat that was conducive to violence, for an incident to trigger a full-scale riot it needs to be linked to the communal division, to be perceived as an expression of the perceived tensions between Hindus and Muslims. Brass (2003: 33) called the people who perform this task 'conversion specialists': the people who convert the meaning of a shocking incident in such a way that the incident acquires a communal overtone and becomes a legitimate cause for retribution against a group of local citizens. In this way, the lead-up to the rioting is characterized by an intense struggle to determine the meaning of an incident like Godhra; Tambiah (1996: 257) referred to this process as 'parochialization', a 'reproduction of national issues in diverse local places, where it explodes like a clusterbomb in multiple context-bound ways'.

The important question here is: who is listened to? Whose arguments carry the most weight, whose rumours are believed? And why do some interpretations of a triggering incident prevail, while the arguments of others fall on deaf ears? Why did respected citizens like Mahendra Vaghela and Tikesh Macwana fail to dissuade people from committing violence, and why did Shailesh Macwana and his neighbourhood workers succeed in mobilizing such large crowds?

As I discussed in Chapter 2, one could come up with quite a number of general answers to such questions: some point to the psychological benefits that a divisive discourse and the rioting itself offer, others point out how a general political atmosphere can raise the susceptibility of inhabitants to the instigation of violence. But such answers do not explain the patterns of rioting; they do not help to understand why violence erupts in some areas while other, apparently similar localities, remain peaceful. To understand this pattern, I believe, one has to look at the local patterns of authority, and the relation of these patterns of authority within neighbourhoods to the structure of patronage networks that provide access to the state. Local politicians' capacity and willingness to spread rumours and instigate riots are shaped by the position of these leaders in the broader intermediary networks that offer access to the resources of the state.

In the earlier chapters I discussed how the capacity to deal with outside authorities contributes to the local standing of an aspiring leader. I discussed the use of the Gujarati word '*prabhav*' ('to have a hold') to illustrate how aspiring politicians and social workers acquire a 'hold' over their constituencies by developing a capacity to perform favours for inhabitants. In poorer localities like Isanpur, where citizens have difficulties dealing independently with state institutions, local leaders are generally those people who can get things done—who have the capacity to influence the activities of the police and local bureaucrats. Because of the dependence of poorer inhabitants on intermediaries to deal with state institutions, residents can become local leaders if they are able to develop influential contacts and show their effectiveness in dealing with authorities. The contacts with influential politicians and bureaucrats enable aspiring leaders to command respect and develop a group of local followers. This 'hold' enables local leaders to influence their neighbours' opinions and voting behaviour. Since local leadership is so closely related to the capacity to deliver, local patterns of authority have been shaped by the practices of patronage that politicians engage in to develop local support. In localities like Isanpur there are few *stanik-netas* (slum- or *chawl*-leaders) who do not owe any allegiance to local or state-level politicians: such contacts are essential to establish one's position as a local leader. As a result, local patterns of authority in areas like Isanpur have become very politicized.

Such patterns in local authority are important to understand the capacity of local leaders and politicians to instigate violence. Shailesh Macwana's speeches tap into feelings of insecurity or frustration that may be common throughout the city; their exhortations to violence tap into urges that may, deep down, dwell inside all of us: the rioting can offer gratifying feelings of superiority, fulfil a need to dominate (Nussbaum 2007), and there can be 'fun' in violence (Verkaaik 2006). But such urges are generally constrained; people do not feel free to act on such desires, whether because of fear or shame, or from inhibitions against inflicting harm on others (see Collins 2008). But when people in a position of authority seem to condone or legitimize the violence, such restraints can temporarily fall away. A position of leadership—whether based on symbolic capital or on a capacity to get things done—can involve a capacity to take away some of the inhibitions that prevent people from acting out their violent urges. For this reason local patterns of authority and the interdependencies that structure these patterns of authority are essential for understanding the spread of violence throughout a city or state.

Shailesh Macwana's ability to deal with government authorities gave him a threefold advantage over opponents like Mahendra Vaghela. First, politicians like Shailesh could command the support of a large group of supporters and local leaders. As we have seen in Chapters 7 and 8, there are social workers, party workers and local *goondas* in almost every street who derive (parts of) their livelihoods and local status from their contacts with politicians. This network of dependents provided politicians like Shailesh Macwana with the infrastructure to spread rumours effectively, and enabled him to bring people out on the street. I will discuss this point in more detail below.

Secondly, the dependence of Isanpur residents on people like Shailesh Macwana to deal with state institutions grants such local leaders the credibility and authority to impose their version of events and, ultimately, legitimize the use of violence. Shailesh Macwana's capacity to 'get things done' enabled him to develop such a 'hold' in his area that he could influence the course of events during riots. In contrast, inhabitants who—like Tikesh and Mahendra—develop no contacts with important politicians or bureaucrats, who do not engage in regular efforts to help inhabitants deal with their daily difficulties, forego an important avenue to develop a similar status and influence. Note in this light that the above-mentioned inhabitants who disagreed with Tikesh and Mahendra mentioned the usefulness of Shailesh Macwana and the relative uselessness of the peace-mongers. As a Hindi saying goes: '*Jiska Jor Hai, Uski Baat Hai*'—he who has power can make his talk heard.

Thirdly, the hold that local politicians have over the bureaucracy and especially the police enables them to silence people who take a different stand in the lead-up to rioting. The control of politicians over the bureaucracy and the police can dissuade people from voicing a different opinion, since such a public stand might lead to severe harassment. Courageous people like Mahendra and Tikesh were willing to take that risk, but other inhabitants can be silenced by a perceived or real threat of future consequences. As a local social worker said about his role during the riots:

> I am living in a Hindu area, OK? So if I do some talking against communalism or I tell the ordinary people 'do not go into the riots' (...) then I would have faced full danger from the Hindus. If there were some worn-out worker like me who has some feelings and tries to do something then he would get beaten up by Hindus. (...) This time the government and the police were on the side of the Hindus, so no one talked about it openly.

In sum, Shailesh Macwana's greater capacity to mobilize people is not only due to the attractiveness of his divisive discourse; it is also related to his prominent position within local patronage networks. This prominence lends him local authority and organizational support, which enabled him to have a bigger impact on the course of events after the incident in Godhra.

To further illustrate this argument, I will turn to a neighbourhood that remained peaceful after the burning of the train coach in Godhra. Despite having a similar population to Isanpur—in terms of its income levels as well as its composition—there has been no communal violence in Raamrahimnagar over the last thirty years.

The world should learn from us

In an otherwise drab office, the award shines like a shrine. The members of the Raamrahimnagar Jhupadavasi Mandal (RJM) have placed their prize in a cupboard in the middle of the room, beneath a drawing of Ram and Sita and a prayer from the Koran. The golden placard in the cupboard is the 'Indira Gandhi Award for National Integration', which national politicians from Congress awarded to the RJM for its efforts during the riots. A picture next to the award shows how Aaljibhai and Kapadiabhai—the RJM's previous president and vice-president—are being congratulated by Sonia Gandhi herself.

By now they have told their story many times. Even the chief inspector of police came to hear about how the residents of Raamrahimnagar maintained the peace in their locality. Not just in 2002; since 1969 Raamrahimnagar remained peaceful throughout the many instances of violence that plagued the surrounding city. As Mr Kapadia, a frail-looking Muslim in his seventies, declares with some pride, 'The world should learn from us. We are famous; we live according to the constitution. We should all live together harmoniously'.

The RJM's methods to preserve peace seem simple enough. When the news about the burning of the train coach in Godhra spread, the 23 members of the neighbourhood committee—both Hindus and Muslims—got together and resolved to defend Hindu-Muslim unity in their locality. They were joined by Taajubanu, a prominent social worker in the locality whose sons are known for their somewhat violent image. Together they toured the neighbourhood, telling people that nothing would happen in the area, and that they should not believe any rumours. They also visited the few VHP and RSS members in the locality. As Aaljibhai relates, 'We told them 'during the riots you have to do our work, otherwise we will beat you up'. They have to pass through these streets so if they do it [create disturbances], where would they go tomorrow?'

The RJM members stayed up all night to quell any disturbance. They sat in front of their office in the middle of the locality, ready to act at the slightest indication of trouble. They instructed local boys to guard the three main entrances to the locality. Anybody who wanted to enter the locality had to ask permission from the RJM members. As Aaljibhai explained the measure: 'We have boys to guard these places to keep troublemakers out. They do not let anybody enter without our permission, because the boys are under our hand, they do what we want'. Some VHP activists did try to enter Raamrahimnagar, and they sent bangles to male residents—female wear to protest at a lack of 'manly' behaviour. But even though several people were killed in nearby localities, Raamrahimnagar remained peaceful. On two occasions a possible troublemaker was beaten up when he tried to enter the locality; apart from that there was no violence in Raamrahimnagar.

Isanpur and Raamrahimnagar provide two very different examples of how a shocking event—the burning of the train coach in Godhra—'lands' in an urban neighbourhood. In Isanpur the people calling for restraint were intimidated and silenced, whereas in Raamrahimnagar the round-the-clock patrolling by RJM members succeeded in keeping all riot-mongers out. In Isanpur prominent politicians were exploiting Hindu-Muslim tensions, while the local leaders in Raamrahimnagar tried to defuse communal tensions.

As I discussed in Chapter 6, the RJM's current local standing goes back to events in the 1970s, when residents fought together to get rid of the local slumlord. That fight brought representatives from different castes and religious communities in Raamrahimnagar together; after throwing the slumlord out these residents founded the RJM, and they came up with a name for their neighbourhood that symbolized Hindu-Muslim unity. After its heroic fight against the slumlord, the RJM could count on the support of many residents. After that, the RJM built up close relations with influential politicians from the Congress party; the RJM campaigned for these politicians, while they helped the RJM in dealing with the bureaucracy in order to improve the facilities in the area. The results of this exchange were noticeable: facilities like water-taps, electricity and a drainage system arrived in Raamrahimnagar much earlier than in surrounding slum areas.

Most other neighbourhood committees in Ahmedabad have long withered away to be replaced by patronage networks around local politicians, but the residents of Raamrahimnagar still approach RJM members on a daily basis to deal with water problems, overflowing gutters, disputes, etc. Their successes in dealing with the authorities seem to keep other organizations out; throughout my stay I could not find many BJP workers, and there are few RSS and VHP activists in the locality. This is a major difference from Isanpur: as I discussed in earlier chapters many residents in Isanpur approached local politicians and their workers directly to solve all sorts of daily problems, while in Raamrahimnagar much of this interaction has been monopolized by RJM members. This local prominence of the RJM is, I believe, essential to understand the absence of violence in Raamrahimnagar. The authority that RJM members have in the neighbourhood enabled them to defuse tensions and prevent violence. They could prevent the spread of rumours and accusations by touring the area, and intimidate anybody who tried to provoke communal tension. In Isanpur it was Shailesh Macwana and his workers who could intimidate those calling for restraint, while in Raamrahimnagar it was the RJM that intimidated anyone with a dissenting opinion. In Isanpur the local boys hung around the houses and offices of VHP and BJP leaders, while in Raamrahimnagar the RJM could tell the local youths what to do. In this sense the situation in the two neighbourhoods corresponds: in both localities those residents who had the greatest capacity to deal with outside authorities had the greatest influence over the course of events.

The crucial difference is that while Shailesh Macwana and his supporters were integrated into patronage networks that benefited from Hindu-Muslim tension, the RJM could operate relatively independently of these networks. Its capacity to solve local issues through Congress channels helped the

RJM to keep the VHP, the RSS and the BJP out. The exceptional peace in Raamrahimnagar cannot just be attributed to a greater belief in secular or humanist ideals among its residents; it is also the result of the integration of its local leaders, the RJM, into patronage networks that had little to gain from the violence. A recent newspaper article warned that Raamrahimnagar's communal harmony would end if local youths could not find jobs; the article quoted disgruntled inhabitants saying that 'had we had SIMI and RSS [a Muslim and a Hindu radical group] workers among us, our children would have gotten jobs'.[7]

Such a focus on the role that changing local patronage channels play in shaping local authority patterns can shed a different light on the arguments that Varshney (2002) advances about a relation between civic engagement and communal harmony. The contrasts between Isanpur and Raamrahimnagar illustrate Varshney's argument; Raamrahimnagar's RJM provides a good example of how an intercommunal civic body can help to maintain communal harmony. At the same time the analysis above points to two other aspects of the relation between communal violence and civic engagement. First, the present predominance of the networks around political leaders and the capacity of these networks to instigate violence are not only due to the decline of civic interaction between Hindus and Muslims, as Varshney argues; the influence of such political networks has also grown because of the gradual encroachment of state institutions on the terrain of intra-ethnic civic activity. In Chapter 3 I discussed how the development of state institutions and the accompanying decline of the *pol panch* and the *mahajans*—consisting almost solely of members of a single community[8]—have enabled the development of political networks as a new interface between citizens and the state. There are at present not so many civic bodies that can, like the RJM, help its members to deal with collective problems while minimizing political involvement. As state institutions gradually assumed responsibility for functions that several civic institutions were performing, the patterns of local leadership changed. Neighbourhoods gradually became politicized as inhabitants became dependent on the political mediators that could provide access to state institutions.[9]

Secondly, the RJM's example suggests that active and strong civic associations can prevent communal violence not just because they can counter rumours and generate incentives to maintain peace, but also because they can limit the politicization of neighbourhoods. As I discussed in Chapter 4, in many localities Hindu-nationalist organizations like the BJP, VHP and RSS gained local prominence by helping inhabitants deal with state institutions because older mediating networks organized around the TLA trade union had collapsed. Neighbourhood life has become politicized as older civic institutions have been replaced by extensive local networks of political agents. The capacity of Hindu-nationalist organizations and their politicians to mobilize people and to spread communal tensions is not only related to the absence of civic organizations to stop their rumours and accusations; it is also related to the increased dependence of the population on the patronage channels that these organizations provide. Raamrahimnagar stands out as an island of communal harmony, not only because its neighbourhood committee has been able to inspire trust and cooperation among its mixed population, but also because that neighbourhood committee has served to minimize the dependence of residents on local politicians and Hindu-nationalist organizations like the VHP, the RSS and the Bajrang Dal. In this way, the RJM did not prevent violence just by maintaining the 'horizontal' relations between local Hindus and Muslims—an argument that Varshney makes—but also by altering the power imbalance that characterizes the 'vertical' relations between political patrons and local inhabitants.

Citizens' dependence on politicians to gain access to valuable state resources—and the absence of alternative providers of (access to) these resources—has made poorer neighbourhoods, in particular, vulnerable to political manipulation and instigation of violence. This, to me, is the reason why communal violence is more often perpetrated by poorer residents in poorer parts of a city: not because poorer citizens are more prone to violence, or more irrational or more infused with a communal ideology, but because, as I argued in Chapter 6, poorer residents are in a more vulnerable and dependent relationship with state institutions, a relationship which is exploited by all kinds of intermediary networks. The dependence of poorer residents on political mediation supplies political actors with contacts, authority and influence in these neighbourhoods, which greatly facilitates the mobilization for violence.

I will now turn to a discussion of the contribution of that varied and large group of VHP, Bajrang Dal, RSS and BJP workers to the organization and instigation of riots. Their specific roles within the 'riot networks' discussed above can also be interpreted in the light of specific ways in which these organizations help their followers deal with state institutions.

The foot soldiers of Hindu-nationalism

An important element in the lead-up to rioting is the dissemination of prejudices and grievances against the target population. During meetings, discussions, rituals, training etc. the perception of a 'threatening other' is slowly built up by a constant stream of accusations and rumours. Such meetings contribute to what Tilly (2003) called 'boundary activation': a repeated emphasis on differences between religious communities serves to bring one aspect of one's identity to the fore, at the expense of other identity dimensions, thereby heightening awareness of tensions between an 'us' and a 'them'. In the last chapter I discussed how politicians contribute to such 'boundary activation' by, for example, addressing their audiences in terms of their caste and religion, and by portraying a political contest as a competition between religious communities.

Such speeches are relatively rare compared to the regular activities that organizations like the VHP and RSS organize. The RSS organizes *shakhas* ('branches') throughout Gujarat in which participants get not only a work-out but also a daily dose of Hindu-nationalist ideas. The VHP and its youth wing, Bajrang Dal, organize weekly training and meetings for local youths, where, in addition to religious texts, the threats posed by Muslims are a recurring topic of discussion. Such discussions are often accompanied by a more military type of training in which youths are instructed on how to fight. These organizations have been very effective in spreading Hindu-nationalist ideology; the organizations now command an unsurpassed grassroots network of thousands of local activists.

Hindu-nationalist organizations stepped up their activities in the months preceding the riots. According to several informants the VHP and the RSS started organizing new weekly meetings inside the *chawls* in Isanpur in the months before the riots, which were then discontinued after the riots. This increased activity of VHP, RSS and Bajrang Dal units was also noted in other parts of Gujarat,[10] which suggests that the preparation for the violence had been under way before the burning of the train coach in Godhra.

Rajesh was one of the local boys who was attracted to such meetings and who, months later, participated in the stoning and burning of a nearby Muslim locality. In his *chawl* Mr Jha, a local VHP leader, had started to organize Sunday-meetings for which he especially invited the local boys. 'A friend of mine took me to these meetings', Rajesh told me later, 'He said if you come once you feel like coming again and again. He said that it is about our religion'. Rajesh was not so much motivated by that topic, but he saw the meetings as a chance to get ahead: 'We thought, the VHP gives us some power that we can use on other people. Like, if I need to fight with someone, for example if had some problem with my teacher, then if I talk to the main leader of VHP then lots of people would gather around me'. Such expectations were not unrealistic; Rajesh has seen how the VHP people move around in his locality: 'In our area the police sit with the VHP people. They listen more to VHP people. These people who got positions [within the VHP] now roam around with the police. They have a salary and they are given a bike, a Hero Honda Splendid. They create the impression that I roam around with the police so I am powerful'.

At that time, Rajesh felt his teachers discriminated against him at school because of his caste. He had hoped that the VHP would help him to end this discrimination. When he and his friends raised such issues at the meetings, Mr Jha and his helpers offered different interpretations of their problems: 'If someone has a complaint about waste, that there is too much waste, they would say that Muslims are the cause of that. If someone says they have a problem with a broken pipeline, they say if you drive out the Muslims living in front of your house, you can live in their house'. Then, when the train coach was burned in Godhra, boys like Rajesh came out on the street and participated in the burning and looting of houses of Muslims who had been living on the other side of the street. Although rioting had also felt good ('the tensions go away and all people are the same'), Rajesh later regretted his actions. He joined a local NGO, which changed his perspective. At the time of writing Rajesh runs a library with a Muslim friend, and he has persuaded his parents to let him marry a Muslim girl.

Rajesh's turnaround is rare: generally boys of his age and background do not have access to different sources of information, which makes it difficult to develop a more critical attitude towards the Hindu-nationalist ideas that are being spread among them. And since their prospects for the future are limited they are easily swayed by the promises of jobs, bikes and status that VHP leaders hold out.

The grassroots-level activity of organizations like the VHP, the RSS and the Bajrang Dal is impressive: there are people like Mr Jha throughout Ahmedabad, whose activities infuse a daily dose of Hindu-nationalist ideology into the hearts and minds of the city's inhabitants. There are good arguments for attributing the popularity of these organizations—and their command over a large number of local activists—to the attractiveness of their ideas: the ideas discussed at the RSS' *shakhas*, or during the VHP discussions and the Bajrang Dal training-camps can generate an attractive sense of self-esteem, of pride, in a threateningly changing world (Basu *et al.* 1993, Blom Hansen 1999, Punyani 2004, Anderson 1987). But the strength of these organizations can also be interpreted in terms of the particular avenue they provide to deal with the extended scope but limited reach of the state. As I argued in Chapter 4, in Ahmedabad organizations like the VHP and the RSS are seamlessly woven into the political patronage networks, and membership of such organizations can often be the first step to launch a political career. The links between Hindu-nationalist organizations and government institutions are not only visible at the top; at that level one can point to the infiltration of the RSS and the VHP into government bureaucracies and the judiciary, as well as universities, or to the many state-level politicians like Chief Minister Narendra Modi or the MLA Shailesh Macwana, who started their careers as, respectively, an RSS *pracharak* (full-time worker) and a VHP organizer.[11] At the neighbourhood level the VHP and the RSS leaders can operate like local patrons; they can offer their supporters beneficial connections to government officials as well as influential (BJP) politicians who often have a VHP background, and who depend on the RSS workers as well as the VHP for their support during electoral campaigns. In Isanpur and Maneknagar the workers of the RSS, BJP, VHP and Bajrang Dal generally belonged to the same patronage network and I met them at the meetings of all these organizations.

In that light, Rajesh's motivation to join the VHP seems not that exceptional: the VHP offers boys like him a chance to develop influential contacts and (by offering them positions within the organization) to become a local leader. Rajesh can see the benefits that VHP membership has brought to older VHP workers like Rajubhai: this prominent neighbourhood worker, who figured in Chapters 6 and 8, could build his career on the contacts that the VHP provided him with. For such workers the VHP represents an important avenue to develop profitable access to government institutions.

In this sense, the limited capacity of state institutions to provide basic services presents Hindu-nationalist organizations with a twofold opportunity to gain a following. First, these organizations are gaining popularity through their efforts to provide alternative services. The VHP and the RSS are very active in the fields of education and health; they run mobile doctor services, ambulance services and even hospitals and schools (Sundar 2004, Jaffrelot 2006, Hansen 1999). Since the government services in these fields are often deficient, the facilities they provide enable the VHP and the RSS to establish a good reputation, and they provide an avenue to disseminate Hindu-nationalist ideology. Secondly, these organizations' embeddedness in political networks enables them to attract supporters by facilitating their dealings with state institutions. The involvement of Hindu-nationalist organizations in efforts to help inhabitants deal with government institutions has been observed by others as well (Simpson 2006), and also in other parts of the country;[12] the VHP, the RSS and the Bajrang Dal as well as the Shiv Sena can reward their followers with jobs, ration cards, electricity connections, preferential treatment by the police, and so on.

Given the degree to which local VHP and RSS workers are, just like BJP workers, integrated into local patronage networks, we need to interpret their contributions to the rioting in the light of the way in which these networks function. The interdependencies between different actors in these networks (see Chapter 6) engender several incentives for local BJP, VHP and RSS workers to contribute to the rioting. Their position within local patronage networks depends on a constant exchange of favours, in which they build up their local standing and their contacts by performing favours for those people who are likely (and able) to reciprocate the favour in the future. To workers involved in this constant exchange of favours, the riots provide a valuable occasion to perform favours, to win gratitude and to become popular. By showing leadership during the violence itself, or by taking the lead in the various relief efforts—such as providing money, food, health care, etc.—during and after the riots, local workers of the VHP, the RSS and the BJP, as well as Congress, can boost their own local status.

Furthermore, through their activities during the riots these VHP, RSS and BJP workers not only gain local fame, but also win the gratitude and support of influential leaders and politicians. Not only is the promotion of an individual worker within the party or organization often premised on how much work he or she has done, but the careers of such local workers often also depend on the support of influential politicians. As I argued in Chapter 6, the regular exchange of favours that these local workers are engaged in often serves to oblige politicians. In this sense the practice of these local workers to gain influence by performing tasks for higher-ups during 'normal' times—by staging rallies, organizing meetings, distributing propaganda, liaising with officials etc.—is continued during the riots. Their practical contributions to organizing the riots—distributing weapons, arranging the gas-cylinders used to set houses on fire, driving and arranging the trucks to move the rioters, mobilizing the rioters, preparing selection of the targets, distributing food parcels—serves to cement the relations between workers and influential leaders, and to improve their access to state resources.

That does not warrant the conclusion that these workers contributed to killing sprees just because they needed to please their superiors. Many of them will have been genuinely convinced that violence was justified. Some might even have enjoyed the tension and intensity of the riots, while some others might have been motivated by a deep fear of the threat that Muslims were posing—some of the approaches discussed in Chapter 2 are useful to interpret the emotions that undoubtedly played a role. But at the same time these large grassroots networks of Hindu-nationalist activists would not have been there had it not been for the capacity ofVHP and BJP leaders to provide their workers with access to government institutions and resources. These organizations can command the loyalty of large number of workers, not just because of the ideology they disseminate, but also because of the promises of power and money they hold out.

The performance of violence

Another aspect of the 'riot networks' discussed above is the repeatedly observed cooperation between politicians and local *goonda*s. As we have seen in Chapter 8, cooperation between politicians and *goonda*s is an inevitable aspect of local politics in poorer localities. Local liquor dealers, small-time extortionists, gambling hall owners etc. have important reasons to cooperate with politicians. They need to be protected from police intervention; since politicians have a certain degree of control over the police, political support is important to prevent police intervention in their more or less openly illegal businesses. Tacit political support can help to streamline a steady payment of *hapta* (weekly or monthly bribes) to keep their businesses open. Local politicians have several important reasons to provide such support to *goonda*s. Their illegal businesses offer politicians opportunities to increase their 'moneypower'; they all create opportunities for politicians to amass a campaigning budget. These local criminals are also useful because of their 'musclepower': local politicians can use such people with a violent image to improve their capacity to solve local issues. I discussed these interdependencies between *goonda*s and politicians in order to explain why it is important and lucrative for a local *goonda* to develop a violent image: it helps to be known as a 'dangerous' and 'violent' person, because this increases the capacity of an aspiring *goonda* to settle disputes, intimidate people, disrupt meetings etc. With such an image an aspiring *goonda* can be useful to local politicians, since this reputation can serve to establish some local authority.

Such an analysis can help to understand the cooperation of politicians and *goonda*s during riots. The nexus between them predates the riots, and has not been established for the purpose of rioting: the links have been established because their cooperation enables both parties to strengthen their local authority and to develop some control over the functioning of state officials and police officers. Because of these links it is not easy for small-time *goonda*s to resist the exhortations of politicians to commit violence: neglecting such requests could endanger important relationships. Conversely, by performing these 'services', by taking the lead in the burning, looting and killing, such local *goonda*s can win the gratitude of people who can help them to stay in business after the riots. As one informant observed: 'In the time of riots they [*goonda*s] become leaders. If they do not take part, they will spoil their image. In normal times, these people do *dadagiri* ['criminal behaviour': illegal activities]. So he feels that if he would not take leadership in riot times, he would suffer for his misbehaviour in normal times. People will say [if he does take leadership] you helped us, so you can go ahead with your *dadagiri*'. The active participation of local *goonda*s during riots is an exercise in maintaining relations: their contribution to the riots allows them to cement the relations with people who are essential to uphold their livelihood.

Furthermore, riots provide (aspiring) *goonda*s with a stage to showcase their capacity for violence. The riots are an opportunity to inspire fear and awe among their neighbours; the active or tacit support of the police allows them to acquire a violent image without too much risk of arrest or retribution. As I argued above, this makes riots a valuable opportunity: such a display of violence can serve to acquire a useful image of being 'prone to violence'. This image can be a source of income since such an image lends an aspiring *goonda* the leverage to settle disputes, engage in extortion, intimidate rivals, and so on. A noticeable performance during riots can back up the threats and intimidation after riots: by demonstrating a capacity for violence, an aspiring *goonda* can acquire the necessary authority to carry on his semi-illegal activities. In this way, violence during riots serves to limit the use of violence after the riots.

Riots thus provide local *mathabare* people with an opportunity to establish and protect their livelihood. The riots provide an opportunity to establish the image that makes local *goonda*s attractive partners for politicians; once local residents become fearful of an aspiring *goonda*, he becomes useful for politicians as a local enforcer of their authority. In this way, the riots can lead to mutually beneficial relations: once an aspiring *goonda* is noticed by local politicians, he can use their support to prevent (some of the) police intervention in their liquor trading, extortion practices, gambling halls, etc.; such political support will help the business to flourish.

Police and the need for 'situational logic'

A similar argument can be made to interpret the complicity of the police in the rioting. A few weeks after the beginning of the violence, rumours started to circulate in the Indian media about a secret meeting in Narendra Modi's bungalow on the eve of the riots. A state minister testified on the condition of anonymity that during this meeting Modi instructed senior police officials to allow 'people to vent their anger'. Despite pleas from the director general of the police, all those present were ordered to stay out of the way of the Hindu-nationalist activists.[13] A recent investigation of phone records has shown that the police and leading politicians (including the office of Chief Minister Modi) were in constant contact during the violence,[14] which suggests that the lack of police intervention was due to political intervention. In an undercover operation the magazine *Tehelka* gathered more support for this claim: in secretly recorded interviews, several perpetrators of violence claimed that Modi had told the police to 'cooperate'. As one Bajrang Dal worker remarked: 'the police was standing right in front of us, seeing all that was happening, but they had shut their eyes and mouths...If they wanted to stop us, there were 50 of them there, they could have stopped us... We had good support from the police... because of Narendrabhai [Modi]'.[15]

Such claims tally with the testimonies of victims who had approached the police for help: they were given responses like 'today we have orders from above that you are not to be saved' and 'they have been given twenty four hours to kill you' (CCT 2002: 37, HRW 2002: 5). When Vadodara's police commissioner was approached by concerned citizens to protest against the inaction of the police, he answered, 'Whose work would your servant do?', suggesting he had to obey the orders of politicians (CCT 2002: 86). The police were not only told to refrain from intervening in the rioting, they were told whom to arrest and release, what intelligence to gather, even how to register FIR's in such a way that the evidence would be useless in court. Usually such political manipulation of police operations during riots remain within the realm of rumours, but the courageous actions of R.B. Sreekumar brought some aspects of this political pressure into the open. During the riots this police official was in charge of the state's intelligence unit, and in that capacity he clashed repeatedly with both his seniors and with leading politicians. Before he was transferred Sreekumar filed an affidavit[16] about the riots, and later he also disclosed his diary and recordings. These documents create the impression of a completely politicized police force, largely incapable of undertaking action during riots without political approval.[17] Sreekumar describes several meetings with police officials and leading politicians, where action against Hindu activists involved in the rioting was discouraged; this was 'against government policy' and the law needed to be enforced 'according to the situation', following a 'situational logic'.[18]

Sreekumar's disclosures illustrate that it is somewhat simplistic to attribute the complicity of the police in the violence to a communal mind-set in the police force. Clearly the police constables are infused with the same amount of anti-Muslim prejudices and communalist ideology as the average Gujarati citizen. But the lower ranking police officers cannot risk their jobs by disobeying orders from their seniors; they can only risk participating in the riots if their superiors have created the perception that their actions will not be punished. As we saw in Chapter 7, there are two aspects of the professional life of a police officer that limit his or her capacity to contravene the wishes of influential politicians. A first aspect is the political control over the posting and promotion of police officers. The capacity of politicians to arrange the transfer of police officers to remote, dull or difficult places (so called 'punishment postings') puts a high price on any refusal to comply with the wishes of politicians, even if such wishes are partially or wholly illegal. Even a local police inspector or a constable has to maintain good relations with the politicians in power in order to safeguard his career. A second reason for local police officials to maintain good relations with politicians is that good relations pay off, literally. Even for a local constable there are quite a number of ways to earn extra income in localities like Isanpur. As I discussed in Chapter 7, the 'regularization' of illegal activities like gambling or the sale of alcohol, offers various opportunities to make money (by collecting *hapta*, for example). This is risky, if not impossible, without the cooperation of elected politicians; the 'regulation' of these illegal activities usually involves both the police and politicians as well as their workers, who share the bribes. As a result, police officers can hardly risk upsetting their relations with elected politicians. Not only do they risk being transferred out, they also risk endangering important sources of income.

Such day-to-day interactions between politicians and police officers limit the scope for police intervention during the riots. The need for police officers to maintain good relations with elected politicians seriously hampers the capacity of the police to prevent or stop communal violence. The control of politicians over the posting of police officers can greatly discourage any attempt to intervene in the rioting, while, on the other hand, cooperation might lead to future benefits. The pattern of transfers and promotions of the police during and after the violence corroborates this: while cooperating policemen such as police commissioner P.C. Pandey were promoted (he became Director General of Gujarat's police force), a large number of police officers who attempted to stop the rioting and who arrested Hindu-nationalist leaders were quickly transferred to other posts which are generally regarded as 'punishment postings'.[19]

Here again we can see the relation between Gujarat's communal violence and the particular development of Gujarat's state institutions. The difficulties of ordinary citizens in dealing with state institutions have generated a political field in which control over the police is an important asset to gain local support and popularity. Politicians have an active interest in using their control over the transfers of government officials, because their political careers hinge on their capacity to influence these officials' operations. Their interference in the operations of the police has not only politicized the police force, it has effectively limited police officers' capacity to uphold the law in the face of political pressure. As a result the police force cannot function as a bulwark against the instigation of communal violence; in effect politicians' control over the police undermines the capacity and willingness of individual officers to function as custodians of the law.

Conclusion

While discussing the operation of a 'riot network' of neighbourhood leaders, politicians, police, local gangsters and Hindu-nationalist activists, I have put forward three more arguments for relating Ahmedabad's outburst of violence to the day-to-day operations of political networks as mediators between state institutions and citizens. These arguments complement the discussion in the previous chapter, where I argued that communal violence serves the need of political actors to engage in a constant manipulation of the importance that voters attach to different social divisions.

First, the linkages between the different actors within 'riot networks' are formed because of a shared need to acquire and maintain a lucrative control over the functioning of state institutions. The contacts between party workers, *goonda*s, politicians and police officers who contribute to the rioting have not been established for the sole purpose of coordinating and organizing riots; they stem from the daily cooperation of these actors as intermediaries between state institutions and citizens. In this sense the difficulties that citizens encounter when having to deal with state institutions are at the basis of these networks: in order to develop the capacity to mediate between state institutions and citizens, local (political) actors need to cooperate with each other. This daily cooperation generates the networks that, at the times of communal tension, can be used to distribute weapons, bring people to the streets, organize relief, and get people released from jail, etc.

Secondly, the daily work of politicians, party workers and neighbourhood leaders as intermediaries gives these actors the authority and influence to spread rumours, create tensions and trigger violence. In the context of a mediated state, political leaders can use their control over state resources to build up a local base of supporters and to develop local authority and credibility. These local patterns of support and authority play an important role in the mobilization for violence: I have tried to show how the capacity to spread (or counter) rumours and increase acceptance of the use of violence is related to the capacity of local (political) leaders to access state institutions and their resources. A civic body with the capacity to negotiate access to state institutions, like the RJM, can reduce the capacity of political networks to instigate violence.

Thirdly, violence helps various local actors to acquire or improve lucrative access to state institutions. I used my earlier discussion of the interdependencies between *goonda*s, political workers, local state officials and politicians to interpret various local actors' contributions to the rioting. I argued that the position of these actors in the patronage networks as intermediaries between state institutions and citizens motivated them in various ways to contribute to the rioting. The incentives to cooperate during riots are generated by the everyday mediation of the state: in the context of a political field structured by the difficulties of ordinary citizens to access state services, the actors within a wide-ranging network come to depend on each other to profit from their control over the implementation of state policies and laws. In this struggle for control over state resources, the career and income of police officers, *goonda*s, social workers etc. depend on a skilful maintenance of relations. Rioting can—depending on the political context in which it occurs—provide a chance to develop and strengthen these relations, whereas the prevention of violence might damage these relations. Rioting is maintaining relations.

CONCLUSION

POLITICAL MEDIATION, COMMUNAL VIOLENCE AND THE STATE

On a cold winter morning I accompany two of my neighbours to the Isanpur market. The market is, as Mahesh and Hasmukh told me elaborately the evening before, an ideal place to meet girls. Under the pretext of buying fruit and vegetables you can talk and flirt in a way that would be impossible in other places. Mahesh assures me that he has even been seeing a Muslim girl in the market, and he looks forward to meeting her again.

The market is the place where social boundaries, so strictly enforced in other places, are most porous. Men and women, Muslim and Hindu, Dalits and upper castes rummage jointly through the piles of lemons, tomatoes and potatoes, and together they complain to the traders about the decreasing quality and the rising prices of their products. After decades of riots the market is one of the few places in Isanpur where Muslims and Hindus regularly interact.

This morning we do not spot any girl of Mahesh's or Hasmukh's interest, but we do run into a group of young Muslim men. This group regularly hangs out at the market, and Mahesh and Hasmukh seem to know them well. Their leader, who sits in the middle on his scooter, is introduced to me as Rajabhai. 'I am the king of this area', he says, referring to his name. Mahesh and Hasmukh do not seem impressed, and they tease him about his new sunglasses. After some further joking Mahesh tells me that Rajabhai is a famous local Muslim *don* [*goonda*]: 'During the riots he was very active attacking us Hindus'. That makes Rajabhai and his friends laugh. Rajabhai responds, 'That all happened, but we are still good friends. During the riots we fight, but normally it is just Hindu-Muslim *bhai-bhai* [unity]'. Hasmukh tells me that they have been friends with Rajabhai for a long time. 'Only during riots we throw stones at each other, otherwise we are friends'. As everybody bursts out laughing, Rajabhai adds 'Yes that is it, we just like to throw stones at each other from time to time'.

I tried to laugh along. The joyous mood of my friends made it sound funny, but these jokes are tragic. Such jokes suggest a feeling of helplessness, an inability to resist the hurricane of communal hatred that occasionally seems to engulf a neighbourhood. Such jokes make it sound as if communal violence is an atmospheric condition—a common Gujarati word for 'riot' is indeed *tofaan*, hurricane. Mahesh, Hasmukh and Rajabhai need such jokes to maintain relationships that are regularly threatened by political speeches and communal rioting. They often run into each other—in a locality where Muslims and Hindus live in such close proximity it is extremely impractical to maintain communal animosities for a long time. Things happen, and then, somehow, you move on. Even if you have seen your friends in the mobs that burned the houses of your neighbours, the mobs that raped and killed several of your family members. Even if you know that your friends are still close to the local leaders who were leading these mobs. Normal relations need to be resumed. You try to forget what you saw, you blame the killing and the destruction on these dirty politicians, you express grief over what happened and then you try to live together as if nothing happened. At that moment it helps to make jokes: I did what I did, and I might be sorry for it, but—and that is a recurring element in these apologetic jokes—I could not have acted otherwise.

In this book I have focused on the processes of mobilization and instigation through which people like Rajabhai and Mahesh end up in clashing mobs. I have used observations from participants and bystanders during the violence, together with various investigative reports, to discuss the organization and instigation behind outbursts of communal violence. In order to understand this mobilization and cooperation during riots, I have studied the functioning of local political networks in three neighbourhoods in Ahmedabad. In two of these neighbourhoods local politicians played a prominent role during the intense rioting that took place in 2002, while in the third local leaders managed to maintain peace. As I followed the daily routines of local politicians and their followers, I have highlighted the continuity between the activities of political networks during riots and their everyday routine as intermediaries between state institutions and citizens. I have argued that the dependence of citizens on political mediation underlies the capacity and interests of political actors to instigate and organize communal violence. This can help understand why the followers follow: the everyday mediation of the state generates incentives for various local actors—local criminals, party activists, police officers, etc.—to contribute to the violence. In this last chapter I will revisit these conclusions. I will suggest that the arguments in this book about the relation between political mediation and communal violence or ethnic violence—I will use the terms interchangeably[1]—may be useful to study other instances of mass violence outside Gujarat and outside India as well.

Political mediation and violence

One might summarize the current academic debate on India's communal violence—reviewed in Chapter 2—as a standoff between top-down and bottom-up approaches. Top-down arguments (Engineer 1989, 1995, Brass 1996, 1998, 2003, Wilkinson 2004) attribute the outbursts of communal rioting to the strategic calculations of political leaders who create communal tensions and provoke communal riots to serve their electoral interests. The various bottom-up approaches to the study of communal violence, on the other hand, focus on the drives and motivations of those who participate in the rioting. These bottom-up approaches focus, for example, on the pervasiveness of a communal ideology (Jaffrelot 2003, Chandra 1987), on social psychology (Kakar 1996, Nussbaum 2007), on the social construction of perceptions of Hindu-Muslim enmity (Van der Veer 1994, Pandey 1992, Hansen 2001), on changes in India's economy (Breman 2002, 2003), and on the decreased strength of civil society (Varshney 2002) to explain the participation of ordinary people in large violent mobs. A central weakness of many of these bottom-up approaches is that they risk losing sight of the deliberate political strategies behind violence. They might serve as 'blame displacement' (Brass 2003) and exonerate the state because they risk obscuring the agency of political actors in fomenting communal violence. The top-down approaches that focus on political elites, on the other hand, risk sliding into 'conspiracy theories': lacking an account of how political leaders manage to bring large violent mobs out on the streets, these top-down arguments cannot fully explain how and why the instigators of violence manage to tap into the existing fears, hopes and drives of those who actually perpetrate violence.

It has been this book's contention that a focus on the everyday mediation of the state can help integrate elements of this divergent literature: on the one hand a focus on political mediation can help to understand the capacity of political actors to organize and instigate communal rioting, while on the other hand a focus on political mediation can also highlight how broader societal changes—such as Gujarat's changing economy, the spread of Hindu-nationalist ideology and the changed nature of its civil society—affect political actors' capacity and willingness to instigate violence. Riot networks are not just 'institutional riot systems', they are in fact versatile patronage networks: the linkages between the actors who organize and instigate riots are a product of the difficulties that citizens face when dealing with state institutions. The networks engaged in the organization and instigation of violence are, to a large extent, the same intermediary networks that help citizens deal with state institutions. In the preceding chapters I have discussed how politicians, party workers, social workers, but also local criminals, state officials and police officers need each other to develop a profitable capacity to manipulate the implementation of government policies. I have argued that the daily functioning of these intermediary networks shapes the mobilization and instigation that take place during communal riots. Their role as intermediaries lends these various local actors the organizational capacity as well as the local authority to mobilize people for violence. Similarly the motivation of local actors to contribute to the violence can be understood in the light of these actors' position within the patronage networks that mediate between state institutions and local inhabitants: the pattern of their interdependencies gives these actors various incentives to contribute to the rioting. In this way Gujarat's communal violence can be seen as an outcome of the particular way in which the state has come to be embedded in Gujarat's society. To substantiate these arguments I have discussed different connections between the dependence of citizens on political intermediaries and the capacity of political actors to instigate and organize communal violence.

First, the dependence of voters on politicians to gain access to state resources can help to explain why communal violence helps politicians win elections. In the context of a mediated state, a candidate needs to convince voters that he or she, when elected, will be most forthcoming in helping people deal with state institutions. In this way a mediated state creates a political arena in which identity symbols are useful political instruments: as voters look for reassurances of the loyalty and potential usefulness of a candidate to improve their access to government resources, identity symbols and issues with a clear identity-related undertone (on the basis of religion, class, caste or even region) are effective means to signal loyalty and commitment to the targeted group of voters. By invoking the social differences among the electorate in this way, a candidate can convince the targeted group of voters that he or she will be most helpful after elections. In a political context where identity symbols are useful to reassure voters that the candidate, once elected, will indeed facilitate their dealings with the state, the importance that people attach to these identity symbols needs to be manipulated constantly. Communal violence serves this purpose: the rioting serves to bring certain identity dimensions among the electorate (Hindu-Muslim, for example) to the fore while relegating other possible antagonisms (on the basis of caste or region, for example) to the background. Politicians who—through their speeches, patronage and use of symbols—target a Hindu-Muslim division stand to gain from Hindu-Muslim rioting, whereas those who target caste or class divisions stand to lose. The invocation of social divisions, political patronage and the instigation of communal riots are thus three coherent political strategies.

Secondly, citizens' difficulties in dealing with state institutions have generated the linkages between the various local actors involved in fomenting tensions and instigating violence. The cooperation and coordination that can be observed during riots between neighbourhood leaders, the police, local criminals, Hindu-nationalist activists, political party workers and politicians should be understood against the backdrop of the daily interaction between these actors as they cooperate with each other to develop and maintain lucrative access to state resources. Their daily exchange of favours shapes and cements the infrastructure that, at times of communal tension, can be used to spread rumours, bring people to the streets, distribute weapons, and prevent the police from interfering.

Thirdly, the capacity of local leaders to access state resources generates the necessary authority and influence to mobilize large groups of people for rioting. The daily functioning of political actors as intermediaries between state institutions and citizens lends politicians and their various supporters the authority, influence and organizational capacity to spread rumours and legitimize the use of violence. Political actors can use their control over state resources to build up a local base of supporters who are instrumental in spreading rumours and fomenting tensions, and the words of those with good political connections simply carry more weight during the intense discussions and speeches that precede the riots.

Access to state resources is, in itself, an important determinant of local authority: local leadership largely depends on one's capacity to deal successfully with politicians and state authorities. In this sense the dependence of poorer citizens on political intermediaries has greatly politicized social life in their neighbourhoods, since local leaders as well as aspiring local party workers need to develop and maintain their relationships with influential political actors in order to cement their own authority. Attention to the functioning of local patronage networks and their integration into supra-local networks can therefore help to understand why some areas remain peaceful while others see repeated outbursts of violence. I argued that intra- as well as intercommunal engagement limits the capacity of politicians and their supporters to instigate violence, because such civic activity can—under certain conditions—reduce the dependence of citizens on political patronage networks.

Fourthly, the motives of those who participate in (the organization of) the violence are shaped by the interdependencies generated by the everyday mediation of the state. Neighbourhood leaders, party workers, criminals and also local state officials have an interest in maintaining good relations with local politicians in order to protect their jobs and their preferential access to state resources. Rioting is an exercise in maintaining relations: the interdependencies between politicians and these various local actors can help to explain the capacity of politicians to instigate riots. For many local inhabitants rioting is actually a beneficial strategy to further their careers and to protect their livelihoods, because their particular contributions to the violence can help to maintain or strengthen relationships with useful politicians. The dependence of criminals, local party workers and social workers on politicians creates incentives for these actors to contribute to the rioting: they can strengthen important relationships by responding to calls to lead a violent mob, spread rumours, distribute weapons etc. Similarly the political control over the posting of police officers affects the capacity and willingness of the police force to stop communal violence.

For these four reasons the recurring outbursts of Hindu-Muslim violence in Gujarat can be seen as a product of the historical development of the channels providing access to state institutions and resources. The history of these channels has been another important theme of this book. As the Gujarat state gradually expanded the range of services it offered to citizens over the last 200 years, inhabitants gradually turned to the state to solve their various daily problems. As a result, older civic institutions—such as the trade guilds (*mahajans*) and the neighbourhood committees (the *pol panch*)—lost their functionality and authority, while the political networks that could provide access to these expanding resources grew in prominence. In this way the gradual expansion of services that the state provides, together with the limited capacity to meet the demand for these services, underlies the current dependence of ordinary citizens on the mediation of political networks. This is a reason why communal violence can be seen as a modern phenomenon: the preconditions for violence that I discussed in this book—democratic political competition, the dependence of citizens on political mediation, and the politicization of neighbourhood life—are all by-products of the development of modern state institutions.

The current prominence of Hindu-nationalist organizations and their ideology can be understood in the light of the way these organizations have gradually developed the capacity to provide their followers with access to state resources. The current polarization of Gujarati society along religious lines has been facilitated by the control that Hindu-nationalist organizations currently wield over the distribution of state resources. This control, and the absence of alternative political mobilization in Gujarat, can help explain the relative riot-proneness of Gujarat. As most voters in India look to politicians to maximize their access to state resources, a strategy of targeting some groups of voters and excluding other groups can be observed throughout India. But while in other states caste, class or regional cleavages have served this purpose, such cleavages have been less prominent in Gujarat's politics since the 1980s. Unlike most other Indian states, Gujarat has not seen a sustained and successful political mobilization on the basis of caste or class divisions over the last thirty years. As the competition for control over the resources of the state often been fought under the banner of religion, a barrage of accusations and grievances have constantly reinforced the tensions between the two religious communities. Both political rhetoric and the functioning of local patronage channels have created the impression that one's religious identity is closely bound up with one's chances of benefiting from the resources and jobs that the Gujarat state provides. This impression that a member of another religious community is also a competitor is dangerous: together with the growing insecurities caused by the integration of Gujarat's economy in global markets, the shifting patterns of state-society interaction helped to create the political atmosphere in which the 2002 Hindu-Muslim violence could take place.

This political atmosphere should also be related to the gradual liberalization of Gujarat's economy. The resulting efforts to reduce labour costs to the lowest possible level have led to the demise of Gujarat's once prominent textile industry and its trade union, and forced the poorer sections of society into more insecure and temporary labour contracts. As Gujarat's textile industry gradually collapsed the Textile Labour Association gradually lost members, which undermined the organizational basis for a political mobilization based on socio-economic interests. The patronage channels around the TLA that offered workers access to state resources collapsed, which intensified the dependence on the channels offered by Hindu-nationalist organizations. Furthermore, the informal and fleeting nature of the employment of the poorest sections of society makes these citizens very dependent on the political networks discussed in this book. In the absence of much other stable sources of income, people have been very dependent on the jobs and resources that the state provides. This has led to a politicization of neighbourhoods and the proliferation of the social workers and party workers that figure so prominently in this book. The dependence on political intermediaries has made poorer citizens more susceptible to the political exploitation of Hindu-Muslim divisions.

Political mediation and violence in India and beyond

It is not just in India that politicians and their supporters play a prominent role during outbursts of communal or ethnic violence. As Horowitz concludes in *The Deadly Ethnic Riot*, a comprehensive study of 150 incidents of communal violence in 50 countries, 'organization without political support rarely produces deadly ethnic riots. Of those riots having a serious organizational element, the vast majority are organized either by political parties or by those who have some connection to parties' (2001: 253). Other recent comparative studies on a wide range of instances of mass violence—from Rwanda to the Armenian genocide, from the war in the former Yugoslavia to the Holocaust—similarly concluded that 'the impetus for mass killing usually originates from a relatively small group of powerful political or military leaders (...) Mass violence occurs when powerful groups come to believe it is the best available means to accomplish certain radical goals' (Valentino 2004: 2 and 66, Mann 2005, Snyder 2000). Compared to earlier studies on mass violence (see Straus 2007), these recent comparative studies have put more emphasis on the relation between democratic political competition and violence. In an impressive study of the incidence of mass violence across the globe, Mann (2005: 502) argues that ethnic cleansing is an unplanned political strategy, most likely to be adopted by elites in weakly institutionalized democracies that function along ethnic lines: 'Modern ethnic cleansing is the dark side of democracy when ethnonationalist movements claim the state for their own *ethnos*, which they initially intend to constitute as a democracy, but then they seek to exclude and cleanse others'. Countries that go through a democratization process are particularly likely to experience violence, because the changing political equations stimulate political elites to invoke ethnic divisions as a means to maintain their grip on power. As Snyder (2000: 22) argued, '[d]emocratization produces nationalism when powerful groups within the nation (...) want to avoid surrendering real political authority to the average citizen'.

But despite signalling a need for a 'sociology of power' (Mann 2005: 9) to understand how elites mobilize ordinary people for violence, and despite various references to the functioning of patronage networks, these comparative studies do not pay systematic attention to the relation between the specific embeddedness of a state in society and the political dynamic leading to mass violence.[2] The occasional observations about the material incentives that patronage channels can offer to participants in violence are treated as a corollary to general arguments about the relation between weakly institutionalized democracies and violence. Such observations are not taken up—as this study has suggested—as important clues to understand why violence occurs in some places and not in other places, nor as clues about the attractiveness of communal or nationalist ideologies. Nor do these studies offer systematic inquiry into how the specific structure and functioning of local patronage channels affect the mobilization that takes place during episodes of mass violence. A comparative and more systematic focus on state-society mediation could serve to better understand the relation between democracy, economic development and violence. A focus on different patterns of state-society interaction—on how historical contingencies, economic development and state policies affect the dependence of citizens on political intermediaries, on how patronage channels come to be organized on ethnic lines, on how a dependence on political mediation stimulates politicians to employ a communal, exclusionary ideology, etc.—can further our understanding of the way the day-to-day functioning of democratic institutions affects the capacity and willingness of political elites to mobilize ordinary people for violence.

In order to illustrate how this focus on state-society mediation might be relevant to study of other instances of ethnic or communal violence, let me use the last paragraphs of this book to compare, briefly, Gujarat's Hindu-Muslim violence with the Christian-Muslim violence that occurred in different parts in Indonesia between 1999 and 2003, and the genocide perpetrated by a Hutu majority against the Tutsi population in Rwanda in 1994. My very brief discussion of these two very different cases will not do full justice to the complexities behind these outburst of violence, but it will, I hope, illustrate the wider applicability of some of the arguments in this book.

At first glance these instances of mass violence might seem hardly comparable to the communal violence that took place in Gujarat in 2002. The killings in Rwanda, in which an estimated 800,000 people died in violence between two ethnic groups, involved a much larger part of the population than in Gujarat and Indonesia, where the violence took place between religious groups. The violence in both Indonesia and Rwanda took place during a turbulent phase of democratization, when new political parties had entered the political arena and more power was being devolved to local state levels. The genocide in Rwanda took place amidst the escalation of a civil war between RPF rebels—associated with the Tutsis—and the Rwandan government run by Hutu hardliners. At the same time the increased political competition between the two main Hutu parties, the MDR and the MRNDD, seems to have stimulated politicians to employ a political rhetoric about 'Hutu power'. In Indonesia the rapid political changes that enveloped the country after Suharto's removal from power in 1998 intensified the competition between local ethnic elites over key government posts. In Maluku and Sulawesi the violence was intensified by the arrival of an outside Islamic militia, the Lashkar Jihad. By contrast such dramatic changes have not taken place in Gujarat, where democratic institutions have been functioning in a more or less stable fashion for decades, with regularly recurring outbursts of violence.

Despite such obvious differences, and despite the very different historical and cultural background to these instances of violence, we can see some illuminating similarities if we limit our attention to the way the violence was organized and instigated. First, the available material about the processes of mobilization for the violence in Rwanda and Indonesia suggests that, as in Gujarat, the networks involved in the organization and perpetration of violence overlapped with the networks of actors that mediated access to state resources. Many observers argue that Rwanda's genocide perpetrated by the Hutu majority on a Tutsi minority was planned and coordinated by a small clique of leaders within Rwanda's ruling party (the MRNDD), a clique referred to as *akazu*, or 'little house'. This clique could make use of its control over the state to command the obedience of government officials: 'most reluctant officials and policemen soon felt forced to cooperate out of fear and anxiety to preserve their career and patronage positions' (Mann 2005: 453). In many parts of Rwanda the genocide was overseen by elected officials like the *bourgmestres* and the prefects in cooperation with the *Interahamwe*, a militia linked to the ruling party. The youths who were recruited by the *Interahamwe*—the organization that committed most of the killings in Rwanda—often seem to have been motivated by promises of material rewards (Des Forges 1999, Boersema 2007): as an organization allied to the ruling political party, the *Interahamwe* could attract youths with promises of access to state resources. Des Forges (1999: 10) argues that 'the organizers of the genocide similarly exploited the structures that already existed—administrative, political, and military—and called upon personnel to execute a campaign to kill Tutsi and Hutu presumed to oppose Hutu Power. Through these three channels, the organizers were able to reach all Rwandans and to incite or force most Hutu into acquiescing in or participating in the slaughter'.

During the various instances of communal violence in Indonesia, existing patronage channels played a similarly important role in fomenting tensions and mobilizing violent mobs. When after Suharto's forced resignation in 1998 the established hierarchies of power in many Indonesian islands became unstable and the competition for control over the state intensified, local patrons began to draw upon the available patronage channels to mobilize support. Under Indonesia's new order the patronage channels in Maluku and

Sulawesi had largely formed along communal lines (Bertrand 2002: 85) and membership of religious organizations had become important to acquire the support of powerful patrons. Van Klinken (2007: 78) argues for example: 'The relationship between a civilian bureaucrat and powerful patrons needed strong personal elements of trust to work (...) religion was an important vehicle for building such trust. All the civilian bureaucrats [in Sulawesi] combined bureaucratic ladder climbing with active religious affiliation'. As a result, the intensified competition for state power quickly acquired communal overtones: in both Sulawesi and Maluku the violence between Christians and Muslims broke out at the time when new appointments and/or election of top positions within the district administration were due. The selection of the top bureaucrats in the region was highly contested: the religious affiliation of the appointee could determine which religious group would have best access to the bureaucracy (Aragon 2001: 57). This motivated both communities to mobilize to press for the appointment of 'their' candidates. Van Klinken (2007: 18) concludes that the violence that affected Indonesia after Suharto's resignation 'was not so much a product of popular grievances as a result of mobilisation of powerful local patrons competing with each other'.

Another similarity is that, like in Gujarat, the authority and influence of those actors engaged in instigating violence in Indonesia and Rwanda seemed to rest on the capacity of these actors to control (and provide access to) state resources. The 'culture of obedience' that Prunier (1999) advances as an explanation for the violence in Rwanda seems to have been sustained by the practice of patronage that helped people to gain access to the limited resources of the state. The capacity to access state resources seemed to have given non-state actors the necessary authority to circumvent state officials when they were unwilling to support the genocide: Boersema (2007), McDoom (2005) and Strauss (2004) show that in those districts where government officials opposed the violence, these officials could be sidetracked by local leaders with strong connections to national politicians.

Van Klinken (2007) describes how the mobilization for the violence in Kalimantan and Sulawesi as well as Maluku mainly proceeded along the lines of pre-existing clientelistic networks and organizations. Local thugs and 'provocateurs' close to important politicians, as well as the Pemuda Pancasila, a political youth group, are said to have played an important role in the violence (see also ICG 2001, ICG 2002, HRW 1999). Aragon (2001) explicitly relates the patterns of the violence in Sulawesi to the structure of local patronage channels: she notes that leaders in the towns could draw on their communal organizations to foment violence in far away districts, while nearby areas in which these organizations were relatively weak remained peaceful. She describes how the violence in Sulawesi spread from urban centres to rural areas through the patron-client networks that linked villages to the main towns.

Such observations invite numerous comparisons with the manner in which the communal violence in Gujarat was organized: I have described in this book how leadership and local prominence in Ahmedabad are similarly tied up with a capacity to deal with state authorities. The integration of such local leaders into broader patronage networks enables these leaders to play a prominent role during the rioting and the intense discussions that precede the outbreak of violence. The spreading of rumours during the riots and the mobilization of large masses of people were facilitated in a similar way by the fact that the instigators could make use of patronage channels that had tentacles in almost every street or village. The motives of various participants in the violence seems similarly related to the prospect of gaining access to state resources, and the motivation of the youths joining the *Interahamwe* might not be too dissimilar from the motivation of those joining the VHP, the Bajrang Dal or the RSS.

With such a brief comparison I cannot do justice to the complexities of the violence in Rwanda and Indonesia, and the scope of this conclusion does not allow me to go deeper into the similarities that I perceive between these different instances of violence. My purpose here is merely to suggest that such comparisons could be fruitful: as the patterns of mobilization and instigation behind communal violence in different parts of the world are shaped in comparable ways by the daily functioning of the networks that mediate between state institutions and citizens, it can be fruitful to compare the relation between political mediation and communal violence in different parts of the world. By focusing on the relation between the occurrence of violence and the specific embeddedness of the state in society we can integrate different approaches to the study of violence, because such a focus can help to understand not only the political dynamic that propels elites to exploit social divisions and employ exclusionary ideologies, but also the mechanisms through which these leaders make use of the desires and fears of their followers. By looking at the specific structure of the networks involved in the mediation between state institutions and ordinary citizens, we can grasp how and why different people can be motivated to contribute to violence.

A comparative focus on political mediation can alert us to the fact that instigators of mass violence often benefit from the particular strengths and weaknesses of state institutions. The patterns of mobilization in Gujarat cast doubt on the often-made claim that communal violence is a result of the weakness or low capacity of the state (see for example Tilly 2003: 26–54, Brubaker and Laitin 1998: 424). This claim could be made more specific because it obscures the fact that the networks that foment violence make use of their control over the resources of the state to mobilize people. As Prunier argued in relation to Rwanda (1995: 354), 'The genocide did not happen because the state was weak, but on the contrary because it was so totalitarian and strong that it had the capacity to make its subjects obey absolutely any order, including one of mass slaughter'. Van Klinken (2007, see also Bertrand 2002) similarly argues that communal violence in Indonesia is most likely in districts where the operations of the state make up a comparatively large part of the local economy, because such dependence on the resources of the state generates an intense competition over those resources. As I have tried to show in this book, the functioning of the local networks of politicians, police officers, local criminals and party workers is shaped by both the range of services that state institutions provide and the difficulties that citizens face when trying to get access to these services. People need these various mediators because the state has valuable services to offer and because citizens have difficulty gaining access to these services. These two aspects, the expanded reach and limited strength of Gujarat's state, underlie the formation and functioning of the local patronage networks involved in the instigation and organization of violence.

Both the scope of the state's activities and its strength to implement its policies in various fields shape the interaction between political actors, state officials and voters, and structure the competition for power over the resources of the state. When states are really weak, in the sense that they have little to offer to citizens, local leaders or 'local strongmen' derive their power more from control over non-state resources, such as trade-flows or natural resources, prestige or wealth. They gain support by offering alternative strategies for survival, independently of the state (Reno 1995, Migdal 1988). But when the state develops the capacity to offer various valuable services—from basic amenities and regulating trade to maintaining law and order—the sources of social control begin to change: gradually control over the resources of the state becomes an important determinant of local leadership. When, in this context, state institutions depend on local leaders to implement state policies and distribute resources, these leaders have an interest in monopolizing the interaction with state institutions: their capacity to facilitate the interaction between those institutions and citizens is an important determinant of their power. In that context country-wide political networks can come into being that link the remotest villages to the centres of power. The existence of these networks, and the dependence of ordinary citizens on them, provide political leaders with the infrastructure needed to spread prejudices and organize mass-violence.

A comparative focus on the nature of patronage channels can also help to understand how a society comes to be polarized along communal or ethnic lines. Not everywhere are patronage networks organized along ethnic or communal lines, and sometimes patronage networks incorporate different, overlapping social divisions. But when the available channels that provide access to state resources are mainly organized on the basis of membership of an ethnic or religious community, competition for control over these state resources can contribute to a heightened sense of distrust and ill-will between different communities: in this context members from another community form a threat to one's chances of securing a government job, a place in a good school, an electricity connection, a license to start a business, etc. When the available patronage channels are organized on the basis of communal differences, members from the other community represent an almost personal threat to one's livelihood and one's chances of progressing in life.

Similarly, a focus on the nature of local patronage channels can help us to understand why rioting occurs repeatedly in some areas while other areas remain peaceful: by looking at the different structure and affiliation of local patronage channels we can improve our understanding of the often seemingly erratic spread of violence throughout a city, region or country. The importance of clientelistic networks during the mobilization for violence suggests that violence is more likely to occur in areas where citizens are most dependent on political mediation, and where local leaders are affiliated to patronage channels that stand to gain from the violence. By looking at the structure of the networks that provide access to state resources, and studying whether these networks are organized along communal lines, we can gain some insight into why political leaders are capable of instigating violence in some areas while they fail to stir up trouble in other areas.

Violence and vulnerability

People like Rajabhai or Mahesh did not just join violent mobs out of intense communal hatred. Ultimately, they joined these mobs because their dependence on political mediation made them vulnerable to the conflict-mongering of politicians and their supporters. The conclusions of this study suggest that the prospects of reducing Hindu-Muslim violence in India are closely tied up with the prospects of reducing the dependency of citizens on political mediation. The political dynamics behind the violence can only be structurally changed if, on the one hand, measures are taken to improve the capacity of poorer citizens to deal successfully with state institutions without political interference and if, on the other hand, economic growth in Gujarat can become more inclusive.

Of course it would help to combat the communal ideologies that fill Hindus and Muslims with hatred and distrust towards each other. And of course it is necessary to criticize political parties that make use of communal tensions for political gain, as it is important to maintain the brave efforts to bring the perpetrators of communal violence to justice.[3] Similarly it remains vital to stir up public debate about the political manipulation of social and religious identities; this book is an attempt in that direction.

However, to some extent that is merely fighting the symptoms of the problem. The exploitation of communal tensions, and the communal ideologies that sustain it, are not intrinsic to one political group or party—these practices are part and parcel of the nature of a political game in which the instigation of violence is a beneficial political strategy. In order to tackle the capacity and incentives to instigate violence, the nature of the political game itself needs to be changed by tackling the dependence of citizens on political mediation. The bureaucracy needs to be made more responsive to the wishes and demands of ordinary citizens without the intervention of political intermediaries. And a more inclusive form of economic growth is needed to reduce the reliance of poorer citizens on state resources: once citizens can find more secure and stable livelihoods, access to state resources (through political intermediaries) will become less enviable and arouse less contention.

Such developments—a more accessible and effective bureaucracy and more inclusive economic growth—could change the dynamics discussed in this book. Poorer neighbourhoods would no longer be filled with workers of political parties, as their relations with politicians would no longer earn them their livelihood—or at least other sources of income would become more attractive. Political actors would no longer be the most influential people in these neighbourhoods, as their role in daily life would be limited. The police would be more active in preventing riots, as the political interference in their work would be reduced, and political leaders might be less inclined to exploit social divisions for political gain: as voters would be less dependent on the cooperation of politicians to gain access to the state, there might be fewer reasons to invoke caste or religious identities in order to ensure the cooperation of politicians.

Such changes do not just involve a gradual development of Gujarat's economy or the capacities of the Gujarati state. They also involve enacting the right policies and, ultimately, political will. The dependence on political mediation is sustained by the currently very limited investment in public services in poorer neighbourhoods. It is sustained by the current unwillingness of political elites to halt the relentless drive to lower labour costs. The dependence on political mediation could be reduced, for example, by addressing the scarcity of basic amenities and by enacting measures to ensure a stricter separation of the executive and legislative wings of government. It could be reduced by reconsidering the central features of the transfer system: as their control over transfers is currently one of the most important instruments used by politicians to control the bureaucracy, a change in this transfer system could limit the political interference in the functioning of the bureaucracy. The dependence on political mediation could also be reduced by developing new ways—through ward committees, NGOs, the press, etc.—of making state bureaucracies more accountable and more accessible to poorer citizens. And, although I cannot fully explore this here, the material in this book also provides some support for current efforts[4] to introduce some elements of a proportional electoral system into India's majoritarian ('first-past-the-post') electoral system, as this could make some of the political strategies discussed in this book—particularly the political exploitation of social divisions and the nurturing of local patronage channels—less beneficial.

Such changes in the relations between politicians and bureaucrats are not easy to bring about, and I am not too optimistic about the necessary political will to enforce such measures: in the end such changes are decided upon by politicians who, themselves, have a large stake in maintaining the dependence on their mediation. As I have described in this book, the strategies adopted by politicians tend to reproduce that dependence. As political careers often depend on the capacity to develop and maintain control over the bureaucracy, politicians might not be expected to enact measures to relinquish that control. But the separate levels of Indian government—the local, the state and the central level—might at least offer some opportunities: measures adopted at a central or state level could affect power relations in local arenas.

I hope the courage and political will can be found to bring about such changes. It has been the rise of the modern Indian state and its complex embeddedness in society that has laid the groundwork for the outbursts of violence between Hindus and Muslims in Gujarat. The future of Hindu-Muslim relations will depend on whether the courage and political will can be found to enact measures to reduce the vulnerability of poorer citizens and their dependence on political mediation. Inclusive economic growth and a more accessible and responsive state can lay the basis for a political arena that is less violent and more conducive to communal harmony.

NOTES

PREFACE AND ACKNOWLEDGEMENTS

1. See for example the repeated threats to journalists of the monthly *Communalism Combat*, or the legal harassment of the weekly *Tehelka*. See also the 2004 report *Discouraging Dissent: Intimidation and Harassment of Witnesses, Human Rights Activists and Lawyers* by Human Rights Watch.
2. Recent examples are the documentaries *War and Peace* by Anand Pardwardhan and *Final Solution* by Rakesh Sharma, which were banned by the Indian Censor Board.

1. INTRODUCTION: RIOT NETWORKS IN AHMEDABAD

1. In an interview with 'Hotline', see Setalvad 2002: 16.
2. According to these figures, released by the Gujarat State government in May 2005, 223 people were still missing.
3. There are good reasons to assume that the government statistics underestimate the number of victims. These numbers are based on reported deaths and injuries at hospitals and police-stations. At the time of rioting it was not always possible for (the families of) the victims to report there: not only was it often dangerous to go to the hospitals, the police were also seen as the perpetrators of the violence. This makes it likely that a number of people who died were never reported to the authorities—even though financial compensation required such reporting. The number of dead I heard about in Isanpur exceeded the official count. A survey done by Action Aid counted 24 deaths in Isanpur alone, while official statistics speak of 29 deaths in Isanpur and two (equally violent) neighbouring wards (see note 9). For a list of the reports of human rights organizations that estimate the death toll at around 2000, see note 6.
4. Or 110 billion rupees. This is the estimate of the Gujarat Chamber of Commerce and Industry. See 'Far from business as usual', *The Hindu*, 5–5–2002.
5. The refugees were put up in 81 relief camps throughout the state. Around ten thousand of those displaced have still not been able to return. See Mander 2006.
6. For detailed descriptions of the violence in Ahmedabad as well as other parts of Gujarat, see the following investigative reports: Concerned Citizens Tribunal, *Crime against Humanity. Volume 1 and 2*, Mumbai: Citizens for Justice and Peace, 2002;

Human Rights Watch, *'We have no orders to save you': State Complicity and Participation in Communal Violence in Gujarat*, New York: Human Rights Watch, 2002; International Initiative for Justice, *Threatened Existence: A Feminist Analysis of the Genocide in Gujarat*, Mumbai: IIJ, 2003, People's Union for Civil Liberties (PUCL), *Violence in Vadodara: A Report*, Vadodara: PUCL, 2002; People's Union for Democratic Rights (PUDR), *'Maaro! Kaapo! Baalo!': State, Society and Communalism in Gujarat*, Delhi: PUDR, 2002; Teesta Seetalvad *et al.*, 'Genocide: Gujarat 2002', *Communalism Combat*, 8 (76), 2002; Siddharth Varadarajan (ed.), *Gujarat, the Making of a Tragedy*, New Delhi: Penguin Books India, 2002.

7. Dalits are those castes that occupy the lowest ranks in India's complex caste hierarchy and who, according to traditional Hindu beliefs, fall outside the Hindu caste system. The term 'Untouchables' and Gandhi's word 'Harijans' (children of God) are sometimes also used to refer to this group.
8. T. Macwana (2002). 'Uncivil War', *Voice of the Weak* (6), p. 6. Tikesh Macwana was a Dalit activist who lived in Isanpur.
9. The descriptions of the violence in Isanpur are based on interviews with local residents, on reports of the riots in Isanpur (*Communalism Combat* (CC) 2002: 39, Concerned Citizens Tribunal (CCT) 2002: 52–61, HRW 2002: 25–6) as well on the FIR's (first information reports) about the incidents that local residents as well as the police submitted at the local police stations.
10. Such brutality against women was widespread. Throughout Gujarat women were stripped naked, mass-raped, had their genitals mutilated, and in some cases even their foetuses ripped from their bodies before they were burned to death (see especially IIJ 2003, Women's Panel 2002 and PUCL 2002). The testimonies of the survivors of these attacks are extremely disturbing, such as this remark from a young girl during an interview in a refugee camp (HRW 2002: 30): "Shall I tell you?', volunteers a nine-year old, 'Rape is when a woman is stripped naked and then burned'.'
11. Of the 29 people who, according to police statistics, died in Isanpur and two neighbouring municipal wards (in the period between 28 February and 22 April), 16 died as a result of police firing. Of these 29 deaths, two were Hindu and 22 Muslim (five unknown). 138 people were injured, 86 of whom were hospitalized ('Polis golibaarma 16na mot', *Gujarat Today*, 22–4–06). It is reasonable to suspect that these statistics underestimate the number of victims; during a survey the NGO Action Aid counted 24 deaths among Muslims in Isanpur alone.
12. "Newton' Modi has a lot of explaining to do', *Times of India* 3–3–2002.
13. Ahmedabad's police commissioner PC Pandey's comment on the riots in *Newshour* (Star News).
14. VHP vice-president Giriraj Kishore in 'Violence result of natural outburst: Giriraj Kishore', *Times of India* 1 March 2002.
15. For an overview of the criminal record of leading Gujarati politicians, see 'Gujarat Election Watch (2002)' by the Association for Democratic Reforms, available at www.adrindia.org.
16. See note 6.
17. See CCT: 56. Human Rights Watch (2002: 23) noted that in the months prior to the riots people had been going around with lists to determine the addresses of Muslim businesses; allegedly these lists were used to target these establishments during the riots.
18. See 'The truth. In the words of the men who did it', *Tehelka* 3–11–2007, for numerous interviews with rioters, politicians, lawyers, and VHP-activists. The

interviewed discuss how they distributed weapons, liaised with the police, trained local cadres, organized meetings to plan a strategy and perpetrated gruesome acts of violence. The quotation is taken from an interview with Arvind Pandya, a lawyer who helped rioters escape jail sentences.

19. See note 6, as well as my article on the spatial distribution of riots in Ahmedabad (Berenschot 2011).
20. In addition to Brass' work (see esp. Brass 2003) there are articles by Veena Das (2005) and Javed Alam (1993) that focus on the different levels of violence between neighbourhoods. I consider their conclusions and ethnographic material—which also illustrates the role of local patronage networks in the violence—to be in line with the arguments presented here.
21. In his book on collective violence Tilly (2003: 5–8) distinguishes three categories: idea people, behaviour people and relational people. Idea people, according to Tilly, focus on ideas as the drive behind violence, while behaviour people focus on the individual motives and impulses of those who engage in violence. A relational approach 'concentrates on ways that variable patterns of social interaction constitute and cause different varieties of collective violence'.

2. EXPLAINING INDIA'S HINDU-MUSLIM VIOLENCE

1. For an encompassing chronicle of the often chilling incidents that took place during partition, see Butalia 1998.
2. The dataset on incidence of communal violence that Varshney and Wilkinson compiled (on the basis of newspaper reports of incidents of communal violence that took place between 1950 and 1995) indicates that communal violence is largely an urban phenomenon; they found that there were more than 15 times more riot-related deaths reported in cities than in rural areas. See Varshney 2002: 96.
3. See Rajeshwari 2004 for an overview of all the major outburst of communal violence since 1947.
4. In India the term 'communal violence' is more commonly used than 'ethnic violence', even though the terms often denote the same phenomenon. Ethnic violence refers to violent conflict between communities differentiated by their ethnicity—i.e. their descent, language, history or physical appearance or religion. In India the term communal violence has been more common to capture violent conflict between religious communities as well as caste groups.
5. This is based on data from 1950–1995; after 2002 Ahmedabad will have surpassed Bombay in this ranking.
6. These numbers were given by the Assistant General of Police to India's Election Commission, and reported by Oommen (2005: 120).
7. This figure is again based on government figures of the number of injured (2,500) and the number killed (1,044) during the 2002 riots, released in May 2005. As victims who did not report their injuries in a hospital or a police station were not counted, one can safely assume the real number to be much higher: during the rioting it was often not advisable to cross the city to go to a hospital or a police station, and since the police displayed such a hostile attitude towards Muslims, we can assume that many felt discouraged from approaching the police.
8. See particularly CCT 2002 (volume 2: 44–8), and Setalvad *et al.* 2002: 94–5. For a list of the different reports on the Gujarat violence, see Chapter 1, note 6.
9. 'Far from business as usual', *The Hindu*, 5–5–2002.

10. See CCT 2002 (vol. 2, 51–9). In the neighbourhoods I studied I came to the same conclusion: in Maneknagar and especially Isanpur the VHP, the Bajrang Dal seemed to have stepped up its activities in the months before the incident in Godhra.
11. See Manu Joseph, 'From the Devil's lair', *Outlook*, 3 June 2002, as well as the interviews conducted by *Tehelka*.
12. A recent investigation into the phone records of police officers and leading politicians brought to light that the communication between them was very intense during the riots (e.g. Ahmedabad's police commissioner Pande received up to 15 calls a day from the office of Chief Minister Modi), which lends further credence to the suspicion that the police failure to intervene in the riots was at the behest of politicians. See Teesta Seetalvad, 'Dial M. for Massacre', *Communalism Combat*, June 2010.
13. 'The truth. In the words of the men who did it'. *Tehelka* 3–11–2007, page 41.
14. See CCT 2002, vol. 2: 26.
15. On the violence against women, see especially IIJ 2003, Women's Panel 2002 and PUCL 2002.
16. The Best Bakery case (about the burning of a family during the riots) and the Bilkis Bano case (of a woman who was gang raped while her family was being killed) are two famous cases that, after the Supreme Court intervened, have been tried outside Gujarat, and have led to convictions. For an overview of major cases, see www.cjponline.org.
17. In secretly recorded interviews with *Tehelka*, VHP activists boast that judge Nanavati is supporting them (see *Tehelka*, 'The Truth. In the words of the men who did it', 3–11–07), while the organization Citizens for Justice and Peace and its lead activist Teesta Seetalvad have criticized the superficial nature of the early SIT investigations (see 'SIT-ting on the Truth', *Communalism Combat*, March 2010).
18. See Mandar 2006. Mandar cites a survey done for the National Human Rights Commission, which puts the number of families living in the relief camps at 10,000.
19. On Hindu-nationalist ideology, see Basu *et al.* 1993, Nandy *et al.* 1995, Van der Veer 1994, Blom Hansen 1999, Anderson 1987, Punyani 2004.
20. For a discussion of these 'education wars' over textbooks, see Nussbaum 2007: 264–302.
21. The following passage can serve as an illustration of how the capacity to instigate violence is often not questioned, but assumed. Brass (1996: 12), describing a sequence of events leading up to rioting, argues: '[the sequence that leads to rioting] is a much more diverse and complex one which may or may not begin with existing social prejudices. Sometimes, those prejudices need to be created first where none existed before, as in the case of Hindus and Sikhs. The second step is the politicization of those differences. The third is the selection or development of sites where it is politically advantageous to allow or disadvantageous to prevent the proliferation of riot specialists and of institutionalized systems of riot promotion. The fourth, which follows as it were naturally, is the transformation of the environment in which all these events are taking place into a social problem'. This—in itself interesting—description of a sequence leading to riots assumes too readily the capacity of various instigators to 'create prejudices', 'politicize differences' and 'allow the proliferation of riot specialists' 'as it were naturally': this anal-

ysis lacks an account of how and why such instigators are capable of bringing about these different 'steps'.

22. Tambiah (1996: 276) advances a similar argument in his study on ethnic violence in south Asia: 'the greater the blurrings of and ambiguities between the socially constructed categories of difference, the greater the venom of the imposed boundaries, when conflict erupts, between the self and other, 'us' and 'them''.
23. Hansen writes (1999: 107) that the 'formation of militant groups often take place (....) when a group or already formed community experiences a pronounced sense of loss of meaning and identity, of humiliation in the wake of dislocations (war, urbanisation, migration, or rapid modernisation)'.
25. The difficulty of completely surmounting this dichotomy can be seen in a criticism that is often levelled at Bourdieu's work; it is often seen as too deterministic because, his critics argue, it leaves too little scope for understanding and interpreting social change (Jenkins 1992). Bourdieu's reaction to this criticism is characteristic of his approach, and betrays an idea of the goal of social science which I share: 'How not to see that by articulating the social determinants of practices... the sociologist creates the possibility for a certain liberty vis-à-vis these determinants'. (Bourdieu 1987: 26, my translation)
25. Bourdieu used the analogy with a market to discuss how there are several competing discourses 'on offer' between which voters have to choose, arguing that 'the well informed politician is the one who manages to master practically the objective meaning and social effect of his stances by virtue of having mastered the space of actual and especially potential stances'. (Bourdieu 1991: 177–8). As I will argue in Chapter 8, in a political field structured by the difficulties large parts of the population have in dealing with government institutions, the space of actual and potential stances is shaped by the necessity to make use of available different identity dimensions (Hindu-Muslim, upper caste-lower caste etc.) to differentiate themselves.

3. THE COMING OF THE CHAMCHAS AND THE POLITICIZATION OF GUJARAT'S NEIGHBOURHOODS

1. Apart from Ahmedabad *pols* can be found in Cambay, Baroda, Vaso, Sidhpur and Patan
2. *Chamchas* are usually men; especially since the enactment of a reservation of seats for women (one-third) in the municipal council, there are female party workers as well, but not so many: since their activities involve the maintenance of many different contacts, and since this often takes place on street corners after dark, women find it difficult to establish these contacts for themselves without getting the image of having a 'loose character'. See Chapter 6.
3. Mann distinguishes infrastructural power from 'despotic power'. The despotic power of a state refers to the extent to which ruling elites can execute any actions within the state's territory without depending on the consent or cooperation of the affected population. The infrastructural power, in turn, refers to the penetration of the state within society: to the extent to which the state can implement legislation and policies throughout its territory.
4. In a very different context Abram de Swaan used the Dutch term '*verstatelijking*' to describe how state institutions gradually acquired a wider responsibility for the care

of the young, the sick and the elderly in Western Europe and the US. With that term De Swaan aimed to describe how state institutions gradually take over functions that were previously performed by family members or by more private care arrangements (De Swaan 1982, 2004). An English equivalent of the term might be 'statification'.

5. In this sense this chapter can be read as an Indian illustration of Elias' assertion that 'the structure and pattern of interdependencies between people who have their home in the same locality change with the development of societies. (...) The development of communities (...) goes hand in hand with state formation processes as well as with the process rather narrowly conceptualized as 'division of labour (...) or, briefly, as 'social differentiation' (Elias 1974: xx, xxxviii).
6. Written material on the functioning of the *pol panches* is scarce. For a comprehensive study on the life in Ahmedabad's *pols*, see Doshi 1974, as well as Misra 1981. Two Gujarati sources, Dalal 1990 (1948) and Ratnamanirao 1929, contain valuable descriptions as these authors have lived in the *pols*.
7. There are some references to some form of organization of neighbourhoods (*mohalas*) in Mughal sources as well, see Misra 1981: 85. And Ratnamanirao (1929: 322) claims that the *pols* were established at the time the city was established, that is, in 1411.
8. On trade in 17th and 18th century Gujarat, see Gokhale 1969 and Gupta 1981.
9. For an overview of Gujarat's and Ahmedabad's history in this period, see Gillion 1968 and Yagnik and Sheth 2005.
10. For this translation from the original Gujarati—as well for as the translations below—I am indebted to the valuable and indispensable assistance of Prof. Raymond Parmar, Shaival Thakkar, and Kiritbhai Bhavsar.
11. On the changing role of the caste *panchayats* in dispute settlement especially, see Cohn 1988a and 1988b.
12. Yagnik and Sheth (2005: 74–80) describe several stories of how in the mid 19th centuries prominent Gujarati writers and reformers were outcasted for travelling to the UK. All caste members as well as their friends were barred from maintaining contact with the travellers; when in one case a friend did maintain contact, his whole caste was expelled from their *mahajan*. Only after undertaking several purification rituals could the travellers (including Mahatma Gandhi) be readmitted by their caste council.
13. Doshi (1974: 69) describes the case of a family who did not regularly attend the condolence meetings held when a *pol* resident passed away. When a member of this particular family died, *pol* residents and even close relatives were instructed not to assist in the performance of the funeral rites. This ban was lifted only after the head of the family begged for pardon and promised to fulfil the obligations at future funerals.
14. The first references to *mahajans* date back to 600 BC; in several Hindu and Buddhist texts from that period rulers were advised not to interfere in the affairs of the *mahajans*. For an overview see Hopkins 1901.
15. Given the importance of the *mahajans* in earlier times, it is surprising that—to my knowledge—there is no historical study singularly devoted to them. This section is based on several useful articles (Mehta 1984, Mehta 1988, Hopkins 1901: ch. 7; Misra 1981) as well as on a number historical studies which touch upon the functioning of *mahajans* (Ratnamirao 1929: ch. 37; Mehta 1981; Patel 1987: ch. 2; Pearson 1976: 123–4, Haynes 1992: ch. 4; Varshney 2002: ch. 9 and 10; and Spodek 1974; see especially Hasan 2004).

16. The artisan guilds would set fixed prices, while of the *mahajans* only the grain-*mahajan* regulated its prices (Hopkins 1901: 198).
17. The artisan guilds often simply lacked the resources to win a dispute. Hopkins (1901: 197) related for example a dispute that arose between a *mahajan* and a potters' guild when the potters decided to raise their prices. The *mahajan* managed to pressurize the potters to lower their prices by buying the right to dig clay in the village lands, on which the potters were dependent.
18. According to Hopkins the tax was a quarter per cent.
19. Ratnamanirao (1929: 548) cites an example of a trader who had, contrary to the rules of his caste, married a widow. He was excommunicated by his caste as well as by the cloth market *mahajan*. Unable to do any business in Ahmedabad, he had to move to another city.
20. This development was closely related to the development and subsequent decline of the Mughal state: as the Mughal empire grew its rulers became more dependent on the merchants to finance its expanding operations (Hasan 2004: 46), while in the 18th century, when the authority of the Mughal empire declined, power become more decentralized (Bayly 1992) and the *mahajans* partly stepped into the resulting power-vacuum.
21. See Misra (1981: 89) who writes, 'the system also limited the role of the state *vis-à-vis* the urban populace. This mediation necessarily introduced a significant element of indirectness in administration, which in fact served to create autonomous enclaves which were internally self-administered and traditionally independent of state power'.
22. For a discussion of the functioning of *kotwals* and *kazis* in north Indian cities, see Bayly 1992. According to Bayly the role of these officials was limited: 'The kotwal and kazi only appear to have intervened when other methods of control or conciliation had broken down or were in doubt (…) only in the last instance would the *kotwal's* authority be introduced and the case be referred to the city court' (1992:310). As the Mughal empire faded, so did the position of these local officials, so that by the beginning of the 18th century the local authority of Gujarat's rulers was severely constrained.
23. See Migdal's 'state-in-society' approach for a discussion on the basis of more contemporary examples on the dialectic between different forms of social control outside the state, and the functioning of state institutions. The social control that various local organisations and strongmen exercise, Migdal (2001) argues, limits the likelihood that the state expands its capabilities, while the functioning of state institutions also shapes the functioning of these local authorities.
24. Of these local bodies found, half were *pol panches*, the other organizations were either a trust, a neighbourhood committee or a youth group. See AMC 2004a.
25. This is the *kadva pol* in Dariapur.
26. According to Mehta (1984: 174) there were 60 *mahajans* in the 1980s. This is an increase: in 1877 the British surveyors recorded only 21 *mahajans*, while Hopkins mentioned the existence of 40 *mahajans* in 1896.
27. For an overview of the history of Ahmedabad's Municipal Corporation, see Ratnamanirao 1929: ch. 28; Rotary Club of Ahmedabad 1940; Boman-Behram 1937 and Gillion 1968.
28. See Haynes (1992: ch. 7 and 8) for a discussion of this shift in Surat, and for a description of a comparable change in local leadership in Allahabad, see Bayly 1971.

29. Some digression on my use of the term 'state capacity' might be useful. Following Fukuyama (2005) I am employing in this book a distinction between the scope and the strength of the Gujarati state. The scope of the state refers to the number of tasks that a state takes up: whether the role of the state is restricted to, say, the maintenance of law and order and national security, or whether the state takes up more complex tasks like the protection of the environment, education, social security etc. State strength refers to the capacity of a state to enforce its laws and to execute its policies in these different fields. Rudolph and Rudolph (1989) implicitly referred to these two aspects when they described the Indian state as a 'weak-strong state': on the one hand the Indian state has the administrative capacity to develop legislation and to perform a great number of functions, but on the other hand its capacity to penetrate and change society through the enactment of laws and legislation is limited. Myrdal's (1970: 208–71) term 'soft state' also refered to limited capacities of the Indian state to enforce its policies and legislation (he saw the 'soft state' as the outcome not only of deficiencies in legislation and law enforcement, but also of a widespread disregard by public officials of rules and directives).
30. This distinction also helps to grasp an important difference from the dynamics that Migdal describes in his earlier work (1988), as well as the 'shadow states' identified in Africa (see Reno 1995). These authors describe forms of social control (under local strongmen, militia-leaders, village headmen etc.) within society, which exist relatively independent of the state, as their authority springs from other sources (age, heredity, wealth, control over natural resources etc.) than control over government resources. Reno's 'shadow states' function largely independent of—and sometimes in competition with—the state. The dynamics underlying the predominance of politicians and their *chamchas* in Gujarat are different: the extended scope of the services that the state provides has led to local patterns of authority that are to a large extent premised on the capacity to access state resources. Local 'social control' in Gujarat's cities is, after the demise of the *pol panch* and the *mahajans*, no longer as independent of the (resources of) the state: much more than in Reno's 'shadow states', local patterns of authority in Gujarat's cities are shaped by the capacity to access state resources.

4. CHANGING PATRONAGE CHANNELS AND THE RISE OF HINDU-NATIONALISM IN GUJARAT

1. For more detailed discussion of the contemporary political history of Gujarat, see Yagnik and Sheth 2005, Sheth 1998, Patel 2003, Shah 1998, Spodek 1989, 2001 and 2008 and Shani 2007
2. For a detailed historical study of the social organization of textile labourers' localities in Bombay in the early twentieth century, see Chandavarkar 1994 and Gooptu 2001.
3. This informalization of labour is best illustrated by the early morning stampedes at a number of street corners ('*nakas*') throughout Ahmedabad. Every working day people gather early in the morning in great numbers at these street corners to wait for a contractor or the owner of a workshop who needs some extra hands.
4. I am grateful to Jan Breman for this insight.

5. THE EVERYDAY MEDIATION OF A MUNICIPAL COUNCILLOR

1. In the vocabulary of Bourdieu we can thus see both the specific capacities of the state in Gujarat to provide resources and a majoritarian democratic electoral system as the 'structuring principles' underlying the 'space of play' of various intermediaries competing for control over the state. The forms of capital in this field are shaped by the need to develop a (perceived) capacity to provide access to state resources: for example, an image of 'being close' to important people as well as a history of favours performed for others are important forms of capital in this field (cf. Bourdieu, 1991; 1992).
2. Especially (but not only) in the slum areas there is limited registration of residence (apart from various ad-hoc surveys). Residents use various documents such as a driving license and especially an election card as a proof of residence; often a residence proof supplied by a politician is required to update or change the information on these. Since most inhabitants work in the informal sector it is not easy to collect reliable information about the income of many citizens. The system that registers land property is often faulty; the registration of property in Ahmedabad is still based on a map that was originally drawn up by the British. Unsurprisingly, the land registration often leads to disputes which are in many cases settled with (lucrative) political interference.
3. See the guidelines of the 'Member of Parliament Local Area Development Scheme' at http://www.mplads.nic.in/, paragraph 2.4. This scheme was enacted in 1993.
4. In 2006. The Budget for the MPs comes from the central government while the budget for the MLA local area development fund comes from the Gujarat state government. The budget of the municipal councillors comes from the Ahmedabad municipal corporation.
5. The quite extensive literature, of the 1970s and 1980s especially, on patronage distinguishes 'traditional' patronage from political patronage: patronage is often defined by referring to a dyadic relationship between a patron and a client, marked by a big difference in power (see Boissevain 1974, Scott 1972). The patron uses his influence and resources to provide protection or benefits to a client of lesser status who can only reciprocate by offering general support and assistance. Such definitions seem more applicable to traditional forms of patronage premised on the personal resources of the patron, and not patronage premised on the capacity of the patron to access state resources (for a discussion see Breman 1991). When electoral or personal support is premised upon the patron's capacity to access government institutions, the network of actors exchanging favours is more complex and dynamic. For this different type of patronage I will use the term 'political patronage', while the term 'clientelism' is also used in the literature. As we will see in Chapters 6 and 7, the political networks that help ordinary citizens gain access to government institutions involve various different actors who are interdependent. The power differential is less salient in this form of patronage as politicians rely on local leaders as much as those leaders rely on them: this form of patronage can take the form of an exchange of favours, when each actor in this network has a certain bargaining position since each makes use of different resources. See also Weingrod 1968, Roniger 1994, Lemarchand 1981 and Kitschelt and Wilkinson 2007.
6. Such political networks may be called 'political machines' (De Wit 1996, Scott 1969, Bardhan 1984: 77–80, Bailey 1970: 136–61), since the exchange of government resources for electoral support is devoid of any political ideology: the mutual support and loyalty between voters, politicians and their party workers is shaped by

an instrumental calculation of costs and benefits. For such machines political ideologies are at best a mask, and at worst an obstacle for the lucrative exchange of favours. Political machines do not always coincide with political parties: parties are often ridden with factions which compete by forming their own patronage networks (Rosenthal 1966, Weiner 1969).

7. Especially in the 1950s and 1960s, the Congress party perfected this system. It had developed such a wide-ranging patronage network through these local leaders, who were so efficient in delivering votes, that scholars spoke about 'the Congress system' (Kothari 1964, see also Weiner 1969). But since Indira Gandhi's rule Congress' patronage networks have become fragmented and decentralized; according to Kohli (1990) this demise of Congress' networks has left an authority vacuum, which threatens India's governability.
8. This use of the term 'shadow state' is somewhat confusing, as the original meaning of 'Shadow State', as proposed by Reno (1995, 2000), referred to the authority structures in Sierra Leone that functioned as an alternative to the state: these structures have emerged in the context of collapsed or weak states, whose failures enabled other institutions to perform state-like functions alongside remaining government institutions. Such an interpretation makes the term 'shadow state' less applicable to India, since the Indian networks of brokers and fixers are clearly geared towards, and dependent on, the resources that the state provides. India's shadow state is not like Sierra Leone's shadow state: as Blom Hansen (2005: 131) writes about the Shiv Sena in Mumbai, using the other interpretation of the term 'shadow state', 'the Shiv Sena never aimed at creating a shadow state or alternative forms of governance. On the contrary, the Shiv Sena's vague programme revolves around the state as the provider of jobs and benefits, recognition, rights, order, etc'.

6. NEIGHBOURHOOD WORKERS AND THE POLITICS OF EXCHANGING FAVOURS

1. While I find Chatterjee's term 'political society' useful to delineate and describe the everyday mediation of the state, I find the way he conceptualizes the term somewhat unhelpful. He conceives political society as a 'domain of mediating institutions "between" civil society and the state' (Chatterjee 2001: 173, 1998: 60, my emphasis added). This is somewhat inconsistent, since one of Chatterjee's arguments for proposing the term is his observation that the domain of civil society is limited to a fairly small section of citizens, as most of India's inhabitants are not 'proper members of civil society' (Chatterjee 2004: 38). I feel that 'political society' is a different mode of relating to the state, next *to* civil society. While civil society-actors can represent their interests on the basis of their status as rights-bearing citizens, in political society citizens secure benefits from the state on the basis of their capacity to enlist the support of various intermediaries; this cooperation is acquired not on the basis of law or persuasion but through a complex exchange of favours in which status, money and votes are important elements.
2. While neighbourhood leaders regularly refer to themselves as 'social workers', these two categories do not completely overlap since, as might be gleaned from the discussion below, social workers could be local fixers who have not (yet) achieved sufficient local standing to be seen as a neighbourhood leader (or local 'big men', see Mines 1996). While engaging in similar activities and in similar exchanges with elected politicians, social workers and neighbourhood leaders could thus differ in

terms of local standing and authority. Krishna (2007) used the term '*naya neta*' (new leaders) for the intermediaries he encountered in Rajasthan and Madhya Pradesh. His '*naya neta*' seem comparable to the social workers I describe here (even though in Gujarat I never heard this term being used).

3. A possible sixth group, local journalists, has not been included in this chapter, because the neighbourhood focus of this study did not allow me to take up this topic in any systematic manner. Nonetheless my occasional encounters with local journalists convinced me that the interdependencies between journalists and local politicians also deserve closer study. Many local journalists maintain, like social workers and party workers, close relations with politicians, and they often engage in a similar exchange of favours: favourable reporting in the press (or the suppression of an unfavourable article) is often reciprocated with lucrative assignments and bureaucratic support. Gujarat's vernacular newspapers have expanded into real estate: several newspapers have acquired various buildings throughout Gujarat with, it is rumoured, political support. In this sense the hold of politicians over the bureaucracy can threaten the independent reporting of local journalists, since control over the bureaucracy offers politicians with effective means to cajole as well as entice local journalists. The interaction between journalists and politicians, and the effects of this interaction on the standard of reporting in newspapers, would be a deserving topic for more ethnographic studies (see e.g. Stahlberg 2006) on journalism.
4. For a classic description of the functioning of these clubs, see Whyte 1993. See also Scott 1969 and Wilkinson 2007.
5. A lot of the dynamic during election day is related to attempts of politicians to find out whether local leaders (and voters) kept their promises. Candidates post their workers inside polling booths to count the number of voters, while others distribute the above mentioned election-slips to gauge support. Thanks to the recently introduced electronic voting, candidates can now study the results in much more detail. They do so to determine which local leader deserves help (and access to governmental budgets) once they are in office. For an analysis of the importance of this kind of monitoring for political patronage, see Kitschelt and Wilkinson 2007 and Medina and Stokes 2007.
6. Maya Kodnani was allegedly involved in the violence in Gujarat and was indicted for this reason by the Special Investigation Team (SIT) of the Supreme Court. In the light of the argument I make in this paragraph it is telling that a woman is currently the only the high-level politician ever arrested for involvement in the 2002 violence.
7. At the time of writing the Lok Sabha is due to debate a Womens Reservation's Bill, which proposes to implement a 33 per cent reservation of seats in the state parliament as well as the Lok Sabha.
8. In his paper Manor conceptualizes political fixers as intermediaries working outside political organizations—as alternatives to strong political parties. I hope the distinction I employed in this chapter, between social workers and party workers, served to illustrate that those working inside political organizations can often also be seen as fixers, as only the terms of their exchange with political leaders are different. In that sense I find it unhelpful to see strong parties or ideologically driven parties as the antidote to fixers—I would argue that in these contexts the fixers are more likely to be party workers (but see Wilkinson 2007 and Krishna 2007). As I argued in previous chapters, in addition to the factors that Manor highlights I

would particularly study the presence of fixers also in the light of the extended scope but limited reach of the services that the state provides.

9. Saberwal (1996: 16 and 150) argues for example that 'the courses taken by everyday [political] events reflect a weak awareness of, and commitment to, the idea of general rules, routines and disciplines'. He also (1997: 94–5) argues that '[w]hen the participants have not learned the logics, the attitudes, and the techniques to enter participative institutions, violent practice invades the 'democratic' routines increasingly'. Kaviraj (1984 and 2001: 317) argues that 'Elite groups, educated in Western style, understand the advantages of social individuation and have the skills of association—i.e., the subtle and in some ways culturally unfamiliar art of getting together and committing themselves artificially and transiently to others with the same sectional interests. People belonging to other social groups do not'.

7. MONEYPOWER AND MUSCLEPOWER: ON THE NEXUS BETWEEN POLITICIANS, STATE OFFICIALS AND *GOONDAS*

1. Suketu Mehta's *Maximum City* (2004: 191) offers various fascinating examples of how *goonda*s in Mumbai function as an alternative for the overburdened judiciary. In a conversation with Mehta, one Mumbai-based *goonda* advertises his services as follows: 'If someone is sitting on your property, whatever is pending for ten or twenty years in the courts, we goondas will resolve [it] in ten days. Whatever the police, the politicians, the courts can't do, we goondas do. When people are tired of the courts, when they are ruined, when they are looking for a way out, they come to us and say, 'do something'. What you have forgotten is yours, we will restore to you'.
2. On the effects of the political pressure on India's police, see HRW 2009.
3. According to a 2007 report, Gujarat's Anti-Corruption Bureau manages only rarely to register a case of corruption against a government official or bureaucrat. In 2006 only 23 cases of corruption were registered in Gujarat against police officials, and only four cases against government officials in Ahmedabad. See 'Police dept most corrupt', *Times of India* 7–3–2007.
4. Although I could not explore this fully, there are indications that over the years the interaction between politicians and administrators in Ahmedabad has changed. According to several informants, local politicians seem to have become more prominent as mediators between government officials and citizens: thirty years ago local administrators seemed to be more open to requests and complaints from ordinary citizens, while now this interactions seems to take place more frequently via politicians. Several older inhabitants in the studied neighbourhoods remembered how at least until the early 1970s government officials were going on daily rounds through the neighbourhood, to check on the gutters, sweeping, the water supply etc.

8. POLITICAL MEDIATION AND TH POLITICS OF IDENTITY

1. In fact, Chandra advances the term 'patronage democracy' as the context in which the success or failure of ethnic parties should be understood. By this term she refers to something quite similar to the term 'mediated state' which I have been using: 'a democracy in which the state monopolizes access to jobs and services, and in

which elected officials have discretion in the implementation of laws allocating the jobs and services at the disposal of the state'. I have been using the term 'mediated state' to include practices of brokerage and particularization that are, apart from patronage, also important aspects of the linkage between citizens and politicians.

2. Shani (2007: 158) makes a similar argument in her analysis of Gujarat's communal violence: 'Large-scale violence in ethnic politics, therefore, has the effect of ossifying the lines of difference between groups (...). Thus, violence has a particular constitutive effect in the formation process of ethnic identities'. In her book she relates the need for 'ossifying the lines of difference' not—as I do here—to the way the state is embedded in society, but to the way upper castes felt threatened by the increased mobilization and social mobility of lower castes: the violence suppresses a threatening antagonism within the Hindu community. As her analysis is largely focused on why upper-caste people came to support 'ethno-Hinduism', this analysis is less convincing in explaining why Dalits—who did not share a similar anxiety—could be drawn to Hindu-nationalist ideology. As I argue below, I would attribute the success of the BJP in winning over Dalits to a large extent, to the need of these marginalized communities to find new patronage channels. See note 6.
3. Abram de Swaan pointed this out to me: his PhD thesis 'Coalition Theories and Cabinet Formations' (1973) on a completely different topic (cabinet formations in Western democracies) discusses the formation of 'minimal range coalitions'.
4. 'Long live Mother India, Salute to the Motherland, May Babasaheb Ambedkar be immortal!'. Ambedkar was a prominent Dalit leader during India's struggle for independence and served as chairman of the committee that wrote India's constitution. He is still revered by Dalits throughout India.
5. 'To get a ticket' is a commonly used expression for being selected to represent a political party in an election. Before the election the 'election committees' of different parties gather information about the popularity, money, contacts and caste background of possible candidates. On the basis of (mainly) these four criteria the candidates in the different constituencies are selected ('given the tickets').
6. In her interesting work Shani (2005 and 2007) advances the somewhat contradictory argument that the BJP started to ally with Dalits because of the growing tensions between upper castes and lower castes. The conflicts about positive discrimination and the increased social mobility of Dalits had led to tensions which, according to Shani, the BJP tried to defuse by incorporating Dalits within the party. This argument is somewhat contradictory since it invites the question that, given this anxiety about changing caste hierarchies among upper caste BJP supporters—often seen as being caused by earlier Congress support for Dalits—how could this anxiety lead to an extension of more patronage to Dalits? Electoral considerations seem to have carried the most weight here: the incorporation of Dalits within the BJP was also the result of an electoral necessity for the BJP to target a social division that could yield a majority of the votes: their earlier image as an upper caste party (and opposed to lower caste interests) would not win them enough seats. The patronage channels that the BJP could offer made this strategy possible: Dalit leaders and Dalit voters could be swayed by the tangible benefits that they secured through these patronage channels.
7. This can, for example, be observed during Ahmedabad's Rath Yatra, the yearly procession in honour of Lord Jagannath: all along the route of the chariot carrying Lord Jagannath one can find banners carrying names of politicians like 'Member of Parliament Harin Pathak welcomes the Rath Yatra'. Several politicians contribute to the food that is traditionally offered to the people who walk the route. Or take

the 'Dhakor Yatra': around full moon day in March thousands of people walk from Ahmedabad to Dhakor to pay homage to Lord Krishna.

8. Different groups of inhabitants were asked to identify whether the areas mentioned in the list were Hindu dominated, Muslim dominated or with a mixed population. Using their mutually consistent answers the financed projects were grouped under these three headings. I am indebted to Thijs Turel for the idea, as well as for the collection and processing of these data. The list was collected from the website of Ahmedabad's municipality, at http://www.egovamc.com/grants/grants_type_1.asp
9. Included were only the areas within the Isanpur electoral ward; since Shailesh Macwana's constituency comprises three electoral wards, a sizeable number of financed projects are grouped under the heading of 'Outside area'.
10. Such targeted use of government resources is not restricted to these MLA budgets: Sud (2007a) describes for example how in Gujarat Muslims and Christians are excluded from various government subsidies, while developmental programmes are used to woo Dalits and OBCs (Other Backward Castes).
11. See Manor (1997) who described such caste solidarity as the 'materiality of caste'.
12. Chandra (2004b) discusses and dismisses the existence of caste-based or regional networks as an alternative explanation for the voters' preference for electing co-ethnics. She argues that the reason why people invest in these networks in the first place is the same reason why people vote for co-ethnics: in the absence of more information about their attitudes the ethnicity of the networks'members is the clearest indication that they will be willing to provide support. As I tried to show in these paragraphs, we also need to take into account the importance that different identity dimensions have acquired in the daily life of people: their migration patterns, their settlement pattern, and their livelihoods, as well as the strength of their caste- or region-based organizations, all have an impact on the importance that people attach to voting for a co-ethnic.

9. THE INFRASTRUCTURE FOR VIOLENCE: RIOTING AS MAINTAINING RELATIONS

1. The debate between Brass, Varshney and Wilkinson was, at times, a heated one, particularly after Varshney's review of Brass' *The Production of Hindu-Muslim Violence* in *India Today* that was, in my view, indeed somewhat unfair. See Brass' angry response to this review at http://www.mail-archive.com/sapac@www.residentlounge.com/msg00137.html
2. For an overview of the complicity of the police in the violence, see Setalvad 2002, PUDR 2002: 34–9, CCT, vol 2: 81–96.
3. A witness (in HRW 2002: 26) described the cooperation between the police and the mobs in Isanpur as follows: 'The Hindus called us outside to fight. When we came out, the police fired at us, twelve to thirteen people died (…) The police were with them and picked out the Muslim houses and set them on fire. They aimed and fired at the Muslim boys. They then joined with the Hindus to set fire to the homes and to loot the homes'.
4. Some of the local youths I met were only acquitted of all the charges against them four years after the rioting. It seems that the police force residents to name participants in the riots, which often leads to false names and fabricated charges.

5. As part of its undercover reportage, the magazine *Tehelka* interviewed the VHP secretary and lawyer Dilip Trivedi who deals with most of the riot cases for the BJP. In the recording that *Tehelka* made he stresses the usefulness of his contacts in high places: 'I just have to call up these people on the phone. Whenever anyone has any problem, they call me on the phone, I think about the right man and then inform the concerned person (...) Yes we get it done...by finding out who has contacts at which place... All God's grace... we have managed at all the places... otherwise the cases were so weak'. 'The Truth. Gujarat 2002', *Tehelka* 3–11–07.
6. The Best Bakery case is only the most famous example of the failure of Gujarat's judiciary to withstand these pressures. After the accused were acquitted in a Gujarat court, India's Supreme Court ordered a retrial in Mumbai, stating that 'the justice delivery system was taken for a ride and literally allowed to be abused, misused and mutilated by subterfuge'. See Bunsha 2006: 161–6 and 'the shaming of Gujarat', *Tehelka* 22–12–2004. For an overview of the harassment and intimidation of witnesses in riot cases, see HRW 2003. On the unequal treatment by the judiciary of Muslims, see Amnesty 2003.
7. 'Unemployment may rob Ram Rahimnagar of peace', *Times of India* 5–8–2007.
8. This holds especially for the *pol panch* and Ahmedabad's *mahajans*. In *mahajans* in Surat there was more participation of Muslim merchants. See Haynes 1992, Chapter 4.
9. While Varshney (2004: 281) concludes from his study that '*intra*communal or *intra*-ethnic associations (...) were not found useful for the purposes of ethnic or communal peace'.
10. See CCT: 56. Human Rights Watch (2002: 23) noted that in the months prior to the riots people had been going around with lists to determine the addresses of Muslim shops; allegedly these lists where used to target these establishments during the riots.
11. At the time of the violence four state ministers were also prominent VHP leaders: Home Minister Gordhan Zapaphiya, Revenue Minister Haren Pandya, Minister for Forests Prabhat Sing Chauhan and Minister for Cottage Industries Narayan Laloo Patel.
12. Banerjee (2000: 125) for example, writes about the Shiv Sena in Mumbai: 'The bonds created by the Sena's dissemination of Hindu nationalism were shored up by economic patronage (...) The Shiv Sena secured jobs, procured operating licenses for vending carts, paved roads, obtained electricity connections, repaired sewage disposal lines, and helped provide other social amenities for its followers in the slums. The Sena's activity in electoral politics expedited its ability to extend such largesse'. See also Heuzé 1992 and 1997 and Hansen 2001 (ch. 4).
13. 'A plot from the devil's lair', *Outlook*, 03–06–2002.
14. See Teesta Seetalvad, 'Dial M for Massacre, *Communalism Combat*, june 2010.
15. 'Their eyes and mouth were shut', *Tehelka* 3–11–2007.
16. Since 2002 Sreekumar has filed five affidavits before the Nanavati Commission, the judicial committee in charge of inquiring into the Godhra incident and the subsequent riots. In the affidavits Sreekumar discussed the biased attitude of the police during the riots. He noted that police officers often dissuaded Muslims from filing complaints about events during the riots, while arrested Hindu rioters were often quickly released 'on account of the partisan stance taken by the government public prosecutor and also due to lack of keenness of the police (....) Whenever prominent Hindu leaders, accused of their involvement in the recent

riots, are released on bail, local leaders of ruling party make arrangements for giving a hero's felicitation to them'. For Shreekumar's affidavits, see www.cjponline.org/gujaratTrials/Statcomplicity.htm (last accessed 26–08–2010).
17. For a more elaborate discussion of Sreekumar's case see Visvanathan 2007.
18. Two years after the riots Sreekumar was called to testify before a judicial committee on the role of the police during the riots. A few days before Sreekumar was to testify he was summoned for a meeting with the state's Home Secretary and the government pleader before the Nanavati commission. Sreekumar secretly recorded how the duo effectively tutored him on how to depose before the commission. He was told 'not to go to deep into the veracity', and Ahmedabad's Police Commissioner, P.C. Pandey, was presented as an example to follow. Pandey—who is said to have prevented the police in Ahmedabad from attempting to stop the riots (CCT 2002: 37), and who had, according to rioters, ordered the secret disposal of 700 bodies to lower the official death toll—had told the Nanavati commission that he could not recollect most of the events during the riots. In the end Sreekumar was told that if he would be 'giving contrary opinion to the government' then a 'notice will be issued by government to you regarding integrity'. Eventually such a notice was really issued; government officials revived some old complaints that were filed against Sreekumar more than twenty years ago, and they argued that these complaints were the grounds for passing him over for promotion. Sreekumar protested, filing a complaint stating that he was denied promotion for political reasons.
19. For an overview of the senior police officers punished for their efforts to stop the riots, and those rewarded for their complicity in the rioting, see Seetalvad 2002: 194–200, CCT 90–91, and 'Carrot & Stick', *Tehelka* 12–03–2005 as well as 'CM 'punishes' officers who didn't toe line, rewards others', *Times of India* 25–3–2002.

CONCLUSION: POLITICAL MEDIATION, COMMUNAL VIOLENCE AND THE STATE

1. In India the term 'communal violence' is more commonly used than 'ethnic violence', even though the terms often denote the same phenomenon. Ethnic violence refers to violent conflict between communities differentiated by their ethnicity—i.e. their descent, language, history or physical appearance. The term 'communal violence' is used in India to describe violent conflict between caste-groups, religious groups as well various tribes. Whether the terms are interchangeable depends on one's definition of 'ethnicity'—whether one regards religious communities or castes as 'ethnic groups'.
2. But see Wimmer *et al.* 2009: this quantitative study on ethnic politics and civil war has highlighted that exclusion of ethnic groups from access to state resources increases the risk of violent conflict.
3. See www.cjponline.org for an overview of the progress of the efforts to bring perpetrators to court
4. Jayaprakash Narayan's Foundation for Democratic Reforms (www.fdr.cc) and CERI (www.ceri.in) are two movements currently advocating the adoption of a proportional electoral system.

BIBLIOGRAPHY

Agnes, F. (1996). 'Behrampada: The Busti that did not Yield'. In J. McGuire & J. Reeves (eds), *Politics of Violence, from Ayodhya to Behrampada*. New Delhi: Sage Publications.

Ahmad, I. (2009). *Islamism and Democracy in India: The Transformation of Jamaat-e-Islami*. Princeton: Princeton University Press.

Ahmedabad Municipal Corporation (AMC) (2001). *Recommendations for the Conservation and Revitalisation of the Walled City of Ahmedabad*. Ahmedabad.

——— (2004a). *Recommendations for the Conservation and Revitalisation of the Walled City of Ahmedabad*. Ahmedabad: Heritage Cell.

——— (2004b). *Statistical Outline Ahmedabad City 2003–2004*. Ahmedabad.

Amnesty International (2003). *Abuse of the Law in Gujarat: Muslims Detained Illegally in Ahmedabad*: http://web.amnesty.org/library/Index/ENGASA200292003 (Accessed 03–08–07).

——— (2005). *Justice, the Victim—Gujarat State Fails to Protect Women from Violence*. London: Amnesty International.

Aragon, L. (2001). 'Communal Violence in Poso, Central Sulawesi: Where People Eat Fish and Fish Eat People'. *Indonesia*, 72, 45–79.

Bailey, F.G. (1970). *Politics and Social Change: Orissa in 1959*. Berkeley: University of California Press.

——— (2001). *Treasons, Stratagems, and Spoils*. Oxford: Westview Press.

Banerjee, S. (2000). *Warriors in Politics: Hindu Nationalism, Violence, and the Shiv Sena in India*. Boulder: Westview Press.

——— (2002). When the 'Silent Majority' Backs a Violent Minority. *Economic and Political Weekly*, 37 (13), 1183–1185.

Bardhan, P. (1984). *The Political Economy of Development in India*. Oxford: Basil Blackwell.

——— (1997). 'Method in the Madness? A Political-economy Analysis of the Ethnic Conflicts in Less Developed Countries'. *World Development*, 25 (9), 1381–98.

Barkey, K. and S. Parikh (1991). 'Comparative Perspectives on The State'. *Annual Review of Sociology*, 17, 523–49.

Basu, A. (1996). 'Mass Movement of Elite Conspiracy? The Puzzle of Hindu Nationalism'. In D. Ludden (ed.), *Contesting the Nation: Religion, Community, and the Politics of Democracy in India* (pp. 55–81). Philadelphia: University of Pennsylvania Press.

——— (1997). 'When Local Riots are not Merely Local: Bringing the State Back in, Bijnor 1988–1992'. In P. Chatterjee (ed.), *State and Politics in India*. Oxford University Press.

Basu, A. and A, Kohli (eds) (1998). *Community Conflicts and the State in India*. Calcutta: Oxford University Press.

Basu, T., P. Datta, S. Sarkar, T. Sarkar and S. Sen (1993). *Khaki Shorts and Saffron Flags: A Critique of the Hindu Right*. New Delhi: Orient Longman.

Baxi, U. (1990). 'Reflections on the Reservations Crisis in Gujarat'. In V. Das (ed.), *Mirrors of Violence* (pp. 215–40). Delhi: Oxford University Press.

Bayly, C.A. (1971). 'Local Control in Indian Towns—The Case of Allahabad 1880–1920'. *Modern Asian Studies*, 5 (4), 289–311.

——— (1985). 'The Pre-History of 'Communalism'? Religious Conflict in India, 1700–1860'. *Modern Asian Studies*, 19 (2), 177–203.

——— (1992). *Rulers, Townsmen and Bazaars: North Indian Society In the Age of British Expansion, 1770—1870*. Delhi: Oxford University Press.

Benjamin, S. and R. Bhuvaneshwari (2001). *Democracy, Inclusive Governance and Poverty in Bangalore*: University of Birmingham Working Paper 26.

——— (2006). 'Urban Futures of Poor Groups in Chennai and Bangalore'. In N.G. Jayal, A. Prakash and P.K. Sharma (eds), *Local Governance in India: Decentralization and Beyond*. New Delhi: Oxford University Press.

Berenschot, W. (2005). '"Hifi" People versus 'Cheap" People: Class Divisions and Ethnic Conflict in Bombay, India'. In T. Zwaan (ed.), *Politiek Geweld: Etnisch conflict, oorlog en genocide in the twintigste eeuw*. Amsterdam: Walburg Pers.

——— (2009). 'Rioting as Maintaining Relations: Hindu-Muslim Violence and Political Mediation in Gujarat, India'. *Civil Wars*, 11 (4), 414–34.

——— (2010). 'Everyday Mediation: The Politics of Public Service Delivery in Gujarat, India'. *Development and Change*, 41 (5), 883–905.

——— (2011). 'The Spatial Distribution of Riots: Patronage and the Instigation of Communal Violence in Gujarat, India'. *World Development*, 39 (2), 221–230.

——— (forthcoming). 'Moneypower and Musclepower in a Gujarati Locality: On the Usefulness of Goondas in Indian Politics'. *Journal of South Asian Studies*.

Bertrand, J. (2002). 'Legacies of the Authoritarian Past: Religious Violence in Indonesia's Moluccan Islands'. *Pacific Affairs*, 75 (1), 57–85.

Beteille, A. (1999). 'Citizenship, State and Civil Society'. *Economic and Political Weekly*, 34 (36), 2588–91.

Blok, A. (1974). *The Mafia of a Sicilian Village 1860–1960. A Study of Violent Peasant Entrepreneurs*. Oxford: Basil Blackwell.

——— (1997). 'Het Narcisme van de kleine verschillen'. *Amsterdams Sociologisch Tijdschrift*, 24 (2), 159–87.

——— (2001). *Honour and Violence*. Cambridge: Polity Press.

Boersema, J. (2007). 'Rwandan Neighbours: History of a Genocide: Ruanda 1990–1994'. Unpublished MA thesis, University of Amsterdam.

Boissevain, J. (1974). *Friends of Friends: Networks, Manipulators and Coalitions*. Oxford: Basil Blackwell.

Bourdieu, P. (1977). *Outline of a Theory of Practice*. Cambridge University Press.

——— (1987). *Choses Dites*. Paris: Les Edition de Minuit.

——— (1991). *Language and Symbolic Power*. Cambridge: Polity Press.

——— (1999). 'Rethinking the State: Genesis and Structure of the Bureaucratic Field'. In G. Steinmetz (ed.), *State/Culture: State-formation after the Cultural Turn*. Ithaca, NY: Cornell University Press.

Bourdieu, P. and L.J.D. Wacquant (1992). *An Invitation to Reflexive Sociology*. Chicago: Polity Press.

Brass, P. (1997). *Theft of an Idol. Text and Context in the Representation of Collective Violence*. Princeton: Princeton University Press.

——— (2003). *The Production of Hindu-Muslim Violence in Contemporary India*. Seattle: University of Washington Press.

——— (2004). 'Development of an Institutionalised Riot System in Meerut City, 1961 to 1982'. *Economic and Political Weekly*, 39 (44), 4839—48.

——— (ed.) (1996). *Riots and Pogroms*. London: Macmillan Press.

Brass, P.R. (1984). 'National Power and Local Politics in India: A Twenty-Year Perspective'. *Modern Asian Studies*, 18 (1), 89–118.

Breman, J. (1999). 'Ghettoization and Communal Politics: The Dynamics of Inclusion and Exclusion in the Hindutva Landscape'. In R. Gupta and J. Parry (eds), *Institutions and Inequalities* (pp. 259–83). Oxford University Press.

——— (2002). 'Communal Upheaval as Resurgence of Social Darwinism'. *Economic and Political Weekly*, 37 (16), 1485–88.

——— (2003). *The Labouring Poor in India: Patterns of Exploitation, Subordination, and Exclusion*. New Delhi: Oxford University Press.

——— (2004). *The Making and Unmaking of an Industrial Working Class: Sliding Down the Labour Hierarchy in Ahmedabad, India*. New Delhi: Oxford University Press.

Brubaker, R. and D. Laitin (1998). 'Ethnic and Nationalist Violence'. *Annual Review of Sociology*, 24, 423–52.

Bunsha, D. (2006). *Scarred: Experiments with Violence in Gujarat*. New Delhi: Penguin Books.

Butalia, U. (1998). *The Other Side of Silence: Voices from the Partition of India*. New Delhi: Penguin Books.

Chandavarkar, R. (2003). *The Origins of Industrial Capitalism in India: Business Strategies and the Working Classes in Bombay*. Cambridge University Press.

Chandra, B. (1984). *Communalism in Modern India*. New Delhi: Vikas Publishing House.

Chandra, K. (2004). 'Elections as Auctions'. *Seminar*, 539 (http://www.india-seminar.com/2004/539/539%20kanchan%20chandra.htm).

——— (2004). *Why Ethnic Parties Succeed: Patronage and Ethnic Head Counts in India*. Cambridge: Cambridge University Press.

——— (2006). Review of *The Production of Hindu-Muslim Violence in Contemporary India* by Paul R. Brass. *Journal of Asian Studies* (65), 207–9.

Chatterjee, P. (1998). 'Beyond the Nation? Or within?' *Social Text* (56), 57–69.

——— (2001). 'On Civil and Political Society in Postcolonial Democracies'. In S. Kaviraj and S. Khilnani (eds), *Civil Society: History and Possibilities* (pp. 165–79). Cambridge: Cambridge University Press.

——— (2004). *The Politics of the Governed: Reflections on Popular Politics in Most of the World*. New York: Columbia University Press.

Chattopadhyay, R. and E. Duflo (2004). 'Women as Policy Makers: Evidence from a Randomized Policy Experiment in India'. *Econometrica*, 72 (5), 1409–43.

Church, R. (1973). 'Authority and Influence in Indian Municipal Politics: Administrators and Councillors in Lucknow'. *Asian Survey*, 13 (4), 421–38.

Cohen, J. and A. Arato (1992). *Civil Society and Political Theory*. Cambridge: MIT Press.

Cohn, B. (1988a). 'Anthropological Notes on Disputes and Law in India'. In *An Anthropologist Among the Historians and Other Essays* (pp. 575–625). New Delhi: Oxford University Press.

——— (1988b). 'Some Notes on Law and Change in North India'. In *An Anthropologist Among the Historians and Other Essays* (pp. 554–74). New Delhi: Oxford University Press.

Coleman, J.S. (2000). *The Foundations of Social Theory*. Cambridge, MA: Harvard University Press.

Collins, R. (2008). *Violence: A Micro-sociological Theory*. Princeton University Press.

Concerned Citizens Tribunal (CCT) (2002). *Crime against Humanity, Volume 1 and 2*. Mumbai: Citizens for Justice and Peace.

D'Costa, W. and B. Das (2002). 'Life and Living of the Vulnerable in Ahmedabad City'. In A. Kundu and D. Mahadevia (eds), *Ahmedabad; Poverty and Vulnerability in a Globalising Metropolis* (pp. 179–206). New Delhi: Manak Publications.

D'souza, J.B. (2002). 'Gujarat: A Civil Service Failure'. *Economic and Political Weekly*, 37 (34), 3492–3.

Dalal, J. (1990 (1948)). *Shaherni Sheri*. Bombay-Ahmedabad: R.R. Sheth.

Das, S. (2005). 'The 1992 Calcutta Riot in Historical Continuum: A Relapse into 'Communal Fury'?' In S. Wilkinson (ed.), *Religious Politics and Communal Violence*. New Delhi: Oxford University Press.

Das, S.K. (2001). *Public Office, Private Interest: Bureaucracy and Corruption in India*. New Delhi: Oxford University Press.

Das, V. (1990). 'Introduction: Communities, Riots, Survivors—The South Asian Experience'. In V. Das (ed.), *Mirrors of Violence* (pp. 1–37). Delhi: Oxford University Press.

Das, V. and D. Poole (eds) (2004). *Anthropology in the Margins of the State*. Santa Fe: School of American Research Press.

Davis, J. (2004)'. Corruption in Public Service Delivery: Experience from South Asia's Water and Sanitation Sector'. *World Development*, 32 (1), 53–71.

Des Forges, A. (1999). *Leave None to Tell the Story: Genocide in Rwanda*. www.hrw.org (accessed 20–10–07): Human Rights Watch. [Also published in book form as A. Des Forges (1999). *"Leave None to Tell the Story": Genocide in Rwanda*. New York: Human Rights Watch.]

Deshpande, S. (2004). *Contemporary India, a Sociological View*. Delhi: Penguin Books India.

Devy, G. (2002). 'Advisis and Dalits: Tribal Voice and Violence'. In S. Varadarajan (ed.), *Gujarat: the Making of a Tragedy*. New Delhi: Penguin Books India.

Doshi, H. (1974). *Traditional Neighbourhood in a Modern City*. New Delhi: Abinav Publications.

Elias, N. (1974). 'Foreword: Towards a Theory of Communities'. In C. Bell and H. Newby (eds), *The Sociology of Community. A Selection of Readings* (pp. ix-xliii). London: Frank Cass & Co.

——— (1978). *What is Sociology?* London: Hutchinson.

——— (1982). *Het Civilisatieproces: Sociogentische en psychogenetische onderzoekingen, deel 1 en 2*. Utrecht: Het Spectrum.

——— (1988). 'Civilization and Violence: on the State Monopoly of Physical Violence and its Infringements'. In J. Keane (ed.), *Civil Society and the State* (pp. 177–98). London: Verso.

——— (1994). *The Established and the Outsiders: A Sociological Enquiry into Community Problems*. London: Sage Publications.

——— (2000). *The Civilizing Process: Sociogenetic and Psychogenetic Investigations*. Malden: Blackwell Publishing.

——— (2001). *The Society of Individuals*. New York: Continuum.

Emirbayer, M. (1997). 'Manifesto for a Relational Sociology'. *The American Journal of Sociology*, 103 (2), 281–317.

Engineer, A.A. (1989). *Communalism and Communal Violence in India*. Delhi: Ajanta Publications.

——— (1995). *Lifting the Veil: Communal Violence and Communal Harmony in Contemporary India*. Hyderabad: Sangam Books.

——— (2002). 'Gujarat Riots in the Light of the History of Communal Violence'. *Economic and Political Weekly*, 37 (50), 5047–54.

——— (ed.). (1984). *Communal Riots in Post-independence India*. Hyderabad: Sangam Books.

——— (ed.). (2003). *The Gujarat Carnage*. New Delhi: Orient Longman.

Fearon, J.D. and D.D. Laitin (2000). 'Violence and the Social Construction of Ethnic Identity'. *International Organization*, 54 (4), 845–77.

Forum Against Oppression of Women (FAOW). (2002). *Genocide in Rural Gujarat: The Experience of Dahod District*: http://www.onlinevolunteers.org/gujarat/reports/rural/ (accessed 07–08–07).

Fukuyama, F. (2005). *State-building: Governance and World Order in the Twenty-first Century*. London: Profile.

Fuller, C.J. and V. Bénéï (eds) (2001). *The Everyday State & Society in Modern India*. London: Hurst & Co.

Gaborieau, M. (1985). 'From Al-Beruni to Jinnah: Idiom, Ritual and Ideology of the Hindu-Muslim Confrontation in South Asia'. *Anthropology Today*, 1 (3), 7–14.

Geertz, C. (1963). 'The Integrative Revolution: Primordial Sentiments and Civil Politics in the New States'. In C. Geertz (ed.), *Old Societies and New States: The Quest for Modernity in Asia and Africa* (pp. 103–57). New York: Free Press.

Gellner, E. (1995). 'The Importance of Being Modular'. In J. Hall (ed.), *Civil Society: Theory, History, Comparison* (pp. 32–55). Cambridge: Polity Press.

Ghassem-Fachandi, P. (2006). 'Sacrifice, Ahimsa, and Vegetarianism: Pogrom at the Deep End of Non-Violence'. Cornell University: Unpublished PhD thesis.

Ghosh, E. and R. Kumar (2005). 'Hindu-Muslim Inter-group Relations in India: Applying Socio-Psychological Perspectives'. In S. Wilkinson (ed.), *Religious Politics and Communal Violence*. New Delhi: Oxford University Press.

Gill, M.S. and G. Deol (1995). 'Patterns of Riots in India'. *Asian Profile*, 23 (1), 59–66.

Gillion, K.L. (1968). *Ahmedabad: A Study in Indian Urban History*. Berkeley: University of California Press.

Gokhale, B.G. (1969). 'Ahmedabad in the XVIIITH Century'. *Journal of the Economic and Social History of the Orient*, 12, 187.

Gooptu, N. (2001). *The Politics of the Urban Poor in Early Twentieth-Century India*. Cambridge University Press.

Grootaert, C. (1998). *Social Capital: The Missing Link*. The World Bank.

Gupta, A. (1995). 'Blurred Boundaries: the Discourse of Corruption, the Culture of Politics, and the Imagined State'. *American Ethnologist*, 22 (2), 375–402.

Gupta, D. (2000). *Interrogating Caste: Understanding Hierarchy and difference in Indian Society*. New Delhi: Penguin Books.

Gupta, I.P. (1981). 'Urbanization in Gujrat During the Seventeenth Century'. In J.S. Grewal and I. Banga (eds), *Studies in Urban History*. Amritsar.

Hall, J.A. (1995). 'In Search of Civil Society'. In J.A. Hall (ed.), *Civil Society: Theory, History, Comparison* (pp. 1–31). Cambridge: Polity Press.

Hansen, T.B. (1999). *The Saffron Wave, Democracy and Hindu-nationalism in Modern India*. Princeton: Princeton University Press.

——— (2001). *Wages of Violence: Naming and Identity in Postcolonial Bombay*. Princeton: Princeton University Press.

——— (2004). 'Politics as Permanent Performance: The Production of Political Authority in the Locality'. In J. Zavos, A. Wyatt and V. Hewitt (eds), *The Politics of Cultural Mobilization in India* (pp. 19–36). New Delhi: Oxford University Press.

——— (2005). 'Sovereigns Beyond the State: On Legality and Public Authority in India'. In R. Kaur (ed.), *Religion, Violence and Political Mobilisation in South Asia* (pp. 109–44). New Delhi: Sage Publications.

Hansen, T.B and F. Stepputat (2001). 'Introduction: States of Imagination'. In T.B. Hansen and F. Stepputat (eds), *States of Imagination: Ethnographic Explorations of the Postcolonial State* (pp. 1–40). Durham, NC: Duke University Press.

Harris, J. (2001). *Depoliticizing Development: The World Bank and Social Capital*. New Delhi: Leftword Books.

Harriss-White, B. (1997). 'Informal Economic Order: Shadow States, Private Status States, States of Last Resort and Spinning States: a Speculative Discussion on S Asian Case Material'. *QEH Working Paper Series*, Oxford, 6.

——— (2003). *India Working: Essays on Society and Economy*. Cambridge: Cambridge University Press.

Hasan, F. (2004). *State and Locality in Mughal India: Power Relations in Western India, c. 1572–1730*. Cambridge University Press.

Haynes, D. (1992). *Rhetoric and Ritual in Colonial India: The Shaping of a Public Culture in Surat City, 1852–1928*. Delhi: Oxford University Press.

Heuzé, G. (1992). 'Shiv Sena and 'National' Hinduism'. *Economic and Political Weekly*, 27 (41), 2253–55, 2257–59, 2261–63.

——— (1997). 'Cultural Populism: The Appeal of the Shiv Sena'. In S. Patel (ed.), *Bombay: Metaphor for Modern India* (pp. 213–47). Oxford: Oxford University Press.

Hirway, I. and D. Mahadevia (2005). *Gujarat Human Development Report 2004*. Ahmedabad: Mahatma Gandhi Labour Institute.

Hopkins, E.W. (1901). *India Old and New*. London: Edward Arnold.

Horowitz, D. (1985). *Ethnic Groups in Conflict*. Berkeley: University of California Press.

——— (2002). *The Deadly Ethnic Riot*. New Delhi: Oxford University Press.

Howell, J. and J. Pearce (2002). *Civil Society and Development*. Boulder: Lynne Rienner Publishers.

Human Rights Watch (HRW) (1999). *Indonesia: The Violence in Ambon*: www.hrw.org (accessed 20–10–07).

——— (2002a). *Breakdown: Four Years of Communal Violence in Central Sulawesi*. www.hrw.org (accessed 20–10–07).

——— (2002b). *'We have no orders to save you': State Complicity and Participation in Communal Violence in Gujarat*: www.hrw.org, (accessed 31–07–07).

——— (2003). *Compounding Injustice: The Government's Failure to Redress Massacres in Gujarat*: www.hrw.org (accessed 3–8–07).

——— (2009). *Broken System: Dysfunction, Abuse, and Impunity in the Indian Police*. New York: Human Rights Watch.

Ignatieff, M. (1999). *The Warrior's Honour: Ethnic War and the Modern Conscience*. London: Vintage.

International Crisis Group (ICG) (2001). *Communal Violence in Indonesia: Lessons from Kalimantan*: www.icg.org (accessed 20–10–07).

——— (2002). *Indonesia: The Search for Peace in Maluku*: www.icg.org (accessed 20–10–07).

International Initiative for Justice (IIJ) (2003). *Threatened Existence: A Feminist Analysis of the Genocide in Gujarat*: http://www.onlinevolunteers.org/gujarat/reports/iijg/2003/ (accessed 3–8–07).

Jaffrelot, C. (1992). 'Les émeutes entre hindous et musulmans: essai de hiérarchisation des facteurs culturels, économiques et politiques'. *Cultures et Conflicts*, 5 (printemps 1992), 25–53.

——— (1996). *The Hindu Nationalist Movement and Indian Politics*. London: Hurst & Co.

——— (1998). 'The Politics of Processions and Hindu-Muslim Riots'. In A. Basu and A. Kohli (eds), *Community Conflicts and the State in India* (pp. 58–92). Calcutta: Oxford University Press.

——— (2003a). 'Communal Riots in Gujarat: The State at Risk'. *Heidelberg Papers in South Asian and Comparative Politics*, 17.

——— (2003b). 'Les violences entre hindous et musulmans au Gujarat (inde) en 2002: émeute d'état, pogromes et reaction antijihadiste'. *Revue Tiers-Monde* (174), 345–67.

——— (ed.) (2005). *The Sangh Parivar: a Reader*. New Delhi: Oxford University Press.

Jeffrey, C. (2002). 'Caste, Class and Clientelism: A Political Economy of Everyday Corruption in Rural North India'. *Economic Geography*, 78 (1), 21–42.

Jeffrey, C. and J. Lerche (2001). 'Dimensions of Dominance: Class and State in Uttar Pradesh'. In C.J. Fuller and V. Bénéï (eds), *The Everyday State & Society in Modern India* (pp. 91–114). London: Hurst & Co.

Jenkins, R. (1992). *Pierre Bourdieu*. London: Routledge.

Joshi, S. (1999). 'Tribals, Missionaries and Sadhus: Understanding Violence in the Dangs'. *Economic and Political Weekly*, 34, 2667–75.

Kakar, S. (1990). 'Some Unconscious Aspects of Ethnic Violence in India'. In V. Das (ed.), *Mirrors of Violence* (pp. 135–46). Delhi: Oxford University Press.

——— (1996). *The Colors of Violence: Cultural Identities, Religion and Conflict*. Chicago: University of Chicago Press.

Kanungo, P. (2002). *RSS's Tryst with Politics: from Hedgewar to Sudarshan*. Delhi: Manohar.

Katju, M. (2003). *Vishva Hindu Parishad and Indian Politics*. New Delhi: Orient Longman.

Katzenstein, M. (1977). 'Mobilization of Indian Youth in the Shiv Sena'. *Pacific Affairs*, 50 (2), 231–48.

Kaviraj, S. (1984). 'On the Crisis of Political Institutions in India'. *Contributions to Indian Sociology*, 18 (2), 223–43.

Kaviraj, S. (2001). 'In Search of Civil Society'. In S. Kaviraj and S. Khilnani (eds), *Civil Society: History and Possibilities* (pp. 287–324). Cambridge University Press.

Kaviraj, S. and S. Khilnani (2001). 'Introduction: Ideas of Civil Society'. In S. Kaviraj and S. Khilnani (eds), *Civil Society: History and Possibilities* (pp. 1–7). Cambridge: Cambridge University Press.

Keane, J. (1998). *Civil Society: Old Images, New Visions*. Cambridge: Polity Press.

Keefer, P. and S. Khemani (2004). 'Why do the Poor Receive Poor Services?' *Economic and Political Weekly*, 39 (9), 935–43.

Keefer, P. and R. Vlaicu (2008). 'Democracy, Credibility, and Clientelism'. *Journal of Law, Economics, and Organization*, 24 (2), 371–406.

Kitschelt, H. and S. Wilkinson (2007). 'Citizen-politician Linkages: an Introduction'. In H. Kitschelt and S. Wilkinson (eds), *Patrons, Clients and Policies: Patterns of Demo-*

cratic Accountability and Political Competition (pp. 1–50), Cambridge: Cambridge University Press.

Klinken, G.V. (2001). 'The Maluku Wars: Bringing Society Back In'. *Indonesia*, 71, 1–26.

——— (2007). *Communal Violence and Democratization in Indonesia: Small Town Wars*. New York: Routledge.

Kohli, A. (1988). 'Interpreting India's Democracy: A State-Society Framework'. In *India's Democracy: An Analysis of Changing State-Society Relations*. Princeton: Princeton University Press.

——— (1990). *Democracy and Discontent: India's Growing Crisis of Governability*. Cambridge: Cambridge University Press.

Kothari, R. (1964). 'The Congress 'System' in India'. *Asian Survey*, 4 (12), 1161–73.

——— (2005). *Rethinking Democracy*. New Delhi: Orient Longman.

——— (ed.) (1970). *Caste in Indian Politics*. New Delhi: Orient Longman.

Krishna, A. (2007). 'Politics in the Middle: Mediation Relationships between the Citizens and the State in Rural North India'. In H. Kitschelt and S. Wilkinson (eds), *Patrons, Clients and Policies: Patterns of Democratic Accountability and Political Competition* (pp. 141–59). Cambridge: Cambridge University Press.

Kumar, P. (2005). 'Communal Riots in Mau Nath Bhanjan'. In S. Wilkinson (ed.), *Religious Politics and Communal Violence* (pp. 244–71). New Delhi: Oxford University Press.

Kumar, S. (2003). 'Gujarat Assembly Elections 2002: Analysing the Verdict'. *Economic and Political Weekly*, 38 (4), 270–5.

Kundu, A. and D. Mahadevia (2002). *Ahmedabad; Poverty and Vulnerability in a Globalising Metropolis*. New Delhi: Manak Publications.

Kundu, D. (2002). 'Provision of Infrastructure and Basic Amenities: Analysing Institutional Vulnerability'. In A. Kundu and D. Mahadevia (eds), *Ahmedabad; Poverty and Vulnerability in a Globalising Metropolis*. New Delhi: Manak Publications.

Lemarchand, R. (1981). 'Comparative Political Clientelism: Structure, Processes and Optic'. In R. Lemarchand and S.N. Eisenstadt (eds), *Political Clientelism, Patronage and Development* (pp. 7–32). London: Sage Publications.

Lipsky, M. (1980). *Street-level Bureaucracy: Dilemmas of the Individual in Public Services*. New York: Russel Sage Foundation.

Lobo, L. (2006). 'Adivasis, Hindutva and Post-Godhra riots in Gujarat'. In L. Lobo and B. Das (eds), *Communal Violence and Minorities*. Jaipur: Rawat Publications.

Long, N. (1989). *Encounters at the Interface: a Perspective on Social Discontinuities in Rural Development*. Wageningen: Agricultural University Wageningen.

Mahadevia, D. (2002). 'Communal Space over Life Space: Saga of Increasing Vulnerability in Ahmedabad'. *Economic and Political Weekly*, 37 (48), 4850–58

Mander, H. (2006). 'Inside Gujarat's Relief Colonies: Surviving State Hostility and Denial'. *Economic and Political Weekly*, 41 (51), 5235–9.

Mann, M. (1986). 'The Autonomous Power of the State: Its Origins, Mechanisms and Results'. In J. Hall (ed.), *States in History* (pp. 109–36). Oxford: Basil Blackwell.

——— (2005). *The Dark Side of Democracy*. Cambridge: Cambridge University Press.

Manor, J. (1990). 'Parties and the Party System'. In A. Kohli (Ed.), *India's Democracy: An Analysis of Changing State-Society Relations* (pp. 62–5). Princeton: Princeton University Press.

——— (1997). 'Karnataka: Caste, Class, Dominance and Politics in a Cohesive Society'. In S. Kaviraj (ed.), *Politics in India*. Delhi: Oxford University Press.

——— (2000). 'Small-Time Political Fixers in India's States: 'Towel over Armpit'. *Asian Survey*, 40 (5), 816–35.

McDoom, O. (2005). *Rwanda's Ordinary Killers: Interpreting Popular Participation in the Rwandan Genocide*. Crisis States Programme Working Paper 77: LSE.

Medina, L.F. and S. Stokes (2007). 'Monopoly and Monitoring: an Approach to Political Clientelism'. In H. Kitschelt and S. Wilkinson (eds), *Patrons, Clients and Policies: Patterns of Democratic Accountability and Political Competition* (pp. 68–84). Cambridge University Press.

Mehta, M.J. (1981). 'Business Environment and Urbanization: Ahmedabad in the 19th Century'. In J.S. Grewal and I. Banga (eds), *Studies in Urban History*. Amritsar: Guru Nanak Dev University.

Mehta, S. (1984). 'The Mahajans and the Business Communities of Ahmedabad'. In D. Tripathi (ed.), *Business Communities of India: A Historical Perspective* (pp. 173–85). New Delhi: Manohar.

——— (1988). 'The Continuity and Change in an Urban Institution; a Caste Study of Maskati Cloth Mahajan of Ahmedabad'. In M. Mehta (ed.), *Urbanization in Western India, Historical Perspective*. Ahmedabad: Gujarat University.

——— (2004). *Maximum City: Bombay Lost and Found*. New Delhi: Penguin Books.

Michaelson, K.L. (1976). 'Patronage, Mediators, and the Historical Context of Social Organization in Bombay'. *American Ethnologist*, 3 (2), 281–95.

Migdal, J. (2001). *State in Society: Studying how States and Societies Transform and Constitute one another*. Cambridge: Cambridge University Press.

——— (1988). *Strong Societies and Weak States: State-society Relations and State Capabilities in the Third World*. Princeton: Princeton University Press.

Mines, M. (1996). *Public Faces, Private Voices: Community and Individuality in South India*. Delhi: Oxford University Press.

Misra, S.C. (1981). 'The Self Administering Institutions in Medieval Indian Towns'. In J.S.Grewal and I. Banga (eds), *Studies in Urban History*. Amritsar.

Mitchell, T. (1991). 'The Limits of the State: beyond Statist Approaches and their Critics'. *American Political Science Review*, 85 (1), 77–96.

Mitra, S. (2001). 'Making Local Government Work: Local Elites, *panchayati raj* and Governance in India'. In A. Kohli (ed.), *The Success of India's Democracy* (pp. 103–26). Cambridge: Cambridge University Press.

Mitra, S.K. (1991). 'Room to Maneuver in the Middle: Local Elites, Political Action, and the State in India'. *World Politics*, 43 (3), 390–413.

Mooij, J. (1999). 'Food Policy in India: the Importance of Electoral Politics in Policy Implementation'. *Journal of International Development*, 11, 625–36.

Myrdal, G. (1970). *The Challenge of World Poverty: A World Anti-Poverty Program in Outline*. London: Penguin Press.

Namishray, M. (2002). 'The Violence in Gujarat and the Dalits'. In S. Varadarajan (ed.), *Gujarat: the Making of a Tragedy*. New Delhi: Penguin.

Nandy, A., S. Trivedy, S. Mayaram and A. Yagnik (1995). *Creating a Nationality: the Ramjanmabhumi Movement and Fear of the Self*. Delhi: Oxford University Press.

Noorani, A.G. (2000). *The RSS and the BJP: A Division of Labour*. New Delhi: Leftword Books.

Nugent, D. (1994). 'Building the State, Making the Nation: The Bases and Limits of State Centralization in 'Modern' Peru'. *American Anthropologist*, 96 (2), 333–69.

Nussbaum, M. (2007). *The Clash Within: Democracy, Religious Violence, and India's Future*. Cambridge: Belknap Press.

Oldenburg, P. (1976). *Big City Government in India: Councilor, Administrator, and Citizen in Delhi.* Tucson: University of Arizona Press.

——— (1987). 'Middlemen in Third-World Corruption: Implications of an Indian Case'. *World Politics*, 39 (4), 508–35.

Oommen, T.K. (2005). *Crisis and Contention in Indian Society.* New Delhi: Sage Publications.

Pandey, G. (1992a). *The Construction of Communalism in Colonial North India.* Delhi: Oxford University Press.

——— (1992b). 'In Defense of the Fragment: Writing About Hindu-Muslim Riots in India Today'. *Representations*, 37, 27–55.

Parekh, B. (2002). 'Making Sense of Gujarat'. *Seminar*, 513.

Patel, G. (2002). 'Narendra Modi's One-Day Cricket'. *Economic and Political Weekly*, 37 (48), 4826–37.

Patel, P. (2003). 'Sectarian Mobilization, Communal Polarization and Factionalism: Electoral Dominance of Hindutva and Voting in Gujarat'. http://www.rsis-ntsasia.org/publications/PDF/Sectarian%20Mobilization.pdf.

Patel, S. (2002). 'Corporatist Patronage in the Ahmedabad Textile Industry'. In G. Shah, M. Rutten and H. Streefkerk (eds), *Development and Deprivation in Gujarat* (pp. 314–28). New Delhi: Sage Publications.

Pearson, M.N. (1976). *Merchants and Rulers in Gujarat.* Berkeley: University of California Press.

People's Union for Civil Liberties (PUCL). (2002a). *At the Receiving End: Women's Experiences of Violence in Vadodara*: http://www.onlinevolunteers.org/gujarat/reports/pucl/receivingend.pdf (accessed 07–08–07).

——— (2002b). *Violence in Vadodara: A Report.* http://www.onlinevolunteers.org/gujarat/reports/pucl/index.htm (accessed 31–9–07).

People's Union for Democratic Rights (cx PUDR). (2002). *'Maaro! Kaapo! Baalo!': State, Society and Communalism in Gujarat.* www.onlinevolunteers.org/gujarat/reports/pudr (Accessed 10–07–07).

Prakash, A. (2003). 'Re-imagination of the State and Gujarat's Electoral Verdict'. *Economic and Political Weekly*, 1601–10.

Prunier, G. (1995). *The Rwanda Crisis 1959–1994: History of a Genocide.* London: Hurst & Company.

Punyani, R. (2004). *Hindu Extreme Right-Wing Groups: Ideology & Consequences.* Delhi: Media House.

Rajeshwari, B. (2004). *Communal Riots in India: A Chronology (1947–2003)*. IPCS Research Papers (3): Institute for Peace and Research Studies.

Ratnamanirao Bhimrao, J. (1929). *Gujaratnu Patnagar—Amdavad.* Ahmedabad: Gujarat Sahitya-Sabha.

Raychaudhuri, S. (2001). 'Colonialism, Indigenous Elites and the Transformation of Cities in the Non-Western World: Ahmedabad (Western India), 1890–1947'. *Modern Asian Studies*, 35 (3), 677–726.

Reddy, G.R. and G. Haragopal (1985). 'The Pyraveekar: 'The Fixer' in Rural India'. *Asian Survey*, 25 (11), 1148–62.

Reno, W. (1995). *Corruption and State Politics in Sierra Leone.* Cambridge: Cambridge University Press.

——— (2000). 'Clandestine Economies, Violence and States in Africa'. *Journal of International Affairs*, 53 (2), 433–59.

Robinson, F. (2005). 'Foreword'. In R. Kaur (ed.), *Religion, Violence and Political Mobilisation in South Asia* (pp. 1–26). New Delhi: Sage.

Roniger, L. (1994).'The Comparative Study of Clientelism and the Changing Nature of Civil Society in the Contemporary World'. In L. Roniger and A. Günes-Ayata (eds), *Democracy, Clientelism, and Civil Society* (pp. 1–18). Boulder: Lynne Rienner Publishers.

Rosenthal, D.B. (1966).'Factions and Alliances in Indian City Politics'. *Midwest Journal of Political Science*, 10 (3), 320–49.

——— (1970). *The Limited Elite*. Chicago: University of Chicago Press.

——— (1974)."Making It' in Maharashtra'. *The Journal of Politics*, 36 (2), 409–37.

Rotary Club of Ahmedabad (1940). *Ahmedabad, being a Compilation of Articles Contributed by Rotarians and Others on Various Subjects Prominently Bringing out Many Interesting Details Pertaining to and Connected with the City*. Ahmedabad: Rotary Club of Ahmedabad.

Roy, B. (1994). *Some Trouble with Cows: Making Sense of Social Conflict*. Berkeley: University of California Press.

Rudolph, L.I. (1965).'The Modernity of Tradition: The Democratic Incarnation of Caste in India'. *The American Political Science Review*, 59 (4), 975–89.

Rudolph, L.I. and S.H. Rudolph (1960).'The Political Role of India's Caste Associations'. *Pacific Affairs*, 33 (1), 5–22.

——— (1987). *In the Pursuit of Lakshmi: The Political Economy of the Indian State*. University of Chicago Press.

Rutten, M. (1995). *Farms and Factories: Social Profile of Large Farmers and Rural Industrialists in West India*. Delhi: Oxford University Press.

Ruud, A.E. (2001).'Talking Dirty about Politics: a View from a Bengali Village'. In C.J. Fuller and V. Bénéï (eds), *The Everyday State & Society in Modern India*. (pp. 115–35).

Saberwal, S. (1996). *Roots of Crisis: Interpreting Contemporary Indian Society*. New Delhi: Sage Publications.

——— (1997). 'A Juncture of Traditions'. In M. Doornbos and S. Kaviraj (eds), *Dynamics of State Formation: India and Europe Compared*. New Delhi: Sage Publications.

Sarkar, T. (2002).'Semiotics of Terror'. *Economic and Political Weekly*, 37 (28), 2872–6.

Scott, J.C. (1969).'Corruption, Machine Politics, and Political Change'. *The American Political Science Review*, 63 (4), 1142–1558.

——— (1972). 'Patron-client Politics and Political Change in Southeast Asia'. *The American Political Science Review*, 66 (1), 91–113.

——— (1998). *Seeing like a State: How Certain Schemes to Improve the Human Condition Have Failed*. New Haven: Yale University Press.

Setalvad, T. and J. Anand, J. (eds) (2002). *Genocide: Gujarat 2002*. Mumbai: Communalism Combat (CC).

Seth, P. (1998). *Political Development in Gujarat*. Ahmedabad: Karnavati Publications.

Shah, A.M. and I.P. Desai (1988). *Division and Hierarchy: An Overview of Caste in Gujarat*. Delhi: Hindustan Publishing Corporation.

Shah, A.M., P. Patel and L. Lobo (2008).'A Heady Mix: Gujarati and Hindu Pride'. *Economic and Political Weekly*, 43 (8).

Shah, G. (1975). *Caste Association and Political Process in Gujarat*. Bombay: Popular Prakashan.

——— (1976).'The 1975 Gujarat Assembly Election in India'. *Asian Survey*, 16 (3), 270–82.

——— (1984). 'The 1969 Communal Riots in Ahmedabad: A Case Study'. In A.A. Engineer (ed.), *Communal Riots in Post-Independence India*. Hyderabad: Sangam Books.

——— (1998). 'The BJP's Riddle in Gujarat: Caste, Factionalism and Hindutva'. In T.B. Hansen and C. Jaffrelot (eds), *The BJP and the Compulsions of Politics in India*. Delhi: Oxford University Press.

——— (2002a). 'Caste Hindutva and Hideousness'. *Economic and Political Weekly*, 37 (15), 1391–3.

——— (2002b). 'Contestation and Negotiations: Hindutva Sentiments and Temporal Interests in Gujarat Elections'. *Economic and Political Weekly*, 37 (48), 4838–43.

——— (2004a). 'Introduction: Caste and Democratic Politics in India'. In G. Shah (ed.), *Caste and Democratic Politics in India* (pp. 1–26). London: Anthem Press.

——— (2004b). *Under-priviliged and Communal Carnage: A Case of Gujarat*. Wertheim Lecture, Amsterdam.

——— (2006). 'Communalization and Participation of Dalits in Gujarat 2002 Riots'. In L. Lobo and B. Das (eds), *Communal Violence and Minorities*. Jaipur: Rawat Publications.

Shani, O. (2005). 'The Rise of Hindu Nationalism in India: The Case Study of Ahmedabad in the 1980s'. *Modern Asian Studies*, 39 (4), 861–96.

——— (2007). *Communalism, Caste and Hindu Nationalism: the Violence in Gujarat*. Cambridge University Press.

Simpson, E. (2005). 'The 'Gujarat' Earthquake and the Political Economy of Nostalgia'. *Contributions to Indian Sociology*, 39 (2), 219–49.

——— (2006). 'The State of Gujarat and the Men without Souls'. *Critique of Anthropology*, 26 (3), 331–48.

Simpson, E. and S. Corbridge (2006). 'The Geography of Things That May Become Memories: The 2001 Earthquake in Kachchh-Gujarat and the Politics of Rehabilitation in the Prememorial Era'. *Annals of the Association of American Geographers*, 96 (3), 566–85.

SK (2000). 'Police and Courts: Perpetuating Insecurity'. *Economic and Political Weekly*, 35 (40), 3561–3.

Smith, D. (2003). *Hinduism and Modernity*. Malden: Blackwell.

Snyder, J. (2000). *From Voting to Violence: Democratization and Nationalist Conflict*. New York: W.W. Norton & Company.

Spodek, H. (1974). 'Rulers, Merchants and Other Groups in the City-States of Saurashtra, India around 1800'. *Comparative Studies in Society and History*, 16 (4), 448–70.

——— (1989). 'From Gandhi to Violence: Ahmedabad's 1985 Riots in Historical Perspective'. *Modern Asian Studies*, 23 (4), 765–95.

——— (2001). 'Crisis and Response: Ahmedabad 2000'. *Economic and Political Weekly*, 36 (19), 1627–38.

——— (2008). 'In the Hindutva Laboratory: Pogroms and Politics in Gujarat, 2002'. *Modern Asian Studies*, 44, 349–99.

Stahlberg, P. (2006). 'On the Journalist Beat in India: Encounters with the Near Familiar'. *Ethnography*, 7 (1), 47–67.

Straus, S. (2006). *The Order of Genocide: Race, Power, and War in Rwanda*. Ithaca: Cornell University Press.

——— (2007). 'Second-Generation Comparative Research on Genocide'. *World Politics*, 59 (3), 476–501.

Subramanian, T.S.R. (2004). *Journeys through Babudom and Netaland: Governance in India*. New Delhi: Rupa & Co.

Sud, N. (2007a). 'Constructing and Contesting a Gujarati-Hindu Ethno-religious Identity Through Development Programmes in an Indian Province'. *Oxford Development Studies*, 35 (2), 131–48.

——— (2007b). 'Secularism and the Gujarat State: 1960–2005'. *Modern Asian Studies*, 42, 1251–81.

——— (2009). 'The Indian State in a Liberalizing Landscape'. *Development and Change*, 40 (4), 645–65.

Sundar, N. (2002). 'A Licence to Kill: Patterns of Violence in Gujarat'. In S. Varadarajan (ed.), *Gujarat: The Making of a Tragedy*. New Delhi: Penguin Books.

——— (2004). 'Teaching to Hate: RSS' Pedagogical Programme'. *Economic and Political Weekly*, 39 (16), 1605–12.

Swaan, A.D. (1982). 'De mens is de mens een zorg: over de verstatelijking van de verzorgingsarrangementen'. In A. d. Swaan (ed.), *De mens is de mens een zorg: opstellen 1971–1981* (pp. 81–115). Amsterdam: Meulenhoff.

——— (1995). 'Widening Circles of Identification: Emotional Concerns in Sociogenetic Perspective'. *Theory, Culture & Society*, 12, 25–39.

——— (1997). 'Widening Circles of Disidentification: on the Psycho- and Sociogenesis of the Hatred of Distant Strangers—Reflections on Rwanda'. *Theory, Culture & Society*, 14 (2), 105–22.

——— (2001). 'Dyscivilization, Mass Extermination and the State'. *Theory, Culture & Society*, 18 (2–3), 265–76.

——— (2004). *Zorg en de Staat*. Amsterdam: Bert Bakker.

——— (2007). *Bakens in Niemandsland: opstellen over massaal geweld*. Amsterdam: Bert Bakker.

Tambiah, S. (1996). *Leveling Crowds: Ethnonationalist Conflicts and Collective Violence in South Asia*. Berkeley: University of California Press.

Tilly, C. (2003). *The Politics of Collective Violence*. Cambridge: Cambridge University Press.

Turel, T. (2007). 'Community Upliftment through Self-sustenance: The Impact of the 2002 Riots on Ahmedabad's Muslim Community's Choice between Political and Self-sustenance Strategies to Improve Access to State Services'. Unpublished MA thesis, University of Amsterdam.

Valentino, B.A. (2004). *Final Solutions: Mass Killing and Genocide in the Twentieth Century*. Ithaca: Cornell University Press.

Varadarajan, S. (ed.) (2002). *Gujarat, the Making of a Tragedy*. New Delhi: Penguin Books India.

Varshney, A. (2001). 'Ethnic Conflict and Civil Society: India and Beyond'. *World Politics*, 53 (April 2001), 362–98.

——— (2002). *Ethnic Conflict and Civic Life: Hindus and Muslims in India*. New Haven and London: Yale University Press.

Veer, P. V. D. (1994). *Religious Nationalism*. Berkeley: University of California Press.

——— (2002). 'Religion in South Asia'. *Annual Review of Anthropology*, 31, 173–87.

Verkaaik, O. (2003). 'Fun and Violence. Ethnocide and the Effervescence of Collective Aggression'. *Social Anthropology*, 11 (1), 3–22.

Veron, R., S. Corbridge, G. Williams, and M. Srivastava (2003). 'The Everyday State and Political Society in Eastern India: Structuring Access to the Employment Assurance Scheme'. *The Journal of Development Studies*, 39 (5), 1–28.

Visvanathan, S. (2007). 'The Wages of Dissent'. *Seminar*, 569.

Wade, R. (1982). 'The System of Administrative and Politicial Corruption: Canal Irrigation in South India'. *The Journal of Development Studies*, 18 (2), 287–328.

——— (1985). 'The Market for Public Office: Why the Indian State Is Not Better at Development'. *World Development*, 13 (4), 467–97.

Weiner, M. (1967). *Party Building in a New Nation: The Indian National Congress*. Chicago: University of Chicago Press.

——— (1989). 'The Indian Paradox: Violent Social Conflict and Democratic Politics'. In M. Weiner (ed.), *The Indian Paradox: Essays in Indian Politics* (pp. 21–37). New Delhi: Sage Publications.

Weingrod, A. (1968). 'Patrons, Patronage, and Political Parties'. *Comparative Studies in Society and History*, 10 (4), 377–400.

Weitering, D. and G. Nooteboom (2004). 'Railway Porters of Mumbai: Social Capital in Practice'. *Economic and Political Weekly*, 39 (22), 2243–50.

Whyte, W.F. (1993). *Street Corner Society: the Social Structure of an Italian Slum*. Chicago: University of Chigaco Press.

Wilkinson, S. (2004). *Votes and Violence: Electoral Competition and Ethnic Riots in India*. Cambridge: Cambridge University Press.

——— (2007). 'Explaining Changing Patterns of Party-voter Linkages in India'. In H. Kitschelt and S. I. Wilkinson (eds), *Patrons, Clients and Policies: Patterns of Democratic Accountability and Political Competition* (pp. 110–41). Cambridge: Cambridge University Press.

Wimmer, A., L.-E. Cederman and B. Min (2009). 'Ethnic Politics and Armed Conflict: A Configurational Analysis of a New Global Data Set'. *American Sociological Review*, 74 (April), 316–37.

Wirsing, R.G. (1973). 'Associational 'Micro-Arenas' in Indian Urban Politics'. *Asian Survey*, 13 (4), 408–20.

Wit, J. d. (1996). *Poverty, Policy and Politics in Madras Slums: Dynamics of Survival, Gender, and Leadership*. New Delhi: Sage Publications.

Women's Panel (2002). *How Has the Gujarat Massacre Affected Minority Women? The Survivors Speak*.

Yagnik, A. (2002). 'The Pathology of Gujarat'. *Seminar*, 513.

Yagnik, A and S. Sheth (2005). *The Shaping of Modern Gujarat: Plurality, Hindutva and Beyond*. New Delhi: Penguin Books.

Zwaan, T. (2001). *Civilisering en Decivilisering: Studies over staatsvorming en geweld, nationalisme en vervolging*. Amsterdam: Boom.

Zwart, F.D. (1994). *The Bureaucratic Merry-go-round*. Amsterdam University Press.

INDEX

www.ingramcontent.com/pod-product-compliance
Lightning Source LLC
Chambersburg PA
CBHW030809310726
48980CB00006B/431/J

* 9 7 8 8 1 2 9 1 2 3 7 5 6 *